PRAISE FOR *ALL I KNOW*

"In *All I Know*, Kai's heartbreaking journey asks us to confront big questions about family and personal trauma: What happens when the people we love hurt each other? How does that shape our relationships with others and with ourselves? How do we move forward when we can't forget the past? LaBarbera's characters are as funny as they are flawed, and I couldn't look away from their struggles to love each other as much as I loved each of them."

—Claire Boyles, author of *Site Fidelity*, 2022 Whiting Award Winner in Fiction and Longlisted for the 2022 PEN America/Robert W. Bingham Prize for Debut Short Story Collections

"*All I Know* captures one woman's heart-wrenching journey in coming to terms with her past, the trials of two, close-knit families increasingly caught in the web of addiction, and the ongoing struggle to overcome a heartbreaking loss. At its core, it is also a gripping tale of an epic love rooted in childhood, the quest to overcome mutual demons, and the courage to transcend dependency to embrace the possibilities of a new kind of love reborn of mutual respect, resilience, and humility. Readers will root for Kai (and Josh) every step of the way!"

—Susan Dugan, author of the short story collection, *Safe Haven*

"*All I Know* is more than a family drama, more than a love story, though it is also both. It's a moving novel of picking up the pieces after a family tragedy, contending with loss, talking to ghosts, and fearlessly pursuing love and happiness. Kai Martin, the novel's heroine reminds us that true connections can never be broken — not by time, change, or even death. Hopeful and unforgettable."

—Caroline Kim, author of *The Prince of Mournful Thoughts and Other Stories*, which won the 2020 Drue Heinz Prize in Literature, was long listed for both the PEN/Robert W. Bingham Prize and the Story Prize, and was a finalist for the Northern California Book Award and the Janet Heidinger Award for Fiction

"*All I Know*, Holly C LaBarbera's immersive coming of age tale, explores what happens to young love as it ages. As we follow Kai through tragedy, transformation, and heartbreak, across the US and Europe, the novel reminds us of the joys and sorrows of self-discovery. A book on grief as much as love, *All I Know* won my heart and kept me up past bedtime until its final pages."

—Amy Meyerson, bestselling author of *The Bookshop of Yesterdays* and *The Imperfects*

"A heartbreaking yet uplifting story of the perils found in all families. LaBarbera deftly shows how childhood wounds and mental health challenges impact adult relationships. Protagonist Kai's struggles will resonate with readers, as will the resilient human spirit that allows her find hope, to overcome, and to grow into an ever-better version of herself."

—Robert Dugoni, critically acclaimed *New York Times, Wall Street Journal, Washington Post* and #1 Amazon bestselling author of the Tracy Crosswhite police series, which has sold more than 8 million books worldwide and the coming-of-age standalone novel *The Extraordinary Life of Sam Hell*

"A tender, thoughtful and heartbreaking story, *All I Know* is a snapshot of the inner heart. You will fall in love with Kai, a child struggling to decipher the complicated messages that come our way in route to adulthood. It's raw, it's real, and it's compelling through and through."

—LEE KRAVETZ, author of the novel *The Last Confessions of Sylvia P.* as well as acclaimed nonfiction, *Strange Contagion* and *SuperSurvivors*

"...a book that amplifies the great feeling of success at knowing the human spirit is resilient.

The author does a brilliant job at explaining how and why Kai makes the decisions she makes, and even if the reader would choose a different path, Kai's point of view is understandable.

The characters are very well developed with care and great depth. Not only are the characters well developed, the feeling the reader gets of family in the book is also deep. When some of the family—real or chosen—are not there, the reader feels the void."

—*LitPick Reviews*

"Young members of intertwined families forge a complicated bond in the tense coming-of-age novel *All I Know*. Early on, the book lingers on one-on-one interactions well, emphasizing its aching interfamily ties...the story is driven by the choices that each of the characters makes, with their complicated family intimacies best established via Kai's maturing perspective."

—*Foreword Clarion Review*

ALL I KNOW

BY HOLLY C LaBARBERA

ISBN: 979-8-98949290-9 (Paperback)

ISBN: 979-8-98949291-6 (eBook)

Library of Congress Control Number: 2023921218

Any references to historical events, real people, or real places are used fictitiously. All characters, incidents, and dialogue are drawn from the author's imagination and are not to be construed as real.

BUCKBERG MOUNTAIN BOOKS
FREMONT, CA

For Alex,
You are a beautiful part of the world.
Keep faith and stay.

PART 1

CERTAINTY

A BLOODY MESS

We'd been sledding all afternoon when the accident happened. I was nine years old that Christmas of 1981, and we were on the hill in front of my house, experimenting with combinations of people on variations of sleds, trying to find the perfect weight distribution to send us shooting down the slope at top speed.

Dad and Rob Tyler were directing the action, as invested as any of us kids in getting the most thrilling run possible. I have no memory of them drinking, but given the lifetime of memories I do have, my guess is they probably were.

The Tylers were with us for the holiday, as usual. In a way, they were our extended family, the adults estranged from their families of origin for various reasons, although I purposely did not think of them as relatives yet. I was waiting for the day I believed was inevitable, the day I would marry Josh and make us an official family. Stephanie and I must have planned my wedding to her brother about a hundred times. I can picture us lying together under the covers with a flashlight, imagining my Princess Diana-inspired dress, layers of satin billowing around me like a poufy cloud, the one romantic kiss, the happily-ever-after of it all. Then we would be sisters, live next door to each other, and raise our daughters to be third-generation best friends.

I was always so sure about things, like my home and family, Santa Claus and summer vacation—and loving Josh Tyler. I knew him my whole life, and while there must have been a time before I thought about liking boys, I can't actually remember not being in love with Josh. At twenty years old, I still love him, despite my disillusionment about most everything else.

Among the kids, Josh was the undisputed leader, and his brothers Bobby and Nick were his primary minions, a three-man pack of mayhem and mischief. Bobby was two years younger than Josh, Nick a year younger than Bobby, with me and Kade, my twin brother, a year after them and Stephanie Tyler a year after that, pretty much a kid a year, like a ladder of children.

So there we were, the day after Christmas, Dad and Kade and I trying to make the jump to light speed. Kade was obsessed with *Star Wars*, so everything we did in those days was translated into galactic terms. Kade was sitting in front of me on the toboggan, aka the *Millennium Falcon*, pretending to enter coordinates before we took off.

"C'mon, Kade," I said, pushing my body up against him. "Let's go already."

"Traveling through hyperspace ain't like dusting crops, kid. Without precise calculations we could fly right through a star or bounce too close to a supernova and that'd end our trip real quick," Kade said, channeling Han Solo.

I collapsed backward against Dad in impatience and irritation.

"Okay, Chewie, hit it," Kade finally said to Dad/Chewbacca, who pushed us off, and we went flying down the hill.

When the older boys took a turn on the toboggan, Stephanie and Kade and I traded off in pairs on an old wooden sled with red metal runners, which wasn't as fast but was easier to steer. Stephanie and Kade were scared if we went too fast anyway, although I never was. I was fearless, invincible.

Dad proposed one last run on the big toboggan on an alternate, riskier course that was fresh snow but steeper, with more trees and obstacles. Josh was in because Josh was always in when my dad suggested something. Bobby, Nick, and I followed Josh's lead as per usual. I was in the front of the toboggan, because we had learned that you went faster when the lightest person was in front and the heaviest person was in back. We started down the hill at top speed, and I was thrilled. With the wind making my eyes water and snow kicking up in my face, I couldn't see anything, including the tree we were barreling toward. My dad pulled Josh off, Josh pulled Bobby with him, and Bobby pulled Nick, but Nick didn't pull me off. It felt like the toboggan had taken flight, so light now with only me on it.

"Jump!" Dad yelled, echoed by everyone else screaming "Jump!" but I was deer-in-the-headlights at that point and couldn't move.

I crashed straight into the tree.

My dad froze in terror when he saw the scarlet puddle forming around me in the snow. Josh was the one who picked me up and started running back to our house.

Rob grabbed my dad by his shoulders and shook him, yelling for him to pull himself together and pushing him in our direction.

Dad quickly caught up with us, taking me from Josh, getting me home and then to the hospital, where he and Mom waited with me for hours before a skilled plastic surgeon sewed my bloody mess of a face back together, doing such a good job that I was left with only a hint of a scar on my bottom lip, where I'd bitten clean through. I needed twenty-seven stitches in total. My nose was broken and one cheekbone had a hairline fracture, all of which was painful but nothing that wouldn't heal.

The rest of that week could have been horrible, but I actually remember it fondly. I was in pain, with bandages that were difficult to see around, and I was on a liquid diet because of my ripped-up lip, so all of that was terrible. But I also got a lot of attention. Kade never left my side. Dad made me his world-famous milkshakes, bringing them to me and quickly scurrying away, avoiding looking directly at my mangled face. Mom made sure I took my medicine and didn't mess with my bandages, made me soup and slept next to me in case I needed anything in the night. One day she started reading to me from my favorite book, *The Secret Garden*, and when something else required her attention, Kade took over for chapter two. It was sweet of him to make the attempt, but he wasn't a good reader, and it was tedious to listen to him try to sound out the words over and over. Josh overheard and offered to take a turn, spending hours over the next few days to read me the rest of the book, admitting how much he liked it once we finished.

Josh and Kade. My two guys.

SUMMER DAZE

By spring, my face had mostly healed, with the few remaining scars fading a bit each day, barely noticeable by June. Dad taught high school, so he was as happy as Kade and I when summer vacation finally arrived. We immediately headed to Lake George, as we had for as many summers as I could remember, to spend a week in a cheap, grimy little rental cabin that we all loved. Dad bought Mom a new bikini every year before we left, and they treated it like a honeymoon, even though Kade and I were tagging along. It was our one and only family tradition that did not include the Tylers.

We spent most days on the water—exploring the miles of coastline, fishing, swimming, simply being together. One afternoon, the four of us were anchored along the shore of one of the small, uninhabited islands that were scattered throughout the lake. Mom was blipping in her little inflatable boat—that's what we called it, not reading or sleeping or doing anything in particular, just blipping. Dad was sleeping on the padded bow of the rented motorboat while Kade and I played with action figures in the stern. When we got bored, we jumped on Dad to wake him, and he pretended to be grumpy about it and threw us overboard. We had life jackets on, so we easily bobbed to the surface, climbed back on board, and begged him to do it again. I remember the joy of flying through the air, the exciting thrill offered within Dad's safe bubble of protection. He threw us a few times, then hurled us close to Mom's raft to splash her. We climbed in and cuddled along either side of her. Then Dad did a giant cannonball to splash us all.

He draped his arms over the side of the boat, touching Mom's arm, which was wrapped around me, and floated along with us in the water.

"This is a slice of heaven right here," Mom said.

"You do love being on the water," Dad said.

"I do," Mom answered dreamily. "Must be from growing up around all those boats."

"What do you mean?" Kade asked.

"My dad was a sailor," Mom said.

"He was?" I asked. Mom never talked about her family. Neither did Dad. I peered over at Kade, who shared my interest in this new bit of information.

"Didn't you know that?" Mom asked.

"I don't know anything about him," I said.

"Lucky you," Dad said.

"He was in the Navy," Mom said. "That's why we were in Hawaii when I met your father."

I'd never thought about what Mom had been doing in Hawaii. I'd heard Dad's story because it was also the Tyler-Martin origin story, but I guess my kid brain hadn't considered that Mom had her own journey. Dad had been in the Peace Corps in the Philippines and met Rob Tyler there in 1966. Rob met Pam soon after, and Dad was best man at their shotgun wedding, then Josh's godfather when he was born a short five months later. The four of them migrated together to Honolulu, where Rob and Dad enrolled at the University of Hawaii to be teachers, which was where they met Mom and eventually where Kade and I were born.

"That man could not stand me," Dad chimed in about my invisible grandfather. "The Navy in him didn't like the Peace Corps in me. Wouldn't give us permission to get married, wouldn't come to the wedding. You guys remember the story of Mom and me meeting?"

"You noticed her because she was beautiful…" I started. This part of the story I'd heard dozens of times, and it always made me happy because I looked like Mom. Kade and I both had her straight brown hair with sun-streaked natural highlights, her small, angular nose, and her well-defined cheekbones. I eventually grew into her great figure as well, but I didn't know that then.

"The *most* beautiful girl on the island," Dad corrected.

"But you fell in love with her because she was arguing with the teacher," Kade finished.

"She was the gutsiest, fiercest girl I'd ever seen."

Mom smiled at him. Looking back, it's funny that the thing that made him fall in love with her was one of the things that ruined them. But that's jumping ahead.

"So imagine her fighting with her dad. That was something to see."

"Why can't I fight with my dad?" I asked.

"Your dad is always right," he said. "Nothing to fight about."

"Well, I wouldn't say that," Mom said, and Dad splashed her.

"What about your parents, Daddy?" I asked.

"Mine were worse." Dad's face darkened for just a second, then assumed a devious look. "Okay, no more hogging the raft, y'all."

He climbed over the side and almost swamped the little boat with his added weight.

"Daddy, there's no room!" I squealed.

"Out with you then." Dad tossed me overboard as I screamed excitedly, then he tossed Kade in after me. He stretched out next to Mom and kissed her.

"Eww! Kissing!" Kade shrieked, and we swam back to our bigger boat and resumed playing with our guys, although I peeked over at Mom and Dad often, watching their kissing and snuggling, then reenacting it with my action figures, despite Kade's protests.

A few weeks later, we were back home with the Tylers, who had taken the well-traveled road trip from their house in Vermont to ours in New York. Stephanie and I were playing Barbies on the back porch, where the shade kept it relatively cool on hot summer days. Kade had used his artistic talents, which were considerable, to transform cardboard boxes into a Barbie dreamhouse and furniture. We told him what we wanted and he designed it for us, directing us in how to help him execute his vision. Once we started actually playing with our dolls, he quickly got bored and retreated to a spot under a big tree in the backyard with his sketchpad and some colored pencils.

Mom and Pam joined us on the porch to sip an afternoon cocktail and enjoy the peace and quiet before the other boys returned from playing football on the field at Dad's school. Mom spread her long legs across to the rattan table and put her feet up, her perfectly manicured toes contrasting with Pam's chipped polish. Pam was plump and rumpled, hair pulled back into a ponytail with strands falling out around her face. Mom was slim, with well-fitting shorts and top, her hair blow-dried and flat-ironed, her face with a bit of makeup on.

Pam was telling a story about one of the boys (not Josh, so I wasn't paying too much attention) while Mom listened, smiling and nodding. My mom was barely halfway through her cocktail when Pam went to refill hers. She had only taken a few sips of her fresh drink when the tranquility came to an end. Bobby and Nick tumbled out of the car and were the first to barrel around the corner of the house, with Bobby inexplicably tackling Nick, then wrestling with him on the grass. Next to round the corner was Rob, followed by Dad, his arm draped over Josh's shoulder, in some deep football discussion about either a well-executed play or something to improve upon. Kade looked up and watched them for a minute, then went back to his drawing.

Josh was not nearly as tall as my dad, but he had grown since Christmas. His face looked older, although his hair was still the wild tangle of blond curls that I imagined working a finger through, pulling a curl straight to see how long it was, how much hair was wrapped up in each tight spiral, watching to see if it would spring back into place when I let it go. That sounds sexual now, to my twenty-year-old self, but at the time I really just wanted to touch his hair and play with his curls.

"Kai!" Stephanie said. "Aren't you playing?"

"Yes, sorry." I pulled my attention away from Josh and back to Barbies. "Let's have a wedding."

As I changed Barbie into her puffy white gown, my attention was only halfhearted. I kept Josh in my peripheral vision. Dad ruffled his hair, then followed Rob up the stairs and onto the porch with us. They sat down in chairs across from the moms, and Pam got up to fix them both a drink. Mom was still sipping on her first, and she wasn't about to get up and fix Dad a drink.

Josh knelt down next to Kade, looking at his drawings. I couldn't hear what they were saying, but Josh was pointing at stuff and seemed impressed. He was still holding the football and somehow convinced my brother to play catch. They stood not far apart, and Josh threw the ball gently to Kade, who dropped it, then picked it up and threw a terrible pass back to Josh, who hustled and stretched to catch it.

"Quite the MVP you got there, John," Rob said. "Don't you ever throw a ball with that kid?"

"He's not interested," Dad said.

"He'd rather draw," Mom said, "which is just fine."

"Still, a boy should be able to throw a ball," Rob said.

I knew better than to butt into the adults' conversation, but I wanted to stand up for Kade, like I always did at school when anyone said anything like that. I'd tell them to shut up and leave him alone, then comfort him if they'd made him cry.

Kade struggled in school as much as athletics. He was smart but didn't learn the way I did, the way most kids did. He'd cry over homework sometimes, and Dad would get frustrated because he was a teacher but couldn't teach Kade. Mom was the one to calm Kade down, then help him figure out whatever was giving him trouble, or give him permission to leave it incomplete and send a note to the teacher.

Josh was being like Mom right now, patiently giving Kade pointers and helping him try to do better with the football. Kade was enjoying his lesson until Bobby said something that made him stop, probably something like what Rob had said. Josh said something to him, and Bobby said something back, and then Josh tackled him and they were the ones wrestling, but more aggressively than Bobby and Nick had been. Josh pinned Bobby with his arm behind his back, then it was over and they were back to throwing the football, but without Kade.

When the dads finished their drinks, they suggested a game of capture the flag. Our house was over a hundred years old, built of stone and stucco, perched all alone on the top of a mountain. We were surrounded by ten acres of our own woods, a mile from the nearest intersection and five miles from a grocery store. It only took an hour to drive south to New York City, but we were a world apart. There were no neighborhood kids, no other houses in sight, and our isolation added to the twin bond Kade and I shared. We were constant companions, exploring these woods endlessly, intimately familiar with every path and meadow and mossy spot.

The expanse of our woods made a game of capture the flag a serious undertaking. The flag could be anywhere, and we'd sneak and hide and spy across acres of trees and bushes, everyone treating the game as if it were a genuine reconnaissance mission. We were a competitive bunch, so things got intense sometimes, but that day was the worst.

About an hour into the game, Josh captured Bobby, which made Bobby mad. He got madder when Nick tried to rescue him but was caught by Kade, who had been secretly guarding the jail. Bobby started yelling that Kade had cheated, which was stupid because you couldn't really even cheat at capture the flag, and for once Kade stood up for himself. I heard the unusual sound of Kade's raised voice and headed toward the kerfuffle. Nick was halfheartedly backing up his brother and teammate, even though I'm sure he knew Bobby was being dumb. Josh crashed through the bushes and started yelling at Bobby, and then they were pushing and shoving and all of a sudden fists were flying.

When Josh gave Bobby a bloody nose, I started screaming. I'd never seen this level of brutality, drawing blood, and I was scared. I was also upset because Josh was the one being mean, hurting his brother, which I couldn't make sense of. The dads heard me screaming and arrived to break up the fight, but that only ended up making things worse. Rob grabbed a branch, lined the boys up, then started hitting them across their hands, even Kade, even though he hadn't been fighting.

I started crying at the first crack of the branch against Josh's hand. I begged my dad to stop Rob, but Dad just picked me up and carried me home. As we walked away, the thwack of the branch faded but my crying became uncontrollable because of the terror I knew Kade was experiencing. Dad had never hit us, and I hadn't ever thought about that happening.

"Daddy, why would Rob do that? How could you let him do that?" I sobbed.

"That's his choice, Kai. He gets to decide his boys' punishment when they're bad."

"But what about Kade? Kade isn't his, and Kade wasn't fighting."

"Kade can use some toughening up, too. He's learning a lesson and he'll be fine."

"But they were hitting and Rob was hitting. The lesson doesn't even make sense."

"Quiet now, Kai. We're done talking about this." I continued crying but didn't say anything else because I was too scared of what had happened and what could happen.

When I got home, I was a mess of sweat and tears, so Mom put me in a cool bath. I told her what had happened, how I had been scared but also angry—first at Josh for hitting Bobby, then at Rob for hitting all of them, then at Dad for not doing anything.

"How could he let Rob do that?" I asked Mom. "If I was bigger, I would have stopped him."

"I promise you that Rob will never hit Kade again," Mom said. "I promise that." She was looking right at me, and I saw the fire in her eyes. Then she started shampooing my hair, massaging my head, which felt nice and helped me calm down.

When she left me, I could hear her talking with my dad outside the bathroom door. Their voices were low, so I couldn't make out the words, but they were somehow still yelling. I floated my head just below the water so I couldn't hear them anymore.

At dinner, it was obvious that my mom was mad at Rob and Dad. The boys were all "yes, sir" and "no, sir" when they said anything at all. Kade hadn't even come to the table. Mom had tucked him away in her room and brought his food there. It was the quietest dinner we'd ever had.

I was on high alert all night, paying attention to everyone's every movement. After dinner and dishes, I saw my mom whisper something to Rob, and he got up off the couch and followed her out the back door. Dad, Pam, and Josh all watched them leave, but nobody moved except for me. I snuck out the front door and circled around the house to keep an eye on what was happening. I was curious, of course, but I also wanted to be sure my mom was okay.

I didn't hear how the conversation started, but Mom didn't seem to have wasted much time getting right to the point.

"Don't you ever touch my son again, Rob," I heard her tell him, in an icy cold voice.

"It was no big deal, Tammy," he said. At least he wasn't mad, which made me less worried, even though I was incredulous that he thought it was no big deal. So was my mom.

"It is a very big deal, and if it happens again, we are done. No more good ole family times. No more vacations together, no more coming to this house. You lose your playmate and drinking buddy if this happens again. Do you understand me?"

Rob tried to stare her down, obviously not used to being talked to like this. The longer he stared at her, the more my fear crept back, goose bumps popping up all over my body.

He finally broke the tension with, "Sure thing, Tammy. Like I said, no big deal. We done here?"

"Yeah, we're done," Mom said.

This was the first time, but far from the last, that my mom stood up for us and my dad did not.

I ducked back around the corner of the house so neither of them would see me and bumped into Josh, who had been spying too. He put his hand over my mouth to keep me quiet until Mom and Rob were both back inside.

"What are you doing out here?" he asked when we were alone.

"Same as you, keeping an eye on things."

"You're nine. What're you gonna do about anything?"

"I don't know. Something. Scream maybe."

"Yeah, you're good at that," he said, an edge to his voice.

"I'm sorry I screamed, Josh. I didn't know that would happen."

"Well, now you know. It happens."

"I'm sorry that happens. Are your hands okay?"

"Yeah, no big deal." He repeated his dad's words but winced when he put his hands in his pockets.

"Well, I was scared. I've never seen anything like that."

"I've never seen anything like what your mom did right there. Never saw anybody stand up to my dad like that."

Later, when Steph and I were lying in bed, I told her what had happened, but she wasn't surprised.

"They're stupid boys," she said. "They fight and break things and talk back, even though they always get spankings. Daddy spanked me once and that was enough for me. I try really hard to be good, but they don't even try."

"My daddy never spanks me."

"You're lucky. Does he spank Kade?"

"No."

"What about your mom?"

"What?"

"Sometimes my dad hits my mom, but only if he's really mad," Steph said.

"But your mom can't be bad."

"I guess she is sometimes. I don't know. Can we not talk about this anymore? I don't think I should talk about this." Steph rolled over as if going to sleep, although I doubted she actually was. I lay there for a long time before finally drifting off.

In the morning, Kade and I headed to the Big Rock, our

favorite spot in the world. The huge boulder was far enough from the house that we felt like we were in the wilderness but close enough to get to easily and often. It had indentations on one side that made it easy to climb, and a nice flat top to sit on. It was where we went when we were mad or sad or just needed some twin time to ourselves. As always, Kade and I sat back-to-back, leaning into one another, having decided long ago that this was how we'd been in our mom's tummy.

"Are you okay, Kade?"

"My hands don't really hurt, but that's not the worst part anyway. I wet my pants when Rob was hitting us, and I think the boys saw. I had bad dreams last night, so I went into Mom and Dad's room, and Dad was mad, which made me cry, which made him madder. Mom let me climb in bed and cuddle with her, but Dad hated that too, so then I was too upset to sleep. I didn't want to bother Dad by being there, but I didn't want to go back to my room because the boys were there. I wish they would just leave."

Kade rarely talked that much all at once. I pushed my body against his, and he pushed back, our mutual show of support.

I told him what Steph had said about Rob hitting Pam, and he was as shocked as I'd been, then seemed more worried, so I told him I'd stick to him like glue for the last two days of the Tyler's visit, thinking I could make him feel safe. That reminded me to tell him about Mom's conversation with Rob.

"Mom's brave," Kade said.

"Yeah," I agreed.

"You're brave, too, Kai." Then, after a minute, "I wish I was brave."

Kade hadn't had a good night's rest since then, but the night after the Tylers left, he was sound asleep on the trundle in my room. I was asleep too, but I woke up when Dad shuffled into the room.

I was an expert at barely cracking my eyes open so he wouldn't know I was awake, and tonight I watched him slide down the wall to sit on the floor near my bedroom door. He had a glass in one hand and a bottle in the other. He finished what was in the glass and refilled it. I closed my eyes again, comforted by his presence.

"John, what are you doing in here?" I heard Mom whisper. I peeked and saw her standing in the doorway. Had I fallen asleep? I wasn't sure how long Dad had been there.

"It's so easy to love them when they're asleep," he whispered back, slurring his words a little. "Nobody disappointing anybody."

Part of me knew I should tell them I was awake, but I lay perfectly still, breathing evenly. Mom slid down the wall to sit next to him, set the bottle aside, and took his hand. Dad told Mom he was sorry, and she suggested he apologize to Kade, which Dad seemed to silently consider.

"I can almost convince myself I'm a decent father when they're sleeping."

Mom leaned her head against his arm and reassured him that he was a great father, that a bad decision here or there didn't make him a bad father. That made me feel better, but it didn't seem to comfort Dad.

"I'm supposed to love them equally and no matter what," he said. "That's how it is for you, right?"

"Yes," Mom said, whispering even more softly than before.

"Loving Kai is easy," Dad said. "She's just like you."

"You love them both, John," Mom said.

"Okay," Dad said, and after a pause added, "but Kai's easier."

I didn't want to hear any more, didn't want to know this. I closed my eyes and tried to make myself fall back to sleep, to stop listening.

Dad continued, "You know, it's not even that I let Rob hit him, it's that he didn't even check with me, didn't hesitate. He knew for a fact that I wouldn't say anything, that I'd let him do whatever he wanted. And he was right."

"You don't have to stay friends with him," Mom said.

"He's like my brother. I chose him to be my new family. I can't lose another family." Dad's voice cracked.

"We're your family, hon," Mom said. She picked up the bottle and stood, reaching her hand down to Dad. "Come to bed, my love."

Dad took her hand, got up unsteadily, and followed her out of the room.

I was wide awake now. I opened my eyes to watch them leave and saw Kade looking at me, his face wet with silent tears.

October 7, 1982

Dear Steph,

My homework today is to write a letter to someone, so I chose you.

How's school going for you? It's okay for me. I wanted to be in a separate class from Kade this year, take a break from watching out for him, but now I'm glad Mom kept us together. My friends have been mean. Do you remember my friend Jennifer? Well, now she's best friends with a girl named Elizabeth. We were all friends last year, but over summer, Jennifer and Elizabeth decided they were best friends and they leave me out all the time. They even made their own name, so everyone calls them Jennabeth. They are both Jennabeth! I told them they were being mean and stupid, but they said they weren't, so I just decided to stop being friends with them. So now I'm glad I have Kade. There's a cute boy in my class named Danny who is new at our school, and he sits next to Kade. I keep telling Kade to be friends with him so Danny will come over to our house sometime, but you know Kade. That probably won't happen.

Mom's still mad at your dad and doesn't want to go to your house for Thanksgiving (Kade doesn't want to either), but Dad and I convinced her it will be okay, so we're coming. Kade's still nervous, so I told him he can hang out with us the whole time if he wants.

Write me back soon!

Love,

Your best friend Kai

October 15, 1982

Dear Kai,

I was so excited when my mom gave me my very own letter! I loved it! I hope we can be pen pals forever and ever!

Jennabeth is so stupid! They are really mean and I hope they get in a fight and then they don't have anyone else to be friends with! My friend Isabelle is in my class again this year and we are best friends at school, even though you are my best friend really! I went to sleep over at her house last night. We stayed up late watching Love Boat and Fantasy Island, which was scary and then I couldn't sleep, so I called Mom to come get me in the night, but she wasn't mad so that was good.

Josh is playing football so he's not home much because they practice all the time. He's acting mean and stupid, like he's so great because he's in high school now.

I hope Kade invites Danny over so he can be your boyfriend

and you can marry him instead of my annoying brother!!

I can't wait to see you at Thanksgiving! Thank goodness you're coming! We'll have lots of fun with Kade, just like always.

What are you dressing up as for Halloween? I'm going as Strawberry Shortcake and hoping for lots of Reese's Pieces... they're my new favorite!

Love,

Your best friend Stephanie Tyler

BUILDING BRIDGES

After another round of holidays, we were all pretending nothing had ever happened, and things felt back to normal. The family gatherings over the past year had been a bit awkward, but the adults drank enough to numb most of the tension. Kade and I stayed away from Rob, and nothing bad happened again, so the memory faded.

One day in July, the Tylers back at our house for their summer visit, Stephanie and I brought a bunch of Barbies down to the pond to play. I would never admit to my school friends that I still played with Barbies when we were going to be starting middle school, but this was just Kade and Steph, so it was safe. Kade came with us because he was helping to design an Amazon jungle fortress for our dolls. The three of us were having a ball together until Dad, Rob, Josh, Bobby, and Nick arrived on a mission to build bridges among the islands in the wooded back part of the pond. The water there was shallow, only a foot or two deep, and there were many islands that were only a few yards apart, begging to be linked by bridges. When I saw their group, I ditched Steph and Kade without a second thought.

I loved spending time with Dad and Josh. I figured that since Josh loved my dad and my dad loved me, something would rub off there if I spent enough time with them together. Plus, Dad and Josh were both fun, and their flow with each other was nice to be around. Rob, Bobby, and Nick started on a bridge from one shore to the first island while Dad, Josh, and I worked on a bridge from the same island to the opposite shore. We hunted for fallen logs long enough to span the distance, small enough for us to lift and maneuver, and hefty enough to hold people crossing over. It took about six or eight logs to make a sturdy bridge, and we had to get them to fit together just so. The bridges were always wobbly, which was part of the fun and adventure of crossing them, but we strove to make them as solid as possible. We broke down the bridges every fall so that we could ice skate when the pond froze, which required rebuilding every summer.

The three of us were a good team. Dad and Josh did the heavy lifting, but I was an expert at finding the right logs. We joked and laughed together, especially when my dad half fell into the water.

At first, I didn't realize Stephanie was mad at me. When I got home from the pond, my mom asked me to husk corn on the cob, then help with the salad, so I was busy until we sat down to eat.

Over dinner, Bobby was talking about how far we'd gotten in building the bridges, connecting the first island to both sides of the shore, and then connecting the first island to the second. I turned to Stephanie, who was sitting next to me as usual, and proposed that I show her the bridges tomorrow, excitedly telling her how sturdy the one I'd helped with had turned out.

"I don't want to see your stupid bridge," she said.

"It's not stupid. It's a great bridge," I replied, confused by her response.

"I'm sure it is. I'm sure you and Josh can walk across that bridge and get married someday. Josh, did you know that Kai wants to marry you? Did you know that's why she follows you around all the time? She couldn't care less about me, but she'd do anything for you."

"Shut up, Stephanie! You're such a liar!" I shouted. I felt my face flushing, an adrenaline rush shooting through my body, my heart hammering.

"Kai, that is enough." Mom was mad. Manners at the dinner table were rule number one for her.

I was mad too, and humiliated, so of course I made it worse. I stood up and pushed my chair back so hard it fell over.

"She's lying! She's just angry that I didn't want to play stupid baby Barbies with her." Bobby and Nick were highly entertained by my outburst. Kade was looking at me with concern, willing me to settle down and listen to Mom. I didn't dare look at Josh or the grown-ups.

"Kai, you are on thin ice." This was my mom's last chance voice, and usually I would have listened to it, but I couldn't stop myself this time, especially after what Stephanie said next.

"I am not lying!" she cried. "You talk about how much you love Josh all the time! But you know what? He never, ever, ever talks about you, Kai. Never ever!"

"Shut up, you stupid baby!"

"Kai Martin!" Dad stood up. "Your room. Now!"

I turned and stomped off to my room, and only after I slammed the door did I start crying. I had never been so ashamed. And now Josh would hate me. Stephanie was supposed to be my best friend, but she had ruined my life. I cried myself to sleep, and when I woke up, I didn't feel any better. I didn't know where Stephanie had slept, but she wasn't in her regular spot on the trundle beside me. I didn't want to leave my room, couldn't bear seeing Josh or any of the boys.

Kade came in to check on me. He sat crossways on the bed, his back against the wall, his legs draped over mine.

"How bad is it?" I asked him, not bothering to move.

He told me that Stephanie had left the table crying right after I did.

"She shouldn't have said those things," he said, "even if everyone knows they're true."

"What do you mean?"

"Everyone already knew you like Josh. You're not very subtle."

"Oh, God, Kade. How can I ever leave my room again?" I pulled the blanket over my head.

"I don't know, but you're going to have to. Mom's going to make you apologize to Stephanie and to everyone else for ruining dinner. It's not fair. What she did was way worse than what you did."

I asked Kade how everyone else reacted, how badly Bobby and Nick had made fun of me. He told me that Bobby started humming "Here Comes the Bride" until Josh asked him if he wanted a beating, which made him stop. The rest of dinner had been relatively quiet. When they were going to bed, Bobby and Nick started to tease Josh again, but he smacked them both across the head and told them they better not mention it again.

Mom came in my room then, asked Kade to leave, and closed the door behind him. She sat down next to me on the bed.

"First off, Kai, that was unacceptable behavior last night. Stephanie is your friend and a guest in our house, and you were mean and rude. You were also disrespectful to me by ignoring my directions and to your dad with all the stomping and slamming and to everyone at that table. That will not happen again, do you understand?"

"But, Mom, she was…"

"Stop right there. We'll talk about that next. But you need to understand that reasons are different from excuses. Even though you had reasons for acting the way you did, those reasons are not excuses. You are responsible for your choices and your behavior, no matter what is going on around you. You made the choice to yell at your friend at my table, in front of our guests, even after I told you to stop. Do you understand that there is no excuse for that?"

"Yes, Mom, I understand."

"Good. You will apologize to Stephanie and to everyone else at dinner tonight."

I looked at her to argue the point, to explain that this was unfair and humiliating and that I couldn't possibly do it. But I saw the look in her eye and knew it was pointless.

"I am sorry for what Stephanie said." Mom's voice was softer now. "There was no excuse for that either, but I'm not her mother."

"Oh, Mom, how am I going to face him?" I fell into her arms and cried. "Stupid Bobby and Nick are going to be laughing at me for the rest of my life."

"I know, sweetie. I know." She let me cry myself out, then handed me the box of tissues. "This is a hard time, Kai, and it's only the first of many. You're going to have to decide what you do when life brings hard times. You can open the door and let hard times come live with you, settle in with the fear, anger, embarrassment, all the yucky feelings, and let them become a part of you. Or you can say, 'Thank you kindly, Mr. Hard Times, sir. Thank you for visiting, but you can go now.' You can hide, run away, give up. Or you can fight those urges and be stronger and more powerful than they are. Personally, I choose fighting. Not everybody is a fighter, but I think you are."

Mom should have been a college basketball coach or something. She could certainly give an inspiring speech.

"I want to be a fighter, Mom, but what do I do?"

"You walk into the kitchen and hold your head up high. You pour juice and eat some cereal and go to the pond with Kade and show him your bridge. You will show that you are strong and resilient and you don't let yourself get beaten down. Then you will apologize tonight to show that you also take responsibility and to make amends. And if those Tyler boys don't respect that, they're crazy."

"Do you really think I can do that, Mom?"

"Of course you can. You are my daughter. Oh, but one more thing you need."

"What?"

"You need Frank, of course."

"Oh my god, Mom." I rolled my eyes. My mom loved Frank Sinatra, especially her personal theme song. She left my room while I got dressed and came back with my brother and the record and put it on my turntable. Kade and I exchanged eye rolls, but we were smiling because deep down, we loved it too.

"That's life," Frank crooned as we sang along with him.

I followed Mom's advice, even though it was hard. Kade and I spent the morning at the pond and the afternoon reading on the Big Rock. I apologized at dinner, even though it almost killed me. I was helping my mom wash dishes when she leaned over and kissed my head and told me how proud she was, and that pretty much made the horrible day worth it. People were starting to play Monopoly, but I went outside to be alone. I wasn't quite ready to rejoin the group, since I didn't yet know how to be around either Josh or Stephanie.

I twisted and twirled myself on the swing, leaning far back, looking at the first few stars appearing in the darkening sky.

"Want a push?" Josh asked, surprising me.

"Why aren't you playing Monopoly?" I said, planting my feet on the ground to stop the spinning. "You love Monopoly."

"Yeah, I didn't feel like it tonight," he said, grabbing hold of the ropes. "So, ya wanna push or what?"

"Sure." I resettled myself on the swing, and Josh pulled me with him as he took a few steps backward, then let me go and started pushing. I loved the feeling of soaring through the air.

"Sorry about last night," he said. "My sister was mean, and I told her so."

"Well, good thing I'm the one who apologized then." Sarcasm was a specialty of mine. It went along with growing up in New York.

"You did what your mom said. Nothing wrong with that. Nothing wrong with anything you did really, except calling her a liar when she wasn't lying."

Thank god he was standing behind me and couldn't see my cheeks burning.

"I thought you'd be hiding in your room all day," he added.

"I wanted to," I said, trying not to cry. "I feel so stupid."

"Well, it doesn't show, and that makes you pretty cool."

"You think I'm cool?" That certainly perked me up.

"Listen, I'm fifteen and you're ten. You're cool for ten, but that's it. Get it?"

"I'm *almost* eleven and you *just* turned fifteen, but I get it. I'm cool."

"The rest of it. Do you get the rest of it?" Josh might have been annoyed, but I was pretty sure I heard a smile in his voice.

"Did you come out here to cheer me up, Josh? Let's stop at the part when you called me cool, okay?"

"You are still ten, right? Sometimes you talk like you're eighteen."

"You'd like me if I was eighteen," I said, grinning. "But then I wouldn't like you. I'd think you were just some little kid."

"Shut up and let me push you, kid, okay?"

I continued smiling and swinging.

I'd started the day feeling like my life was ruined, and now I was as happy as I'd ever been, especially because I had done it for myself. Okay, a little help from Mom because she hadn't given me a choice on parts of it, but still mostly me. It reinforced what I already believed at this age—that I would always be able to make things work out for the best. I wonder if all children have this grandiose belief or if it was unique to me.

"And make up with my sister tomorrow, okay? She's stupid but she is sorry."

So that's what I did the next day, in equal measure because Josh asked and because she was my best friend and we had plans to go to the movies together.

MIDDLE SCHOOL MESS

Kade and I were in different classes for the first time in our lives. Our elementary teacher had recommended different tracks for the two of us as we started middle school. Kade called his the dummy track. I tried to tell him that wasn't true, but it kind of was. I got to take French, and Kade took study skills. I was with the Talented and Gifted kids for enriched learning in our core classes, and Kade was with the remedial kids, trying to learn the foundational concepts he hadn't yet mastered.

I missed having Kade with me, especially when war broke out in my homeroom. I knew a lot of the kids in my class from elementary school, but the rest were from other schools that fed into this bigger, more intimidating one. The year started with an election for class representative, and I thought I had it in the bag but lost to a girl named Debbie, who became my arch nemesis. She called me Loser and got some other kids to join in. I wasn't about to let her bully me, though, and formed my own team against her. Added to our rivalry was the fact that we liked the same boy, Billy O'Malley. He was no Josh, but he was cute and age appropriate.

I was sure my birthday party would give me the winning edge. Our birthday was September 15, and the celebration was historically a kind of kick-off-the-school-year event as well. We'd invite kids I considered our joint friends, even though Kade viewed most of them as my friends. Mom threw us a big party that year because I convinced her that we had to make a splashy impression on all the new kids we were meeting. Kade didn't want to invite kids from his class, so we ended up with about half of my homeroom and other kids we'd known through the years, about twenty of us in all.

Mom was always good at birthday parties. She'd come up with a theme and decorations and games and make a cake to match it all. That year, her idea was a space theme. A few months prior, Sally Ride had been the first American woman launched into space, on the maiden flight of the Space Shuttle *Challenger*, so that was big news. The month before, *Return of the Jedi* had come out, completing Kade's favorite movie trilogy. The best part was that it was going to be a nighttime birthday party, which felt very cool and grown-up.

The science teacher at Dad's school brought telescopes. Mom made a rocket-ship cake and planet cupcakes and arranged them on a black tablecloth that Kade had painted in a space motif. We made "moon rocks" with crumpled-up aluminum foil and then divided guests into teams to see who could take home the most moon rocks by shooting them into "space ships" that Kade had created out of cardboard. Dad bought foam tubes and cut them into light-saber lengths, and we painted them with phosphorescent paint so they would glow in the dark when we had a mammoth fight between good and evil. Dad even dressed up as Darth Vader and let us all attack him. Billy was there laughing with a couple of his friends, and Kade had as much fun as everyone else for once, so the night seemed like a huge success.

I found out on Monday that I had it all wrong. A lot of kids told me how much fun they'd had at the party, but I also started noticing snickering and sideways glances, especially from Billy's friends and Debbie's team of supporters. By Tuesday, Debbie's nickname for me had evolved from Loser to Baby Loser, and I realized that Billy and his friends thought the party had been a stupid little-kid thing.

Debbie and I got into it on the blacktop at lunch on Wednesday. I walked right up to her and told her to shut up and get off my case. She made crying baby noises, which I told her was a weak comeback. Our showdown basically ended when she told me that Billy had asked her out because she wasn't a baby or a loser. I told her they deserved each other and walked away and didn't cry until after school, when I was safe at home.

The next weekend, I found Kade in the woods starting on his first in a series of paintings of a leaf. He'd end up with about twenty variations, and then move on to pinecones and branches and nests, but this was the start of his obsessive painting phase. I asked him once how he knew when he'd finally gotten it right, since they all looked amazing to me, and he told me he never did. He said eventually he simply accepted failure, gave up, and moved on to a new subject.

"I hate Debbie Fuller," I said. He already knew the whole story because I hadn't stopped talking about it all week.

"Billy's been calling me Darth Baby Loser Junior all week," he said as he mixed shades of green for his leaf.

"Why didn't you tell me?" I asked, carefully ripping an actual leaf, trying to tear it right along the veins.

"Because you would have said something or done something and that would only make it worse, having my sister fight my battles for me."

"What did you do?" I stopped my careful tearing and looked at Kade, who continued to mix paint.

"Nothing. I tried to pretend I didn't hear. I thought he'd stop if I ignored him, but then he saw me crying because he's right—I am a stupid baby—so he started doing it even more and getting his friends in on it too."

"He's such a jerk," I said. "Both of them. We have to get them back." I was brutally shredding leaves at this point.

"Please don't do anything, Kai," Kade said, tears forming.

I didn't reply, not wanting to make a promise I wasn't going to keep but also not wanting to upset Kade. He did have a point. I'd stuck up for him plenty of times in the primary grades, when kids made fun of him for missing a kick in kickball or not knowing an answer when the teacher called on him or crying about any of those things, but that was when we were younger and being a boy or girl didn't matter as much. The last few years, kids had been nice to Kade because they'd gotten to know him and liked us both. Things were different now.

"Darth Baby Loser Junior," I finally said. "They're so stupid. How did they get into the TAG class if they couldn't even think up better insults that that?"

"They're obviously smarter than me," Kade said, a tear slipping down his cheek.

I scooted around to push my back against his.

"You're obviously nicer," was all I could think of to say.

The next week started pretty quietly. Debbie's focus was exclusively on Billy, and they seemed to have lost interest in bothering me, probably because I'd proven that I wasn't an easy target. Kade, on the other hand, had shown that he was.

A bunch of classes joined together for PE, including mine and Kade's, and on Thursday we were playing dodgeball, which Kade historically hated. Our teacher had taken a girl to the office with a bloody nose, so we were left without supervision for a few minutes. Billy and Kade were the last two people left on their team, so everyone was watching to see the dramatic ending to the game. But instead what they saw was Billy sneak up behind my brother and pull his pants down, underwear and everything.

Kade froze, and before he recovered himself, everyone had time to see him on full display. He panicked and started running before pulling his pants up all the way and tripped and fell on the blacktop, his bare butt sticking up in the air, knees and hands scraped and bleeding.

I ran over to Billy and punched him in the face. He was so surprised he didn't fight back. I pushed him and he fell to the ground. I had never hit anyone before, so I don't really even know where that reaction came from, other than pure self-defense for my other half.

The PE teacher came running and grabbed me before I could kick Billy, which I was about to do. Most of the kids were staring in shocked disbelief at everything they had witnessed. Kade was crying, in a ball on the blacktop, but with his pants back up in place at least.

My parents both came to the school that afternoon for a very serious meeting. The principal didn't know what to do, because while I would normally be suspended for fighting, he also understood that my parents had every right to make a big stink about what Billy had done to Kade. In the end, I was suspended for a day because my mom insisted on consequences, although it was kept off my official school record. Billy was suspended as well. Kade wasn't in any trouble, but he stayed home from school the next day anyway.

That night at dinner, Mom repeated her lecture about reasons not being excuses and reiterated that there was no excuse for fighting.

"Isn't that right, John?"

"There's certainly no excuse for Kai fighting," he said. "It's not what *she* should have been doing, that's for sure."

Kade stayed perfectly silent, but it was clear to all of us that Dad thought he should have thrown the punch.

Kade locked his door that night so I couldn't get in, which had never happened before.

I sat outside Mom and Dad's bedroom door, trying to eavesdrop, although I could only hear angry whispering tones, not any actual words.

Suddenly, Dad opened the door and almost tripped over me. "Goddammit, Kai. Can't you mind your own business for once?" he said before continuing down the hall toward the kitchen, most likely to refill his empty glass.

Mom came out and took my hands to pull me up, then walked me upstairs to my room. "You've had a rough day," she said as we both sat down on my bed.

I immediately started crying, and she held me tight.

"I was trying to help, Mom, but now everyone's mad at me."

"I know you want to help, sweetie, but sometimes there's nothing you can do."

I'd never considered that before and dismissed the possibility. "But I have to try. Kade doesn't even try. Dad either. Why don't they at least try?"

Mom told me about fight, flight, or freeze, explaining that animals and people react to stressful situations differently, that it's about instinct, the way someone is wired. Some people fight when they feel threatened, while some freeze, hoping that if they stay very quiet and still, trouble will move on by. Other people run away. She said that all three can work for different people in different situations, that it wasn't about one being better than another.

"Which one is Dad?" Clearly Mom and I fought and Kade froze.

"Dad does a different kind of running away. But he freezes sometimes too."

"I hear him fighting with you, though."

"True. Dad does a little bit of all of them. We all do. We might have one that's more of our go-to, but they all come up for all of us in different situations. You need to learn to fight less, Kai, and not at all at school."

"I know. Do you think Kade can learn to fight a little more?"

"Maybe. I hope he develops a bit more fighting spirit, but at the same time, I love him exactly as he is. You too, Kai. I love you exactly as you are, fighting or not."

She kissed me goodnight, and I heard her knock on Kade's door. I was relieved when he let her in. I might not be able to help, but I knew that Mom would.

Later that night, I woke up when Dad leaned too far back on my desk chair and almost fell over.

"Dad? You okay?" I mumbled, groggy from sleep.

"Uh-huh. Sorry I woke you, sweetheart." His words were slurred. He got up and stumbled over to me, giving me a kiss on the head that left the familiar scent of liquor lingering behind him. I could have been annoyed at his being in my room, or being drunk, or waking me. But it felt kind of nice to know that he'd been sitting there, watching over me as best he could.

Kade didn't talk to me for the next few days, although he met up with me at the Big Rock on Sunday afternoon, taking his place leaning against my back. I apologized for what I'd done, for embarrassing him, for acting on impulse. He forgave me and confided that he wished he wasn't such a wimp. I insisted he was simply nicer than me and thought for two seconds before doing stupid things.

"Well, that's true," he said. I could hear the smile in his voice, which brought me some relief, though it only lasted for a moment. "But what you did wasn't stupid, it's what I should have done. Dad can't even look at me." Neither of us said anything for a little while. I was watching a chickadee jump from branch to branch, wishing I could erase the past few days and weeks for both of us.

We talked about what we thought things would be like back at school tomorrow and each shared our worries.

I leaned into him, pushing against him, and he did the same. "I got your back, brother."

"Yeah, but that's part of the problem, isn't it?"

November 4, 1983

Dear Steph,

Middle school sucks. I'll give you all the gory details when I see you at Thanksgiving, but I hate it. The only good part is that I started taking French, which I love because my teacher is really nice and fun and loves French stuff so she makes us love it too. At the end of next year, we get to go to Quebec! My new dream is to go to Paris.

Kade's not doing so well. I still make sure he sits with me at lunch, but some days I can't find him. He sneaks off and disappears. He says he's fine, but I know he's not. The other day I suggested he join the art club at school, and he told me to shut up and leave him alone. He's never told me to shut up before. Mom's worried about him too, but she doesn't seem to know what to do either.

Anyway, that's what's going on here. How's school going for you? How's everyone there?

Love,

Kai

November 17, 1983

Dear Kai,

I'm so sad!! We aren't seeing you guys for Thanksgiving. The boys' stupid football team is in some state champion tournament, so I have to go watch them play and be freezing cold and bored all Thanksgiving break instead of seeing you.

School is okay. I'm not in the same class with Isabelle, so that was hard at first, especially because she's in the same class with all our other friends, so I'm the one left out. I've made some new friends, which is good but not the same.

Everyone here is fine, but I know you're really asking about Josh, so I'll tell you this bit of bad news...he has a girlfriend. They went to the Homecoming Dance together, and she's really pretty. Sorry, Kai.

See you at Christmas!

Love,

Your best friend Stephanie

NO MORE NORMAL

ON A FRIDAY NIGHT TOWARD the end of May, Mom, Dad, Kade, and I were eating dinner when the phone rang. Dad answered, and his tone immediately alerted us that something was up.

"Pam, calm down, what's going on?" Dad looked worried and confused. "Pam, please, I can't understand what you're saying."

He pulled the phone into the other room to hear better, even though Mom, Kade, and I were all completely silent, practically holding our breath.

"It's okay, it'll be okay. We'll figure it out." He closed the door. Now it was about privacy, not quiet, which meant it was something really bad.

When he came back into the kitchen, he announced that Josh was coming to stay with us for a while. Mom gave him a look but didn't say anything, not at the dinner table.

Kade and I sped through the dishes so that I could go eavesdrop on our parents' conversation about Josh. By the time I got to their bedroom door, the conversation had already escalated into a fight, something they were doing a lot more lately.

I heard Mom yell, "You didn't even talk to me! Not one second of 'Hold on, Pam. Let me check with Tammy.' Just you making decisions with Pam or Rob and expecting me to go along. Just like always."

"I never thought you'd be heartless enough to say no! He needs us. They all need us."

"I'm sorry for them, but having him here is a bad idea."

"How can you say that?"

"What about Kai? And Kade?" Mom asked.

"What about them?"

"Well, for one, it would be nice if you cared about your own son as much as you care about Josh. He's going through a hard time, and he needs you too, but you don't jump through hoops for him." Mom had a valid point, but I didn't think it was helpful to her argument, since I'd heard her lose this fight several times already.

"He has you and Kai, and that's enough for him."

"You are so wrong, but I'm not having that fight again right now." Good move, Mom.

"And what about Kai? She loves having Josh around."

"Yes, exactly. That could be a problem."

"What are you talking about?"

"She's boy-crazy, and Josh has always been her number one crush. Having him here without the buffer of all the other kids is asking for trouble."

"You're crazy. He's like her brother."

"Not to her. You do know that your view of things is not the way everyone sees them, right? Not all people align with your take on how things work."

"Oh, here we go again! Me and my selfish ways. Okay, let's hear how thoughtless and self-centered I am."

I moved away from the door because I knew this part of the fight by heart. Kade was watching *Magnum, P.I.* in the living room, and I sat down on the couch next to him.

"So what's the scoop?" he asked at the commercial break.

I told him that Josh was coming but that I'd missed the part of the conversation that gave any details or explanation. I told him they were fighting.

"And?"

"And she thinks it's bad for you and me if he stays with us."

"You'll love it."

"Yeah, Mom thinks I'll love it too much."

"Well, that's probably true." He grinned at me.

I grinned back but then turned serious. "Will it be bad for you?"

"What do you mean?"

"The way Dad is with him."

"Whatever," Kade said. "Josh is hard to compete with."

"You shouldn't have to compete, Kade. I know Dad's not good at showing it, but he definitely loves you more than Josh."

"If you say so." I knew Kade didn't believe it, and I wasn't sure I did either, but I wanted it to be true.

Josh was on an overnight train. Pam had apparently rushed him to the station as soon as she hung up with my dad, which meant whatever was going on was really bad. I set my alarm to wake me before dawn, and although Dad was clearly surprised to see me that early in the morning, he didn't say anything about it. There was no traffic at five a.m. on a Saturday, and we sailed down the Palisades Parkway toward the city. Dad navigated the relatively deserted city streets and found a parking spot near Penn Station in plenty of time to meet Josh's train.

I was shocked when I saw him. He had a black eye, which wasn't even the worst part. He obviously hadn't slept and had been crying. He looked ragged and raw. He dropped his two big bags and hugged my dad, who held him tight. I never saw my dad hug anyone like that. He wasn't a big hugger. Josh began sobbing in my dad's arms, and I couldn't believe any of this was happening.

When they parted, Josh gave me a quick, embarrassed "Hey, Kai."

I stuck with, "Hey, Josh," and left him alone.

He and Dad each picked up a bag and carried it to the car. The ride home was silent. Josh fell asleep as soon as we started moving, and neither Dad nor I wanted to disturb him. When we got home, Josh settled himself in Kade's room, on the extra bunk, and fell back asleep until after lunchtime.

When he woke, Mom fed him. Despite the argument about his coming, she saw what a wreck he was, and her mom instincts automatically kicked in. And anyway, she loved Josh too.

Dad suggested they take a walk in the woods after Josh finished eating. He specifically told me to stay put, but of course I snuck out and followed them. I'd played hide-and-seek and capture the flag so many times in these woods that I was a stealth prowler. They stopped and sat together at one of our favorite soft mossy patches while I snuck close enough to listen.

"Thanks for letting me come stay," Josh said, sounding like a little kid.

"You're always welcome here, Josh," Dad replied. "You're part of the family."

"Did you know he hits her, Mr. Martin? Did you know that?" Yes, I thought, I knew that. I wished I didn't.

"That's not my business. It's not my place to get involved and it wasn't your place either. You can't take a swing at your dad."

"I'm not going to let him hit my mom anymore. I don't care if he punches me and I don't care if he kicks me out. I'm not going to live there and let that happen." I was proud of Josh for protecting his mom, angry and confused by Dad's take on things.

"You don't know what it's like," Josh continued, staring at the ground, his voice cracking.

"I do, though," Dad said, silent and thinking for a while, rubbing his hands together nervously. "My house was kind of like yours, but worse. Your parents are better people."

Josh looked at my dad, then looked away. "Jeez, I didn't know that."

Neither did I.

"Yeah, well…" Dad obviously didn't know what to say now. "He's not perfect, but your dad loves you guys and he tries. He messed up but he's still your dad."

"He told me to get out."

"I talked to him this morning. He regrets what happened yesterday. He and your mom worked it out, and he's not going to do that again."

"I don't believe him."

"I believe him, Josh."

I wondered if my dad actually believed it. Maybe he said it because he wanted to believe it, or maybe he knew something I didn't, but mostly I thought he was just trying to resolve the problem and wrap things up. This was already more discomfort than I'd ever seen my dad hang in there for. I'd never heard him have such a heart-to-heart conversation.

My feet were falling asleep from crouching behind the rock where I was hiding, but I didn't dare move.

"I think you should stay here with us until our camping trip. There's only a few more weeks of school, and I'm sure we can arrange a way for you to do your work from here to finish the term, or you can come to my school for the last few weeks. Then we'll meet up with your family and things will have blown over."

Josh was quiet, thinking about it. He'd picked up a stick and was digging at the moss with it. "My dad doesn't want me home, right?" It was kind of a question but not really, since he knew the answer.

"He'll cool off."

"Did he say I can come home after camping?" Josh sounded like a little kid again.

"He didn't say you couldn't." Dad put his arm around Josh's shoulders and gave him a squeeze. "He'll miss you and want you home by then."

"And my mom's going along with it? She's fine with me staying here?"

I wanted to cry for Josh but I had to stay quiet.

"I assume so. I haven't talked with her since last night."

They were quiet again for a while. "There's one more thing," Dad said, moving his arm away from Josh and looking down at his hands. "You have to apologize to him."

"No fucking way!" Josh flung his stick off into the woods. "You've got to be kidding me! Look at my fucking face! I'm not apologizing for doing the right thing!"

"Hey, hitting your dad is never the right thing. You have to respect him."

I almost stood up right then to take Josh's side and argue for him. I was so mad at my dad. How could he love Josh so much and still not take his side?

"I don't," Josh said. "That's the point."

Their eyes locked for a beat or two, then Dad looked at his feet.

"Okay, so we'll round back to that. Tempers are high. Let's leave it alone for now. You're staying here for the next few weeks, and then things will work themselves out. It will be fine, Josh. You both just need some time apart."

My dad patted Josh's leg and got up. He had reached his hard-stuff limit. "I'm headed back. Take your time out here." Which meant, Calm down, and we're not talking about it anymore. I knew that and so did Josh.

As my dad walked off, Josh lay back on the moss with his arm over his eyes. After a while, he said, "You can come out now, Kai."

I was embarrassed to be caught, but glad to stand up and get my blood circulating again.

"How did you know I was here?" I asked, moving toward him.

"I grew up playing in these woods too, remember?" His voice was monotone, and he didn't move, lying still, defeated.

"I'm sorry. I'll go."

"No, you don't have to go." There was a plaintiveness to his voice that I'd never heard before. "I'd rather not be alone actually."

I sat next to him, taking my dad's place. I had butterflies in my stomach, unsure of what to say. "I'm sorry I heard all that. I wanted to know what was going on, but now I wish I didn't."

"Yeah, you're too young to hear all that."

"No, I'm not. I just don't want you to be embarrassed."

Silence.

"My dad's wrong, Josh. You did the right thing."

"It doesn't feel like it. I think I made things worse for my mom. She was more upset when my dad and I were hitting each other than when he hit her."

"But you couldn't just let him do that."

"I guess. But now I'll have to apologize, which is bullshit. Sorry."

"That's okay. I say bullshit all the time."

Josh grinned for a minute under his arm. "Yeah, sure you do."

"I wish that hadn't all happened to you," I said, "but I'm glad you're here. You'll like being here, won't you?"

"Of course I will. It's nice of your mom and dad to let me come stay, but I feel bad invading Kade's space."

"Kade won't mind. He's out here in the woods painting all the time anyway."

I sat quietly next to Josh, listening to the breeze rustle the leaves around us, my chin resting on my knees.

"You think I could be alone for a while now?"

"Sure." I got up and started walking but turned around in a burst of courage. "I think you are a brave and strong and wonderful person, Josh." Then I ran off down the path before he could respond.

The next day, Kade left a present in my room, a painting of Josh and me in the woods. The way he'd captured light and shadow perfectly reflected the conflicted mood of that moment in time. Apparently, I wasn't the only spy.

Josh did all he could to make himself useful. His school sent packets of work, which he did at our house, and they sent his finals to my dad at his school, where Josh went to take them. The work didn't take him long, so he started helping Mom with projects around the house.

I ran up our driveway every day after school but didn't always like what I saw when I got there. Mom and Josh became like best friends, always working together on one thing or another when I got home. First he prepped the garden for her, since Dad hated that job—turning the soil, clearing rocks, building a fence to keep out the deer and other hungry creatures. Then they started painting the kitchen together, something my dad had been promising to do for years. One day, Mom had Frank Sinatra blasting and they were singing "That's Life"—our song, right out loud. I banged around that afternoon to show that I was mad, but they didn't even notice.

Another day, Kade and I heard Mom and Josh talking through the open kitchen window before they knew we were home. Josh was upset, saying something about how he'd messed everything up, and Mom was reassuring him that he'd done the right thing. She told him that she'd called Pam the day he got here and said that if she wanted to leave Rob, she and the kids could all come stay with us, but Pam had said she was fine, that she and Rob had worked things out.

Then Josh and Mom talked about how Dad, Rob, and Pam acted like everything was normal and fine when it so clearly wasn't. How unsettling it was to see the world one way when everyone around you was seeing something completely different. Josh told her how hard it was to never know what was coming; even if it didn't happen often, you just never knew when it might. It sounded like Josh started crying, and then his voice was muffled, like Mom was hugging him.

It was one thing for Josh to love Dad, but I didn't like this sudden intimacy he had with my mom. I looked around for something to stand on so I could see inside, but Kade shook his head, not wanting to blow our cover. He pulled me away from the window, and we went to the Big Rock to talk about what we'd heard.

I told him I didn't like Mom and Josh being BFFs, and Kade pointed out that Josh seemed to need a mom right now and that perhaps it was selfish of me to deny him that, even in my thoughts. I had to admit he had a point, but I still didn't like it.

May 30, 1984

Dear Steph,

Your brother is all settled in here. He seems happier now than he did the first few days. It was awful what happened. Are you okay? How's your mom? You must all miss Josh, but we're happy to have him here (me especially!). I can't wait to see you for camping. I'm going to bring the camera I got for Christmas and take tons and tons of pictures. You have to take lots of pictures to get good at it.

Love,

Kai

June 11, 1984

Dear Kai,

My brother was stupid, as usual. He made a big deal out of nothing. Everything is fine here. I'm fine, my mom's fine. We're all good. Can't wait to see you too. Can I be your model? We'll have lots of fun taking pictures.

Love,

Your best friend Stephanie

FIRST KISS

WHEN JOSH FIRST CAME TO our house, he volunteered to babysit so my parents could go out on the weekends. I hated the word babysit, since I certainly didn't need a babysitter at twelve and three quarters years old. Instead, I turned it into playing house with Josh, except Josh didn't know that. I helped him cook dinner for us, then took care of cleaning up. Kade knew exactly what I was doing, so he mostly stayed in his room, out of my way, although he mostly stayed out of the way regardless. Josh and I would watch TV together until my parents got home, unless I fell asleep first.

One night after Josh had been with us for about a month, my parents were out especially late. It was one of the last Saturday nights before camping with the Tylers, and they were taking advantage of their live-in nanny with a night out in the city. It was after midnight, and I was out cold on the couch. Josh wanted to go to bed but didn't want to leave me there. He tried waking me up, but I didn't budge.

I woke as he slipped his hands under me, but I pretended to still be asleep. He carried me to my bed, and it felt like I was floating in a dream. I was so happy to be in his arms. He was strong and didn't struggle to carry me, even up the stairs to my room.

He lowered me down onto my bed, and our faces were so close that I kissed him, a quick peck on the lips. He dropped me the last few inches in surprise.

"Jesus, Kai. Not cool," he said before barreling out of the room.

I stayed hiding under my covers for as much of the next morning as I could. By then, the joy of the kiss had been replaced by the horror of Josh's reaction. I was usually up by eight or nine o'clock, but it was past ten when my mom brought me juice and sat down on my bed.

"I heard what happened last night."

I buried my head in the pillow and started crying, and she rubbed my back. "Does he hate me? Does he think I'm the stupidest girl who ever lived?"

"No, of course not, but you did upset him. He's beating himself up, thinking it's his fault."

"It wasn't his fault. Don't be mad at him."

"Oh, I'm not," she said. "I know who was one hundred percent responsible for that kiss."

"I'm sorry, Mom. I just couldn't help it. I love him."

"I know you think so, Kai."

"I do. I always have and always will."

Mom kept rubbing my back while she thought of what to say next.

"Even if you love him, you can't go around kissing people who don't want to be kissed. Did you think he wanted you to kiss him?"

"I don't know. I wasn't really thinking. I just wanted to do it."

"Here's your first lesson in love, Kai," Mom said, seeming to take me seriously. "Don't lose your head. Love makes you want to stop thinking, but you can't do that. You have to be smart if you want to have any chance at love."

I rolled over and sat up. "Do you think I have a chance, Mom?"

She looked me straight in the eye and studied me for a minute. "Honestly, honey, I don't think so. I think he sees you as another little sister."

"I think you're wrong," I said. "I love him, and someday he'll love me too."

Mom took a deep breath and studied me again. "Maybe." She handed me my juice, and I took a few gulps. "For now, though, you and Josh feel differently, so maybe it would be smarter to tuck your love away in your back pocket, like a map you're going to pull out when you get to the trailhead. But live your life now, as a twelve-year-old girl. Date boys your own age. Don't look desperate for Josh, because that will make him less and less interested in you. You're too old for the cute crush thing now, and after last night, it will feel creepy to him. But you can be friends. Play it cool and keep the connection but pursue other options while you wait to grow up."

I wanted Mom to be wrong. What did she know about love? She didn't seem to handle it very well herself, what with all the fighting and complaining about Dad. Still, she did make some strong points. Josh didn't love me yet. And Tommy Baker at school was cute. Maybe I would like kissing him first and then Josh later. I'd be a better kisser if I practiced.

Mom let me mull it over as she got up from the bed and started picking clothes up off the floor and putting them in my laundry basket.

"I know you have stuff to think about, sweetie, but right now we need to figure out what you're going to say to Josh. And to your dad. They're both pretty upset."

I hadn't even thought about Dad. Mom told me that Josh had waited up for them last night and that Dad hadn't reacted well to the news of our kiss. He'd been angry, which upset Josh even more than he already was.

"I can handle Dad."

"Oh really?"

"Dad likes problems to go away quickly, so all I have to do is tell him I'll make the problem go away, and he'll be fine."

"Who's the smart one now?" Mom asked with a grin, but it faded quickly, and she sat back down on the bed. "Do you always just tell Dad what he wants to hear?"

"Usually," I answered.

"You don't have to do that, you know. You are allowed to speak your mind, tell him what you think and feel."

"When you do that, the two of you end up fighting."

"Fighting is necessary sometimes."

"I guess." I didn't really think the way Mom and Dad fought was necessary. I thought it was generally pointless and often mean, but I kept that to myself. "I do tell Dad what I'm thinking, just not everything, not the stuff that would upset him."

"Do you do that with me?" Mom asked.

"Not as much. You listen and understand, and then you're okay, so I tell you most stuff. Some things are private, though."

"As well they should be. You are entitled to your privacy. You are also entitled to share what you want to share without worrying about how the other person will react."

"I don't think that's true," I said firmly.

"How so?" Mom asked.

"I shared a kiss and it freaked Josh out. Pam shared something and Rob hit her. Josh did something and he got hit too. You yell at Dad and he yells back and then goes and drinks and you have the same argument the next day and the day after that. I think you *do* need to worry how the other person will react. I think it's smarter to keep some things to yourself and say what the other person wants to hear sometimes."

Mom got a little teary-eyed and thought for a minute before

responding. "I wish that wasn't true, but maybe sometimes it is. You have a strong spirit and a powerful voice, though, baby, and I want you to use them."

"But not to tell Josh I love him."

"True, not for that. I don't know. This stuff is complicated. It's hard to be true to ourselves sometimes, but I think it's important to try."

We both sat silently with our thoughts for a few more minutes, then Mom stood up. "Okay, let's fix this. First your dad, then Josh."

I lay back down and pulled the covers up around my shoulders. "What do I say to Josh? Do I have to talk to him today? Can't I go to Julie's house and come home after dinner? Deal with it tomorrow?"

"No chance," Mom said, patting my leg in a way that meant I needed to get up. "The longer you wait the worse it will be. And we're not going to torture Josh all day either. You're going to find him and tell him you're sorry for making him uncomfortable. Tell him you were half asleep and thought it was a dream. That's a little bit true, right?"

"Yes, but it's so embarrassing."

"That ship has sailed, sweetie. Long gone, halfway across the Atlantic. Yes, it is embarrassing. So just own up to it. It will be awkward for a day or two, and then it will be fine. Apologize and tell him it won't happen again and that you want things to get back to normal as quickly as possible. Josh is a good kid, and he'll forgive you."

"Okay, fine." I didn't like it but didn't seem to have much of a choice.

"Get dressed and talk to your dad first. He's in the kitchen. But before anything, you know what we need."

"Please don't say Frank," I begged.

"Of course we need Frank." Mom smiled and put on "That's Life" while I got dressed. I didn't want to encourage her by singing along, but I couldn't help myself. It's a catchy tune, and it did make me feel better.

Dad was reading the *New York Times Book Review* at the table, and I immediately apologized, taking full responsibility for the kiss and exonerating Josh. He looked up at me for a minute, then looked back at the paper and said, "Okay."

I made some toast and sat with him at the table. When I finished my toast and rinsed my plate, Dad said, "Josh is off in the woods somewhere, avoiding us all. Go find him and make this right, Kai." I knew he wouldn't mention it again.

I walked slowly through the woods, in no hurry to face this awkward reckoning, distracting myself by thinking about how much I loved springtime on my mountain, the anticipation of summer, knowing something great was right around the corner. In spring, the woods came alive with color. Variations of pinks and purples bloomed on lilac bushes and mountain laurel. Dogwood trees blossomed in white and pink. Forsythia glowed bright yellow. Purple and yellow crocuses would be the first flowers to peek out, putting them at risk when there was a late frost or snow. Hundreds of daffodils grew wild throughout the woods and on the side of the hill in front of our house, in all combinations of yellow, orange, and white. I loved the daffodils, but my favorite flowers were lily of the valley, delicate little white bells that smelled gloriously sweet, although the honeysuckle smelled even sweeter.

After stopping to smell my twentieth flower, I took a deep breath and headed to the mossy spot I knew Josh liked. I found him lying with his arm over his eyes, his distressed pose. I sat down next to him, my stomach in knots.

"Sorry, Josh."

"Okay."

"It won't happen again." At least not for a while, and hopefully he would be the one to kiss me next time.

"Okay."

He was lying perfectly still, probably afraid to move around me now. I was a bundle of jittery nerves, sitting there rocking my legs from side to side, tapping my feet together.

"Can we go back to normal?"

"Okay."

"That's not very convincing."

He moved his arm to look at me. "My life is *so* not normal right now, Kai. And you just made it weirder. I would love for things to go back to normal, but I don't think that's going to happen." He put his arm back over his eyes. I felt like I was going to cry but held it in.

"I really am sorry. I didn't mean it."

"Don't bullshit me, Kai. If you want to apologize, at least be straight."

"That will make it even weirder. I'm trying to make it easier and better for you." The way I handled Dad wasn't working here. "What do you want me to do? I'll do whatever you want."

He sat up, looked at me, then looked off into the distance. "I know you have feelings for me, and you know I don't feel that way."

He paused. I was pretty much holding my breath because it felt like breathing might lead to crying, and I really didn't want to cry.

"But I do care about you, and I hope you know that too."

I let out a long breath, feeling like this might actually be okay.

He picked up a branch and poked at the moss and dirt, then added, "You just have to stay in your lane, okay? We're like cousins, siblings, friends. That's how it is."

I picked up a stick and dug in the moss too, thinking about that.

"I'm okay with friends. And, like, second cousins twice removed. Not siblings. Can that be how it is?"

He grinned and squinted over at me. "Okay, second cousins twice removed." He tossed the branch aside, lay back down, and put his arm over his eyes again. "Your dad was not happy with me."

"Me neither, but he's fine now. My dad likes to avoid messy stuff, so you'll never hear about it again." I dug in the dirt for a few minutes while we both pondered things.

"You are a brave girl, Kai. And clever. You put yourself out there and get what you want most of the time, huh?"

"Most of the time. Eventually. Sometimes I just have to be patient and wear people down." I grinned and lay down on the moss next to Josh.

I felt different, older.

"This has been a weird day," I said.

"You're tellin' me," Josh answered.

"I had a talk with my mom that was different than ones we've had before, and this is different too, talking with you like this. But I talked to my dad and that was just the same. I don't know, it's just got me all confused."

"Confused about what?" He turned his head toward me, his arm shading his face but not blocking his eyes now.

I kept looking up at the sky. Watching the light through the leaves made it easier to articulate my thoughts.

"Is it better to tell people what you think or to tell them what they want to hear?"

"Dang, that's a serious question." He rolled back into his contemplative position, arm over eyes. "I have no clue. I usually tell my dad what he wants to hear and do what he wants me to do, and my life goes along just fine. Then I stand up to him, and I get punched in the face and kicked out of the house."

"Yeah, that's what I mean. Mom said I should use my voice, not worry about what other people want to hear, but then she told me what I should say to you and Dad, and it was what you both wanted to hear, not what I really wanted to say." A breeze rustled the leaves above me, and I squinted as the sun poked through the fresh spaces.

"I usually tell my dad what he wants to hear because he fights with my mom when she says what she actually thinks," I continued. "It works better my way, but I don't really like how it feels. I came out here to tell you what you wanted to hear, but then I told you what I really thought and that felt better." I rolled my head to look at him. "It's confusing."

"It's confusing because it's bullshit."

"Is that your favorite word?" I teased.

"It's my life right now," he joked back, although it wasn't really a joke.

"It's like they say to do it one way, but they don't really mean it and they definitely don't do it that way," I said.

"I've been thinking about all this since my mom put me on that train in the middle of the night, and I still don't have a clue," Josh said. "The one thing I do know is that some people clearly don't want to know what we're thinking or how we feel. Some people definitely want us to tell them what they want to hear. And if we want to live with those people without causing problems, we better do it their way."

"You're going to do it that way with your dad?"

"You bet, but I'm also going to get out of there as soon as I possibly can. College, work, whatever, I'm out of there one year from now. I can keep my mouth shut for a year, but then I don't want to be like that. I want to be someone who means what I say and does what feels right."

"I want to be that kind of person too. Maybe just not with my dad."

"Yeah, probably not with our dads."

"But maybe with each other?"

"Maybe." Josh peeked at me again. "As long as you stay in your lane."

I smiled at him and looked back at the sky. I wasn't going to say anything that wasn't true, so I kept my mouth shut. I saw him shake his head a little, grinning at my intentional nonresponse.

I was thinking all these deep and profound thoughts, but mostly—really, truly, predominantly—I was thinking about Josh lying next to me, how someday maybe he would reach over and take my hand or roll over and kiss me, but how right now it was nice to just lie here next to him and know that he knew what I was thinking and feeling and that he was still there beside me. He didn't like it, it wasn't ideal, but he was hanging in here with me, and that meant a lot.

CAMPING

Two weeks later, we arrived at High Point Campground in the Adirondacks. The lake there was small but had lots of little inlets to accommodate about thirty campsites, all situated along the meandering shoreline, nestled among tall trees and thick brush. We'd picked a site that was walking distance to the little beach but not too close, because we didn't want to be bothered by people walking back and forth all the time. The site was also not far from a wide-open meadow where we could play football or wiffle ball or Frisbee. And it was close to bathrooms, always an important consideration.

Josh was helping Dad set up our tent when the Tylers pulled into the adjacent campsite. Dad walked over to greet Rob while Bobby and Nick bounded out of the car and ran over to Josh, pulling him into a three-way bear hug. They immediately started play-punching him to mask their emotion at seeing him again. Pam was right behind them with tears in her eyes, pulling Josh to her briefly, before Rob called out for him to come help set up camp. No "Hello, son," no "Nice to see you," just "Get to work"— oh, and don't hug your mom too long. My heart broke for Josh, who had swallowed his pride to call and apologize to his dad weeks ago, all for this lousy reunion. Josh seemed disappointed but not surprised and merely proceeded to corral his brothers into helping him.

I hugged Stephanie, who started talking right away about something or other. I wasn't paying attention because I was watching my mom hug Pam, who looked like she had gained thirty pounds since Christmas. She was crying, Mom was whispering in her ear, and I wished I could hear what she was saying.

My dad came back to our campsite and greeted Pam, ending their moment. He called Kade to take Josh's place setting up. Mom noticed me watching everyone and sent me and Steph to go fill our water jugs at the pump, which was a few sites away.

"Steph, is your mom okay? She was crying."

"Kai, I told you, everything's fine. She's happy to see Josh, that's all."

"You must be happy to see him too. Did you miss him?"

"Not really. Everything has always been about Josh in our house. The past few weeks, it's been about me for a change. Mom was so sad when he left, but I cheered her up. Bobby and Nick were staying out of Dad's way because they're always Team Josh, so Dad and I did stuff together too. I had a great time actually."

"How could you hang out with your dad after what he did? Weren't you scared or mad or anything?" I couldn't believe what she was saying.

"You're not listening to me at all. Did you even read my letter? I told you everything is fine."

"It's not fine! Your dad hurt him!"

"That was Josh's fault for hitting Dad. Josh only thinks about himself. All you have to do with my dad is walk away and leave him alone, but Josh doesn't like to do that, so he gets in trouble."

"How can you say that? He was trying to take care of your mom. He's always thinking about all of us."

"Of course you would say that. You're another member of

Team Josh. For once, people picked me. Mom and Dad picked me."

"They didn't pick you," I said. "You were just the only one there."

She turned and stomped back to her campsite and helped her mom unpack while I got the water myself, which was for the best because I would only have said something even meaner if she'd given me the chance.

I escaped with Kade as soon as I could and told him what Stephanie had said. "I don't get it. I think she's been brainwashed by her evil dad."

"I guess," Kade said. "None of it makes any sense. Did you see how mean Rob was to Josh? Not even saying hi?"

"Of course I did. Poor Josh. How can Dad still be friends with Rob?"

"I don't know. Like I said, it makes no sense."

"Well, I'm not talking to Stephanie. If she's going to be mean to Josh, then I don't even like her anymore."

"That's gonna make it a boring week for you."

"No it won't. I have a plan."

I told Kade my idea to use my new camera to take pictures of everyone this week as a cover story for spying on them. I thought it might be the best way of figuring this whole thing out. Kade didn't share my optimism that I would find any answers, but he agreed to help.

Our first subjects, later that afternoon, were the Tyler boys. We surreptitiously followed them to the meadow, Kade and I positioning ourselves among the trees and bushes that bordered the grass. Josh, Bobby, and Nick tossed the football around for a while, and I took a few pictures of them. I'd always been so focused on Josh that I never realized how much the three of them looked alike, particularly when you took into account their similar mannerisms—tilting their heads in tandem, running in matching strides. Josh was the cutest, of course, but they all shared their dad's broad shoulders and muscular build, their mom's rich brown eyes and attractive face. Josh had the blond curls, Bobby's brown hair was buzz-cut, and Nick had straight brown hair reminiscent of Han Solo. I noticed that Bobby was now taller than Josh and wondered when that had happened.

The key moment for my investigation came when they sat in the shade right near where Kade and I were hiding. He looked at me nervously because they were so close. I made the universal shushing signal, finger to lips, and kept myself as still as possible, not daring to click the camera shutter.

"So what's it been like at home?" Josh asked.

"Ya know, all puppies and sunshine, Josh, as usual," Bobby said.

"How's Mom been?"

"She's been okay," Bobby said.

"She missed you a lot," Nick elaborated. "But at the same time, Dad was in his nice-guy, make-it-up-to-her mode, so that was going on too."

"And how about you guys?"

"Please…we can take care of ourselves," Bobby said.

Again Nick was more forthcoming. "It sucked not having you there, Josh. That was bullshit to send you away."

I smiled at the bullshit comment. Was it a family thing or just a teenage boy thing?

"Yeah, that was bullshit," Bobby agreed, probably just so he could say the word too. "You know what wasn't bullshit?"

"What?" asked Josh.

"That shiner you gave Dad. It was a doozy. I think it's why he's still pissed. I don't know what you looked like, but you got him good." They were all smiling now.

"Were you okay?" Nick asked.

"Yeah, John and Tammy took good care of me. Missed prom, though."

"Yeah, Becca went with Trent," Bobby said. "Asshole."

"Yeah, she broke up with me."

What was this all about? I hadn't heard about any of it. I looked at Kade and he shrugged.

"Dad's been better, though, Josh," Nick said. "I think he did feel bad about what happened. He seemed to know he took it too far."

"What makes you think so?" Josh asked.

"Mostly what he let Bobby and me get away with."

"Yeah, man, Nick and I were pushing it with him, especially right when you left. Wouldn't look at him, wouldn't talk to him except to answer a direct question. But he just ignored it. Never did anything about it, and we were asking for it. I was dying for him to start something with me." Bobby was all tough guy.

"That was stupid," Josh said, although he was smiling again and seemed touched by their loyalty.

"Yeah? Look who's talking!" Bobby said.

They all cracked up at that, relieving the tension of the past weeks as much as anything, because it wasn't all that funny, and I couldn't help but snap a picture. They didn't hear the click above their laughter.

I followed Josh around a lot that week, but not for the usual reason. Mostly because I wanted to be sure he was alright. If I wasn't watching him, I was keeping an eye on Rob, but I preferred watching Josh.

I took a beautiful picture of Josh with his mom the morning after we got there. Dad and Rob had gone fishing, as they usually did in the early mornings. Kade used to go with them, but he stopped after the whole hitting-him-with-a-stick thing. Staying away from Rob was something Kade wised up to long ago. Josh used to go with them too, but not this year.

The men were gone and we were all eating breakfast when I noticed Pam put her hand on Josh's shoulder. He looked up at her with such love in his eyes. She suggested they take a walk, and I snuck along a few minutes behind them. I never got close enough to hear what they were saying, but it was beautiful to watch. Pam had her arm looped through Josh's, and they were strolling slowly, completely focused on each other. The picture I love from that walk was one where Pam rested her head on Josh's arm, leaning into him, soaking up the physical presence of her son beside her. Just before they got back to the campground, they shared the biggest, longest hug I'd ever seen, surpassing Dad's with Josh at the train station. I almost cried watching them, and Pam was clearly crying, and I thought I saw Josh wipe his eyes quickly when they separated, although I wasn't sure. They took a walk every morning of our trip while the dads were fishing, but I never followed them again. It was too private, too intimate, and anyway, I knew that Josh was perfectly safe with his mom.

I was proud of the pictures I took that week. They were not the posed pictures that go along with most family vacations. I discreetly took pictures of everyone showing the emotions of the week—anger, disappointment, sadness, loss, and worry. I didn't take any pictures of Rob. It was my way of cutting him out, even though no one ever knew that but me. Mom didn't talk to Rob all week, and that was a much more obvious statement. It made things awkward, but Mom didn't care. She was mad at Rob, and I think she also did it to support Josh and Pam, and to show me that she wasn't going to pretend.

A few days into the trip, Dad and I took a canoe out on the lake together, a little father-daughter tradition we had. I was in the front of the boat and wasn't saying much, still confused and generally irritated with my dad for palling around with Rob as if nothing had happened.

"You're unusually quiet, Kai. Something on your mind?"

I was surprised he asked and wasn't about to pass up my opportunity to tell him exactly what was on my mind. I turned around suddenly and almost tipped our canoe.

"Whoa! Talk, don't move," Dad said, and I turned back around, thinking it might be easier for him if we talked like this anyway, without eye contact. That was always easier for Kade.

"How can you still be friends with Rob?" I said. "He hurt Josh and Pam, but you act like nothing happened."

Dad continued paddling.

"Are you going to say something?" I asked after a minute.

"It's complicated, Kai."

"I doesn't really seem that complicated to me. He's mean, so don't be friends with him."

More paddling.

"Dad!" I yelled.

"Okay, I'm going to tell you some things, but give me a minute. It's complicated for me because Rob is my family and he's trying his best. I know he is, even though that's hard for everyone else to see."

Now it was my turn to stay quiet and paddle, waiting for Dad to tell me whatever he was going to tell me. Eventually he started talking. He told me a story about the Philippines, when he and Rob were first friends. One night, they were walking around the town where they were living and working, and they saw a guy hitting his daughter over and over with a bamboo pole. She was screaming and crying, and Dad wanted to go tell him to stop. Rob told him not to get involved and tried pulling him away, but it made Dad think of things his dad had done and how badly he'd wanted somebody to stop it, and how nobody did, including Dad, and how he just had to stop this beating. He went up to talk to the guy, who was obviously shocked and embarrassed that my dad had called him out, and for a moment Dad felt good, like he'd changed something by making the guy see the error of his ways. But as they were interacting, the guy's adult son came out of the house and started yelling at Dad, who didn't understand most of it because he only knew a little Tagalog, but the son was basically pissed that my dad had shamed his dad, since his sister's beating was well-deserved in their minds. Anyway, one thing led to another, and that guy started punching my dad. Rob came out of nowhere and beat the crap out of the son.

Dad and Rob went back to their place and nursed their minor injuries, and after a few drinks Dad explained why he'd felt compelled to get involved. They ended up playing a drinking game comparing terrible childhoods. Dad told me that his didn't hold a candle to Rob's. Dad's dad hit him and his mom, but nothing terrible, nothing that left permanent scars, according to Dad.

Rob's dad, on the other hand, had a shed in back of their house where he would take Rob and his mom and his sister and do all kinds of awful things to them. Dad didn't give me details because he said he still wished he didn't know. One day, a new neighbor moved in, heard shrieks from the shed, and called the cops, who came and arrested Rob's dad and took Rob and his sister away, and he spent his teen years moving from one foster home to another, many of them not much better than his parents' house.

"He's so much better than his dad, Kai. He's moved so far beyond where he came from. He could be angry all the time, but he works really, really hard to control himself, and I get it that it's not good enough, but that's why I forgive him. It's why I'm his friend no matter what, because I know how hard he's trying. It's also why I stay out of it. People getting involved, trying to save other people, just doesn't work anyway."

I was crying in the front of the canoe. I hated that I cried so often and easily.

"I'm sorry, Kai," Dad said behind me. "But things are complicated."

"I wish it wasn't all so complicated," I said. "I wish there were good guys and bad guys and a hero who could save everyone." I usually wanted to be grown up already, but right then I wanted to be a naïve, innocent kid again. Part of me still wants that.

"Me too, honey," Dad said. "Me too."

I turned around, slowly and carefully this time. "Thanks for telling me, Dad." I knew how hard and unnatural it was for him to talk like that, and it made me feel like I mattered to him. "I kind of wish you hadn't, but I'm mostly glad you did. It helps me not be so mad at you at least. I'm still mad at Rob, though. It's not okay, what he did…what he does. No matter what happened to him, it's not okay."

"I know that, but he's like a brother to me. Is there anything that would make you turn against Kade?"

I couldn't think of anything, but I didn't want to admit that to Dad, so I stayed quiet.

"I have talked with him," Dad added. "I really think he's going to do better."

"Okay." I wasn't sure if either of us believed it, but what else was there but to hope it was true.

About halfway through the week, I made up with Stephanie, even though I didn't really want to. I wanted some things to stay black-and-white. Yet as much as part of me thought Stephanie had come down on the villain's side, against my hero, another part of me knew now that it wasn't so simple. Also, Kade begged me to make up with her because she was driving him crazy. She'd decided that Kade would take my place as her Martin twin, and she'd been following him around doing her nonstop babbling thing, and Kade wanted some peace and quiet. So there was that, although neither Kade nor my own critical thinking could ever change my mind as powerfully as Josh, who intervened next.

I was lugging the water jug back from the pump one afternoon when he came up behind me. For once, I hadn't been tracking him.

"Hey, Kai," he said, taking the jug out of my hand, making my stomach lurch a little when his fingers brushed mine.

"Hey, Josh," I said. "Water's my chore. You've got plenty of your own."

"That's okay, I have a favor to ask in return."

"What's that?" I wanted to say yes right away but figured I should let him tell me the favor first. Plus, that would lengthen the amount of time I got to walk and talk with him. We hadn't really interacted now that he had his brothers back.

"Fix whatever's up with my sister?"

"Really? Can't you ask me a different favor?" I kicked a rock that jumped ahead of Josh.

"Nope, that's the favor." He kicked the rock back into my path. "What's the deal anyway?"

I didn't want to tell him that Stephanie had turned to the dark side. I thought it would hurt him and make him feel like even more of an outsider in his family to hear that his baby sister was against him.

"She just said some stupid stuff that made me mad," I said, kicking the rock again, accidentally making it skip off into the woods.

"About me?" Josh asked.

"Why do you think that?"

"If it was anything else, you would have just told me. And she's been weird with me too."

"Yeah."

"What'd she say?"

"Basically, she just took your dad's side in the whole thing, which is bullshit."

Josh tried not to laugh at me. "You can't say that."

"I told you I say it all the time."

"Now that *is* bullshit," he said, smiling at me. "Please make up with my stupid sister."

"Fine," I agreed, happy that I'd made him smile, even if he was kind of laughing at me.

I found Stephanie when we got back to the campsite, and although we didn't exactly work it through, we did apologize to each other and start hanging out again. It had gotten boring without her anyway. Over the next few days, we swam together and braided each other's hair and I told her about kissing Josh but not about our conversation afterward, because that was mine and his and I liked having something private between us.

We hadn't done much all together that week, people taking hikes at different times, going fishing around the lake in groups of two or three, swimming in various clusters. But on the last day, I think we all realized this was our final shot at making amends and coming together, so we made an effort to do that. I don't even remember anyone suggesting the plan; we just all ended up at the little campground beach. Everyone seemed happy finally, and I was capturing smiles with my camera for a change. Our dads and Josh were grilling hot dogs for lunch, Pam was sunbathing, Mom was blipping. Stephanie was floating peacefully too, until Bobby and Nick started splashing her. Even Kade joined in the splashing, like an evil spell had been broken and we were alright again. After a while, I noticed that Josh had drifted off, so I went to look for him. I found him on a bench at the far end of the beach, watching everyone from afar.

"Say cheese," I said for the first time that week.

"Don't start that," Josh said, holding his hand up in front of his face. "You were doing so well at not being annoying with that thing."

"What're you doing down here all by yourself? Everyone's having fun for once."

"I know. I'll come back down soon. I just had to take a minute so I didn't cast a dark cloud over the festivities."

"What do you mean?"

He scooted over to make room for me on the bench, and I sat down next to him.

"My awesome dad just informed me that I'm not coming home with them."

"What?" I was stunned.

"He got me a job as a camp counselor for the summer. One of his teacher friends runs the place. They're dropping me off on the way home. I don't even get to go to Cape Cod." Going to the Cape for the first week of August was another Tyler-Martin tradition that we'd had for as long as I could remember.

"No! That's not fair! You apologized. You did what he said."

"Yeah, and he said it wasn't enough. He said that chilling at your house wasn't really a punishment. The money I earn this summer will go toward college, which he'll consider paying for if I toe the line for the next year. So I don't get to spend the money, I don't get to see my friends, I don't get to go to the Cape. He actually spelled it out in detail and said *that* is what a punishment feels like." Josh was looking out at the lake as he talked, almost like he wasn't even there.

"He already gave you a black eye. Did you remind him of that punishment?"

"That would not have been smart."

"What did you say?"

"I said, 'Yes, sir.'"

"Oh, Josh. I'm sorry. Again."

I knew my mom or his mom would touch his arm or give him a hug or something, but that seemed out of my lane, so I sat on my hands instead.

"Let's not do a Josh pity party, okay?" he said.

"Didn't my dad say anything?" I knew the answer but hoped for a different one.

"Nope. He just stood there sucking on his beer."

That was the first time I ever heard Josh sound upset with my dad.

"My mom helps me look at things differently when they don't go my way," I said after staring at the water for a while. "Wanna do that?"

"Sure." He seemed unconvinced, but at least he was willing to let me stay and talk.

"You have senior year, then you'll be off to college. You can do that. It's just a year, right?"

"And what about the summer?"

"You'll have work experience, which will help you get another job later. Maybe you'll like being a camp counselor. You're used to bossing all of us around. And that will be two fewer months that you have to spend with your dad."

"Are you really this smart?" he asked, squinting at me with a little grin.

"Yes." I smiled. "You should remember that for later."

"Why? What happens later?" He was still grinning, while also giving me a skeptical look.

"You never know. Just remember that I'm smart. Just in case."

We both looked back out at the water.

"I love Cape Cod," Josh said after a bit.

"How about if I write to you about it?"

"Like pen pals? Like you and Stephanie?"

"Sure, if you write me back."

"That would be nice, help me be less lonely all summer."

"You won't be lonely. People always like you. You'll make friends with the other counselors in two seconds. Probably girls too, but don't write to me about them, okay?"

"Deal."

I loved the idea of being pen pals with Josh, although I didn't think he would actually write. I was wrong.

July 1, 1984

Dear Kai,

I'm sending the first letter so you'll know I was serious and to give you my address here at Camp Lots 'O Fun. It's not bad, actually. You were right that I've made friends already. Plus, this camp is all about outdoor adventures like hiking and rock climbing and obstacle courses and stuff that I love, so that's fun. The kids can be a pain, but not as much as you (ha!) and most of them are alright. We do storytelling under the stars a couple of times a week, and I'm learning that I'm good at that, which is new. I may even start writing some of my stories down. We'll see. No comment on girls...ha! I hope you write back. Even though I'm busy and not lonely, it's not the same as home.

J

July 5, 1984

Dear J,

I was so happy to get your letter. I'm glad the camp isn't so bad. It sounds like fun really. I'm sending you some of the pictures I took when we were camping. I like that nobody is looking at the camera. I hope you like the one of you and your mom...sorry I was spying on you, but maybe it's okay because of how good the picture is.

My summer is okay. It's really hot, so that's annoying. Mom took Kade and me to see a play called The Wiz in the city last week, and it was so good! It was the story of the Wizard of Oz but with Black people and different music. We got the record and have been listening to it over and over again. There's this song called "Home" that made me think of you because it's at the end when Dorothy just wants to go home. It's sad but happy because she does end up going home, just like you will at the end of the summer.

Write me back! Send me one of your stories.

K

July 22, 1984

K,

Thanks for your letter. It was great. I hope you all have fun in Cape Cod. Don't be missing me. I'm fine here. The play sounds great, although I hate going to the city. Your pictures were amazing! You captured what everyone was feeling and they didn't even know it. You're a really good photographer, although you should be less sneaky about it! Take lots of pictures at the Cape and send them to me so I don't completely miss out.

I'm sending you the first story I've ever written down. It's probably stupid, but I'm pretty sure you'll be an easy critic, so I'm sending it to you. The kids liked the story when I told it, but I'm not sure it works on paper.

Big news...I've decided to quit football senior year, and you're the only person I'm telling why, so don't tell anyone. I'm quitting because it's going to crush my dad. He loves that we all play football because he did and because it proves we're such tough guys, just like him. But I don't want to be like him, and I definitely don't want to give him the satisfaction of watching me play again. So I'm quitting. He can't know why because it'll piss him off all over again, so I'll have to come up with a different reason. But I'll know why, and that's enough for me. It gives me a little bit of control over something again, which I need. Don't tell!

    J

Red Flame Extinguished
by Josh Tyler

There was once a boy named Paxton who lived on a pirate ship. His mother was the kindest, sweetest woman in the world, but his father was the most brutal pirate on all the seas. No one knew his real name, for as long as anyone could remember he was known as Captain Red Flame. He had earned this name by the evil pleasure he took in burning down each village or town that denied him what he demanded, be it fresh water or wine, bread or meat, pillows or pineapples. If anyone refused him anything, he struck a match and burned everything down.

So how did this kind, sweet woman end up on Red Flame's ship? He must have kidnapped her, right? Taken her away against her will and locked her in the bowels of his ship.

But no, she loved him.

How could that be, you ask?

Magic is how. These were the days when magic was still real and working everywhere, all the time.

Paxton's mom lived in a village along the sea. When Red Flame anchored there, he demanded that the townspeople board his ship and clean the filth of their many long voyages. He wanted a clean and sparkly ship, and Paxton's mom was a diligent worker, so the townspeople sent her to Red Flame's cabin to clean there, since it needed to be spotless so that he wouldn't burn down their town.

While cleaning, a mouse ran out of a corner where he had been living happily in a pile of discarded clothes and papers and food. Anyone else would have smooshed that mouse, but Paxton's mom was such a gentle soul that she made a little nest for the mouse and put him on a high shelf where he would be out of harm's way.

But you see, the mouse was magical. He appreciated this kind gesture, and decided to grant a wish to Paxton's mom. Instead of asking her, he magically looked into her heart to see what she most desired. And what she most desired was to be loved, so the mouse placed a magical spell to bring her what she wanted.

When Red Flame walked through the door of his room, expecting to berate whomever was working there, he instead fell in love with Paxton's mom. The mouse realized that he had made a small mistake in his magic, since he knew the evil in Red Flame's heart, so he cast a second spell to make Red Flame the gentlest, kindest man in the world when he was in this room with Paxton's mom.

So they fell in love and sailed off happily together, leaving the village whole and well. Red Flame was terrible and mean in the whole wide world except when he was in his cabin with his love, and then he was kind and gentle.

Of course, no one understood exactly what was going on, but everyone knew that magic happened, so most people just assumed that's what it was.

Now, when Paxton was a baby, he lived in the cabin with his mother, and saw his father as a kind and gentle man. His mother hoped to keep him in the cabin forever, although she knew that could never be. One day when he was about your age, he snuck out to the main deck to see the world around him. The ship was docked, and Red Flame was pillaging the town, demanding all their winter supplies.

Paxton saw his father's true self, his evil attacks on people and his final order to burn the village to the ground. Paxton cried out to his father, ordering him not to do this terrible thing, expecting the kind and gentle man who came into their cabin each night, not the evil man who struck Paxton and tossed him overboard, discarding him as if he'd never seen him before, although he knew perfectly well this was his son. His true, evil self simply didn't care.

That night, in the magical cabin, he cried with Paxton's mother at what he'd done, but that didn't matter because he had done it, and nothing he could do would make that right. At that moment, the magical mouse scampered by, and Red Flame stepped on the mouse and killed him. Apparently, the spell hadn't made him as kind and gentle as Paxton's mom, and he had enough meanness in him to kill a mouse when he saw one.

As soon as the mouse was dead, the spell was broken and Red Flame became his terrible, horrible self once again. He blamed Paxton's mom for the fact that he'd killed his own son, and he took all his anger and hatred out on her. Then he cast her out of the room and into the brig, with plans to make her walk the plank the next day.

But never fear. For as I said, magic was not uncommon in the world at that time, and Paxton was not truly dead. He had been saved by a mermaid who'd heard the kerfuffle with his dad and rescued him from drowning. Her magic revived him and when he told her all about his evil father, she agreed to help Paxton kill him. Paxton didn't want to kill his father, of course, but sometimes drastic measures are required. Paxton was kind and gentle like his mother, but he knew his father's brutality was bad for his mom and bad for the world, so he was willing to do what must be done.

The next morning, Paxton and the mermaid watched his mother walk the plank, and of course they rescued her as soon as she dropped into the sea. And as soon as his mother was safe, the mermaid struck up a storm to end all storms, lightning and thunder, whirlpools and wind.

As the ship went down, Paxton and his mother watched from the safety of a protected island the mermaid had made for them. His mother cried for the kind man she had loved, even though that man had been an illusion. Paxton comforted his mother, but wasn't sad and had no regrets. He'd made the world a better place by eliminating one evil man, and now there was that much more room for kindness and love.

Paxton and his mom lived happily together on the island for many years, with frequent visits from the mermaid, until they were ready to go back into the world and look for new people to love.

July 23, 1984

J,

I loved your story! And not just because I'm me and you're you. It was like a Grimm's Fairy Tale, darkly twisted but still for kids. You're not planning to enact your story, are you? If so, can I be the mermaid?

I love your real-life plan too, and I will never tell! Quitting football to beat your dad is something I would do, which makes it brilliant! You could double your impact by deciding to do something super-geeky instead of football, like join drama or choir or band.

Kade and Dad and I have been building bridges at the pond and we made it to the fourth island. We've never gotten back that far, but the water's higher this year, so that last gap was shorter than usual. I went to the mall with my friend Meg yesterday to buy a new bathing suit for the trip next week. We'll all miss you, but I'll do my best to make sure everyone has fun. And I'll take pictures to send you.

 K

STORM CLOUDS GATHER

A SHIFT BEGAN DURING JOSH'S stay with us. After that, I didn't feel like a kid anymore. I'd learned things I didn't know about our families, and I was also growing as I moved through middle school over the next years. I played spin the bottle for the first time and had my first mutual kiss with Tommy Baker, who was my boyfriend for a month or so in eighth grade, until our French class trip to Quebec, when I decided I liked Jimmy Middleton more.

I couldn't wait for high school, and it started out exceeding all my expectations. I had lots of friends and liked my classes, and Troy Buckman, a cute wide receiver on the football team, asked me to the Homecoming Dance.

I was filled with self-confidence, so much so that when I saw an ad in *Seventeen* magazine for their Undiscovered Covergirl contest, I convinced my parents to let me enter. Dad asked the photography teacher at his school to help, since he had a side business doing portraits and weddings and graduation pictures. Mom did my makeup and applied more than she normally let me wear, and Dad took me to this park where we did a whole photo shoot. I felt like a professional model already.

The one troubling thing during this time was Kade, who didn't have such a successful transition to high school. He had terrible acne, which made me feel bad because my face was clear. He was taller than me now and incredibly skinny. His hair was long, not as a style choice but because he hardly ever got it cut, and since he didn't wash it often either, it was greasy and stringy. I was initially excited to see him hanging out with a new group of kids, since he hadn't had many friends in middle school, but I became concerned as time went on. They all dressed in black and I never saw any of them smile, although I hoped they smiled when other people weren't around. I asked Kade about them, but he wouldn't say much, which added to my unease. He wasn't talking to me a whole lot in those days, mostly sitting in his room drawing and painting. At least he was taking art class, and I knew he liked that.

About a month after sending in my pictures for the contest, Dad came home from work with an ear-to-ear grin on his face, waving a big, thick envelope from *Seventeen* magazine. I screamed with excitement when I opened it and read that I was a finalist in the contest. I hugged Mom and Dad and danced around the kitchen singing Kool and the Gang's "Celebration." Dad congratulated me, showering me with assurances that there wasn't a more beautiful teenager out there. Mom suggested a celebratory dinner at our favorite Italian restaurant, where we went for all special occasions, and Dad agreed.

Mom was reading the letter more closely, flipping through the packet they'd sent, which explained that we'd have to call to schedule a time for an official shoot with their photographer in the city, and said something about paperwork we had to read and sign tomorrow. The winner would be on the cover, but all five finalists, me included, would have a picture in the February issue. I guess this was important information, but all I cared about was that I was going to be in the magazine!

I bounded upstairs to tell Kade my news, bursting into his room. He glanced up long enough to give me a dirty look, then resumed drawing. When we were younger, he'd mostly painted watercolor scenes of the woods—chipmunks and squirrels darting up and down trees, birds in their nests, autumn leaves and spring flowers, landscapes of the view of the Hudson River from our front porch. The past few years had been recurring studies of inanimate objects, and all around his room were stacks of discarded art pads and canvases with imperfect apples and shells and trees. His room had always smelled like paint, although the scent was fading, replaced by adolescent boy smell. Kade was mostly sketching in pencil only now, working on parts of the body. He'd sketch eyes over and over and over for days, or hands, or feet. Today it was ears.

"Dammit, Kai, you gotta knock." He was in a mood, as usual.

"You wouldn't be able to hear me over *The Wall* even if I did." Kade was obsessed with Pink Floyd, keeping it loud enough to drown out the rest of the world. "Guess what."

"What," he said with no actual energy or curiosity at all.

"I'm a finalist in the *Seventeen* cover contest! Can you believe it?"

"Of course you are," he said, not even looking up from his drawing. "I'm sure you'll win."

I was staring at him, trying to figure out if he was happy for me or not.

"Everything goes your way, so I'm sure this will too," he said, still drawing.

"What's that supposed to mean?"

"You're the winner twin. Little Miss Perfect. You get the grades, the friends, the boyfriend. I'm sure you'll get this too."

"Are you serious right now?" I asked. "You're not even going to pretend to be happy for me?"

"Nope." Still sketching, not acknowledging me more than was absolutely necessary.

"You are such a jerk! I watch out for you all the time! Your whole life! I'm always helping you out and building you up." As usual lately, I was irritated by his lack of appreciation and hurt by his lack of attention.

"I never asked you to watch out for me, and there's no one more sick of it than me, so you can stop anytime."

"Fine," I said. "I'll be busy enough with my modeling and all my friends and my boyfriend. I have plenty to do besides take care of you."

"Great," Kade said. "Is that it?"

"We're going to Bruno's for dinner," I said, although I was barely excited anymore.

"Have fun." Kade's voice remained flat. "Bring me back a doggie bag. I'm used to living on scraps."

When I went back to the kitchen, Dad was already halfway done with the drink he'd poured. Mom saw my face and immediately asked what was wrong.

"Kade's being a jerk," I said. "He's not even happy for me, just jealous and hating his stupid life."

"Honey, I'm sorry." Mom pulled me in for a hug. "He probably just had a bad day. I'll go talk to him."

"Stop making excuses for him, Tammy," Dad said, taking another swig of his drink.

"I'm going to take this stuff to my room and look it over by myself if that's okay," I said, putting everything back into the ripped envelope. "Maybe we can just have dinner at home?"

"No, this calls for a celebration, and we are not going to let your brother ruin it," Dad insisted. "We are going to Bruno's. We'll deal with the paperwork and your brother later."

"Maybe she doesn't feel like celebrating now, John," Mom said.

"No, Dad's right, Mom. It'll be fun." I wanted to go to my room and cry, the excitement wiped out by anger, which had morphed into disappointment and sadness. Yet I didn't want Mom and Dad to fight. Plus, if I didn't go, Dad would definitely go yell at Kade, and I didn't want that either. It was easier to go along with the plan, even if it no longer felt like a celebration.

We ended up having a nice time. Mom and Dad gushed over me, and I felt happy and excited again while we were out. We got home late, and I washed up and got ready for bed. As soon as I laid my head on the pillow, I started crying, the mixed emotions of the day overwhelming me. I heard my door open and felt Kade climb in bed next to me, his back pressed against mine.

"I'm sorry, Kai," he said. "I am happy for you. I'm glad you won."

"I'm just a finalist," I said.

"Okay, but don't say it like that."

"Like what?"

"Like you're trying to make me feel better. You get to be happy and excited and proud. You deserve it."

"You deserve it, too, Kade. You deserve the good stuff as much as I do."

No response.

"Do you hate me, Kade?" I asked.

"No, I hate me."

I started to roll over.

"Don't," he said. "Let's just stay like this, okay? This calms me."

"Me too," It was true. Back to back with Kade made me feel connected, not only to him, but also grounded in the world.

February 16, 1986

Dear Steph,

So what was it like to see my face on the cover of your

Seventeen magazine!?! It was THE WEIRDEST THING for me! I am like the most popular girl at school right now! Troy bought me a necklace for Valentine's Day with half of a heart and he has one that's the other half of the heart. I love it! I also love kissing him! He's a really good kisser. We haven't done much more than that, except I did touch his you-know-what the other day and I let him put his hand up my shirt. He wants to do more, of course, but that's it for now.

Ok, so since you'll have to burn this letter after you read it so nobody ever sees that, I'll tell you something else that is top secret. Kade's been smoking pot and drinking with his new group of "friends." I don't like them at all, and they definitely aren't good friends, but whatever. I was momentarily happy that he was going out on the weekends for a change, but then I realized what was going on. He won't talk to me about it, so I don't know how much he's drinking or smoking, and I don't like all the secrecy. Why not just tell me? It's not like I'm gonna tell Mom and Dad. Why doesn't he trust me anymore? The other thing that has me worried is his art. You know that Scream painting by that Munch guy? Well, that's nothing compared to the twisted stuff my brother's got going in his bedroom.....mutated, distorted faces that are creepy to say the least. Mom keeps admiring them (they are good) and encouraging him to express himself, but they are really disturbing and Mom seems to be completely ignoring that fact. Of course, Dad hasn't even looked at them. He and Kade rarely even talk. It's not like they're mad at each other exactly, it's like they've both just accepted that they have nothing to say to each other. It's really sad and messed up. So I'm worried about Kade and sad for him, but I also keep getting really mad at him because he's being stupid.

Oh, one other great thing that I almost forgot to tell you! I have another modeling job! It looks like I may get more now too, after the cover. I'll keep you updated.

Love,

Kai

March 4, 1986

Dear Kai,

Wow, your life is so exciting right now, and mine is not at all.

Richie Maddox asked me out last week, but Dad said I'm not allowed to date until I'm sixteen. It's so not fair! Josh and Bobby and Nick dated all through high school, but of course I'm not going to say that to my dad.

Anyway, nothing else going on here, just boring old Vermont.

Love,

Your BFF Steph

April 5, 1986

Dear Steph,

Sorry things are boring there. I hope you're not jealous. Boyfriends aren't so great. I broke up with Troy because he wanted to touch me down there, and I wouldn't let him and he kept trying all the time and I was sick of it. I didn't give him his necklace back, even though I took it off and will never wear it again.

I'm doing a lot of modeling now, and it's almost like a regular job. I'd like to tell you it's not so great, but it really is. I love going to the city! I love the attention, the makeup, the clothes, the excitement of the photo shoots! It's awesome! Sorry, I don't mean to make you feel bad. I just really love it, if you couldn't tell. I know it's a pain for Mom, because she usually gets stuck driving me, since most of the shoots are during the week and Dad's working. She's the best! Luckily, neither of them mind me missing school as long as I'm still managing B's and C's, but that's been hard. I wish I could just stop school altogether, but I know they won't go for that. Kade's barely passing, and there's enough drama about that. I don't know what's going to happen there, but when Mom's not driving me to the city, she's going to the school for meetings about Kade. She tries to talk to Dad about it, but it usually ends up in a fight. Kade and I are up and down...sometimes getting along and sometimes not. He used to always be so nice, but now he gets really angry and mean. So nothing to be jealous about on the family front, Steph.

I can't wait for the school year to be over! Can't wait to see you!

Love,

Kai

CAPE COD

OUR ANNUAL TRIP TO CAPE Cod that summer was not as idyllic as in years past. We were staying in a house we'd rented before, one of my favorites. It was in Wellfleet, less than a block from a quiet, tranquil bay beach, so close that we could come and go as we pleased rather than waiting until everyone was ready to load up cars and lug coolers and umbrellas and toys and towels back and forth from parking lot to sand. In this house, you could head out whenever you were ready and meet up with whomever was there ahead of you. Dad and I were usually eager to get to the beach early, loving every second we could claim in the water and the sun. The others usually trickled down throughout the morning. When you wanted lunch, you'd head back to the house, then return to the beach for the afternoon. It was gloriously free and easy to leave with a towel and tanning oil and know that if you forgot something, you could just run back home and grab it.

I generally preferred the thrill of body surfing in the wild waves at Marconi or White Crest Beach, but one thing I did love about the bay beaches was the dramatic tides. At high tide, the strip of sand would shrink to almost nothing, and at low tide, the sand stretched out as far as the eye could see. When we were little, Stephanie, Kade, and I used to load our Smurf collection in buckets, and Dad would walk us out as far as we wanted during low tide, helping us create villages for the blue plastic figures, then playing with us for as long as we wanted. The Tyler boys usually played football with their dad on the open expanse of sand, but sometimes they would join in too, and we'd construct huge cities. When all the boys were involved, there would always end up being a battle. It wasn't worth it for me to tell them that Smurfs didn't fight like that, because I didn't have any say-so in that group.

Josh was nineteen that summer and I wasn't quite fifteen, so still not at all on his radar romantically. I was a late bloomer, my lean body an advantage for modeling but not for grabbing the attention of a nineteen-year-old boy. Plus, he had been away at college that year, so he'd moved past all of us to another level. Bobby had just graduated and Nick was going to be a junior. Kade and I were going to be sophomores and Stephanie was only starting high school this coming year.

Kade was mostly off on his own. He would take long walks on the beach with his sketch pad and oil pastels—his new preferred medium, as they gave his melting faces a more nightmarish affect—setting up somewhere far away to draw. We'd been getting along worse and worse, and he clearly didn't want to be around any of us, even me.

Nights at the house, we would eat a big dinner together and play games. The parents drank a lot, often ending up pretty sloshed, even Mom. She didn't drink much at home, but over the years, when we were with the Tylers, she joined in the excess imbibing. Some nights they were loud and raucous, embarrassing us with singing or dancing in the living room. Sometimes it meant somebody got sick. Sometimes one of the dads would pass out on the couch. By now we'd all realized that this was not normal for family vacations. But in the past few years, Josh and the boys had been taking advantage of the way things were, sneaking off with beers or a bottle once the parents were too buzzed to notice. The only time Kade hung out with anybody that summer was when he drank with the boys.

On our third evening, after several glasses of Chablis, my mom started bragging about my modeling work, about my latest shoot and how impressed everyone was with my energy, attitude, and maturity. She brought out my portfolio, and I was happy that Josh would have a chance to see because I knew I looked beautiful in those pictures, if not much like my normal self. Stephanie had already seen them all, but she oohed and aahed like a good friend anyway.

"Guys, come look," Steph said, another excellent friend move.

Steph flipped to the front of the album and started again. Josh looked over her shoulder for a few pages, then moved away. The other boys, as always, followed his lead.

"Doesn't Kai look pretty?" she asked.

"Sure," said Bobby.

"Mm-hmm," grunted Nick.

"Josh?" Steph was really working this for me.

He gave her an annoyed look. "I guess. I'm not into all that makeup and fashion and stuff. I like the natural look better." Josh had a newfound college hipster vibe going, all about the environment and backpacking and bucking conventional thinking.

I was trying not to cry or punch him in the face.

"Well, I think she looks real cute," said Pam.

Cute. Perfect. Exactly the look I was *not* going for.

"Kai, let's do pedicures. The sand destroyed my toes." Stephanie took my hand and pulled me upstairs before I threw a fit.

"I thought we were playing Monopoly," Josh said.

"You go ahead, jerk," said Stephanie under her breath as we walked past him.

The next day at the beach, I was still moping. I didn't usually hold on to things for long, especially at the beach, yet a cloud hung over me, despite the clear and bright morning. I'd been soaking up the sun for about an hour when the Tyler boys arrived. Bobby and Nick threw their stuff down, kicking up sand as they raced past and straight into the water. Josh held back.

"Hey, Kai, wanna take a walk?" he asked.

My head snapped up to see if he was kidding. "Really?" Josh didn't take walks on the beach, certainly not with me. I looked at Stephanie, who was equally shocked.

"C'mon," he said, striding off.

"Yeah, sure." I scrambled to my feet and followed him.

We walked for a while in silence, until we were well away from the others.

"I wanted to talk to you about last night," Josh started.

"Okay," I said, surprised that he was going to apologize, that he'd even given it a second thought.

"I'm worried about your brother."

I stopped walking and looked at him. "What?"

"I'm worried about Kade."

"You want to talk to me about Kade?" I was immediately pissed. "That's what you want to talk about?" My voice was rising.

"Yeah. Why? What's wrong with you?" Josh was standing there with a look of confusion on his face.

"You hurt my feelings last night, stupid."

"What are you talking about?"

"You didn't like my pictures."

"No, I didn't." He shook his head and resumed walking.

"What the hell, Josh?" I called, standing where I was. "You just say it like that and you don't think that hurts my feelings?"

He stopped and turned back to me. "Jesus, could we not do this?"

"Definitely." I stood, feet planted, looking him straight in the eye. "What about Kade?"

"He drinks a lot."

"Ha!" I rolled my eyes and shook my head. "Yeah, welcome to this family."

Josh walked the few steps back to me.

"Goddammit, why does what I think about those pictures have to matter so much anyway?"

I looked down at my feet, embarrassed now. "It just does."

"Fine, let's talk about your stupid pictures first so you can actually listen to me about something important."

"Whatever, Josh."

"Don't go trippin' over what I'm gonna say here, okay?" He waited for me to look up at him and nod, then studied me for a minute to make sure I knew he was serious, which I did. "My problem with those pictures is that you're prettier in real life, without all that shit all over you. I also have a problem with your mom allowing you to be used to perpetuate our sick cultural views of beauty and womanhood."

Oh my god! Josh had just called me pretty and a woman! This was the new best day of my life.

"See, you're trippin'. I can see it all over your face. I'm not saying that because of feelings or anything. It's just a fact, okay? Can you not make it into a whole thing?"

"Sure, of course. No big thing at all," I said with a huge grin on my face. I turned to continue our walk, relishing his words, playing them over in my mind a few times before moving on with the intended conversation.

"So what about Kade?" I asked after a while.

"He's been drinking with us this week. At first, I didn't notice how much he was drinking because he's always so background. Last night, though, I made a point to pay attention. He drank so much more than Bobby or Nick, and he seemed less drunk. Like he drinks a lot."

"Tolerance," I said. I knew a little something about alcohol abuse. "He's been hanging out with losers at school this year. They drink and stuff, but I thought it was cool that he had some friends."

"Yeah, I get that. He's such a sad, lonely kid."

Tears sprang to my eyes, the happiness evaporating. "He has me, but I guess I'm not enough. I haven't been around much, with the modeling and all. Plus, he's always in a bad mood, so even when I'm home, I avoid him sometimes."

"Hey, this isn't your fault." Josh looked at me, but I kept walking, looking straight ahead.

"Of course it is," I said. "I'm Kade's person."

"Still, you're a kid. It's not your responsibility."

"Except you know it is. That's why you're telling me."

Josh stepped in front of me and put his hands on my shoulders, which didn't even thrill me because I was now only thinking about how I was failing Kade.

"It's really not," he said. "Kai, look at me."

I didn't want to look at him because I felt awful, but as usual, Josh eventually got his way.

"I'm telling you because I wanted to see what you thought before I talk with your dad. I was kind of hoping you'd convince me it was no big deal, that I was overreacting."

Clearly, I didn't think that.

"My dad won't do anything," I said, my emotions about Kade receding a bit as I became more aware of Josh touching me.

"He might." Josh moved his hands away, and we continued walking.

"You love my dad because he's fun and cool, but that's not what makes a good dad. You can't rely on my dad for the hard stuff. You should know that."

"I'm still gonna talk to him. Maybe he'll surprise us."

"Either way, thanks for talking to me about it. I need to pay closer attention to Kade."

"That's not what I'm saying," Josh said.

"I know it's not, but it's still what I'm gonna do."

That night, Josh cancelled the drinking plan for the kids. He obviously couldn't control the parents, but he always led the way for us. We played Risk instead, although Kade didn't join. I was the first one to be defeated, so I went in search of my brother and found him outside lying on one of the trifold lawn chairs in the backyard, looking up at the stars. The plastic crinkled and scrunched as I stretched out on the chair next to him.

"You are such a goody-two-shoes, Kai," he said, still looking up at the sky, not moving an inch.

"God, Kade, can't you be nice to me for two seconds?" My seemingly constant reaction to Kade lately, simultaneously angry and crushed.

"Not when you go ratting me out to Dad."

"I didn't say anything to Dad." I sat up straight and tried to catch his eye, but he wouldn't even glance my way.

"Well, someone told him I have a drinking problem, and he got all on my case about it."

"It wasn't me," I said, not about to rat out Josh.

"Whatever," he said.

After a minute, when Kade still didn't budge, I lay back down, the lounger crunching and stretching beneath me.

Once I was settled, he said, "It was pretty funny, actually, although Dad didn't see the humor."

"I'll bet," I said, off-balance and unsure which version of Kade was talking.

"Picture it, though." He looked at me then, with a glimmer in his eye, a liveliness and mischievous enjoyment I hadn't seen in a long time—my Kade. "Dad—our dad—telling me that *I* have a drinking problem. I couldn't help but laugh at him."

I was smiling now too. He did have a point. Plus, I was happy to feel connected to him, sharing an intimate moment for a change.

"I'm guessing that didn't help," I said.

"It actually kind of did." His eyes looked misty before he turned away again to look at the sky. "Dad said something to the effect that he had no idea how to talk to me and walked away muttering about no respect and idiot kid."

"I'm sorry, Kade," I said.

"See, it never takes long for us to circle back to you feeling sorry for me."

I didn't want our moment to be over, but it already was. I'd stepped on an unseen emotional landmine once again.

"I'm worried about you, that's all."

"The classic one-two punch, pity and worry."

Another one. How could I avoid upsetting him when I didn't even understand why he was upset?

"Is that so bad, for me to care about you? I didn't tell Dad, but I've thought about telling Mom. I don't want you drinking. It's bad for you, especially because of Dad. Getting high too."

Kade didn't say anything, just kept looking at the stars.

"Why do you do it?" I asked after a while.

"It's the only time I don't feel miserable. Drinking and smoking quiet the nonstop voice in my head telling me I'm a worthless piece of shit."

His words were breaking my heart, but I didn't want to overreact, didn't want to step on another mine and blow either of us away. Yet I couldn't say nothing either.

"But you're not. You're amazing." I sat up again, on the edge of my chair, looking at him even though he wouldn't look back at me. "Why can't you see what I see? What Mom sees?"

"Because you are the only two who see it, which means it's not really there. You're seeing what you want to see, a reflection of you that's an illusion. What you see in me isn't really there." His voice was monotone, as if this was a simple fact, no emotion at all except that tears were creeping down his face.

"It *is* there!" I insisted. "What about your art? You say that I'm perfect and you're worthless, but I can't do one single thing as well as you can paint."

"Yeah, but that is my one single thing. Nothing else."

"Don't you feel happy when you're drawing?"

He didn't answer.

"Kade, look at me," I demanded, but he didn't move.

"Kade." I pulled on his arm, and he turned his head to me finally. I could see my Kade in there—the hurt, scared kid who was my brother. The person he hated.

"I used to feel happy when I was drawing and painting, but I don't anymore." He took a ragged breath. "I used to feel happy with you, but that's gone too. It scares me that I never feel happy anymore. Only mad and sad." Another ragged breath. "Or numb, when I'm wasted, which is better."

I tried to lean in and hug him, but he rolled away.

"Okay, fine, scoot over then," I said, and he did. I squeezed myself onto the chair beside him, pressing up against his back. I didn't know if it comforted him at all anymore, and I couldn't bear to ask. But it did help me, so I stayed there as long as he put up with it.

END OF DAYS

BY THE TIME WE LEFT the Cape, I'd decided I was done with modeling. I told my family that it took too much time and that I wanted to be a normal kid and concentrate on school and my friends. Really, I stopped so I could be around for Kade. I missed it for a while, but it felt more important to be close to my brother. I couldn't enjoy being happy and successful when he was so lost and miserable.

Josh had apparently talked with my mom about Kade too, but the only thing that accomplished was that my parents spent August and September fighting about him. I didn't trust the situation at home, so I stayed there most of the time, and tried to watch over Kade at school as best I could.

By late October, things seemed to be getting better. Kade's room was back to smelling like paint rather than BO. He had more energy and smiled sometimes. He was almost in a frenzy of creating strange combinations of figures and objects—strange but not disturbing or depressing, abstracts in the vein of Picasso or Dali. We laughed, shared school stories, stayed up late together on weekends again. I felt like I'd done the right thing in choosing to pay more attention to Kade, like I was helping him find his way back to himself.

Then, right before Thanksgiving, Mom found cocaine in his room. Apparently, that was why he'd perked up. She found a treatment center for him, but Dad refused to send him there.

That was the fight to end all fights, and Kade and I heard every word through our open bedroom doors. I didn't even have to try to eavesdrop.

"We can't afford that place, Tammy," Dad yelled. "You took the stuff, and we'll make sure he doesn't get more. Kai can watch him at school and he'll come straight home. That's the end of it."

Dad walked from the living room to the kitchen to refill his drink, and Mom followed him.

"You are living in a fantasy land! You can't even say cocaine! It was cocaine, John!"

"I know what it was! Jesus, you've said it a million times!"

"You drink away reality and now our son is doing the same thing! He's becoming just like you!"

"He is nothing like me!"

"You're an alcoholic, John! Our son is an alcoholic and a drug addict! You need to face facts."

"I am not an alcoholic. I like to drink. Kade is a moody teenager acting out for attention because he's jealous of Kai."

"I can't do this anymore," Mom said, in a definitive tone I rarely heard her use with Dad. "I will not let Kade end up like you. He needs professional help, and I am going to get that for him. You can get on board, or you can get out of my way."

"What are you saying?"

"I'm giving you the choice to stay and be in this with us or to run away and hide like you always do."

"I've never gone anywhere!"

"You run away into a drunken stupor anytime things get hard! You need to stop drinking, stay present, and be a role model for your son!" I heard the desperate pleading in her voice, but Dad only heard an attack.

"Fuck you, Tammy! I've done everything for this family! I provide for us, I've been here every step of the way."

"Tell yourself whatever you need to, John." I heard a chair pull out from the kitchen table and assumed Mom had sat down, which seemed to give her strength for her next words, spoken decisively, with no more room for discussion.

"I won't keep having this fight because it wastes energy I need to save my son. If you're not in, then get out."

I heard a glass shatter—probably Dad threw it against the wall—and there wasn't another word.

Dad left and officially moved out a week later. They didn't get legally divorced for a few years, but that was the end of their marriage, the end of our family. Mom sat us both down and told us that it wasn't our fault, but that didn't change anything. Kade knew it was because of him.

On December twenty-first, Kade attempted suicide for the first time. We were staying at Dad's apartment in town. Kade snuck out in the middle of the night and slit his wrists. Some kids messing around at the park found him and called 911, and he was in the psych ward of the hospital for two weeks. Merry Christmas and Happy New Year. He started taking Prozac and was transferred to an addiction treatment center, the one Mom had found for him months ago. He was there for five weeks.

Mom didn't want me to visit him at the hospital, so I didn't see him for those first two weeks. I'd never gone two weeks without Kade, and I cried myself to sleep every night. It was like a piece of me had been amputated.

I was allowed to visit him at the rehab center, and I went once a week with Mom. She visited more often, the max they would allow. One day she was sick with the flu, so Dad picked me up and we went together. He said a quick hello to Kade, then left the two of us alone to talk, sitting together at a table in one of the visitation lounges. We hadn't been alone in over a month, and it took a while for either of us to say anything. Mom had been guiding our conversations through safe topics that wouldn't upset Kade.

"I hate that it feels so awkward to be with you," I said finally.

"Me too," he said. We sat in silence for a few beats longer.

"I'm sorry, Kai."

That broke the floodgates for me, tears pouring out.

"How could you do that, Kade? How could you even think about leaving me?" He slid the tissue box across the table toward me. There were tissues everywhere in this place. "What would I do without you?"

"I can't talk to you like this," he said, and we moved to the floor, sitting back to back, finally feeling reconnected. I brought the box of tissues with me.

"Okay, so now you have to talk," I said, trying to joke through my tears.

"I honestly thought you'd be better off without me," he said, not joking at all.

"Kade," I started, but he cut me off.

"Please don't say that's not true. I know you don't think it's true. I guess I believe it less now, now that my head's a little clearer."

I wiped my eyes and blew my nose. "I've hated not having you around, Kade. I couldn't live my whole life without you."

He pulled a tissue from the box for himself.

"I'm such a pain in the ass for everyone, though." He was crying hard now, but I didn't move because I didn't want him to stop talking. "You and Mom worry about me all the time. Dad hates that he has to come here, has to pay for this place, has to take care of me, has to look at me even. I make life harder for everybody, including me. It reached a point that it just didn't seem worth it to put us all through that forever and ever."

"It won't be forever, Kade. It's just for now. You're going to feel better soon, and then we'll be happy again."

"What if I don't get better? What if I'm never happy?"

"You will. You will be." It was all I could think to say, and I one hundred percent believed it was true, which was why the next thing he said was so devastating.

"I can't actually remember feeling happy."

That brought on a fresh round of tears for both of us.

"Remember when we were little and the leaves fell off the trees and we'd go outside and rake them into pathways and mazes for each other to follow? And making houses with rooms and furniture out of leaves?"

"Yes," he said. "I was happy then."

"Remember that Halloween after *Empire Strikes Back*, when you were Luke and I was Leah? And that was before we even knew they were twins."

"And Dad was Darth Vader."

"Yup. And how about learning to swim at Lake George? Well, Lake George in general really."

"Yeah, why did we stop going there?"

"No idea," I said, wishing we hadn't. We spent the next hour or so reminiscing about the good times in our childhood, laughing at the ridiculous moments and avoiding the ones we didn't want to think about. I felt hope and love in being one with my other half again.

Kade came home at the beginning of February, and things were better for a while. He was seeing a therapist weekly, and it gave Mom and me a sense of comfort to know that someone else was watching over him. It's not like he was suddenly happy-go-lucky, but he seemed like his old self again, quiet and introverted but not particularly sad. He was both sketching and painting, a seemingly healthy variety of subjects, normal people with all their body parts intact and in the right places, a few landscapes of our winter woods. We even went ice skating at the pond once or twice. He wanted to go back to school, which stressed Mom out, but I told her I'd keep an eye on him, so she agreed. I thought he would be more depressed sitting home all day with Mom hovering over him. I thought I could keep track of him, but it was a big school and we were on different sides of campus half the time. I always looked for him at lunch, but if I couldn't find him, I'd join my friends and try not to worry too much.

One day, after missing him for a few lunches in a row, I looked harder. I found him smoking pot with his group at lunch, just off school property, along the fence behind the softball fields.

"What the hell, Kade?" I yelled.

"Kai, can we do this later?" He tried to ignore me.

"We can do this with Mom at home."

"Chill, Kai," one of Kade's stoner cohorts said. "We're just chillin'."

"Shut up, loser! You know my brother was in the hospital! He can't just chill with this shit."

"Kai, don't tell Mom," Kade said, looking at me finally. "She'll pull me out of school and then I'll have nothing, and I really will kill myself."

"You can't say that, Kade!" I didn't want to cry in front of these idiots. "Don't put that on me."

"You can handle it. You're the strong one, remember?" His eyes were stone-cold. "You're the smart, fun, pretty, perky one. You'll be fine. Just keep your mouth shut and let me be." He looked away and took another hit. "Let me have this one thing I actually enjoy. You have everything else in life to enjoy."

I turned and walked away before I screamed or punched him or fell down sobbing.

I didn't tell my mom. I hate myself for that now, but I thought I was doing the best thing for Kade at the time. Or maybe I was just mad at him. I didn't want to help him in that moment because I was sick of it all. I knew how upset Mom would be and what a mess everything would become, so I convinced myself that maybe he could just get high with some friends once in a while and be fine.

We avoided each other as much as possible for a week or so, but gradually things improved. We resumed watching *The A-Team* together on Tuesday nights and *Dallas* on Fridays. We went to movies with Mom. We saw Dad here and there, but we didn't stay at his place anymore. Kade stopped going to therapy because things seemed better and because therapy was expensive and money was tighter than ever now that Dad was funding two households and still paying off Kade's stay in rehab, which wasn't fully covered by insurance.

I began to notice Kade deteriorating, but I pretended it wasn't happening. Pink Floyd was back on repeat. He spent more time in his room and was starting to smell, not showering regularly. His paintings were less tangible, swirling masses of blacks and greys, like dark clouds about to let loose a storm. He'd stopped talking with me for the most part and was arguing with Mom again, but she seemed to be ignoring the danger signs as well. We were hoping it would go away, that he would just be okay again.

One Saturday afternoon late in May, I was home alone with Kade, and I went to his room to ask if he wanted some of the mac and cheese I'd made for lunch. He was sitting on the edge of his bed holding a knife and staring at it. My heart was pounding so hard it felt like I would burst the buttons of my shirt.

"What are you doing, Kade?" I asked. I'd never been so scared, and although I think my voice was shaking, I was trying to sound calm.

"Leave me alone, Kai," he said, without any energy behind it.

I walked toward him slowly. "Give me the knife, Kade."

He just kept staring at it like a zombie, ignoring me.

I leaned forward to take it from him, and he lunged at me, cutting me twice on my arm.

I was the one bleeding, but he was the one who screamed. "Now look what you made me do! Why can't you just leave me alone?"

He ran past me and off into the woods with the knife. I didn't know how to reach my mom or dad, and I was afraid that he was going to hurt himself, so I called 911.

The police came with an ambulance. The cops searched the woods while the paramedics bandaged my arm. The cuts weren't too deep, didn't require stitches.

Mom got home while the police were still searching for Kade. She tried to care about my arm, but she was completely panicked about my brother. We were both thinking the worst until the police finally found him, unharmed, loaded him in the ambulance, and took him to the hospital.

Dad showed up drunk at our house later that night while Mom was still at the ER. I thought he'd come to check on me, to make sure I was okay or give me an update. But that wasn't why he'd come. He was in a drunken rage.

"How could you call the police?" he screamed at me. "What did you do to push him so far, Kai? What did you do?"

He didn't ask about my bandaged arm, didn't ask if I was okay, and something in me broke. I was so angry—at Dad, at Kade, even at Mom for not finding a way to fix all this a long time ago. My anger came pouring out, and I screamed back at my dad for the first and only time ever.

"What did *I* do? What did *you* do?"

Dad stood there in stunned silence, looking at me with his glassy eyes, which enraged me more.

"Why is it *my* job to take care of *your* son? Why couldn't *you* be here for Kade? Where were *you*?"

Dad started to stammer something, but I cut him off.

"Oh, wait, let me guess. You were drinking. The one and only thing you give a shit about."

"So you've officially become your mother, huh?" Dad sputtered with contempt.

"Better her than you," I said.

And then he smacked me. Hard. Right across the face.

My dad had never been physical with any of us, no matter how drunk he was. Tears streamed down my face, but I didn't feel like I was actually crying. I was staring at him in shock, disbelief, and hatred, ignoring the heat and pain in my cheek.

He simply walked away, got in his car, and drove off. I thought about calling the cops on him too, making a day of turning my family in to the authorities, but I was too exhausted, too drained to do anything other than lie down on the couch and fall into a comatose sleep. I never told anyone that my dad hit me, because by the time I woke up, all I wanted was to hold on to the pitiful remnant of family I had left and not make anything worse than it already was. Everyone assumed my cheek had been bruised in the scuffle with Kade.

May 25, 1987

K,

I'm sorry your life sucks right now. I can't imagine what you're going through. Please remember that none of this is your fault. I know you'll still think it is, but I wanted to say it at least. You can do what you can do, but the rest of it is up to Kade and your parents and the doctors. Don't take this all on yourself. You're doing the best you can.

J

May 27, 1987

Dear Kai,

I am so sorry for cutting you. You know you are my one person, and I feel like shit that you are the one I hurt. I didn't mean to, wasn't even thinking really, but that doesn't matter because what happened happened, and it's my fault. I don't blame you for not coming to visit. I don't even want you to because it would make me feel worse. I'm sorry for the mean things I've said to you lately. I hate myself so much that the hatred oozes out and spills over onto you, since you are a part of me. You're the only good part of me, the best part of us, and I do love you. I hope you can forgive me.

Love,

Kade

June 3, 1987

Dear Kade,

I forgive you. Can you please forgive yourself?

I love you too. Can you please love yourself?

You are my person too, and I need you back.

Please get better and come home. I'll see you then.

Love,

Kai

June 18, 1987

K,

You've never not written me back, so things must be even worse than I thought. I'm worried about you. Please write me and let me know how you're doing, even if it's terrible and depressing. You are allowed to keep living your life, you know. You can move forward even if Kade's stuck right now. Just sayin'.

J

AND THEN THERE WAS ONE

Kade was only in the psych hospital for five days. He hadn't actually tried to kill himself, and he said he'd cut me by accident, so they didn't keep him as long as before. Mom took him back to the rehab center, and he was there for three weeks. I never went to see him. I was angry and hurt and confused and thought we would make amends when he got home. Mom tried to be positive around me, but I could hear her crying at night in bed.

One afternoon, Kade called our Dad from the center and asked him to come pick him up. I'm sure he said all the things he knew Dad most wanted to hear: the place was useless and a waste of money; he might drink and get high now and then, but it wasn't the big deal Mom made it out to be; Mom was overreacting and taking her anger at Dad out on him; his meds were helping his mood and he would be fine if he could just get out of the prison he was in; he wanted to come home and apologize and make it up to me. I can practically hear him on the phone, giving a perfect sales pitch, telling Dad exactly what he wanted so badly to believe. No addiction problem, everything was all better, Mom was wrong and Dad was right. Dad could be the cool hero and make Mom the bad guy, and he didn't even have to do anything hard, just go pick Kade up and bring him home.

So that's what he did.

He had full legal rights, so he signed Kade out as easily as Mom had signed him in.

That night, Kade took the bottles of hydrocodone and Ambien that my dad had in his medicine cabinet from when he'd had hernia surgery a few months before. He swallowed all those pills with a bottle of Dad's Jack Daniels.

Dad found him dead in bed the next morning.

I moved through the next few months like a zombie, only aware of bits and pieces of what was going on around me. At first, I tried to tell myself that the overdose was an accident, because I couldn't believe Kade would leave me without saying goodbye. I searched his room, went through every drawing to look for hidden messages, but there were none. I spent a lot of time in his room actually, organizing his paintings by mood and age and subject and style: childhood watercolors, adolescent series of leaves and pinecones and birds and nests, sketches of eyes and noses and hands, demented creatures, abstract unknowns.

I started sleeping in his bed. I'd prop pillows against my back to try and pretend he was there, going over and over the last few exchanges we'd had.

Eventually I realized that his letter from the hospital had been his goodbye. He'd never believed he would get better. We found my return letter to him unopened with his things. He'd never even read my last words to him.

Mom hardly got out of bed for weeks. Friends brought food, I guess, because we did eat, even though I don't remember either of us ever going to the store. We had a funeral, but I don't remember that either. I'm sure Josh was there, but I have no memory of seeing him, so that's how checked out I was. I must have seen my dad, but again, it's a blur. Mom thought about selling the house, but I begged her not to. She thought it would be too hard to live with all the memories, but I couldn't bear to leave them. In the end, she didn't have the energy even to talk to a realtor, and we stayed where we were. Neither of us had any fight left in us, so we froze. We huddled in bed for days at a time, sometimes together in Mom's bed, sometimes me in my own bed, often me in Kade's bed. On good days, we'd make it to the couch to watch daytime TV: *Ryan's Hope*, *All My Children*, *One Life to Live* and *General Hospital*—we couldn't even turn the channel. Started on ABC and stayed there all afternoon, trying to drown our devastation in the melodrama of the soaps.

Sleeping in Kade's bed one night, I had a dream that became a recurring one. I was in the woods with him, sitting on the Big Rock, and he was painting me, a picture full of color, light, and sunshine. It was springtime and everything was in bloom. There were chipmunks and chickadees in the picture, cardinals and squirrels. The painting was brimming with life. He was smiling at me, and it felt like he was pouring every bit of hope and joy he'd ever had into me. Then he walked over and reached out to hand me his paintbrush, but I woke up before I took it. I've never taken the brush, not once in the hundreds of times I've had this dream.

August 5, 1987

K,

Cape Cod sucks without you guys. Obviously not as much as your life sucks right now, but you know what I mean. It's really quiet here. I'm so sorry about everything, Kai, although I'm sure you're sick of hearing that from people. I keep thinking about last summer and that Kade was here and now he's not. Sorry, does it make it worse for you if I write about him? Anyway, I've been thinking a lot about all of you. We went on a whale watch boat yesterday, but the only spouts we saw were far away and the whales were gone by the time we got there. I hope you're back next year.

J

August 10, 1987

J,

Thanks for your letter. It's nice that you mentioned Kade. Hardly anybody says his name around me, and I don't say it around Mom, so it's actually really nice. I don't have much to say. Things are quiet here too.

K

August 30, 1987

Dear Steph,

Thank you for coming to visit! I'm not sure when I would have left the house again if you hadn't come. You got me back out into the world, and I appreciate that because we both know my mom can't do it. You helped her too, though, because at least she got dressed while you were here. I'm so glad we went shopping because it makes me feel more ready to start school. I really want to focus and try to pull my grades up. I need to have something to look forward to, so I've decided to make that college. Maybe college in California...a change of scenery would be nice, although I'm not sure I can leave Mom. Anyway, that's far off, and I'm not really up for planning too much for the future. Don't really see the point, if you know what I mean.

Thanks again for being the most amazing best friend.

Love,

Kai

September 5, 1987

Dear Kai,

I'm so glad I came to visit too! It was great to see you and your mom, even though you both looked like hell when I got there. It will get better. Your mom has always been a tough nut, and she'll bounce back. I don't think mine would, but yours will.

School started, and I have a boyfriend! Remember I told you about Ryan? He asked me out and we went to the movies and held hands and then he kissed me! It was amazing! Mom knows, but we're not telling Dad.

I hope you are doing okay, Kai. I'm thinking about you. I know your birthday is going to suck, so I won't even say happy birthday. Sorry.

Love,

Your BFF, Steph

September 18, 1987

Dear Steph,

Mom and I agreed to completely ignore my birthday this year. I couldn't face it without him, and I know Mom couldn't either, so it was just another day. Didn't hear from Dad.

Yay for Ryan!! I'm excited for you! That's so cool! This guy Craig asked me to go to the Homecoming dance. I'm not really interested in him, but the dance sounds like more fun than anything else has in a while, so I'm going. I'm almost happier about the fact that Mom is taking me to shop for a dress, which will be her first big outing in months.

I convinced my school counselor to let me switch into mostly Honors and AP classes this year. I've summoned my stubborn self to do what it takes to go away to college. I have so much homework all the time, but it's good because it keeps my mind busy so I can't think of other things. I see my friends at school and I've gone to the movies once, but my classes keep me pretty busy and it's still hard to be out with people who are happy and haven't had their worlds shattered.

Sorry to get depressing. I'm generally doing better, but it's still hard.

Love,

Kai

November 30, 1987

K,

Sorry I haven't written until now. I didn't know what to say. How are you doing? How's your mom? We missed you here for Thanksgiving. Your dad came and looked terrible.

I'm not sure if I told you I'm a journalism major (I had to pick something!), and I started working at the school paper this term, which is really cool. I've met some awesome people and am learning a lot, but I'm not sure if this is what I'll end up doing. I kind of can't wait to get out of here and travel the world, to be honest, so that's as far as I'm planning for now.

Oh, Steph made sure to show me a picture of you with your date for Homecoming. You both looked great. Have I been replaced? Ha! I hope you're happy is all.

J

January 21, 1988

J,

School is kicking my butt this year, but it's kind of nice to actually work and learn stuff rather than just getting by. At least I feel smart and proud of myself, and it keeps my mind occupied. My goal is to ace everything this year to bring up my GPA, since I have pretty much straight C's from freshman and sophomore years. I want to go away to school. I could use a change of scenery. Mom is doing better, although Christmas sucked big time for both of us. She gets out of the house more often and is starting to talk about maybe getting a job.

Homecoming was fun, but people in general are hard for me right now. I'm not sure I'd say I'm happy, but I am less sad.

K

ON THE MEND

THAT NEXT SUMMER, STEPHANIE BEGGED me to return to Cape Cod with my dad. There would be a smaller group, more subdued, since Bobby was studying abroad for the summer. Steph wanted to make sure I was reengaging in life, but I also knew she'd been bored at the Cape without me, and it felt like a good friend would go and keep her company. A lot of my choices were based on what it felt like a normal person would do, since I often didn't care much one way or the other.

I'd seen my dad occasionally, but not much. He was drinking more than ever and couldn't pull himself out of his hole of guilt and grief, on top of all his old baggage. I decided to go with him to the Cape because as furious as I was, I also felt sorry for him. I was all he had left.

The week was quiet and pleasant, with lots of sunbathing and board games. I took long walks on the beach, collecting shells to bring back for my mom. Josh, Nick, Stephanie, and I made an easy foursome, my past infatuation with Josh now mitigated by grief. I didn't feel big feelings anymore, and that applied to Josh as well.

Dad took me to Provincetown for lunch one rainy day when we couldn't go to the beach. The conversation was strained at first, but we eventually found a groove, talking about the disappointing start to the Yankees season and Florence Griffith Joyner's domination at the Seoul Olympics. I shared some of my academic plans for senior year and beyond, which was as personal as either of us wanted to get. It was a safe conversation, which was what we needed. He didn't drink at lunch, which I knew was for my benefit, so that felt nice, even if he did open a beer as soon as we got back.

By evening, he and Rob and Pam were as inebriated as ever. I didn't want to be mad about it, so I walked to the beach alone. We were staying on the bay side that year, so there were no loud waves crashing, just quiet and stillness. Kade's favorite.

I was standing with my toes in the water, looking out at the reflection of the full moon, when Josh came up beside me.

"I hope it's okay I followed you. I wanted to be sure you were safe out here."

"It's okay." I gave him as much of a smile as I could muster.

"Beautiful moon," he said.

"It is." It was strange how everything had changed. I didn't feel hopeful or excited or anything at all about Josh following me out here, standing with me in the moonlight. I was just a person having a conversation with this nice guy I'd known forever.

"How are you?" he asked. "I mean, how have you been doing?"

"Maybe we should sit if you're going to ask me that." We backed away from the water's edge and settled down on dry sand. "I'm okay, better than this time last year."

"I can't imagine what you've been through. I'm so sorry. I'm sorry I barely even talked to you at the funeral, and I'm sorry I haven't written more. Do you even want to talk about this now? Sorry."

"Wow, that's a lot of sorry's."

"Sorry." We both smiled when he said it.

"I don't even remember the funeral. I was not okay then. I

thought my life was over."

"And now?" he asked.

I looked at the water, dug my toes in the sand, thinking about how to answer. Most of the time, I answered questions like this with some variation of "I'm fine" or "I'm getting by," but I didn't want to do that right now.

"My whole life, I was ruled by my emotions, but now they barely register, just tickle at the edges now and again."

"That's gotta suck," he said. "Especially since it's so not you."

"Maybe it's the new me. Maybe Kade took the colors with him. Everything feels faded and dull now."

Josh was drizzling sand from one hand to another. He stopped to look at me, but didn't say anything.

Talking about colors reminded me of my recurring Kade dream, and I told Josh about it.

"So in the dream you're full of life and color."

"Yeah," I said, kicking the sand I was burrowing my feet into.

"And you never take the brush?"

I shook my head, watching the sand spray out in front of each kick.

"What do you think would happen if you took it?"

I drew a blank.

"You were always the colorful, lively one. Kade's painting you that way in your dream. I'm curious what it means that he's trying to hand you the brush."

"I know what it means," I said, surprising myself, looking out at the water. This was something I hadn't thought about, hadn't realized I knew. "I don't think it's a regular dream, Josh. I think it's actually Kade." I glanced at him to see his reaction, but his expression didn't change. "I think he's trying to give me my spirit back, but I don't want it. I want him, not some lame afterthought gesture. I don't want him doing me any favors now."

"You know what, Kai? Everything you just said proves you haven't changed as much as you think."

"Still as crazy as ever, you mean?" Digging my feet deeper and deeper into the cool sand.

"Nope," he said, smiling but serious. "First off, you're mad as hell at Kade, which is a big emotion, in case you didn't know. So not so numb after all."

I stared out at the moon on the water.

"Second, you still have that stubborn streak. You were always so sure about things, had this faith I wished I had. Now you're sure your brother is still out there somewhere, and there's a comfort in that. It must be nice. I only have faith in what I can see, what's right in front of me."

"That's not really faith then. That's just sight."

"Yeah, I guess that's my point."

I thought about that for a while. "I don't know what I believe in anymore."

I put my head on his shoulder and sat like that for quite a while, and he let me lean against him as long as I wanted.

"I've been seeing a therapist," I said. "Do you think I'm crazy now?"

"Nope. I think you're brave. Always have."

I smiled at that but didn't move. "My therapist thinks I should write Kade letters. I told her I liked writing letters, so she suggested I write to Kade."

"Well, that's a little crazy," Josh joked.

"I know, right? But I can't stop thinking about it."

"You should do it. You obviously want to. So what if it's crazy? Plenty of crazy floating around these parts. Writing to your brother is more harmless than most of it."

I squeezed his arm for a second, continuing to lean against him.

"Will you write to me too, though? I'm leaving for Antarctica in September, and I've heard it can be pretty lonely." Josh had already told me and Dad about his job at a science station for the next year. He'd be doing mostly grunt labor to keep the station running, but he was thrilled to be adventuring in the great unknown.

I picked my head up and looked at him. "Of course. I'd do anything you asked. You know that."

He held my gaze, and I could almost hear his inner debate about whether or not to kiss me. At any other moment of my life, I would have leaned in and kissed him. The thought of missing the opportunity would have been too much for me. But right here and now, it didn't matter to me. He would kiss me now, or he would kiss me later, or not at all. None of it mattered all that much.

He put his hand on my head, pulled me to him, and kissed the top of my head, and it was just right. I was seventeen and he was twenty-one and we had plenty of time.

LETTERS TO KADE

August 23, 1988

Dear Kade,

When my therapist, Jill, first suggested that I write to you, I thought it was the stupidest, craziest thing I'd ever heard. When I decided to try it, I still thought it was crazy and stupid. And then as soon as I wrote, "Dear Kade," I started crying. So I guess I still think it's crazy but maybe not so stupid.

I miss you, Kade. Jill thought I should write to tell you how angry I am, but that's really not so much the problem. The problem is that I miss you. How am I supposed to live the rest of my life without you? Didn't you think about that? Didn't you think about how much I would miss you?

Oh, there it is! There's the anger. Wow! I can't believe you'd leave me. I would never have left you. Never, ever.

And yet, as mad as I am, I'm mostly really, really sad. Mom is so sad. Some days we just lie in bed together and cry on and off all day. Did you know how much we loved you, Kade? I don't think you did, or you would have stayed with us. Maybe you thought we didn't love you enough, but I don't know how much would have been enough, because I don't know how I could have loved you more.

Okay, that's all I can write at the moment. I'll write again, though, because as weird and awful as it is, as much as I can barely see what I'm writing because I'm crying so hard, it also feels good because it makes me feel close to you. It makes me believe you're not utterly, completely gone, even though I know you are.

I love you, Kade.

September 30, 1988

Dear Kade,

Okay, so Dad. The only person I'm more mad at in the world than you is Dad. And since you're not actually in the world anymore, that leaves Dad. I blame him for what happened and I think he blames me. He and Mom are even more messed up than before, and while I will grant you that most of that isn't your fault, it's definitely worse now. Mom actually hit him...twice. Once right after, at the hospital where they brought you. Then again one time when Dad came to see me. I wouldn't see him, didn't talk to him for a long time and barely talk to him now. But he wanted to take me out, not sure why he was so insistent that day, since he goes weeks without calling or seeing me whenever he feels like it, but whatever, he was insistent. Mom told him to leave about twenty thousand times, in between lots of other terrible things she told him. Then she pushed him, and he yelled that if she was so perfect, then why didn't she save you. And she slapped him hard. He left then, and we didn't hear from him for over a month. Jill says I'm going to have to face that sometime, but I ignore her. Mom doesn't care if I ever see him again or not. I've asked her about it and she says to do whatever I want. She doesn't give such good advice anymore.

I love you and I miss you.

November 3, 1988

Dear Kade,

I wonder if I would tell you this if you were still here.

I'm trying something new…sleeping with guys to make me feel better. They fill me up inside…ha! Get it?

Jill thinks this might have something to do with my relationship with Dad and with you. She's brilliant, huh?

Sorry, I'm in a very sarcastic mood today. Probably from that tiny little bit of anger that eats away at me every day.

Sex distracts me from that. Maybe that's a little bit like what you had with drinking and drugs, except that stuff made you feel numb, which was better for you. For me, sex is the one time I actually feel something other than this overwhelming emptiness. I'm doing my best, Kade, although sometimes it's not so good.

I love you, stupid.

February 7, 1989

Dear Kade,

Do you remember Tony Hernandez? You'd say he was an asshole because he's cool and popular, but he's also my new boyfriend. I've discovered that if you put out, you get cool and popular boyfriends. Who knew? So now, in addition to studying and working at Shop Rite to save for college (adding to the nice little bundle Mom tucked away from my modeling), I'm sleeping with Tony Hernandez and going to parties and stuff with him and his friends, which is actually fun. You'd hate it, but it's fun for me.

Okay, I'm going to stop here because this is the first letter I've written where I haven't cried, so I think I'll quit while I'm ahead.

I love you and miss you.

(Dammit, now I'm crying. I guess I didn't quit soon enough, unlike you who quit way too soon.)

May 5, 1989

Dear Kade,

I didn't get into college. Thanks for screwing up my life in a new and unexpected way, bro. Are you happy about that? Now I'm not the smart one either, just a dummy who's going to Rockland Community College with the other losers. Speaking of losers...Tony broke up with me. He decided he needed his freedom to screw Theresa Malloney, so they're living the dream now. Luckily, I get to stay right here in this town and keep running into them all summer and all next year at RCC. Fun, fun, fun.

Speaking of fun, I also decided to stop having sex. Not permanently, but not like I was. I'm going to take better care of myself than other people I know. I'm going to bust my butt studying and transfer to a school in California next year. I can hardly stand being here for another year, but I'll do it, and then I'll be off. I'm going to do things, Kade. I'm going to do things for both of us.

Love you, I guess, even though I'm pissed again right now.

June 21, 1989

Dear Kade,

I graduated yesterday. I went back and forth about going to graduation. I thought it would suck without you, which it did. I also thought it would be worse for Mom, but she said it would be worse for her if I missed out on important things in my life, so I went. You should have been there, that's all I'm saying. Not gonna go over all that old ground again. I don't really feel like crying right now.

Dad was there at graduation, but all I said to him was hi because I could smell the liquor on his breath. Mom's back to giving advice and says I should forgive him, even if I don't want him in my life, but I don't want to forgive him. Jill says forgiving him would free me, but I guess I don't care about being free. I want to stay mad at him. You're not here, and I have to be mad at someone, otherwise I might not feel anything at all. I forgive you, though. I guess that's the point of this letter. I'm so mad at you, and lonely and sad without you, but I forgive you. I'll set us both free on that one, if that's really a thing.

Damn, I can't keep writing to you if I keep crying every time. Or maybe that's the point. I don't know. I miss you. I really missed you at graduation.

I love you, Kade.

December 5, 1989

Dear Kade,

I'm following the plan, studying hard and acing college. Things are generally better around here, which I think is why I haven't written in a while. I didn't want to give you the satisfaction of telling you we're doing better. I want you to think we never got over it, that you ruined all of us forever. But that's pretty mean, and it's not feeling as true anymore, so I'll tell you the truth instead.

First off, Mom joined a grief support group and it's helped her a lot. She's made some really close friends there, which is nice for her. She also got a job at Saint Thomas Aquinas College in the student services office. She helps kids figure things out at school, and she likes it okay. I think she likes having someplace to go and something useful to do. She's met a few people there too, and gone out for happy hour with them once or twice, even though she's pretty much given up drinking. We don't have alcohol here at home anymore, but she'll have a drink when she goes out sometimes.

Speaking of drinking, you need to sit down for this one. Is there a sitting down wherever you are? Probably not. You probably don't have a physical form, huh? Anyway, Dad stopped drinking. He's going to AA and says he hasn't had a drink in almost four months. Shocking, I know! The fact that he stopped and the fact that he even brought it up. I'm pretty sure that's the first time he's ever mentioned his drinking to me. He actually seems good, and it's weird, kind of like back to the old, old days except you're not here. He even took me to a Yankees game over the summer and didn't have one beer. It was strange to spend a day with him like that, especially without beer, but it was nice too. It's so confusing, Kade. He offered to go see Jill with me, and I'm thinking about forgiving him. I'm still so mad at him, but he's also still Dad, you know?

Same for you, still mad but you're still you.

Love you.

February 12, 1990

Dear Kade,

Wahoo! I got into Cal State Long Beach! My first choice—sun, beach, and a good school—the perfect trifecta! I told Mom first, but you are the second person I'm telling because that's how it would have been, and I want to think some things are still the same. I'll call Dad later. I'm hoping he'll help pay for some of it but I'm not sure. He fell off the wagon, big surprise, but he's trying again. Guess how it happened? Hanging out with his good buddy Rob at Christmas. What is it with those two?

Anyway, I'm going to go celebrate, just wanted to let you know. I wish you were here to join the celebration. Mom and I are going to Bruno's. Really, Kade, this is a time I really, really wish you were here. I miss you so much right now.

I love you, brother.

August 22, 1990

Dear Kade,

I'm freaking out right now. Mom flew with me to LA and

helped me settle into my dorm, but she just left and now I'm all alone. I haven't felt this alone since you left me. I feel sick to my stomach. I wanted to get away so badly, but now I don't know what I'm doing here. I'm so scared this was a mistake. What if I hate it? What if no one likes me? What if Mom can't bear to be without both of us and gets depressed again? Okay, deep breath. I can do this, right?

I'm not sure I can. I'm not really sure of anything anymore. Huh, wonder why that is. But I'm here, so I'm gonna try and make it work. Wish me luck.

Love you.

March 4, 1991

Dear Kade,

I know it's been forever since I wrote, and that's because things are awesome and I am so busy having fun that there's no time to write to my dead brother. Sorry, I don't know where that came from. I keep thinking I'm done being mad and sad about you and then harsh things like that slip out and I know I'm not. Anyway...

To catch you up on the main facts, it was a bit of a rough start here at first. I met some nice people but didn't really click with anyone until Danielle. She's a fresh-man and lives in my dorm, but we didn't meet until we ended up being two of the pitiful stragglers who didn't go home for Thanksgiving. I couldn't afford it, because Dad is being cheap and stupid about money, and I was going home for Christmas a few weeks later anyway. Danielle's messed-up family is rich, but they went to France for the month and left her behind. We ate at Denny's, then flirted our way into a skuzzy bar where we bonded over beers and judging the other losers who were there on Thanksgiving night. From then on, we've been inseparable. Her roommate is our third musketeer. Jaimie had a happy childhood, has parents who love each other, siblings who are mentally healthy and alive, but I like her anyway. She's sweet and fun and a good listener. The three of us are looking for a house to move into together next year.

Probably the best part of my life right now is how much I laugh. Danielle is hilarious and crazy, and we crack each other up. Danielle and I are quite skilled at picking up guys at parties, although it's not hard at all to convince a frat boy to have sex with you. It's pretty much the purpose of their life, so barely a challenge really. But it is fun. Flirting is fun, having guys want me is fun, and then the actually doing it is fun. You really missed out on this, Kade. You should have at least stuck around for sex. You might have decided living was actually worth it.

Okay, I don't want to take that dark turn here. The main message is that things are great. I love Long Beach and love my new friends. Oh, and school is going fine too. I like my psychology classes...can't imagine why! Jaimie is a psych major and I'm thinking of doing that too. I'm also intrigued by religious studies and philosophy classes, helping me think about faith and what it means to believe in things. So I'm really studying you, Kade. Trying to figure it all out, even though I don't expect I ever will.

I love you.

November 26, 1991

Dear Kade,

It's 3am and I can't sleep. Josh is coming here tomorrow, and although I usually avoid thinking about the past, tonight I can't stop. When I first climbed into bed, I had sweet memories of blipping and splashing and laughing in Lake George and Cape Cod; climbing the pine tree in front of the house, our fingers sticky from the sap; Mom reading Little House on the Prairie before bed and Dad draping an extra blanket over us later, when it got chilly. But the longer I toss and turn, the darker everything becomes, and I want it to stop before the danger and ugliness reach the point of no return.

It's all such a tangled mess—the good and the bad, you and Josh, hope and heartbreak. I can't believe I haven't seen him in three years, haven't seen any of them besides Steph in such a long time. Did you ever think we'd go so long without seeing them? Then again, I never thought I'd go so long without seeing you.

Dammit, Kade, I used to be so sure about things, but now nothing makes sense, including writing you a letter I know you'll never read. God, I miss how it all used to be, even the bad parts, because at least I felt like a whole, solid person. Maybe seeing Josh will make me feel better, although it could also make everything worse, since there's no way not to remember around Josh.

I love you,

Kai

PART 2

DOUBT

A PREVIEW

Josh Tyler is in my shower right now.

I'm fidgeting in the kitchen, wiping invisible crumbs off the counters for the umpteenth time while Danielle complains about how disgusting Josh and his friends are. They're crashing at our place for a few days on the tail end of their months-long hike along the Pacific Crest Trail. Dani's been looking forward to having a group of hot single guys staying with us, but after the two-hour ride from the trailhead with their stinky bodies smooshed together in her car, she isn't so sure. She's wondering if I'm crazy for crushing on this caveman for so many years.

I've been back and forth about what I want from the next few days, part of me fantasizing about hooking up with Josh, of course, but another part wary about getting close to anything that might stir up serious feelings, which is definitely a risk with this particular boy. I've decided to just wait and see what happens, which is how I approach most of my life at this point.

Dani and I talk often about how we refuse to make plans for our future since it seems pointless, so many things ending up not at all the way we wanted. We don't wallow, but we are cynical. We're not bitter, but we are careful. We're dedicated to not falling in love, not becoming attached to anyone who will let us down (excluding ourselves, somehow knowing we won't let each other down).

The complaining stops when Josh and his buddy Tim enter the kitchen cleanly shaven, hair still damp from their showers, looking and smelling like different people. It's hot, and Tim is shirtless, his lean, muscular frame and defined abs on full display. Josh is as good-looking as ever, equally lean and muscular, but not showing it off as much as Tim.

Dani raises her eyebrows and smiles at me with a "Now-that's more like it" look, and I return it with a "Told you so" smirk. She commences flirting with Tim, full of sexy confidence, and Tim happily reciprocates.

I pull some beers from the fridge and pass them around. Danielle and Tim head out to the backyard while Josh and I perch on barstools at my kitchen counter. I'm trying not to focus on his long, wet, blond curls and how much I would still like to run my fingers through them.

"God, that's good," Josh says, taking a big gulp. "I love being out on the trail, but there is something to be said for a hot shower and a cold beer. Aren't you too young to have alcohol, though?"

"Maybe legally, but I'm pretty much old enough for anything now."

He ignores my flirtatious remark, which is a relief because I'm not sure I want to be flirting, although it's possible I don't know how to talk to guys without flirting anymore.

"Thanks again for having us here, especially for Thanksgiving."

"It's like old times," I say.

I ask about his hike, and he tells me how they started the trail at the Canadian border on the Fourth of July, the opposite of the route most people take but the one that worked out best for their schedule. He describes the scenery through Washington, Oregon, Northern California, telling me about Mount Shasta,

Lassen, the whole Tahoe basin.

"I can't imagine being out there for months and months. Did you ever want to quit?"

"I guess there were moments when I was really sore and tired and ready to pummel Teddy or Tim for some stupid thing, but overall it made me feel invigorated and peaceful in the same breath, alive and completely Zen. I would live on the top of some mountain if I could. I've actually considered it."

We're on our second round of beers when Teddy, the third member of the hiking crew, comes into the kitchen. I fill a pot of water for pasta and put it on the stove to boil, then pull vegetables out of the fridge to toss a salad. Teddy offers to help, washing and tearing lettuce while I chop carrots. Josh escapes the work of the kitchen, as always, joining Danielle and Tim in the backyard.

We eat our spaghetti at the picnic table outside. There are little patches of worn grass in the backyard, and an orange tree and a hammock on a stand and a few random lawn chairs strewn about. Jaimie, Danielle, and I moved into this run-down little house in Seal Beach over the summer, but Jaimie's not here because she's gone home for the holiday. The house has three tiny bedrooms, a hot-water tank that only suffices for quick showers one at a time, and a front porch with several rotting boards that require a careful approach to avoid falling through. We usually use the back door.

It's a beautiful night, typical southern California weather perfection, about seventy degrees now that the sun's gone down. The five of us are sharing anecdotes, laughing in our beer buzz. Danielle and Tim are generating their own heat.

The guys fill us in as to how they became a trio. Josh and Tim both worked in Antarctica and started traveling together after they left the ice. They met Teddy in Machu Picchu, where he was vacationing with his parents to celebrate getting into Yale Law

School. His parents weren't thrilled when he decided to defer his admission to hike with Josh and Tim, first in New Zealand, then the PCT.

"Teddy's dad is cool, though," Josh says. "He's an editor at a new magazine called *Outdoor Adventures*, so he doesn't really mind Teddy having a few adventures of his own. Plus, he's been reading some stuff I've written about our hikes, and he might hire me to write a story at some point."

"Yeah," Teddy agrees. "He really wants me to go to law school, but he's okay with this for now. He's even considering hiring me as Josh's photographer for said future story."

"Teddy takes great pictures, Kai," Josh says. "You have that in common."

I smile at the compliment but try not to make too much of it.

"I'm just hiking," Tim says. "No work for me."

"Yeah, except you're going full-on adult after this," Teddy says.

"True," says Tim. "I'm headed home to find a real job after the holidays. Enough with the bumming around. Gotta get on track."

"So you better live it up now, huh?" Danielle asks.

"I sure hope so," Tim replies, the heat between them notching up a few degrees.

Danielle prompts the guys to share the most embarrassing, the most terrifying, and the most fucked-up things that happened on the trail.

"Oh, me first," Tim says. "Most embarrassing was Teddy getting poison oak."

"Dude!" Teddy says, and Josh laughs, choking on his beer.

Danielle and I look confused, and Tim explains that Teddy squatted in poison oak when nature called and had an itchy butt for days, so uncomfortable that he stripped off his pants to sit shivering in an ice-melt little creek. By the end of the story, we're all laughing.

"Nice," says Teddy, blushing. "These are my best friends. Very nice."

"Ohhh," I say in sympathy, and Danielle and I lean in and give him kisses on his cheeks. "Poor baby," Dani adds.

Tim seems annoyed that Teddy got the kiss he's been angling for.

"You misread that one, bro," Josh says, chuckling.

"Next story please," Danielle says.

"I've got most scared." Teddy has mischief in his eyes.

"Alright, I know what's coming," Tim says, "and I deserve it."

"We saw quite a few snakes on the trail," Teddy says, "a couple of them rattlers. And every single time, Tim here would shriek like a little girl."

He and Josh shriek in imitation as they bust up laughing.

"So where's my sympathy?" Tim asks Danielle.

"Oh, baby, that must have been so scary," she says in a baby-talk voice, and then she gives him a full-on kiss on the lips.

"Ha!" he says to Teddy as he puts his arm around Danielle, who says, "That's most fucked-up to you, Josh," snuggling into Tim.

The flirting and kissing are looking good to me, but when Josh starts his story, my mood shifts.

"That would be Forester Pass, a couple of weeks ago." The other two guys look dead serious now, no more laughing or joking around. "That's in Sequoia National Park, and it's the highest elevation on the trail. We had to cross a creek on our way up, so we were wet and cold. It's frosty at those high elevations this time of year. I got major altitude sickness, along with a bit of hypothermia, and it was not good. My head was pounding and I was really dizzy and light-headed, couldn't even walk a straight line."

Teddy jumps in. "Yeah, that was actually the scariest part of the hike. I take Tim's stupid shrieking back. Josh was fucked up.

He started throwing up, which made him dehydrated, and we were trying to get him to drink water and rest, but we weren't sure if it was better to stop or to keep going to get him to a lower elevation."

"That was the only time on the trail that I was really freaked out," Tim says.

"I don't know, man, you were pretty freaked out by the rattlesnakes," Josh jokes.

"Yeah, but I thought you could die, dude," Tim says. "We decided to make camp for the night, and he stopped breathing twice. He'd go from panting to nothing, then wake himself up with a huge gasp. Fucking scary."

I feel like I might throw up, the spaghetti in my stomach turning to a sickening mass.

"Okay, okay, let's not get too dramatic," Josh says. "I was better by the next morning. My body adjusted and we hiked out just fine after that."

"It's kind of hilarious now though, because Josh thought he was Mr. Wilderness and he was the one who almost went down," Tim says.

Danielle notices my white face. "Enough. You guys are freaking Kai out. He's fine, Kai, alive and well right here."

Josh looks over at me, and we have this moment of something, probably historical empathy.

She quickly changes the subject. "So how much trail do you have left?"

"We're almost done," Josh says. "Only another three weeks or so now, and no more elevation to speak of." I feel like he's trying to reassure me, which is nice.

We throw around ideas on what to do over the next few days, but the conversation starts to wane, and Josh picks up a stick, breaking it into three pieces to draw straws with Tim and Teddy for sleeping arrangements. Teddy picks the longest stick and gets Jaimie's vacant bed, Tim picks the short stick and is relegated to the floor. Josh gets the middle stick and wins the couch.

Tim complains lightheartedly about sleeping on the ground again, and Dani whispers something in his ear that makes him grin widely. He stands up and takes her hand. She smiles and leads him to her room.

"Hey, he lost!" Teddy protests.

"Doesn't seem like it," Josh says, taking the last gulp of his beer. "I'm sorry, but I can't keep my eyes open. I'll see you in the morning. Thanks again for everything, K."

"Glad to have you here," I say. "Goodnight."

Neither Teddy nor I are sleepy, and we talk late into the night. As we're clearing away the empty beer bottles, Teddy leans in and kisses me. I kiss him back for a minute, and it's nice, but I pull away.

"Sorry," Teddy says. "Did I misread that?"

"I don't really know what that was about." I'm talking about the pulling away, but he thinks I mean the kiss. "I'm sorry too."

I'm confused. I'm also annoyed that Josh obviously didn't say anything about me to these guys, although what would he say? That I'm off limits? Of course not. But we do have some kind of history that he obviously didn't even mention. I mean, Dani would never have kissed Josh. She knows he used to be a thing for me. And that brings back the childhood hurt of knowing that I wasn't a thing for him. I'm mad at myself for not simply hooking up with Teddy, since I don't want anything serious anyway. But I know that's not going to happen, which makes me feel guilty for leading Teddy on and making him worried and uncomfortable.

"I hope this doesn't make things weird," he says.

"Not at all." I kiss him on the cheek to prove it. "Thanks for helping clean up. You're sweet."

I sleep late the next morning and wake to an empty house. As I sit sipping coffee on the couch, I hold Josh's pillow to my chest, breathing in the scent of him.

Danielle comes through the door, glistening with sweat from her run.

"Morning, stalker," she says, smiling.

"I don't think I can stalk someone in my own house." Thank god she's the one who caught me. So stupid. I throw the pillow aside.

"Arguable," she says. She stretches while telling me about the wild night she had with Tim and her new admiration for mountain men, as long as they're clean.

I tell her about my kiss, and she encourages me to forget about Josh and hook up with Teddy instead, but I tell her it would be too weird.

I ask after the guys, who borrowed Danielle's car to make a supply run to REI and to get groceries to make us dinner tonight. I smile at the thought of that, since I have never seen Josh take part in anything productive that happened in a kitchen, other than helping my mom paint. I'm guessing Tim and Teddy are the cooks.

I rinse my coffee cup in the sink before getting ready for work, the lunch shift at Walt's Wharf, a popular restaurant in Seal Beach's Old Town. The tips are good, and the owners and customers like me, the perfect job to help defray student loan debt.

"I'll be back for dinner," I tell Danielle. "Call if it's looking like a disaster, and I'll bring something home from the restaurant."

My shift lasts until six, and when I walk through the door, my house smells like dinnertime in Vermont. I'm shocked to find Josh in the kitchen, the rest of the crew out back drinking beers.

"Is that your mom's chili mac and cheese I smell? God, I love that dish!"

"That's why I made it."

This makes my heart beat a smidge faster, but I tell myself to settle down. He's simply paying me back for letting him crash here.

Now he's filling the sink to wash the prep dishes and wiping up stray scraps on the counter.

"I'm sorry, but I don't even recognize you," I say. "Cooking and cleaning the kitchen? Who are you?"

"Who are you?" he asks. "Last time I saw you, you were still a kid, and now…"

"Now what?" My eyes lock onto his.

"Now you're not," he says, and shifts his focus to the dirty dishes. "Food should be ready in a half hour or so."

I leave him in the kitchen to go take a shower, smiling and reevaluating my plans for a celibate weekend.

After dinner we head to Clancy's, our favorite bar. More like our only bar. Dani and I hooked up with the bartender and bouncer a while ago, both of whom are fifth-year seniors at Long Beach, and they always let us in and serve us, never asking for IDs we don't have. Dani and Tim are tearing it up on the dance floor. Teddy, Josh, and I are nursing beers in our booth. Teddy asks me to dance, and I look at Josh to gauge his reaction, but he doesn't seem to have one, so I accept. I love to dance, and Teddy's a good dancer. I'm having fun until I look back and see that Josh has been joined in the booth by an attractive co-ed throwing back a shot and laughing with him. That was quick. Laughing already? I'm pissed and jealous (and pissed at myself for feeling those feelings), so I do what any normal twenty-year-old would do, start grinding on Teddy. I look over at one point and see Josh looking at us while the bimbo leans into him, whispering in his ear.

We dance for quite a while, then head back to the table to find

Dani and Tim but no Josh, who has apparently left. I wonder if he's with shot-girl, thinking he'd better not be with her on my couch. But then I spot the girl flirting with someone else, and relief washes over me.

Dammit, I really wish I didn't care. I'm distracted, though, when a group of our friends arrive and more drinks are ordered.

I leave the bar definitely drunk, feeling that wonderful dreamy sensation of not-quite-reality, everything soft and fuzzy around the edges. Dani and Tim walk home with me, all of us giggling at nothing in particular. Before we left the bar, I engineered a hookup between Teddy and my friend Naomi, since I had to extricate myself from the situation I'd created with all the grinding. He only momentarily seemed to mind the change of plans, then happily readjusted and went home with her.

Dani and Tim head to her bedroom as soon as we walk through the door. I go to the kitchen for a tall glass of water, then to the living room, where Josh is sleeping.

I tiptoe over to the couch and kneel on the floor near his head. I creepily stare at his beautiful sleeping face, contemplating my next move. I've wanted him my whole life, and here he is, in my house in the middle of the night. No parents, no siblings, both of us consenting adults. True, he is asleep, so not consenting yet, but still.

I touch his face and his eyes open.

"Kai," he says groggily. "What's up?"

"Me. And now you."

"You're drunk."

"Yes, but just the right amount drunk."

"Go to bed, boozer." He closes his eyes again.

"I will if you come with me."

"Jesus, Kai." His eyes fly open. "Don't make this weird."

"Too late. I was just staring at you sleeping, so it's already weird." He doesn't respond to that. "Can I ask you something?"

"Can I stop you?" He rubs his hand over his face.

"What if we were strangers who met tonight at Clancy's? Would you have noticed me? If I'd been the one to sit down next to you and do a shot and ask you to come home with me, would you have come?"

"That's not a fair question." He pauses. "That's not who we are." Another pause as he thinks about what to say. "And I said no to that girl."

"Why? She was pretty."

He turns his head to look at me. "I didn't want her."

I take a breath and gather my courage. "Do you want me?"

He looks up at the ceiling, his arm bent over his forehead in his thinking pose.

"We aren't two strangers who just met at the bar tonight," he says finally. "We have history."

I'm happy and sad and scared when he says this, but I push all that down and concentrate on how badly I want him, redirecting my feelings firmly toward sex and only sex.

"We do, but that wasn't my question." I lower my voice to a sexy whisper. "Do you want me?" He doesn't say anything, but holds my gaze. "I want you. I want to kiss you and undress you and climb on top of you and take you inside of me. Can I do that please? I'm pretty sure you'll like it."

He moves his head in an almost imperceptible nod, so I lean in and kiss him, softly at first, just brushing his lips with mine to see how he'll respond. Then I nibble gently on his lower lip and kiss him again. He remains unsure, not pulling away but not really kissing me back. I increase the pressure slightly and ease his lips apart, sneaking my tongue just barely into his mouth, and then he starts to respond, his lips pressing harder and his tongue dancing with mine, taking my breath away.

I want to take him to my room, but I don't want to give him the opportunity to think twice about what we're doing, so I move up onto the couch next to him, kissing him all the while, tangling my fingers in his curls the way I've always wanted, twining my legs around his. He's timid at first, not wanting to get ahead of me, push me, or assume too much. I stop kissing him long enough to take off my shirt and bra, his shirt, then settle myself on top of him to press my bare breasts against his chest. He groans, and I feel excitement rise up in me. His hands are in my hair, then on my back, then on my ass, pulling me closer to him so that I feel his hardness pressing into me.

Now I lead him to my room, my bed.

I take off the rest of my clothes as he watches, his desire wrestling with lingering uncertainty. I decide to make a bold move, make him understand that I'm a sexual woman who knows exactly what she's doing. I strip him down and push him onto my bed, kneel over him and take him in my mouth. Another deep groan. I relish the pleasure I give him until his final release.

I lie next to him with my head on his stomach, soaking in the fact that I am naked in my bed with this particular man. After a few minutes, a switch seems to flip and he decides he's in this with me. He kisses me hard and intently, making my head spin. He moves his hands over me, cradling my breasts, squeezing them gently, playing with my nipples until they're hard and stiff. He moves his hand down between my legs, bringing me alive and making me crazy. I move my hips under his touch, moaning as my arousal builds.

He never moves his mouth off mine except to ask, "Hey, K, wanna come together now?"

"I really, really do," I say.

I pull a condom out of my nightstand drawer, and he quickly puts it on, then pushes into me. I've waited for this moment for so long and am immediately lost in the pleasure of it. I'm present but at the same time outside myself, relishing every sensation while also being overwhelmed by it all. I've had plenty of sex, but I've never had this sense of completion, of rightness, which is awesome and simultaneously scares the shit out of me.

THANKFUL

I **wake up when** I feel Josh shifting in bed next to me. We exchange good mornings and he wishes me a happy Thanksgiving, a strange new way to start a holiday with Josh.

I reach over him to grab an Altoid out of my nightstand and offer him one as well. He makes fun of my drawer full of breath mints and rubbers, but I'm not offended. Teasing makes things feel more natural.

After a while, he says, "We should probably talk about this, don't you think?"

"About what?" I don't really want to talk, don't want to look too closely at it all.

Josh gives me a skeptical look.

"No, really," I say. "I wanted you. You wanted me. We had sex. Let me just ask you this. Did you like having sex with me?"

"Wasn't that obvious?" He smiles.

"See, so nothing to talk about." I kiss him and wrap my hand around him, rubbing and pulling on him.

"I know what you're doing."

"I hope so," I say. "Otherwise I'm doing it wrong." I roll on a condom, mount him, and guide him inside me. He pushes up and into me with mounting intensity. The sun is streaming in

146

through the thin curtain over the window, yet I'm not shy or self-conscious about my body. I like that he can see me, that he's looking at me longingly, admiringly. I want him to see the body of this woman on top of him, taking the place of any memories he has of the little girl I'd been.

After he comes, I stay sitting on top of him.

"That was awesome," he says, grinning at me. "But I still think we should talk."

"I'm not expecting anything from you, J. I'm not looking for anything serious." I'm not faking this attitude. I feel happy and confident right now, the way I often do after sex, but even more so.

"I live in the moment, Kai. I don't make long-term plans or commitments. I'm not going to live like that. I like having jobs that last a season, maybe a year. I'm with people, and then I move on. That's how I want it to be."

"Here and now. I get it. I'm with you." I am with him. This is exactly where I'm at in my life too, yet even so, I can't help but feel a twinge of disappointment.

"I don't want to hurt you, K."

"I can take care of myself," I say, "I do it all the time."

I grab his hands and move them over my hips, up along my waist and over my breasts, caressing myself with his hands and mine. My skills at using sex to deflect emotion are practiced and serve me well right now. "I can take care of myself in every single way, J, but that doesn't mean it's not more fun to have someone else take care of things now and again. Can you maybe commit to fucking me for the next two days? Or is that too much of a long-term commitment for you?" I feel him getting hard again inside me.

He flips me over so that he's on top and pulls out of me long enough to put on a fresh condom, then pounds into me again, for longer this time, giving me a chance to enjoy each thrust, the thrill of him moving in and out.

Danielle is tapping her fingers on the counter, waiting for the coffee to brew, and greets me with a grin when we walk into the kitchen. Josh heads outside to hang with Tim.

"So, was it everything you ever dreamed?" she says.

"It was pretty damn good," I tell her.

The guys sense when the coffee is done and join us back inside. Danielle pours and passes mugs around as we all settle at the kitchen table. I open the red-and-white-checkered *Better Homes and Gardens Cookbook* my mom gave me when I moved in here and look up roasting times.

"When did you learn to make turkey?" Josh asks. "My mom always made the turkey."

"After," I say, and we both know I mean after Kade, after we stopped having Thanksgiving together. My life divided into before and after Kade.

Josh asks about my mom, and I tell him about her new Thanksgiving experiment. When Mom joined her grief support group, she made some really good friends who started a tradition of going on a cruise for Thanksgiving, to avoid thinking about the things for which they were not grateful, for all they had lost. My mom joined them this year and is now cruising in the Caribbean.

"I'm glad she's having fun," Josh says. "Your mom is amazing. I miss her."

"Tammy's a hoot," Danielle chimes in. "I love hanging out with her." Mom was here to help us move into our house, and Danielle came home with me for spring break. She and Mom are pals. She loves my mom's presence, her caring attention, and she's a little jealous of it too, since her parents' idea of showing affection is through money. I'm occasionally envious of her luxurious vacations around the globe and her designer clothes, although I borrow those, so it balances out. We share in a way that helps fill up each other's empty spaces.

"Yeah, Mom's pretty great," I say.

"My mom's always bitching and moaning about something," Danielle says, "and she hasn't been through half of what your mom's been through."

"Your mom was always tough," Josh says. "Never took crap, just like you."

"Thanks, Josh," I say. "I'd love to think I was as strong as my mom, that I could get through what she's been through."

"You did," he says. "You have."

"It wasn't my son, though. It was worse for her."

"Maybe. Maybe not," Josh says. "He was your other half."

Teddy comes through the back door as I wipe away a tear.

"Howdy, y'all," he says. "Everybody have a good night?" He obviously did.

"Oh, thank God." Danielle gets up and pours Teddy a cup of coffee. "That was getting way too depressing."

"Definitely," I say, getting up as well, shaking off the melancholy before it takes hold. I pull the turkey out of the fridge.

"Holy shit!" Tim says. "That is a big bird!"

"Well, half of Long Beach is coming over," Danielle says. "I think Kai invited every person who told her they couldn't make it home for the holiday."

"It'll be fun," I say. I know the loneliness feeling and don't want anyone else to have to suffer through it on Thanksgiving.

"No doubt," Danielle agrees. "But a lot of work."

"C'mon, Dani, how much work are you going to do?" I tease.

She smiles sheepishly. "Well, a lot of work for you." Growing up with maids and cooks, she has no skills or interest in household tasks, although she buys takeout for the three of us a lot to make up for it.

"I'll stick with Danielle," Tim says unsurprisingly as they head into the backyard.

"I'll help," Teddy says. "I'm just going to take a quick shower and then I'm all yours, Kai. Whatever you need."

When we're alone in the kitchen, Josh gets up and joins me in inspecting the turkey.

"I'm helping too." I look at him with surprise, still not used to the cooking version of Josh, and he adds, "I'm not leaving you in here alone with Teddy, that's for sure."

"What do you mean?" I ask, playing innocent.

"You know exactly what I mean," he says.

"I didn't think you noticed or cared." I'm grinning ear to ear and wish I didn't care so much.

"Well I did and I do."

I kiss him then, a quick little peck that's special because it feels easy and natural. I feel my cheeks flush, which is stupid after everything we did last night and this morning.

"What do you want me to do?" he asks.

"Would you pull the innards out? I hate that part."

Josh shoves his hand into the turkey and pulls out the neck and giblets, waving them toward me.

"Ew, gross," I whine, backing away.

"See, there's the girl I remember," Josh says as he throws the innards in the garbage.

"Oh, yeah?" I pull him to me and kiss him deeply.

Teddy walks in as we're kissing. "Oh, now I get it." He doesn't seem mad, more like things suddenly make more sense. "Dude, I didn't mean to make a move on your girl."

"She's not my girl."

Ouch, that hurts, dammit.

"That's not what it looks like from here." Thanks, Teddy.

"Josh, I thought we agreed that we're a couple for these few days. Don't break my heart before Saturday."

"Kai…" There's a worried look on his face.

"Kidding, Josh. Nobody's heart's getting broken. Let's get this turkey going. Any tips, Teddy?"

"Yup. We gotta melt some butter in water and pour it all over the skin before we put it in the oven. Then establish a frequent basting schedule."

"Jeez, dude, you're like a turkey expert," Josh says.

"I am. So much more useful than you. Sorry, Kai, but you clearly made the wrong choice here."

"Clearly," I say, happy that we're all fine. The three of us work well together throughout the day. Cooking is interspersed with watching football and playing a big touch-football game in the street once our other guests have arrived.

Josh and I take a quiet moment together in my room to call home. He talks to his mom first, his love and warmth toward her obvious as they chat about the hike and the family. She passes the phone to Rob, and Josh's face and tone change. He relaxes again when Stephanie gets on, although they don't talk long before she wants to talk to me. She's jealous that Josh and I are together while she's stuck home with the parents and Bobby and Nick, who have no interest in talking on the phone. Steph has no idea how together we are, and I'm not planning on telling her. She passes the phone to my dad. As usual, I'm assessing to see if he's been drinking, but it's hard to tell during this conversation, since he keeps it brief. Our relationship is cordial at this point, but not particularly warm. I'm not sure either of us would have called the other today if Josh wasn't here, another reason I'm glad he is. It's nice to talk to Dad without either of us having to be the one to make the move.

After dinner, I suggest a game of Risk, which is one of Josh's favorites, and we have plenty of willing participants. The game goes on for hours, as Risk can. I last until about the midpoint, and Josh is one of the last two standing, but ends up losing to Teddy.

"Ha! I beat you there at least!" Teddy jokes.

"Yeah, I'll take Kai over a Risk win any day," Josh retorts, and I appreciate the compliment because I know how competitive Josh is when it comes to board games.

That night, we're back at it. The sex is good, but it's almost better after, when he's holding me, talking, his finger running over my arm.

He tells me about his plans after they finish the trail. He'll go home for a bit and try to round up a temp job for a few months. Then he and Teddy are going to Alaska to work the tourist season at Denali National Park.

"You do keep moving," I say.

"There's a whole world out there. Why stay in one spot?"

Josh surveys my room.

"I like the paintings. Is that us in your woods?" His gaze has settled on two pictures I have hanging over my dresser, both created by Kade. In the first, I'm on the swing that's still hanging in the big oak tree in front of our house, leaning back with my long hair blowing in the breeze, laughing with joy at the feeling of my body flying back and forth. The second is the one Kade painted of Josh and me in the woods when Josh came to stay with us.

"Yeah, Kade painted those. He was spying on us that day you came to stay."

"You mean he was spying on you spying on me."

"Well, if you want to get all technical about it." I unexpectedly feel tears in my eyes and wipe them away. "I look at those paintings every day. I don't know why I'm so emotional all of a sudden."

Josh pulls me closer.

"Nobody here knew him," I say. "Nobody's ever seen those woods, seen that swing. You were there for it all."

He traces the scar on my bottom lip, the scar from the toboggan crash. "You know what I remember about the day you got that?"

"What?"

"Being scared," he says, which surprises me. "I think it was the most scared I'd ever been."

"What are you talking about?" Josh was the one who sprang into action when I lay bleeding in the snow after crashing into that tree. He didn't seem scared. I also can't entirely get my head around the fact that he's thought about that day, that it meant anything at all to him.

"My dad was always a loose cannon, you know?" he says, and I nod. "I never knew what he was going to do, which made my house unstable." He readjusts himself in the bed beside me. "John was my steady point, my ideal father figure. I knew I couldn't count on my dad, but up until the second you hit that tree, I thought your dad would always come through. When he froze like that, saw you bleeding but didn't scoop you up and take care of you, it terrified me because it felt like there were no reliable men, like the world was even more unsafe than I thought."

"You kept me safe," I say. "You scooped me up."

"Yeah, but right then it felt like no one would be there for me."

I hug him tightly, since there's nothing to be said.

"I loved your dad, though," he goes on. "Still do. Just thought he was something he wasn't."

"Ditto," I say.

We lie together in silence for a while, before I say, "I love talking about our shared past, J, but could we maybe not talk about my dad while we're naked in bed together? It's a little weird."

He grins at me. "Oh, is that what makes this weird?"

We spend the next day at Seal Beach, my favorite place here. I go to the beach a few times a week, sometimes every day. It's the whole reason I chose Long Beach in the first place. I'm living up to my name, chosen by my parents because Kai means sea in Hawaiian, making the ocean a part of my life.

Dani and Tim, Teddy and Naomi, and Josh and I head out just after noon. It's November, but it's also LA, so the weather is eighty degrees and sunny. We play beach volleyball and toss a Frisbee. Josh and I body surf and splash together in the waves. We've been playing together all our lives, so it feels natural, yet in a new, more intimate way, because there is no space between us. We lie in the sun tanning and nap to the sound of the surf and seagulls and squealing kids.

We watch the sunset, build a bonfire and roast hot dogs, then marshmallows later. The breeze picks up and the temperature drops to about sixty degrees, but we've brought sweatshirts and blankets, and with the fire we're cozy and warm. It's a new moon, so it's pitch-black except for our fire. We stay late at the beach, enjoying the company and the sound of the waves crashing against the shore. I've always loved listening to the surf at night, when you can't see it and the sound feels more mystical and disembodied, like it's all around you, everywhere at once.

Eventually, we head home. Josh and I make love again and sleep naked in each other's arms.

The next morning the guys shower and pack up, and Danielle and I drive them to the same spot where we picked them up.

"Great to be with you, Kai," Josh says.

"You too, Josh."

He kisses me, a beautiful kiss, settling in that perfect place between a quick peck and making out, meaningful but not going anywhere. "I'll be seeing you, K."

"See ya, J."

And off he goes with Tim and Teddy, to finish the PCT and start another adventure, always moving.

I tear up as we drive away.

"Damn, Dani," I say. "I really tried, but that was not a casual hook up."

"I know," she says. She lets me cry for a few miles, then adds, "What do you need? Beach or party?"

"Beach," I say, and that's where we head when we get home.

January 1, 1992

K,

Sorry I haven't written. Christmas was great. I haven't been here for the holidays for a few years, so it was nice to be home. Your dad seems good. He brought a lady friend and didn't drink at all while they were here, so that was certainly different. Don't worry, my dad drank enough for both of them. Nice of him to support his friend, huh? Bobby and Nick are still the same bozos, even though they are both out of school, with steady girlfriends, and working real jobs. I guess they're more grown-up than me, although they certainly don't act like it! Stephanie was happy to have us all here. It didn't seem like you told her about us. Did you? She didn't say anything, and I know she can't keep a secret, so I'm assuming she doesn't know. I'm substitute teaching while I'm home for these next few months. Can you believe that? I actually like it, which I have trouble believing. I hope you are okay. This is all good with us, right? We're fine, back to normal?

J

January 6, 1992

J,

I'm perfectly fine, although I can't really say we're back to normal because I don't know what that means. I didn't tell Steph about us (is there an us?) because if I told her, then everyone would know, and I figured that wasn't ideal. Glad the holiday was good. Yes, my dad seems happier with Debbie, which is nice for me too. I don't want him to be miserable, even though it's hard for me not to be mad at him.

This semester is kicking my butt! I'm taking mostly upper division classes, so there's a lot more reading and writing and studying. Psychology is the perfect major for me, even though it won't be my career. I love the classes and gaining knowledge about how the mind works (and doesn't). It helps clarify things for me. But it's also intense because I think about Kade a lot, and about my dad and his addiction, and about your family and those messed-up dynamics. It's a lot to process, and it drains me sometimes, but it's mostly good. Okay, gotta get back to work. Great to hear from you, J. I'm guessing I may not hear from you again before you leave, so good luck in Alaska. Drop me a note when you have an address there, if you want to stay in touch. And say hi to Teddy!

K

January 19, 1992

K,

Of course I want to stay in touch, stupid. And of course there's an "us." Did you think having sex would make us less of a thing? I'm not saying this is leading anywhere, since I have no idea when we'll see each other again, but don't think our time together didn't matter to me because it did. Good luck with the studying, although you were always smarter than the rest of us, so I'm sure you'll be fine. I'll drop you a postcard with my new address once I'm settled in Denali. And no, I'm not saying hi to Teddy for you.

J

January 15, 1992

Dear Kade,

You are never going to believe this, but I slept with Josh! Ha! Did you just fall off your cloud or whatever? You don't get details, but let's just say it was something. It kind of messed with my casual approach to men for a sec, but don't worry, Dani got me back in the groove again, and let's just say it's been a satisfying few months since then.

Mom was here with me for Christmas which was nice. We both missed you a little less being here. I still miss you all the time, but it's worse at home. Speaking of... Mom's selling our house. I cried a lot over it, but I understand her decision. She only stayed there for me. Too many ghosts for her all alone. Anyway, I probably won't see the house again. I'm trying to be okay with it for Mom's sake. She needs a fresh start, so I want to support her in that.

Miss you and love you, as always.

GROWING UP

DAD OFFERS TO BUY ME a plane ticket to join him in Cape Cod this summer, and Stephanie begs me to go, so I go. Soon I'm starting my senior year of college, and it feels like my last chance to be a kid on the Cape, with others shopping and cooking and paying.

Stephanie, Nick, and I are the representatives of our generation, which is a new combination that turns out to be unexpectedly fun. Part of the time I feel like a little kid, going mini-golfing and eating ice cream, blipping in the bay and splashing each other. Part of the time, I feel like a teenager again, tanning and watching movies on the VCR late into the night.

Stephanie and I talk nonstop, the way girlfriends do. She tells me all about the sorority she pledged in the spring, the sisters she likes and despises, and the Greek house she's living in next year. She's struggling to pick a major, and I empathize with the problem of deciding what you want to be when you grow up.

I'm rubbing tanning oil on Steph's back one afternoon at the beach while she tells me about the boy she's been fooling around with. She's trying hard to be casual about it, but I can tell how much she likes him. It makes me think of Josh, and I immediately feel guilty that I haven't told Steph about us. When she takes a turn applying oil to my back, I nonchalantly mention that I happened to sleep with her brother last year.

She slaps my back and squeals. "Tell me everything." Then, before I can start talking, she takes it back. "No, wait, don't tell me. I don't think I want to know."

It occurs to me how different Stephanie is from Danielle, sweeter and more naïve, dedicated to a pursuit of avoidance and denial that Danielle would never consider. Steph knows my history because she witnessed it, and we're linked because she loved me through it all. Yet she understands me less in some ways because she's never really wanted to know the whole story. Danielle is a realist who wants to know every messy detail. She shares my cynicism about the security of the world and the reliability of people, particularly men. We don't talk about it all the time, but we are well aware of each other's wounds and disillusionment in a way that Stephanie doesn't acknowledge, a quality that has allowed her to her maintain this beautiful optimism that is unavailable to me now, even though it's a nice place to visit when I'm with her.

Instead of pushing the Josh subject, I suggest we have a photo shoot. I've been rediscovering my love of photography on this trip, and Steph is happy to pose and posture, both of us giggling as she vamps in her bikini, me behind the camera and her in front of it.

I try capturing shots of less voluntary participants when we all go whale watching the next day. As the boat pulls away from the dock, I'm thinking about the first time we did this, years ago. We saw our first humpback within an hour that day, and I was mesmerized by the arching back, the slow and graceful movement through the water, the beauty of the tail poking through the surface just before the whale submerged. I was moved in a way that seven-year-olds aren't used to being moved—deeply and profoundly. I began listening intently to the naturalist on the boat, teaching me about those beautiful behemoths. Rob had worked on a whale watch boat when he lived in Hawaii, and Nick and I were enthralled with the stories he shared. We saw quite a few whales that day, none of whom were bothered by our boat. The captain cut the engine each time we approached, not chasing them or invading their space, watching from a respectful distance. After that, I was a whale lover for life.

This is another exciting day filled with humpback sightings, giving me plenty of opportunities to practice with my camera. One beautiful whale swims right up to the boat to say hello to us, then swims off and bursts out of the water in a dramatic breach, her massive body exploding straight up toward the sky, then twisting and landing with a spectacular splash. I hope I've succeeded in catching it in one of the dozens of shots I attempt, but I'll have to wait to get the pictures developed. Despite all the complicated history, I like being there all together, a shared experience we've always enjoyed. The water as a healing salve. We buy a postcard for Josh in Provincetown and all write on it.

The next day, Dad invites me to a Cape Cod Baseball League game, just the two of us. We've been fans of the Chatham Anglers since we started coming to the Cape. It was always a dads-and-kids outing, giving the moms an afternoon or evening of quiet relaxation. I'm anxious about spending an entire afternoon alone with Dad, since I have no idea what we'll talk about, but once we're at the ballpark, we settle into a comfortable flow. Dad hasn't been drinking for over a year, another reason I agreed to come on this vacation, so we sip on Cokes with our hot dogs and peanuts. We talk baseball while he fills in his scorecard. He tells me for the twenty thousandth time that Thurman Munson won the MVP playing here in 1967. I smile at the memory of all the other times Dad's told me that, but it's bittersweet because Thurman

Munson was Kade's favorite Yankee, so now Kade's here with us too, which makes things complicated.

I'm not sure if Dad realizes it or not, but I kind of think he does because he starts reminiscing about our seventh birthday, when he took Kade and me to game three of the World Series. The memory is crystal clear to me because it was one of the most fun, exciting days of my life. The Dodgers had won the first two games in LA, so this was a must-win for the Yanks. Going to the Bronx for games was always an adventure, driving into the city, parking our car in some sketchy spot and hoping it would still be there in one piece after the game, walking under the train tracks past all kinds of interesting characters and rowdy bars on the way to the stadium. Add to that the quest to repeat the championship victory against the Dodgers the year before, but with our team two games in the hole already, and the tension was palpable. The Yankees scored right away and kept the game well in hand, so the tension was quickly replaced by a joyful thrill that resonated throughout the park.

Dad was a baseball fan to the core, and he'd groomed Kade and me to be Yankees fans along with him. That was easy to do in the 1970s because they won the World Series twice. The three of us knew their lineup backward and forward. Kade loved Munson, the catcher, which made sense because Kade had that catcher personality, very aware of everything going on but also kind of a background character. I loved Graig Nettles because he was the cutest and because he made these big, dramatic plays at third base. Dad loved Reggie Jackson, who hung out in right field and didn't do much except hit big, huge homers when it mattered. Oh, and he looked like a guy who could throw them back, so maybe that appealed to my dad too.

That World Series game was one of those magical days. Nettles made some amazing defensive plays, which I loved, and Dad and Kade got to see Munson and Jackson hit some important RBIs to assure our victory. We were all happy that day, and it makes me happy to remember it now. I can't remember the last time I felt happy and at ease with my dad, and I soak it in like I soak in the sun.

As we're walking to our car after the Anglers' extra-inning victory, a fight breaks out in the parking lot, and I turn cold thinking about another memory that I push to the back of my mind. I don't want that one to ruin my mood, but it's too late. The dark clouds have blocked out the sun and I'm cold again.

That night, Nick, Steph, and I go out to the Beachcomber bar in Wellfleet, which is a bit of a drive from where we're staying in Orleans. The thing that makes it worth the drive is that we're pretty sure we can get in, even though Nick is the only one who's actually twenty-one. We met a guy at the bike rental place the other day who's also a bouncer at the Beachcomber, and he gave us a flyer for his brother's band's show tonight. Stephanie and I flirted enough that we're pretty sure he won't ID us, which he doesn't.

The three of us have been acting like kids all week, and now being out drinking together—drinking a lot—and dancing in the mosh pit as the band plays is a whole new level of merriment and bonding. Stephanie makes out with the bouncer/bike renter, and Nick hooks up with a cute girl, and I don't want to be left out, so I have some semi-innocent fun with the drummer in the band. We end up calling my dad to come pick us up, and we go collapse on the sand dune next to the bar to wait for him.

"So was that drummer a better kisser than Josh?" Steph asks out of nowhere, the alcohol overriding her avoidance filter.

"Wait, what?" Nick says, popping up from the dune.

"Kai went all the way with Josh last Thanksgiving when he was at her house. He stuffed her turkey." This cracks Steph up, even though it doesn't even make sense. She's giggling and rolling around on the dune. Her hair is going to be caked with sand.

"Nice job with that secret, Steph," I say, although I already knew she couldn't keep a secret. "What was that, two days? A personal record for you."

She continues giggling and rolling, drunker than Nick or I.

"Well, this is awkward," Nick says, and we both laugh a little too.

We sit quietly for a while. It seems like Steph may have fallen asleep.

"Hey, Nick, can I ask you something?" I say.

"Sure."

"Do you remember that last Anglers game we all went to?"

"Of course," Nick says. It feels like bringing it up has sobered us both. "One of the shittiest days of my life."

"Yeah," I say, and fall silent. I lie there looking up at the stars, thinking and remembering.

"I was never so scared in my whole life," Steph says, not asleep.

It was one of those summers when Josh was working at the camp and not with us on the Cape. Dad and Rob, Bobby, Nick, Kade, Steph, and I were at a night game and the moms were relaxing at home. It was a pitiful game, the Anglers behind early and falling further back each inning. To make up for the awful game, and because no moms were there to slow things down, Rob and Dad were downing beers at a lightning pace. They were loud and rowdy, yelling things they might have intended to be encouraging to the team but were really just obnoxious.

And of course they weren't the only ones loud and drunk. It started off kind of funny, with all of us kids kind of rolling our eyes at them and laughing at how stupid they were being. Then it got embarrassing, and we tried to ignore them and pretend we weren't with them. Stuff like this had happened before, so we all had practice at putting up invisible walls between ourselves and our drunk dads.

This time, though, things escalated fast. A nearby fan asked Dad and Rob to take it down a notch, which quickly turned into yelling and cursing, then pushing. In a flash, my dad and Rob were in a full-on fight with another group of drunk angry men. Bobby joined in even though I knew he thought they were being stupid, because he also didn't want them to be outnumbered.

Steph and I were crying, and Kade was frozen in shock. As Nick pulled us away from the fight, I could see in his eyes that he was debating returning to the fray, especially when Bobby got punched in the eye and blood started gushing down his face. Luckily the cops arrived right then and broke it up. They took Bobby to the hospital to get stitches and took the rest of us to the police station, arresting Dad and Rob and three other guys. We spent a god-awful couple of hours waiting for our moms to pick us up. Nick comforted Steph, who didn't stop crying the whole time. I was trying to prevent Kade from having a complete breakdown, reminding him to breathe, distracting him from the disturbing goings-on around us while distracting myself from worrying about what was going to happen to my dad.

Pam went straight to the hospital for Bobby, and Mom came to pick us up. She walked in and hugged us all, checking to be sure we were okay. Then she went to talk with the officer in charge, signed the forms that needed to be signed, and turned to leave the station.

"Mom, what about Dad?" I asked.

"What about him?" she said coldly, never breaking stride. Kade was sobbing and shaking as Mom walked us all out the door, leaving Dad in jail.

When Pam got home with Bobby and learned that her husband

was still behind bars, the color drained from her face. She poured a drink and swallowed it down quickly, then got back in the car to go bail out Dad and Rob. Mom brought Kade and me to sleep in her room and locked the door behind us. When we got up in the morning, Dad was on the couch and the Tylers were gone.

I really don't know how we all got past that one, but avoidance and denial are powerful allies with which we were very familiar. Except Kade wasn't good at them. He had night terrors for a long time after that, screaming and waking everyone except himself, battling demons in both his sleeping and waking hours.

"I had fun at the game with my dad today," I say, pulling myself back to the present. "Then, when we were leaving, there was a fight in the parking lot, and I remembered all that bullshit and got mad that I'd let myself enjoy being with him. He doesn't deserve it."

"I don't know who deserves what, Kai. Lots of us don't deserve what we get," Nick said. "But maybe it's okay to find joy where you can, since it doesn't stick around for long."

"Yeah, like my brother," Steph says, giggling again. "Fun and then gone." This time, it's less about being drunk and more about actually acknowledging that Josh and I were together. "Was it fun, Kai?"

"Yes, it was very fun." I say, blushing, but it's too dark for them to see.

"Oh, thank god," Nick says as my dad pulls into the parking lot. Nick reaches out a hand to me and Steph and pulls us both up. I was worried Dad would be mad that we called and woke him up so late, but he seems glad to be the responsible parent for once, and I let that sink in too.

Overall, it's a good trip, and I'm glad I went, but the memories are hard to leave behind. I usually try not to think too much about the past or the future, to keep myself firmly rooted in the present and have as much fun as possible. It takes a bit of work to get back in that zone when I return to Long Beach, but Danielle helps because that's what works for her too.

A few weeks later, as senior year is starting, I inexplicably, unexpectedly feel myself falling into a dark hole, dropping down a little deeper every day. I go to class and to work, but it's a struggle. Getting out of bed in the morning is a battle I've won every day so far, but it doesn't really feel like winning, it feels like just barely hanging on. I've seen what happens at the bottom of this hole, and although that's not where I am, I'm sinking. When I call and tell Mom, she's worried enough to take time off work and come pull me out.

On her first day at our house, she has a strategy session with Danielle and Jaimie while I'm at class. They're worried about me too because I'm not talking with them or going out. I barely have energy for work and school, and I sleep every minute I'm not doing one of those two things.

On day two, Mom takes me to the beach. She knows that's my place and if I'm going to figure this out, the beach is the most likely spot for that to happen. It's a Tuesday morning in October, so there's barely anyone else here. It's a warm and sunny day, and we settle onto our beach chairs. Mom begins the conversation by asking when I started feeling down, trying to figure out what's triggered my sudden gloom.

"I think it was around my birthday," I tell her. "Danielle and Jaimie threw me a great party, and everyone was there, and it should have been fun, but it wasn't." As I say it, I'm convinced that it was literally in that moment, when I realized I should be having fun but wasn't, that everything shifted. Strange that I hadn't realized it before now.

"It was Kade's birthday too, honey. Not just yours."

Tears start as soon as she says his name. "It's not the first birthday I've had without him, Mom. Why now?"

We're both looking out at the water, which makes it easier to open up and also easier to take long pauses to think.

"Maybe it's twenty-one?" Mom speculates. "You're an adult now, in every way, and Kade never made it here. You'll have to be an adult without him."

Tears are streaming down my face now. Mom pulls out a big box of tissues, takes a few for herself, then hands the box to me.

"That's an unusual thing to pull out of a beach bag, Mom."

"I thought we'd need them."

We watch the waves and I cry for a while. I realize how scared I am to be an adult. On the one hand, I feel like I've been an adult forever, but on the other hand, I don't feel like I know what the hell I'm doing. What in the world am I going to do after I graduate?

Mom is awesome. I expect her to come hug me or something, but I think she knows I need to cry and be really, really sad without prematurely comforting me. But of course just her being there is comforting, and she knows that too.

"I feel like I have to live for both of us, Mom, and I don't know how to do that. Especially because most of the time I only feel like half of myself."

"You are your own person, honey, and you only have to live for yourself. If Kade had wanted to live, he'd be here." That's when Mom cries too.

I close my eyes and listen to the surf, feel the sun on my face, dig my toes in the sand. I think about Josh, about the day we spent at this beach last year, and I tell Mom about it. She's surprised but takes it in stride, holding off questions or comments and letting me make the point I want to get to.

I tell her about a letter I received from him a few days after my birthday. He said that he and Teddy were headed to Thailand and Nepal after their contract ended in Denali. They'd be backpacking and hiking, and he might get a chance to submit an article about it to Teddy's dad's magazine, which Josh was hoping could lead to a career of travel and adventure. When I got his letter, I'd been happy for him, but now I realize that there might be more feelings there.

"I don't want to care about that, Mom."

We sit and think quietly, taking time to digest each new nugget of insight.

"You were always so certain about Josh," Mom says. "I was always waiting for it to pass, but you were so sure."

"I'm not sure of anything anymore," I say.

"It's probably tempting to latch onto Josh, to be sure about that one thing again."

I don't want that to be true, but maybe it is a little bit. I reflect on those few days we were together. "It was wonderful to be with him, easy and natural like old times, but also new and exciting. It was nice to be with someone who knew Kade and who knew me before everything changed."

More silence, more digesting.

"Being with Josh kind of felt like a movie trailer, Mom, like the preview for a great show that you can't wait to see but you're also fine with waiting because you know it's not out yet. That's how it felt. But now I see the release date coming, and Josh will be in Asia."

"You can't build your life around Kade or Josh, honey," Mom says, understanding precisely. "You have to figure it out for yourself."

"But that's so hard!" I whine, feeling overwhelmed. "I liked when I just knew things, when I was sure about what I wanted and my ability to get it. I know it was childish, but I miss it."

"I know." She takes my hand and holds it while I cry some more.

"Graduation is eight months away, Kai. Anything can happen in eight months. You can't predict the future or control it, and that is scary as hell."

We listen to the surf again for a while.

"You've got to just ride the waves, baby." She looks at me and smiles. "You love riding waves."

I squeeze her hand. "Thanks, Mom. Thanks for coming here and taking care of me. I hate to be a burden."

"I know, but I really hope you'll let that go. You have good friends here who want to support you, and you need to let them help. I'd never have gotten back to myself if I hadn't found my group and let them help me. We all tried to do it alone, and that didn't work. It doesn't work, Kai. Helping each other in the hard times is what connects us. Not just the fun and the parties."

"I know. I just hate feeling weak."

"Who doesn't? We're strong, Kai, we're fighters, but that doesn't mean we can't be vulnerable too. We've got to allow for both because no one feels strong all the time."

The rest of the week begins to restore me. Mom cooks my favorite meals, and the two of us have long talks at the kitchen table with Danielle and Jaimie. I'm sad and nervous when Mom gets ready to leave, scared that I'll slip back into my hole, knowing I'm not completely out of it yet. After dinner on her last night in Long Beach, Mom surprises me with a gift, something she says I need for times like these.

"Oh my god, Mom," I say, rolling my eyes when I unwrap the package and see the CD inside.

"Why is that always your reaction to Frank?" Mom teases.

"What is it, Kai?" Jaimie asks.

"Frank Sinatra's 'That's Life.' It's Mom's theme song. She played it every time any of us hit rough waters. It's so cheesy, Mom."

"So what's wrong with that?" she asks.

"Let's crank it up," Danielle says, and we head into the living room and pop it into the CD player. Mom and I start singing along right away as Jaimie and Danielle find the lyrics on the sleeve and join in.

"Tammy, I hate to say this, but the ending of that song is fucked up," Danielle says when it's over. I laugh because in all the years Mom has played that song, we've never acknowledged that although it's primarily about resilience, getting knocked down and back up again, at the end Frank is ready to throw in the towel and die if things aren't better by July.

"I ignore it," Mom says.

"How can you ignore it?" Danielle says. "It goes against the whole point of the song!"

"I like the song, young lady, and I choose to ignore the ending."

"Oh! A 'because I said so' Mom thing, huh?" Danielle teases.

"Exactly," Mom agrees.

It's healing to laugh and sing together.

Danielle tells Mom that the three of us have our own theme song, and Jaimie finds the record and puts it on. The Beatles should really only be played on vinyl. We all belt out "Ob-La-Di, Ob-La-Da," my mom loudest of all.

Life goes on.

January 15, 1993

Dear Kade,

I bought you a birthday card but then I couldn't send it. I wasn't doing so well around our birthday. I got a little taste of depression and it sucks. I realize you already know that, and I'm sorry you had more than a taste. It must have been so terrible for you. I had my best friends right here with me, trying to help, but I wouldn't let them, so I get it a little more now. Thing is, Mom came and pulled me out. I still wish either Mom or I could have pulled you out. I wish you would have let us, but I know it was so much worse for you.

I can't believe I'm starting my last semester at college! I needed some extra credits so I took some photography classes last semester and a few more this term. I love them! I'm learning a lot and getting so much better at it. I can't wait to graduate, but part of me wishes I could stay and do more of this.

I dated this guy, Steve, for a few months, and I did really like him. He was fun and nice to me, but he started talking about a future for us after graduation, and I just didn't see it, so I ended things. I have no idea what's going to happen next, but I'm not worried about it anymore. At least, not all the time, and not in an existential crisis kind of way.

I love you, Kade.

May 5, 1993

K,

I know you haven't heard from me in a while. I've been pretty off the grid. Not much mail service in the Himalayas. I talked to Steph yesterday and heard some unbelievable news...you and I are going to be in Hawaii at the same time! I'm going there to do an article about Volcanoes National Park (yes, I am an official journalist now!), and I heard your mom is taking you to celebrate your graduation. Congratulations, by the way. Where will you be? Can we meet up? This is my address in Kathmandu for the next month. I'm doing some work for a local tour company, helping them write some material for their English language brochures. Teddy headed home already. He's starting law school in the fall, bailing on me. He's going to study environmental law to help save all these amazing places we've been.

Hiking to Everest base camp was amazing! The people we met were even weirder than the Antarctica people. Wait, maybe not weirder, but pretty weird. Awesome and inspiring, but also weird. I love adventure, but that is something even I wouldn't aspire to do.

Let me know about Hawaii. It would be nice to reconnect.

J

May 17, 1993

J,

By reconnect, do you mean have sex? Because if so, then yes, I'd like to reconnect as well.

My mom is taking me to Honolulu for a few days to do my personal history tour, see where we used to live and everything, so that will be interesting and fun. Then we're going to the Big Island to this secluded bay where she went with my dad on their honeymoon. She says it's one of her favorite places on earth, so I can't wait to see it. She rented a little cottage for a month! It's going to be amazing! You are welcome to join us, but you have to suck it up and sleep with me even though my mom will be there. I guess you could sleep on the couch, but that would be lame since my mom already knows we had sex. Don't worry...I didn't tell my dad!

Please say you'll come stay with us. Here are all the details of our trip. I hope I see you.

K

P.S. So you're an ad man now? What a sellout, J!

May 30, 1993

K,

Damn, you are something else! Have you ever heard of playing hard to get? I can't believe you told your mom! That's awkward!

However, in spite of your sluttiness (or maybe because of it!) and your weird boundaries with your mom, I accept your invitation. I may regret it, but I doubt it. I think it will be amazing to see you and to reconnect over and over again.

J

ALOHA

I'M DRIVING TO THE KONA airport in our rental Jeep to pick up Josh. The ocean stretches out beyond me in one direction, while on the opposite side of the road the landscape looks like the surface of another planet. It's bleak and sparse, low scrub bushes and trees, with Mauna Kea volcano looming in the distance.

Mom and I had a great time in the bustling metropolis of Honolulu. We toured her alma mater, University of Hawaii, where she met my dad. Then she showed me some of the places where they used to hang out, the ones that were still there anyway. We drove past Queen Kapiolani Hospital, where Kade and I were born, and the apartment building where we lived downstairs from the Tylers. We also spent time on Waikiki Beach and went to the Arizona Memorial.

The Big Island of Hawaii is a different world entirely, quiet and laid back. It's not the expected vision of tropical lushness, which is probably why it hasn't become a tourist mecca like Honolulu. There aren't so many great beaches, but the coastline is beautiful, the terrain rugged and open, with little pockets of undeveloped paradise.

One of those pockets is Kealakekua Bay. The cottage where we're staying overlooks the water, the backyard a part of the coastline. A pod of dolphins lives in the bay and greets us most mornings with an acrobatics show, jumping and playing as we sip our coffee on the shore. Some mornings we take kayaks and paddle out to join the dolphins, swimming with them in the tranquil clear blue. They've become our companions over the two weeks we've been here. We haven't felt the need to do much besides enjoy our amazing surroundings, although we did go to Kona for dinner and shopping one night and toured the City of Refuge another day. We also found a picture-perfect beach about an hour up the coast and have gone there a couple of times. After the past few years of hectic school and work, this nothingness pace is heaven to me. It's also wonderful to spend so much uninterrupted time with my mom.

I pull into a parking space at this tiniest of tiny airports. Everyone here is most likely waiting for the same flight I am, as there's only one arriving right now. I buy a lei and sit with my eyes closed, feeling the sun on my skin, until I hear the sound of an approaching plane. My stomach flutters in anticipation of seeing Josh after almost two years.

The plane taxies up to the terminal, which is merely a small thatched building. A staircase is rolled over to the plane, and people start getting off. I smile broadly when I see Josh, who's looking great as always, his curls long enough to cover his neck, his body lean and hard from all his hiking. He walks over to me, and I put the lei over his head with the requisite kiss on the cheek.

"Aloha, J."

He pulls me against him and kisses me for real. "Aloha, K. Lookin' good."

I am tan and relaxed and happy, and I know I look good. I'm in great shape from running with Danielle, and I've been blessed with Mom's terrific curves, which are on full display in my short shorts and tank top. My hair is longer than usual, thick waves falling over my shoulders and down my back, natural highlights from the sun in Long Beach and Hawaii better than any salon could formulate.

We get Josh's bag, and he takes my hand as we walk to the car. We seem to be doing the full-on couple thing here in Hawaii, which mostly makes me happy and excited but also a little nervous. I squeeze his hand.

We climb into the Jeep and head back toward our cottage. It's hard to talk in the open car, so we keep the conversation to the essentials. I suggest we stop for a swim on the way back, and Josh enthusiastically agrees. I pull off the main road not far from the airport and follow a small road to a smaller pullout that looks like nothing.

"Grab your suit!" I say, hopping out of the Jeep and slinging some snorkel gear over my shoulders. I lead him down a winding path that opens onto a little bay. It's the middle of the day on a Wednesday, and the tiny beach is empty. This is a place frequented by locals, not a tourist attraction, not that there are many tourists around this part of the island anyway. It isn't an especially nice beach, rough pebbly sand, and I see Josh's skeptical reaction.

"Trust me, J." I peel my clothes off down to my bikini and head into the water with two sets of snorkels and masks, swimming out to a sand bank a bit farther from the beach. Josh is quick to follow.

As we approach the ridge, I hand him a mask and snorkel and put mine on, and then we submerge to watch at least a dozen sea turtles swimming all around us. They are huge and beautiful and couldn't care less about us. We bob and point and enjoy them for a long time before they eventually swim away. Only then do we head back to shore and spread out on towels to let the sun dry us. I take note of his body, which is toned without being sculpted, showing that he is in constant motion but not concerned with actual working out. His face is tan from being outside so much, but his body is fair, needing time in the tropical sun to catch up.

"That was amazing!" he says.

"I know, right?" I tell him about meeting a cool waiter in Kona who brought us here the other day. I take pleasure in his note of jealousy before explaining that the waiter was interested in Mom, not me. I tell him that she's considering a date with the guy, which I'm all for. A vacation fling would do her good. Josh adds that having Mom out of the house might be nice for us too, and I tease him about why that might matter. He hints that we could have more fun if nobody else is around, and I point out that nobody is around right now.

I put my hand down his swim trunks.

He moans and lies back as I stroke him. I take off his trunks and he quickly pulls off my bikini, mounting me. I wrap my legs around him and pull him in to kiss me. We move together briefly before he comes.

"Damn, you are hot," he says as he rolls off me.

"Why, thank you sir." I reach for my suit, but he yanks it away.

"Oh, no, no, no. You haven't had your turn yet. You know how I feel about playing fair." He rolls back toward me, kisses me, touches and plays with me in a most satisfying way. I've never been with a guy who cared about me coming after he's done, so I appreciate that, but I appreciate what he's doing down there even more, fingers working magic right where it counts.

"You're going to have to be quieter at the house, or I'm not going to be able to do that," he says.

"Oh, you are definitely doing that again," I say, still breathless. "Jesus, J, I missed you. I'm so glad you're here." I want to roll into him to cuddle, but I can't quite move yet. We're still lying side by side, Josh's hand resting casually on my hip.

"Me too," he says. Then, a moment later, "You sure your mom's glad? I am busting up your mother-daughter bonding time."

"We've had a great time together already, and she's excited to see you. She loves you and she's missed you."

"Same," he says.

Talking about Mom certainly moves me out of my post orgasmic reverie. "We should probably head back. I told Mom we'd stop and pick up groceries on the way, since there's nothing close to our house."

"Okay," he says. "Do we have time for one more quick fuck first?"

"Does it have to be quick?"

The next morning, I wake up to Josh tracing his finger over my leg.

"Whatcha doin' there?" I mumble.

"Trying to wake you up gently," he whispers. "I really want to be inside you."

"Gee, Josh, do you think that's a good idea?" He didn't want to have sex last night, feeling awkward with my mom in the next room, so I feel it's necessary to give him a hard time now. "I don't want to make you uncomfortable."

He takes my hand and puts it on his erection. "This is more uncomfortable," he says.

"Okay, okay," I say. "If we must."

"You have to be quiet." He sounds worried, and it's cute.

"I'll do my best." He touches me and I catch my breath. I groan a little and he stops.

"I'm serious. I don't want your mom to hear."

"Touch me, please, Josh. I'll be quiet," I whisper in his ear as I nibble on it. He does his thing, and I am quiet. Then he's inside me and I stay quiet. After we're done, he's lying beside me and I yell out, "Oh, Josh, baby, do it now!" I laugh, but he's pissed.

"I can't believe you just did that!" He gets up and puts on his shorts and a shirt, hoping to escape the house before my mom is up and about, but when he leaves the room, Mom is in the kitchen, trying not to laugh.

"Morning, Josh."

"Your daughter is a pain in the ass," he says before walking out the back door.

When I join Mom in the kitchen, she admonishes me for embarrassing Josh, although she's still trying not to laugh. We hear him yelling excitedly for us from outside, obviously having spotted our dolphin friends. I grab coffee for the two of us, Mom brings hers, and we join Josh to watch the morning acrobatics show.

After days of kayaking and swimming with dolphins, reading and relaxing together, we leave our secluded bay for the two-hour drive to Volcanoes National Park. Mom went on her first official date with our waiter friend, Tomi, a few nights before, and he's joining us for the day as well. He and Mom take his car and will return tonight. Josh and I are in the Jeep and will be spending the night in the park, compliments of *Outdoor Adventures* magazine.

We start our day at the Kilauea Visitor Center with the rest of the tourists. We watch the introductory video and learn about Pele, the goddess of fire, and how she formed the Hawaiian islands. She is still forming this, the baby island in the family, still sculpting and molding, melting and reforming as she sees fit.

After the movie, we follow the park ranger's suggestion to start out on the Sulphur Banks trail, heading toward the Kilauea caldera. Steam vents line the wooden boardwalk, with warning signs everywhere not to leave the path, as visitors have sunk into the unstable earth and been scalded by the steam. The smell of sulphur is overpowering and disgusting, the rising steam making the landscape eerie and otherworldly. There are plants and flowers along the trail that exist nowhere else in the world; the hapu'u, ohi'a lehua, and ohelo look like they should be in a Dr. Seuss book. Mom stops to read about each and every one of these plants, and I humor her until she tells us about the naupaka flowers, which legend says is a symbol of lovers torn apart and never reunited.

As the four of us walk along, the relatively barren sulphur fields become lush with trees and plants, and then suddenly we are standing at the edge of the caldera. How could something so huge and significant sneak up on us like that? Yet here we are, speechless and in awe of this massive volcanic crater stretched out in front of us. I've already taken tons of pictures, but I take at least a hundred more of the caldera as we follow the trail around its edges. I have to keep stopping to reload my film, losing track of how many rolls I've gone through on this one hike. I've never seen anything like this, and each new angle seems unique and worth capturing. I offer an internal moment of thanks to my dad, who gave me this amazing new camera and two expensive lenses for graduation.

The trail leads to the hotel where Josh and I will be spending the night, right on the lip of the volcano. Josh checks in while I visit the gift shop to buy more film and some postcards. We eventually pull ourselves away from the caldera to see more of the park. We walk through the Thurston Lava Tube, which is cold and eerie; hike to the floor of Kilauea Iki Crater, which feels like we're on the moon; then drive along the Chain of Craters Road to the Holei Sea Arch. It's almost sunset, and the light from the lowering sun is ethereal, glittering off the water and bathing the arch in a surreal luminescence. I take another few rolls of film right there, including a picture of my mom looking out over the water that I know will be fantastic. She looks happy and peaceful, which is nice to see.

Tomi recommends a small restaurant just outside the park, the Lava Rock Café, a casual burger joint. He tells us about life on the island, the quirks of the people there, the antics of tourists. He's a great storyteller, funny and interesting. He's also attentive to Mom, calling the waitress to refill her iced tea when it gets low, checking on how she likes the food. It's cute to see Mom enjoying his attention and watch them make googly eyes at each other.

After dinner, we head back to see the Kilauea crater at night. In the dark, we can see the glowing, bubbling lava. Well, we aren't close enough to actually see the bubbling, but it's implied. The bright reds and oranges emanating from the crater, and the steam rising into the night sky are unbelievably captivating. And the stars! We are in the middle of nowhere, darkness all around us, and I have never seen so many stars. I grew up in the woods, but I guess we were still too close to civilization for it ever to get this dark. Or maybe the trees just limited the expanse of sky we could take in. Here we can see from horizon to horizon, the blackness of space dotted with hundreds of thousands of sparkling pinpoints of light.

Mom and Tomi drive home late that night, while Josh and I stay shivering outside for as long as we can bear, soaking in the peace of the stars juxtaposed with the turbulence of the lava.

We return to our hotel and order tea before heading up to our room. We climb into a steamy tub together to continue the warming process, which leads to major heating up. I lean back against him as he fondles my breasts gently, almost absent-mindedly at first. He moves his hand lower, touching me, arousing me.

"You don't have to be quiet here," he says.

I turn around and kiss him, then mount him as water splashes out of the tub.

"God, Kai," he groans.

After a minute, we leave the tub, dry each other off, and get in bed, taking full advantage of our night alone together.

The next morning, while Josh is in the shower, I write a few postcards—one to my dad, one to Stephanie. I'm writing one to Kade when Josh comes back in, wrapped in a towel, and I quickly slip that postcard under the others.

"Whatcha doin' there?" he asks.

"Just sending some postcards."

"What's that one?" He obviously saw my not-so-stealth move. "Do you have a boyfriend back in Long Beach or something?"

"No, no boyfriend." I like that he sounds a little jealous, but I don't want him to actually think that.

"So what's with the secrecy? Since when do you keep secrets from me?"

"I don't want you to think I'm crazy."

"That hasn't stopped you before," he teases.

I study him for a few minutes.

"You don't have to tell me," he says, turning to get dressed, genuinely offering me some privacy if that's what I want.

"It's for Kade," I say to his back.

Without missing a beat, as he's stepping into his shorts, he says, "So you took your therapist's advice, huh?" I can't believe he remembers that from a conversation years ago.

"Yeah, I know it's crazy, but I write to him sometimes. It's nice to feel like we're still in touch." I look away with tears in my eyes. "I haven't told anyone else about it. Not even Mom."

Josh pulls me up out of my chair and hugs me. "Can I write something, too?"

"What?"

"Can I say hi on your postcard?" Josh asks.

I pull back to look at him, and see that he is serious.

"I get it," he says. "How could you not want to hold on to him? He's a part of you."

"Josh…" I don't know what to say.

"So, can I say hi?"

I slide the card out from under the other ones, and he writes "Hey, Kade. Hawaii is awesome, especially with your sister. Wish you were here." I start crying again, and he pulls me onto the bed and holds me.

"I know you wanted to save him. I wish I could have saved him too."

"Everyone says there's nothing I could have done. My therapist said that, Mom says it. The only person who didn't say it was my dad, who actually thinks I could have."

"No he doesn't."

"He said it once, right after Kade went into the hospital the last time. He yelled at me for not taking care of him."

"He was drunk, right?"

"Yeah, but still, he thought it. Then he hit me."

"Fuck, Kai." Josh's whole body tenses, and he looks at me in shock. "I didn't think your dad did that."

"Only time ever, but it pretty well underscored his point of view."

"Nobody gets it," Josh says, settling down and holding me tenderly again. "Part of me knows I couldn't protect my mom, but this other part of me knows that I should have tried harder, that it was my job, that there was something I didn't think of that would have changed everything."

I wait for him to keep talking, since there's nothing I can add to that. He nailed it exactly.

"Instead, I left. I left her there with him because I couldn't watch it anymore, so who knows what happens now. If something terrible happens, that will be on me, and then I'll probably kill my dad, which will be pointless because it will be too late anyway."

"Yeah." What could I say to that? "I get it."

"Yeah, I know." He pulls me closer.

It means so much to me that he doesn't try to tell me it wasn't my fault. I know he doesn't think it was my fault, but I love that he also understands that I do, that I will always feel responsible for what happened. We both know that experience.

"I think we can't really make choices for other people," I say.

"There is some evidence to support that," he says.

"It would have been nice if they'd chosen us, though. I wish he'd lived for me, if not for himself." Another thing I haven't said out loud before.

"Yeah, our dads pretty much choose themselves too, time and time again." Josh strokes my hair until I'm done crying. "You know, it's kind of nice being with someone who knows my whole life."

I crane my neck up to kiss him.

"Still weird sometimes." He smiles, wiping tears from my cheeks. "But mostly nice."

We cuddle a little longer before he asks, "So what do you do with your letters to Kade?"

"I mail them."

"Really? You don't keep them?"

"No, it would mess with the illusion that he actually gets them."

"Do you use an address."

I don't say anything.

"It's fine if that's private, if it's between you and Kade."

"I put his name and then 'Big Rock, NY.' Somebody probably just throws them away. I mean, what else would they do with them? But I pretend they somehow get to him."

"There it is again." He kisses the top of my head. "Always with the faith."

It's funny that he sees my faith when I don't feel it myself anymore.

LEAP OF FAITH

We explore a bit more of the park, but nothing is nearly as amazing as what we've seen already, so we depart on a mission to find a hike farther north that Tomi told us was a can't-miss experience.

We park the Jeep at a little turnout that we pass twice before finally locating it. Tomi's directions were good, but it is an un-marked, tricky spot to find, although the trail is easy to locate once we're parked. The landscape is lush with more bizarre plants unique to these islands, some looking prehistoric and some look-ing alien. I take pictures of everything as we make our way along. We hear birds and water over rocks and the sound of our feet on the trail, but the rest of the world is silent. After about forty min-utes of hiking, we reach our destination, Kahuna Falls.

The waterfall cascades down about twenty feet from the stream above to the pool below. We didn't see anyone along the trail, but there's a group of twenty-somethings here taking a dip. Josh and I quickly strip down to our bathing suits to join them. The water is brown from the churning of the waterfall, so not the crystal blue fantasy of swimming beneath a waterfall, yet refresh-ingly cool and beautifully real.

We immediately hit it off with the group, four of them locals and the other two friends visiting from UCLA, where two of the four locals go to school, so we trade SoCal stories. After swimming for a while, we sit together on the shore and share our snacks. A few of the local guys mysteriously sneak off, reappearing a few minutes later at the top of the waterfall. They leap off into the pool and burst out of the water hooting and hollering on an adrenaline high. My heart is pounding. They swim back and challenge the rest of us to try.

Josh pops up, ready to make the next jump.

"Hey, wait for me," I say, which sparks a vague memory tickling at the corners of my mind.

When we get to the top, we have to walk across slippery rocks along the edge of the stream to get to the launch point. Josh takes my hand to steady me, and the memory becomes vivid.

I was eight maybe, and we were at the Tylers' house on a hot, sticky summer day. Josh suggested rock hopping along the water we called Tyler Lake and headed off with Nick and Bobby, then rounded back to where Kade was drawing alone and encouraged him to join them, which I remember noticing and appreciating, both for Kade's benefit and mine, since it meant I could go too. I grabbed Stephanie's hand and pulled her along with me.

The boys picked out a route along the shore, jumping from boulder to boulder, skirting the edges of the water. They bounded off ahead of us, and I was happy for Kade that he kept up with them easily. Even Stephanie was ahead of me. I was going slowly, being especially careful because of my inherent lack of coordination. Before I knew it, the boys were leaping past me, having finished their course and started over, obviously racing this time. Josh was uncharacteristically bringing up the rear, perhaps to insure that Kade didn't come in last, an unusual move for competitive Josh, but he'd probably won this race plenty of times and figured he would win again on the next go-round.

When he jumped past me, an essence of momentary closeness made me almost fall. He noticed my stumble and came back, taking my hand to help me balance. My world felt different in that moment, and even though it was a long time ago, I remember the sensation clearly.

When Josh takes my hand today, it feels nice and natural, but not like the world is different. The world is what it is. Nobody's hand is going to change that.

Right before we leap, Josh kisses me, looks me straight in the eye, and asks me if I'm ready.

"Let's go," I say, squeezing his arm as we jump off the cliff together. The thrill of it is exhilarating.

We surface and I kiss him long and deep, pulling him close and pressing my body against his, wrapping my legs around his waist.

"Fuck, that was exciting," Josh says.

"Yes, I agree. I am excited."

"Maybe we should pack it up here and find a more secluded spot somewhere down the trail. What do you say?"

We bid our momentary friends farewell and head back in the direction we came from. I remember a potentially private spot from the hike in, and when I see it, I pull Josh into the tangled tree that's grown in and around itself in such a way that it's formed what looks like a big nest in the middle. It isn't particularly comfortable with all the intertwining roots and branches, but it is relatively private. The combination of the adrenaline rush from the jump and the uniquely unusual setting makes this a wild sexual experience that needs no further foreplay. We simply strip and go at it. I don't even try to keep quiet.

We get back to our bungalow on the bay late that night. Mom is already asleep. We dreamily make love once more before drifting off in each other's arms. We lie low the next few days, and Josh works on writing his volcanoes article, which has a deadline approaching. The three of us are completely comfortable with each other at this point, and Tomi fits right in too when he's around, which is more often as the days go by.

Tomi puts me in touch with a photographer friend of his on the island who agrees to let me use his darkroom for next to nothing. Josh comes with me to develop the hundreds of pictures I've taken over the past weeks. He keeps me company while I work and wait for the film to process. I make contact sheets and he helps me pick the best shots to make into prints. We leave with about fifty photos and scores of developed negatives.

We share them with Mom over dinner, and I relish their admiration, lighting up with pride and a bit of embarrassment with each accolade. Josh asks if he can send some in with his story, to see if the magazine might publish them. I insist they're not good enough, that I'm not a professional, that it's a ridiculous idea. Josh disagrees, contending that my pictures perfectly illustrate everything he's written and that they'll make his words come alive. Although I do not share Josh's optimism, I give in because it's easier than fighting about it. We spend the next hour selecting our favorite dozen pictures to send in with his story to *Outdoor Adventures*, and the next day we drive to the Kona post office and put them in the mail.

The four of us go to Hapuna Beach later in the week, a few days before we're scheduled to leave the islands. It's a perfect Hawaiian beach with soft golden sand, palm trees, a steady surf, and few people. I'm blipping on a cheap inflatable raft we bought in Kona, rising and falling as the waves approach the shore, far enough out that they won't break over the top of me. I'm trying to push away thoughts about what's going to happen between Josh and me when we leave Hawaii, wanting not to care about it as much as I do. Suddenly I am flipped off the float and come up sputtering to find Josh climbing onto my vacated spot.

I splash him. "What was that?"

"Don't be a baby, Kai. You know that aimless floating makes you fair game to be dunked. Those rules were established way back when."

"Yeah, by you. You set all the rules."

I drape my arms over Josh's stomach and rest my head there, sharing the buoyancy of the float with him. His hand rests on my back, and we drift along like that for some time.

My mind wanders to Cape Cod, to the plethora of days we spent on beaches together throughout our lives. I remember our Smurf villages, bodysurfing with Josh and Dad, the conversations we had with the ocean as a witness. The riptide of all those memories pulls me under, sucks me back to where I started and where I am again.

"I love you, Josh." I say out of nowhere, the words like soap slipping out of my hand in the shower.

He's quiet for an awkwardly long time, then says, "I don't know where I'm going next, Kai. My life is so uncertain and unpredictable. It's not really conducive to a serious relationship."

His answer enrages me. I flip him off the raft and start swimming back to shore. He surfaces, grabs the raft, and starts after me, more slowly with only one hand available for swimming.

"You don't like my answer so you throw a fit?" he yells from behind.

"That was a bullshit answer," I yell over my shoulder, although it's hard to yell when I'm swimming, so I slow down and turn to him, treading water. "I tell you what's in my heart and you give me some line about not committing? We're more than that. I deserve better than that."

"See, that's the problem," he says, almost catching up to me. "This means too much to you. I mean too much to you. I'm not up for it."

"God, Josh, you are so full of yourself!" I turn and swim away from him as fast as I can, kicking at the water.

When I reach the shore, I run and grab my towel and stalk off down the beach. Josh throws the raft down on the sand and follows me.

"Leave me alone, Josh."

"Jesus, Kai. Calm down."

"You think I want to be in love with you?" I yell. "Well, I don't."

"Oh yeah, since when?" he yells back, as if he has a right to be mad. "You and Steph have planned our wedding a thousand times!"

"When I was seven!"

"Oh, right, like it was only once, not an ongoing pastime for years."

"In case you didn't notice, some shit's gone down since then, so you can get the hell over yourself. I've had other things on my mind besides you. If you don't want me to love you, fine. Got it. Done."

I storm off down the beach toward the Four Seasons resort at the far end. Mom and Tomi went there for lunch, and I know there's a bar, which is where I'm headed. I wave to them when I see them sitting at a table in the café but don't join them. Mom will see that I'm upset, and I don't want to talk about it. Instead, I head to the poolside bar and order a mai tai.

I'm mad at myself as much as I'm mad at Josh. Why did I say that? Honestly, I'm more angry that I even feel it than that I said it.

A tall, tan, well-built guy named Lucas offers to buy me a second drink, and I accept. By the third round, I've been introduced to his friends and we're having a great time together. Lucas's arm is draped around my shoulder and I've forgotten Josh exists.

Until he's suddenly right in front of me.

"What the fuck, Kai?" he asks, rage bubbling through every word.

"Just keeping things light and non-serious, J," I answer.

"Is there a problem, dude?" Lucas asks.

"Yeah, *dude*, that's my girlfriend you're groping," Josh snarls.

"Ha!" I spit out. "Girlfriend! An hour ago you didn't want a relationship and now I'm your girlfriend? That's convenient."

Josh and I glare at each other while Lucas and his friends wait to see what's going to happen, except Lucas gets tired of waiting and pulls me in closer to him.

"Sounds like you had your chance, man," he says. "My turn now."

"Like hell," Josh says, shoving Lucas hard.

They start swinging at each other, and then big, burly Tomi is there pulling Josh away and settling everyone down. I'm sure he and Mom were watching all this unfold. Mom tries talking to me as she leads me back to pack up our beach stuff, but I don't want to talk.

The car is silent on the long drive home.

I go straight to bed and sleep for several hours, and when I wake up it's dark and quiet in the house. I can hear the surf against the rocks through the window, and it calls me outside to think. Josh is out there too, sitting on the seawall, his back to me. I pause for a moment, debating whether to avoid this conversation until tomorrow, but instead I step through the cool, damp grass toward him. It must have rained while I was asleep, because my butt is wet as soon as I sit down, a little ways from him on the cement wall, which is hard and uncomfortable.

"I can't end up like my dad, Kai," he says. An abrupt start to the conversation, but he seems to have been out here having a discussion in his head without me, and I just happened to show up at this particular point.

"You are nothing like your dad, J."

"But I can be. I reminded myself of that today. His anger and violence are in me. My dad settled for a life he didn't want, and it made him mean and dangerous. I can't do that."

"So don't. Be a different person. Live a different life." I now regret leaving the space between us on the wall, wishing I was closer to him.

"I don't want to settle down, K," he says. "Not ever. I don't want to get married, have kids, a family. I don't want to buy a house and have a nine-to-five job. I never want to be that person."

"Nobody's talking about marriage, J. I'm twenty-one years old, and I don't want to get married or have a family right now either. I have no idea what I want my life to look like. Since Kade, the only thing I planned for was college in California, nothing beyond that. So don't think I've been dreaming of a future with you my whole life, because I stopped dreaming of the future five years ago."

He scoots closer and takes my hand.

"I didn't mean to say those words today," I tell him. "The last thing I want is to be in love with someone, especially you."

"Thanks a lot," he says, attempting to lighten the mood. I try smiling at him, but it's halfhearted at best. After a minute, he asks, "Why especially not me?"

"Too much history, too big," I say, letting go of his hand and adjusting my position on the bumpy wall, pulling my hair back and trying to twist it into a bun, fidgeting to delay saying the next thing I need to say. "I've made it a point not to fall in love, because losing people you love hurts too much."

"I don't want to hurt you but I'm afraid I will," Josh says, running his own hands through his curls.

"Can we just forget I said it?" I ask, already knowing the answer.

"I don't want to forget it." He turns and straddles the wall, facing me. He motions with his finger for me to spin and face him too. Then he looks me straight in the eye. "I love you too, but I don't have anything to offer, and I'm pretty sure I'm going to let you down."

I smile then for real. "Can you please say that again without the pessimistic, depressing part?"

He smiles back at me. "I love you, Kai Martin."

"I love you, Josh Tyler."

The next morning, we are woken by the ringing of the phone. We assume it's Tomi calling for Mom, since that's the only person who's called us all month long. I'm surprised when Mom knocks on our bedroom door and calls Josh to the phone.

When I join them in the kitchen, Josh is finishing up his conversation with an editor at *Outdoor Adventures*, which is obviously going well, since Josh is beaming and thanking him repeatedly.

I'm stumbling toward the coffee when he hangs up and grabs me, lifting me a few inches off the floor in an enthusiastic squeeze. He starts babbling about how much the magazine loved his story and my pictures. Josh doesn't babble, so it's clear he's excited, but before caffeine, my brain isn't working fast enough to keep up with his tumble of words. He has to repeat himself twice before I register that he's telling me the magazine is buying my pictures. Not only that, they want us to do another piece together. Once I realize what he's saying, I jump back into his arms.

Mom shares our excitement when we tell her what we know about our first official assignment together in Yosemite National Park, where we will be heading straight from here. She tells me at least a dozen times how proud she is of me, which feels great.

It's less great later, when Josh is showering and Mom voices concerns. She reminds me that only yesterday I was flirting with someone else and Josh was in a fight and we weren't talking—as if I need to be reminded of all that. I'm annoyed with her for ruining my mood and frustrated that she doesn't trust me to make the right choice. I tell her that Josh and I talked and worked everything out last night, but I don't give her details because I'm irritated, so it doesn't make her feel much better.

She adds her two cents about the Yosemite plan in particular, recalling that I was never the biggest fan of roughing it, that I frequently complained during camping trips and always preferred the comfort of clean sheets and running water, acting as if she knows me so much better than I know myself.

"So you have no faith in me to make a good decision, is that it, Mom?" I ask, sounding like a whiny teenager.

She tries to tell me that she does trust me but that doesn't mean she can't also have concerns. She tells me she just wants to talk about it, that she wants me to think things through before running off with Josh.

"I don't want to talk about it or think about it," I say. "For the first time in a long, long time, I'm not feeling that massive, gaping hole inside me, and if that's because of Josh, then I'm sticking with Josh."

I don't think that convinces Mom it's a good idea, but she doesn't have a response, so at least it ends the conversation.

August 1, 1993

Dear Kade,

Yosemite is amazing! Josh and I have been staying in these tent cabins, so at least we're sleeping on platforms rather than on the ground for two weeks. I don't love the occasional showers and looking like a wreck all the time, but I do love being with Josh. And I love taking pictures, knowing there's a purpose behind it. I've been thinking a lot about you and what it must have felt like for you to draw and paint.

I'm not going to tell you everything about our time here because I'll send you our article...IN THE MAGAZINE... in October! That's so cool to say! Our volcanoes story will be in the September issue, which will be coming out in few weeks. On top of all that, we also got another assignment! We leave here tomorrow to fly to Ketchikan, Alaska. We're going to be staying there for two weeks, then going back in October and writing an article comparing the town during the tourist season and the off-season. They're putting us up in a local resident's house both times, so we can hopefully get the inside scoop on things. I'm just happy we'll be indoors, with plumbing! Josh is amazing, and we are loving being together. I'm really happy.

I love you.

Hey, Kade, your sister shares your artistic talent, dude. She sees things through her lens that makes the world look exactly as it is, yet fuller and more alive somehow. You'd love Yosemite. So much you could capture with your paint and canvas. I love being with Kai, man. Glad I finally wised up to that one. We miss you.

August 30, 1993
Dear Steph,
Wow, I love being with your brother! I love taking pictures and being with him all the time. We just got back

from Alaska, which was unbelievably beautiful. I've enclosed a few pictures, hopefully ones that make it into the magazine. We won't be done with this article until we go back in October, since it's a compare and contrast kind of thing, so we're in a little bit of limbo for now.

As you know, Danielle and Jaimie don't graduate until next spring, like you, and we have the house for another year. Josh is staying with me and the girls for now, and I'm back to waitressing at Walt's to earn money between stories for the magazine. Good luck with senior year!

Love,

Kai

October 13, 1993

Dear Kai,

I know we always talked about you being with Josh, but now that you are, it's so weird! I'm happy that you're happy, though. Are you guys coming to Thanksgiving? You better come! Your dad will be here. No kissing in front of me, though, okay? I'm not ready for that!

All is well here. Senior year is looking tough. I'm doing an internship as well as a full load of classes, so I won't have much time to write. All the more reason for you to come visit so we can catch up! Oh, one more thing, your dad was drinking again in Cape Cod. And he and Debbie broke up, in case you didn't know. Sorry.

Love,

Steph

THANKSGIVING REVISITED

Josh and I fly to Vermont for Thanksgiving. Although I've never been a nervous traveler, I'm freaking out on the plane, anxious about the family dynamics, about how it will be with Josh and me as a couple. I've tried to talk with Josh about it, but he can't understand why I'm worried, since we've spent half a lifetime of Thanksgivings together. But Stephanie's letter makes me think that it will be uncomfortable for us and everyone else. Josh tells me to relax and act normal, although he's avoided clarifying whether he means normal for the family or normal like we've been these last six months as a couple.

Dad is waiting for us at baggage claim. He hugs me, then shakes Josh's hand. We make small talk, but I already feel awkward, and I can tell Josh does too. He keeps a bit of distance between us, carrying both our bags as props. I pretend to sleep in the car, and Josh and Dad relax into a conversation about the Patriots' prospects this season.

We get to the Tylers' just before dinner, everyone gathered in the living room and already slightly buzzed. For once in my life, I am grateful for the alcohol flowing around me, and I down a quick drink to settle my nerves.

I like that Josh is watching me from across the room, even though he's huddled up with his brothers. We are apparently going with the old normal around the family, which is fine, except that I wish we had actually decided that rather than Josh just keeping away from me.

When we sit down for dinner, Stephanie pulls me down next to her and Josh sits at the other end of the table. These are the spots we've pretty much always sat in, but it feels weird now not to be sitting together. I help Pam and Steph clean up after dinner while the guys continue drinking in the living room. After that, it's game time. Tonight is Monopoly, which typically starts out fun but then drags on endlessly, always with someone getting mad somewhere along the way. The game comes down to Josh and Nick, who is thrilled when he beats his older brother. Josh heads off to bed with him and Bobby without even saying goodnight to me. I haven't missed a goodnight kiss, much less slept without him, for six months, and although Steph chatters about her life as we settle into bed, I am quietly seething and can't focus on anything she says.

The next morning I sleep late, primarily due to jet lag. When I go downstairs, Steph and Pam are putting away groceries.

"Sorry I overslept. What can I do to help?"

Pam hands me a mug of strong, dark coffee and tells me to relax and take my time waking up. She asks about Mom, and I tell her about the annual Group Gals cruise. Pam shares how much she misses my mom, how much she regrets that she was forced to choose sides, but I assure her that Mom understood, that there were no hard feelings. I explain that it probably would have been too hard for her to be around everyone without Kade and Dad anyway, although Pam disputes that anything could be too hard for my mom, expressing her admiration for Mom's strength and resilience, which I echo.

I ask where everyone else is, and Steph tells me they went to play football. She's expecting them back battered and bruised any minute, so I sneak in a quick shower before they return.

When I come back downstairs, the guys are sprawled around the kitchen table, telling their gridiron tales. Nick has ice on his face from some skirmish along the way. Josh smiles at me but doesn't get up or greet me.

"Good morning, sweetheart," my dad says, standing to give me a kiss on the cheek.

"Morning, Dad." I glare at Josh, but he doesn't seem to notice.

"Ready for pies, Kai?" Stephanie asks.

For the next couple of hours, I'm busy in the kitchen rolling dough and slicing apples and mixing pumpkin pie filling.

Josh reappears in the kitchen around three o'clock, when we're just finishing cleaning up. He and his mom do the same little dance they do every year—Josh asks for some pie, Pam says not until tomorrow, and then she pulls out the apple turnover she always makes for his special treat. What a mama's boy!

After he devours the turnover, he looks at me. "Wanna go for a walk?"

"Are you talking to me?" I ask.

"Yes, ma'am," he says, thinking he's being cute.

I don't want to just give in and go for a walk as if I'm not mad, but I also don't want to make a scene in front of Steph and Pam, so I get my coat and we head out. It's about forty degrees here in Vermont, quite a change from Long Beach weather. Most of the leaves have fallen, and it feels like winter is right around the corner.

As soon as we're away from the house, Josh leans in to kiss me.

"Are you fucking kidding me?" I yell, pulling away from him.

"What's wrong with you?" He looks genuinely confused,

which makes me even angrier.

"You're serious? What's wrong with you? You haven't talked to me since we walked into your house, and now you want to kiss me?"

"I always want to kiss you," he says, which does not help.

"Really? It sure doesn't seem like it. It seems like you're embarrassed to be with me."

"You were the one who was worried about us being here together. I was trying to give you space."

"Don't you dare put this on me," I say. "You were all cool about acting normal, and this is not normal." He's about to say something, but I cut him off. "You better not tell me you're acting normal. You didn't say goodnight to me, you haven't touched me or sat next to me once. You didn't even say good morning. You have completely ignored me for the past twenty-four hours."

He stops walking and turns toward me. "You're right. I'm sorry. I'm being an asshole."

That's better, but I'm not ready to forgive him quite yet. "Go on."

"You were right, this is weird. It's weird to be here with you. I love you, but it's weird to be your boyfriend when you've always been like my sister in this house."

"I thought we agreed on second cousins, not siblings. Remember?" I kiss him then, and we give each other a nice, long, healing hug.

When we part, I ask, "So how do we do this?"

He takes my hand and continues our walk. "How do you want it to be?"

"I wish I knew! Can I start with how I don't want it to be?"

"You don't want us to be strangers."

Ah, yes, he gets it. "That would be a good start." He kisses me again, and we keep walking.

"Can we be like we were with my mom?"

"I honestly don't think so," he says. "This group is way more complicated than your mom."

"True." I think for a bit as we walk. "How about we start with you talking to me? Saying goodnight and good morning, sitting next to me."

"Yes, I can do that. I should have done that. I'm sorry. Are you prepared for my stupid brothers making fun of us?"

"Been there, done that."

"For the record," he says, "I am not embarrassed to be with you. You are beautiful and talented and smart and funny, and I am lucky to be with you. As awkward as it is or will be, as much as I haven't been acting like it, I am glad you're here with me."

"Thank you," I tell him. Those words matter to me. We make out a little and walk a little, enjoying the time alone together before heading back to the house.

Josh stops for a minute right before we walk through the door. "You ready?"

"I am." He squeezes my hand and keeps hold of it as we enter.

Nick, Bobby, and our dads are sitting at the dining room table playing cards.

"Josh, c'mon. We're playing poker," Bobby calls.

"Later," he says. "I'm gonna help in the kitchen."

Bobby looks over and sees us holding hands.

"Oh, I get it," he says. He looks to me and says, "You finally got him whipped, huh, Kai?"

I hold tight to Josh's hand so he doesn't go punch his brother. "He just grew up and realized what he'd been missing, Bobby. Your brother always was the smartest of y'all."

Bobby laughs, Dad smiles, and I feel Josh relax beside me. So far so good. We head into the kitchen holding hands. Pam is cleaning beans but looks up and smiles at us as we come in.

"I'm here to make myself useful, Mom."

"Well, it's about time," she says, although I don't think she's talking about cooking.

That night, Josh and I freak out his brothers with a serious good-night kiss. Then Steph and I retire to her room, the room that I've shared since we were little kids, and it's like having a slumber party with my best friend. I ask her to repeat most of what she said last night and explain why I was distracted. She agrees with my assessment that Josh was being stupid, and admires my calling him out on it. Then she tells me about the start of her senior year in college. She's happy she chose communications as her major and is enjoying her internship at the Isabella Stewart Gardner Museum. She's helping to organize and promote events at the museum and says she's learned more there in these few months than she has in all her classes at Boston University. She's glad she moved out of the sorority house this year, since an apartment with her two closest friends feels more grown up and is more conducive to sleeping with the guy she's been seeing. We spend the rest of the night talking about boys, hers and mine. As we talk, it gradually becomes less weird that my boy happens to be her brother.

December 26, 1993
Dear Kade,
I'm saying Merry Christmas to you from 35,000 feet! Josh and I are on our way to Idaho for a last-minute article for the February Olympics double-issue. It's about a skier named Picabo Street, and I'm excited to photograph my first person professionally, rather than all nature all the time.

Mom came to Long Beach to celebrate with me and Josh, Danielle and her new boyfriend Marcus, and Jaimie and Nate. Nate and Jaimie are engaged, did I tell you that? This was the first time we'd all been in the house together for a major holiday, and we had the best time. We had a bonfire on the beach on Christmas Eve, all bundled up in hats and gloves, even though Mom and Josh made fun of us because it wasn't actually that cold and we are all spoiled California wimps.

Mom made cinnamon rolls for Christmas morning. Do you remember how delicious they are? And the smell? I'll bet you miss those! Josh gave me a beautiful necklace with a wave charm. "You are my sea," his card read, and I love it so much. Best present since your painting of us in the woods.

I missed you so much yesterday, but of course I miss you every day.

I love you, Kade.

Sorry to be an asshole, man, since you're dead and all, but I hate that you make your sister cry. That was a dick move, as I'm sure you know by now.

CRACKS

THE NEW YEAR STARTS OUT badly. We get home from Idaho on December 30, and that night I wake with a fever of a hundred and two. I stumble to the bathroom and take Tylenol, drinking down a glass of tap water, and put a cold washcloth on the back of my neck. I eventually fall back to sleep, only to awaken a while later with chills. My shaking wakes Josh, who is concerned and attentive. He finds sweats and helps me into them, gets an extra blanket out of the closet and puts it over me, then cuddles up to try and warm me. I tell him to stay away so he doesn't get sick, but he ignores me, for which I'm grateful, since his body heat helps me stop shivering. I drift back to sleep but am soon sweating again, and I push him and the covers away. He gets me the cold cloth this time and puts it gently on my forehead, replacing it every few minutes with a fresh one.

I spend New Year's Eve in bed, our fun plans canceled, but Josh doesn't seem to mind. He takes excellent care of me, and I'm reminded of when I had my sledding accident and he spent hours reading to me when he could have been outside having snowball fights with his brothers.

By the next day, the fever develops into a nasty head cold, and I'm so stuffy I can barely breathe. Josh rounds up extra pillows from Danielle and Jaimie, who are avoiding me and my germs, and gets cold and flu medicine from the drugstore. He massages Vicks VapoRub into my chest and washes my sweaty pajamas so they're fresh the next time I get chills.

By January second, the fever is gone, but I'm still stuffy and am now coughing, which is almost as exhausting as the fever. Josh goes to Blockbuster, and we lie in bed all day watching videos. We start with *Schindler's List*, which is nominated for the upcoming Oscars, but crying makes me more stuffy, so we have to turn that one off before the end. We watch *Sleepless in Seattle* and *Jurassic Park* and *True Romance*, which are almost as different as three movies can be. Despite being sick, I'm happy lying in bed all day next to this man who is perfectly accepting of my sweaty, phlegmy, gross self, patiently attentive to what I need, entirely willing to get up and fetch me soup and tea and cough drops and tissues, seemingly content to be exactly where we are, doing exactly what we're doing.

I'm happy to be living in this dilapidated house near the ocean with friends and the man I love—waking up in our shared bed, eating in our kitchen, shopping for groceries and cooking together. He fits right in with my friends, who have evolved from the three musketeers to a six-pack, including Jaimie's fiancé Nate and Dani's boyfriend Marcus, both of whom practically live here too. The guys teach Josh how to surf, and they watch sports together as often as we let them control the TV. The six of us laugh watching *Seinfeld* and share endlessly incorrect theories of what is possibly going on with *The X-Files*. We go to the beach at least once a week and play touch football on the sand, part of the thrill for me being when Josh grabs me and holds me to him for a minute before resuming the game.

It feels to me like we're living together, but every time I refer to this as our home, he'll slip in a qualifier about it being mine and the girls' or about it being temporary. I tease him that he could at least pretend to be settled down here with me, but the joking is a mask for his restlessness and my unease about that.

Outdoor Adventures magazine has been steadily growing in circulation and reputation, but that ends up being a bad thing for us. As the magazine becomes more popular, it attracts more experienced and esteemed writers and photographers, who end up with the bigger and better assignments. I fall off their radar completely, and Josh is relegated to local SoCal pieces about mountain biking in the hills around LA, deep-sea fishing off the coast, or popular surfing spots. Josh hikes nearby and escapes for weekends of backpacking now and then, sometimes alone and sometimes with Nate or Marcus, writing articles about those outings and submitting them, although it's unclear if any of them will make it into the magazine, so our career has definitely hit the doldrums. I'm still waitressing and bartending at Walt's, which covers rent and expenses, but the lack of work makes Josh edgy and irritable, and we end up fighting about stupid little things on a more regular basis. We don't have sex as often, and when we do it feels like an afterthought, like we do it because there's nothing better to do. I figure this is just a part of long-term relationships, and I try not to dwell on it.

In April, Josh is offered a writing assignment without me. One of the magazine's new big-shot photographers is doing a spread on Costa Rica, and Josh has been tapped to write the accompanying story. It's an amazing opportunity, since it will probably make the cover, and Josh is thrilled, as he should be. I try my best to be happy for him, since he hasn't been this excited in a long time, but it's hard because he's leaving to do a job without me.

A few nights after he gets the news, the six of us are drinking beer and playing cards at the kitchen table. Josh is telling everyone about his trip and the research he's been doing on Costa Rica.

"How'd you sweet-talk Kai into letting you take this job without her?" Nate asks.

"She knows how much this means to me," Josh says, "and she's fine with it, right, K?"

"I'm happy for you," I say, looking around the table. "It's fine." I see that Danielle's going to challenge me since she knows I'm upset about it, but I give her the stink eye and she keeps her mouth shut, which is unprecedented.

Nate laughs. "Ha! Never trust a woman who says she's fine!"

"I second that," Marcus agrees. "Not that Danielle would ever say anything is fine. She busts my balls at every turn."

"I thought you liked what I do with your balls," Danielle says, putting her hand on his crotch.

"Dani!" Jaimie says, always the first to be offended by raunchiness.

"We're different," Josh says. "We've known each other forever, so there's no point in holding things back. We're straight up with each other."

"Okay, if you say so, dude." Marcus suppresses a smirk.

"Plus, we don't need to ask each other permission to do things," Josh adds. "We're two individuals who can do what we want."

"Oh, now I know you're trippin'," Marcus says.

Later, as we're lying in bed in the dark, Josh asks me if I'm really okay with him taking the job.

"Of course. Like you said, you don't need my permission."

He sits up and turns on the light. "You sound pissed. Are you?"

"Not really." He stares at me intently until I say more. I tell him that my head one hundred percent wants him to go, that I know how much he's hated being stuck here and how great the job will be for him, but that another part of me wishes he'd rather stay. I'm hoping he'll tell me that he likes our life, that he hasn't felt stuck, but he doesn't say that. Instead, he tells me what a great opportunity this is for him.

"You don't think I know that?" I ask, my voice rising a bit. "You've said it about a hundred times, so I'm well aware of how great this is for you."

"What's that supposed to mean?" he asks, anger brewing behind his eyes.

"It means what about me? Have you thought about me at all?"

"What about you?"

"About how it might feel for me to be left behind? For you to be so excited to get away? For you to tell me one day that we're partners and the next to take a job without even talking to me first?"

"Oh, so I do need your permission, is that it?" He's yelling now.

"Not permission, just the courtesy of thinking of me and considering how I might feel!"

"Sorry, Kai, I thought you'd be happy for me. That's how I thought you'd feel."

"See, you don't actually want to know how I feel. You just want to tell me how I should feel, which I already know. I know I should be happy for you, and I know that's how you want me to feel, so that's what I told you to begin with. We should have just left it at that."

"Yeah, maybe we should have," he says, turning out the light and rolling away from me.

I lie there unable to sleep, wallowing in my anger and disappointment, and something else that I can't quite put my finger on. I hear Josh's breathing change and know that he's fallen asleep, which makes me livid. How can he sleep? I get up and go to the living room, where Danielle and Marcus are still awake, watching a movie in the dark.

"Everything's fine, huh?" she says, obviously having heard the yelling.

I tell her I don't want to talk about it and start to head outside to lie in the hammock by myself, but Danielle pulls me down onto the couch with them. She doesn't say anything, doesn't pressure me to say anything, simply knows it's better for me not to be alone.

The next morning the fight resumes. I wake up on the couch and find Josh in our bedroom packing.

"I can't believe you just fell asleep last night," I say coldly. "Like you don't even care about us at all."

"I can't believe you want me to miss this chance," he says. "I've been sitting around playing house with you for months, and when I finally convince them to let me do something, you're pissed."

"Wait, what?" All along, Josh has made it sound like the magazine approached him to do this story, that he couldn't pass up the opportunity they offered him. It makes so much more sense that he's been begging for it, and I feel stupid that I didn't see it before.

"Don't act like it's a surprise that I want to travel and write, Kai. You knew that was my plan. I know you don't care about it one way or the other, but this is important to me."

That sends me into another dimension of fury. "*You're* important to me, asshole. And you lied to me, J, straight-up lied to me."

He turns away, which confirms that he knows he was wrong. I lean against the wall, arms crossed. "Well? You have nothing to say?"

"I'm a lying asshole." He turns back to me with rage in his eyes. "What could I possibly say?"

"How about you're sorry?"

"Me? What about you?"

We stare each other down, and then he stomps out the door toward the kitchen. I follow him. He tells me to leave him alone, but I can't. He's banging cabinets open and closed, grinding beans and making coffee.

"Why did you lie to me?" I demand.

"Jesus, Kai, don't make me say it." He won't look at me, which pisses me off even more, which is hard to do because I'm already so monumentally pissed.

"You don't want to be here, right? That's what you don't want to say?"

"Right, I don't want to fucking be here. I can't stand being in one place for so long. But that's not about you, which of course you won't understand."

We're yelling again, and I should be considering the fact that we're going to wake up our roommates, but I don't care.

"Oh, you didn't think I'd understand that you not wanting to be with me doesn't mean you don't want to be with me? Huh, why would I have trouble with that? Have you even been asking for assignments together? Or have you been looking for the opportunity to slip away without me?"

"Goddammit, Kai. I've been stuck here because I *have* been waiting for a joint assignment, but they don't want to hire you because you're not a real photographer."

That hits me hard, mostly because I already know it's true, but I'm not going to give Josh the satisfaction of showing him that he hurt me. Instead, I swing back.

"Oh, and you're a real writer? You've written what? Maybe a dozen articles? And half of those were one-column blurbs on hikes in LA. You're no great journalist either, Josh." As the words tumble out of my mouth, I know I shouldn't say them. It's almost like I'm outside myself, one version of me knowing how mean they are and wishing I would stop, another version wanting to hurt him as much as he's hurting me.

We continue yelling at each other, but I don't even know what we're saying, it's just painful noise in my ears. The fight starts to feel like being sick and thinking there's nothing left to throw up but dry-heaving anyway. There are a lot of fuck you's and accusations that if we really loved each other we'd do this or that. The last thing I remember saying is something about how this isn't love and if he doesn't really love me, he should just leave and be done with it.

The coffee is almost finished brewing, and Josh has a mug in his hand. He's been tapping it agitatedly on the counter, and now he slams it down full force, shattering it in his hand. I'm startled into silence as he grabs another mug out of the cabinet and smashes that one too, then hoists the steaming pot of coffee and launches it across the kitchen, not exactly at me but in my direction, sprinkling me with hot spray that stings but doesn't actually burn me. At that, Danielle, Marcus, Jaimie, and Nate barrel into the room. I'm not sure when we woke them, but they've obviously been listening from the other room for a while and have decided that things are now out of hand.

Nate and Marcus hustle Josh out into the backyard while my girls surround me. I think I apologize to them, offering to clean up the mess, but it's kind of a blur because I'm in shock, not believing what just happened, not believing Josh and I could be so mean to each other.

Danielle gets me dressed, and we walk the few blocks to the beach, just to get out of the house, to create some distance between me and Josh. Jaimie hangs back to clean up the coffee and act as middleman. It's cold and foggy at the beach, perfect for how I'm feeling. One thing I love about Danielle is that she says whatever's on her mind up until she knows that there are no helpful words. She's a great judge of when I need silence and unspoken, unconditional support. We're at the beach for a few hours, mostly trading variations on "That was fucked up" and "What's next?"

Jaimie brings us sandwiches for lunch and makes us eat before she'll tell us what's going on at the house, before saying, "Josh left."

I feel my heart crack and my stomach lurch. I'm afraid I'm going to puke up the sandwich I just ate.

"Nate and Marcus and I tried to convince him to stay and talk things out with you, but he was pretty rattled. I think he freaked himself out by throwing that coffeepot. He's ashamed and mad at himself, and he kept saying how terrible he is for you, how you'll be better off without him. He was packing like a robot on autopilot, repeating over and over that he had to leave."

"Where'd he go?" I ask.

"Marcus took him back to his place for the night. He leaves tomorrow anyway. He made me promise not to let you go to Marcus's, although he knows there's nothing I can do about it if you want to see him."

"Why would I want to see someone who doesn't want to see me?" Part of me feels like crying, part of me wants to hit something, and another part of me just wants to go to sleep for days and days and days.

Jaimie scoots up close beside me and puts her arm around me, and I rest my head on her shoulder, which brings on the tears. "I'm sorry, Kai," she says.

I try to compose myself. "You know, Dani and I have been sitting here repeating how we can't believe what just happened, but I actually think I've been waiting for it. I somehow convinced myself I could have some happily-ever-after with Josh, that we'd just glide through all our fucked-up childhood shit and float along on an uncomplicated life full of travel and love and sex, and that was stupid. The whole idea of us was stupid." As I'm talking, anger takes the place of sadness, anger at myself for not knowing that Josh would leave me. I look at Danielle with fire in my eyes. She knows that look of determination and fierceness. She's perfected it.

"Dani, will you please go to Marcus's and tell Josh that if he leaves like this, without even talking to me first, then we're done, and I don't want to see him again."

"Kai, maybe you should slow down and think about it," Jaimie says calmly, holding me tight. "You're heartbroken, and that's not the best time to make big decisions. Maybe it's better to leave it alone right now, when you're both so upset. You can circle back and work it through when he gets back."

"In a month, Jaimie?" I say. "No way. We resolve this now or it's over. I can't wait a month."

"Fuck that," Dani chimes in. "Josh was an asshole. The temper, the leaving. As much as I really do like him, if you're done you're done. Plenty of fish in the sea." She waves her hand toward the water, trying to lighten the mood.

"He wasn't just some fish, though," Jaimie says.

"Jaims, don't be a downer," Dani says, "even if you're right." She scoots close to me on the other side and puts her arm around me. Now I'm sandwiched between her and Jaimie, silently thinking while we stare out at the waves. After a while, I find myself hypnotized by the waves, not even thinking anymore. But I need to think, so I lie back, pulling my musketeers with me, wanting their bodies pressed against me on both sides so I can feel their love and support. We lie there getting sand in our hair until I know what to do.

"I'm going to say something terrible right now, so you have to promise to love me anyway, after I say it." They each take a hand and give a squeeze to let me know they love me no matter what. "Sometimes I wish that my brother had killed himself the first time he tried." Surprisingly, saying this doesn't make me cry. Instead, I feel numb.

"He came home from the hospital, and I thought he was better. I believed it was going to be okay after that. I had faith. And that made it so much worse when he did it again. Sometimes I wish he'd saved me from hoping it would be okay, because part of hoping was that I thought I could save him, and I couldn't. I couldn't do one single thing to make anything different."

"I understand completely what you're saying, Kai." Dani looks at me seriously, which is rare. "I also don't believe you. You wouldn't give up one single day you had with Kade, even the bad ones, even the fucking horrible ones. I'm sure part of you might want that, but you would never actually make that wish."

I cuddle into Dani's side, feeling so touched and grateful that someone sees me so clearly, knows me so well. And my old grief washes over me once again, for the only person who knew me better.

Finally, I pull myself together. "I still think it's better to cut my losses with Josh here and now, before it's so much worse."

"I back you up one hundred percent, Kai. Always," Jaimie says. "But I just want to say that it is possible this isn't the same thing as Kade. This is a different thing."

"I guess." I turn my head to look at her, smiling sadly. "But it feels the same."

"Okay," Dani says, correctly sensing that my contemplation is over, and I'm ready to take action. She sits up and pulls me and Jaimie with her, scooting around so we're in a little circle. "So what are we going to do?"

"I want you to go to Marcus's and tell Josh it's now or never. He'll refuse to talk, and that will be that. I'm going home and going to bed and staying there until work tomorrow night."

They both study me for a while, and then Dani claps her hands like we're breaking from a huddle after calling the next play.

It goes as I predicted. Dani tells me that Josh was in such a state of self-loathing that he was convinced I'd be better off without him, so he was done. I lie in bed for the next thirty-six hours, and Dani and Jaimie bring me water and coffee and food every now and then. When I have to, I get up and go to work and resume my life.

That night, as Josh is flying to Costa Rica, I have the most vivid, horrible nightmare I've ever had. I see Josh's plane crashing. I see him screaming and burning, gasping for air, and I wake up fighting for breath myself. It feels so real, and the terror sticks with me, a part of me sure it was actually a vision, that Josh is already dead. I toss and turn but can't fall back to sleep. I keep checking the clock, waiting until it's finally time for the morning news so I can see if there's been a plane crash, which there has not.

Jaimie is up for an early class and can see I'm upset, so I tell her about my dream. She reassures me that Josh is safe, which I try to believe. She suggests that maybe I'm more worried about losing him than I thought, that maybe we should at least talk when he gets back, which I don't want to consider, so she lets it go. Jaimie has always been a great listener, which is why she'll make a fabulous therapist someday. She offers to skip class to stay with me, but I don't let her do that. It was just a dream after all.

The thing is, I have nightmares all that week and the next. Dreams of Josh getting malaria and dying of a fever all alone in the jungles of Costa Rica, of him getting eaten by a leopard, of him falling off a cliff and smashing against the rocks below. These vivid, horrifying dreams feel completely real, but there are nonsensical ones that feel even worse. There's a black hole that sucks me into it, over and over. I struggle and fight against the pull of the darkness, but every time, it pulls at me until I disappear. Jaimie kicks Nate out onto the couch and makes me sleep with her after I wake up screaming in my room one night, dripping with sweat.

I feel like I'm losing my mind, becoming absolutely convinced that something awful has happened to Josh. I call Steph after the first week of nightmares, but nobody there has heard from him. She can tell I'm worried and reassures me that they never hear from him, that they only ever know what he's doing because I pass along his news. By the end of the next week, I call the magazine, but our editor hasn't heard from either Josh or the photographer, not that he expected to. He says he doesn't usually hear from them until they submit their story, which isn't due for another few weeks.

None of that makes me feel better, although Dani points out that if something terrible had happened, those are the people who would know first. Her stance is that no news is good news, and she takes on her usual role of fun distracter. She drags me out to bars and the beach, and sometimes I get drunk enough to pass out and not dream for a night.

The worst dream comes after weeks of the near-nightly variations on Josh's death and my own obliteration. It's the least disastrous, but it destroys me. Josh is in heaven hanging out with Kade. They are laughing and happy and having a grand old time. There are girls, and Josh kisses someone. I come into the dream, and they don't know who I am. They've both forgotten me, or maybe I never existed at all, but then I realize that everything happened exactly as it happened but it just doesn't matter to them one single bit. I don't matter. I never mattered to Kade or Josh.

I wake up shaking. My heart is pounding, and I'm the most terrified I've ever been. Jaimie thinks I'm having a panic attack, and that sounds right. Danielle gives me a shot of tequila, but it doesn't calm me down at all. I'm sitting on the floor by my bed, rocking back and forth, unable to stop fidgeting and crying. Marcus pulls out his bong, and they convince me to take a hit. I don't usually smoke because I blame pot for Kade's demise. It's irrational, since he drank and did other drugs and there's all that family history—pot probably contributed the least to his overall problem—but the way I see it, everything shifted when he started smoking pot with that group of people, so I generally stay away from it.

This night, though, I'm thankful for it. After a couple of hits, I calm down, the world becomes less sharp and painful, my thoughts float away. The dream becomes just a dream instead of the defining truth of my life.

I sleep through half of the next day, and when I wake up, I'm surprised to find Dani and Jaimie home.

"You guys didn't need to stay home for me," I say. "I'm okay."

"Debatable," Dani says.

I stick my tongue out at her as I'm pouring coffee.

"It's not just that," Jaimie says, and I see an envelope in her hand. I recognize the handwriting immediately. I reach for Josh's letter, but Dani grabs it first.

"Are you in any kind of shape to read this letter, Kai?" she asks. "You were a fucking basket case last night."

I smile because I know this is how Dani shows her love, being brutally honest and then backing me up no matter what.

"Either way, I want to read the letter," I say.

She hands it to me, then leads me to the couch, and we all sit together while I read it.

May 15, 1994

Dear Kai,

I don't know what to say about what happened. Every time I try to write to you, the words seem lame and stupid. I'm on my way to Iceland for another story, hoping that more time and distance will give me clearer perspective, but that seems lame and stupid too. Writing you a story somehow seemed to make the most sense, which probably proves how senseless I am right now. I miss you like crazy. I want to come home to you, but I also don't trust myself now, so I don't know what to do.

J

Residue of Red Flame

There once was a wise, kind, beautiful mermaid named Leilani who fell in love with a boy named Paxton. She first saw him when he was sinking in the water, drowning, his evil pirate father having tossed him over the side of his ship. Leilani saved him, then helped him save his mother. Then they killed his father, eliminating that particular strain of evil from the world.

However there is always more evil out there. Goodness is always being threatened. That is nothing new. The surprising part of this story is that the evil was lurking within our hero, lying dormant, but always there.

Leilani loved Paxton from the moment she saw him. But he was caught up with other concerns and didn't really see her. He only saw what she did for him, which was not at all the same thing. She built him an enchanted island, gave him a home, took care of him. Yet she also brought him back to civilization when that's what he wanted, even though it meant she would no longer see him every day, even though she would miss him for all the time he was away.

Paxton traveled the land doing good deeds, protecting those who needed protecting, trying to make the world a better place and make up for the evil his father had done. When he became weary or wounded, he would journey to the sea and Leilani would meet him, magically knowing that he needed her. Being with her would make him strong again, give him hope, and remind him what mattered. He soaked up her love and carried it out into the world with him, but he didn't give any back to her.

On one of their visits, Leilani asked him to stay with her. She offered to enchant a new island so that she could walk its shores with him and he could swim in the depths of the waters surrounding it with her. But that was not Paxton's life, and it was not Leilani's life either, so Paxton left her once again and returned to his wandering, do-gooding ways.

Soon after, there came a day when Paxton's village was attacked by a marauding tyrant. By the time Paxton heard the news and rushed home, it was too late. The village was burned to the ground and his sweet, loving mother was dead. He carried her lifeless body to the sea and begged Leilani to revive her, but that was beyond the mermaid's magic, although Paxton didn't believe her. He convinced himself that Leilani was punishing him for leaving, and he was enraged.

As much as the mermaid had done for him, as purely as she had loved him, right then he hated her. He couldn't forgive her for letting him down, for not being able to take away his pain and make things better as she always had before.

That afternoon, his dad's wicked heart began beating in Paxton's chest. He tracked down the marauding tyrant and murdered him and all his men, even the ones who begged for mercy. He saw no point in mercy, saw no further purpose in good deeds. He'd spent his life on good deeds and ended up with a dead mom and a ruined home and a wicked heart.

He built a ship and made a plan to become a pirate—grief, anger, and pain turning him into someone he never thought he would be. But before he could begin to plunder and terrorize seaside towns and peaceful sailors, the mermaid saved his life again. This time she did it by almost killing him. She brought on a storm as brutal as the one that had sunk his father's ship, and it left him clinging to life and the few remaining planks.

Leilani surfaced near Paxton and asked him what he was going to do. He studied her and soaked in her love and goodness, and he cried in shame. He had no faith in himself that he could be the person she saw. How could he be worthy of her love? He begged her forgiveness and she gave it to him, then sent him off to find forgiveness in himself, to find his own faith.

It took him years to do that, to prove to himself that he was worthy, before he found his way back to her and let himself love her the way she'd always loved him.

May 28, 1994

J,

I told you a long time ago that I would be your mermaid, and although many things have changed, that is not one of them. But waiting years isn't going to work for me, so you better forgive yourself quicker than that. I'll be at my mom's in a few weeks. Meet me there and we'll figure this out together.

K

RESET

I CHEER FOR DANIELLE AND Jaimie, Nate and Marcus, as they graduate from Long Beach, and then it's time to pack up. End of the lease, end of an era. Jaimie and Nate move to San Diego together to live near her family, start their careers, and plan their wedding. Danielle and Marcus break up amicably, their relationship having run its course, and she heads to the Amalfi Coast to spend the summer with her parents before moving to New York City, where she will start job hunting while her parents cover her first year's rent. She jokes about the benefits of parents whose love comes from an ATM, and I hear the pain behind her wisecracks.

We have a huge yard sale to sell our furniture, and I stuff the rest of my belongings into my 1980 Ford Fiesta and cry for the first hour of my cross-country drive back to New York. I'm temporarily staying with Mom, who now lives one town away from where I grew up, in a cute little three-bedroom ranch in a typical suburban housing tract, with flower beds in the front yard and a vegetable garden in the back.

Josh's Costa Rica article makes the cover of the July issue, which is delivered to Mom's house shortly after I arrive. It's amazing, and I can tell already that this will be a turning point in his career. I'm both happy for him and sad for myself because I'm pretty sure he'll choose the work he loves over me. I'm not sure I can forgive him for leaving anyway, not sure I'm prepared to risk being hurt that deeply again, not sure I want to hope again.

Although I spend hours rehearsing what I'm going to say to him, the words fly away when I open the door and he's right there in front of me. All I can do is fall into his arms and hold on to him for dear life, unable to imagine anything that will make me let go again. My arms start shaking because I'm holding him so tightly.

He loosens his grip on me only enough to move his hands to my face and kiss me frenetically. The plan was to be smart and logical and set my emotions to the side while we talked through everything that happened. Instead, we end up in my bed having sex before we even say hello. It's a hungry, frantic lovemaking; we don't even undress, simply push clothing out of the way so we can come together as quickly as possible.

"Well, I'm glad we worked that all out," Josh says after, and we both crack up, laughing until tears run down our cheeks. When we catch our breath, he adds, "I really did plan to talk first. I practiced a whole script."

"Me too," I say.

We roll onto our sides, locking eyes.

"Kai, I am so sorry," he starts. "I'm sorry I lied about asking for that story. I actually begged for it, if I'm going to be completely honest. I knew it would hurt you, and I didn't want to hurt you. I just couldn't do it anymore…that version of a life." He looks away then, but I put my hand on his face and turn him back to me.

"That does hurt, J," I say. "I'm not gonna lie. I just wish we could have talked about it instead of erupting like that."

"I'm sorry for that too," he says. "I have my dad's temper, and it scares the shit out of me."

"Hey, you are not your dad."

"I could have burned you with that coffee. Or worse. What if everyone hadn't come in right then and broken it up?" I don't want to think about that, so I don't say anything. "My whole life, I've felt it there, bubbling below the surface. The potential that in a moment of rage, I could be just as brutal as him."

"You never will be," I say firmly, believing it with everything in me. "It's impossible."

"How can you be so sure?" he asks, and I can hear in his voice how badly he needs a strong answer, so I think carefully about my response.

"I know you, Josh Tyler. Yes, you lose your temper sometimes. People do that, especially people who've seen it happen. But that's not who you are. I have never once, not even that day, been scared of you. You are thoughtful and kind. You always watched out for Kade and Bobby and Nick and Steph and me, and probably a bunch of other people I never even met. You are aware of the issue and have set an intention to live your life differently."

He ponders that for a while, then says, "I feel calmer when I'm out in nature. The rage fades away."

I realize that we are about to start talking about our future, and I'm suddenly terrified. I'd had this whole backup plan to go live with Danielle in the city, and that sounded great. I'd really thought that if Josh and I couldn't fix things or reach a compromise, I would be fine parting ways and moving on with my life. But now that's impossible. The desperation and longing when I saw him at my door are churning inside me, and I know I will do whatever it takes not to lose him again.

"What was the speech you rehearsed?" Josh asks.

"Mostly that I'm sorry too." My talking points had been about needing an equal partnership and us being honest with each other. I'd planned to tell him that I didn't know if I wanted to be an outdoor journalist photographer sidekick, away from my friends and the world, but I don't want to say that now. Being with Josh feels more important than total honesty.

"That's a short speech," he says, and I can tell he knows there's more.

"I missed you," I say because that is true. "I had nightmares about you for weeks, couldn't sleep at all, until Marcus started getting me high." I know that will break the tension, which it does.

"How is everyone?" he asks.

I tell him about graduation and the breakup and my move. He tells me about Costa Rica and Iceland and how he's gained a lot of esteem at the magazine with those stories, which he's leveraged to line us up a series of assignments together.

"Will you come back?" he asks. "Be my partner again? I proposed our first story specifically for you, as an additional peace offering in case I wasn't enough on my own."

"You will always be enough, J," I say, and kiss him. I'm at least eighty percent happy, probably closer to ninety percent, and I ignore the ten or twenty percent of me that knows I'm selling myself out a little.

We lie in bed talking for most of the afternoon. He tells me about the assignment he pitched to the magazine for us, and I love him even more for it, since it's entirely for me. We undress each other and make love again, this time slowly and tenderly. When Mom gets home from work, we all have dinner together, and it's like nothing ever happened. Josh was planning to drive back to Vermont tonight, but instead he stays with us for a week, and we make plans to resume our life together, starting with Josh's olive branch.

We head back across the country to Puget Sound and spend a few weeks with Ken Balcomb at his Center for Whale Research, learning about the orcas that he's spent decades studying and protecting. Most days we're on a small boat in the Salish Sea, getting to know the three pods of Southern Resident killer whales that Ken and a crew of staff and volunteers know intimately. I cry more than once when witnessing the beauty of these amazing creatures. And the photos! I capture the curiosity, joy, and love in the orcas movements and social interactions, although I am repeatedly warned not to anthropomorphize the whales. I figure since I'm not writing the article, it does no harm for me to believe these whales are my new best friends. I think my perspective makes the pictures even better, but I keep that to myself.

We are scheduled to be at the research center for two weeks, but I convince everyone to let us stay another week because I can't bring myself to leave. I have a connection with the whales, especially the more I get to know them, learning about them from the staff and simply by watching them with unwavering attention. I am in a constant state of wonder, happy even on the days it's raining and the boat is tossed around on rough waters and I'm cold and soaked to the bone. The joy feels spiritual and encompasses Josh and the whales and all the people here. I feel the least alone I've ever felt, filled with love and gratitude, like I'm a part of something bigger than myself. Josh feels it too, which makes it even more amazing. We talk about it every night. He explains that this is how he feels when he's in the woods, out in the middle of nowhere, alone yet innately connected with everything around him, and I get it now. Sex becomes spiritual too, like it's happening between our souls and not just our bodies. We leave here more bonded and in love than ever.

Next, we head back to Yosemite, which feels like restarting our professional partnership, since that was our first official assignment together. We're doing a piece about rock climbing for the Summer Adventures issue. We stay for two weeks, interviewing climbers, park rangers, emergency rescue workers. It's fun for me because I'm able to take both scenery shots—the sheer faces of El Capitan and Half Dome, the amazing waterfalls and wildflowers—and people pictures of the climbers. At night, we sit by our campfire and read aloud to each other, making our way through John Irving's *A Prayer for Owen Meany*, comparing those dysfunctional families and tragedies to our own. It's my favorite time of day, Josh and I alone together with the fire and a great story. If I'm reading to him, he rests his head in my lap, stretched out perpendicular to me, and I play with his curls while I read. When I lie with my head resting on him, my world becomes his voice, catching me up entirely in Owen's story. I forget about how dirty and smelly I am, how much I hate living like a cave woman, how not sexy I feel even though Josh still wants to have sex every day.

Today, we're on a hike that has nothing to do with our assignment, a backcountry trail to Sentinel Dome that Josh has been wanting to explore. We haven't seen anyone else out here, which is the main reason Josh chose it. He loves to be as isolated as possible.

"When do you think you're going to be done with this article, Josh? I have about a zillion pictures, so I know we're not waiting on me to get back to civilization."

"Civilization is seriously overrated."

"Really? Plumbing? Refrigeration? Electricity? None of that appeals to you?"

"C'mon! How can you not love it out here?"

"I love you. Does that count?"

"You love it. You're just griping."

"It is gorgeous, J, but enough already. Can we please go home and shower and sleep in a bed and go to a restaurant?" I rarely complain, but I want to go home.

"You are disgustingly domesticated. Where's your wild side?"

"It's right here. Look at me—hairy legs and stringy hair—I'm completely wild, and I'm over it."

"You're beautiful," he says. I believe he means it, but I also know it's not true.

We get to the top of Sentinel Dome late in the afternoon, and the light is perfect. We have a beautiful view of Half Dome and the valley, and I take a ton of pictures. Josh is sitting against a rock, looking out over the panorama. I sit between his legs, my arms resting on his bent knees, snapping a few more shots.

"I thought you had plenty of pictures," Josh teases, and I lean against him and pull his arms around me.

"I do, but this light is spectacular."

"See, we could stay here forever, and the light would always be different."

"I really like taking pictures, J," I say.

"You take amazing ones," he says.

"I need to tell you something that I didn't want to tell you before." We're in this beautiful spot, happy and secure, and I feel brave enough to open up. "When we got back together, I agreed to be your partner again because I wanted so much to be with you. I didn't care about ever taking pictures again. I didn't care about having this career. I just wanted to be with you."

He lets me talk and simply listens, which I appreciate.

"This lifestyle isn't my favorite. I wouldn't choose to live in a tent if it wasn't for you. So I guess what I'm saying is that it *is* for you, at least that part of it, and I want you to know that. But I also want you to know that I'm starting to actually feel like a photographer, starting to care about it, and I like that."

"I want you to be honest with me, K." He squeezes me with his arms and legs. "I want to know how you're feeling."

"Even when it makes things messy?"

"Even then." He kisses the top of my head. "I know you're

making sacrifices for me. Thank you," he says, nuzzling my hair. "I know you don't always love being out here in the wilderness, but I don't want to be out here without you. We have different ideas about what we want our life to look like. We may not agree or feel the same way about things. We're gonna have to figure out how to deal with that."

"I know," I say, content that we're acknowledging the truth of how things are.

RESIDUE

FOR THE NEXT SEVERAL MONTHS, time is a blur. We're traveling so much that I often wake up not knowing where I am. But Josh is beside me, and that's all that matters.

A park ranger tracks us down while we're camping in the Everglades to tell us that Pam's had an accident and is in critical condition at the hospital in Rutland. I try to comfort Josh, but he wants no part of it. He is all action, no time for feelings. We break camp in record time and catch the first flight we can from Miami to Vermont.

Josh barely says a word on the drive to the airport, or as we wait for our flight, or on the plane. We haven't been able to get through to anyone, so we have no idea what's going on or how Pam is. He lets me hold his hand, but otherwise he is in his own world. I assume he's scared and sad and upset that he isn't right there next to his mom, but I have no idea that he is also in a rage. I don't realize that until we arrive at the hospital and walk into Pam's room in the ICU.

Josh stops for a moment in the doorway, taken aback at the sight of his mom's bandaged and swollen face as she lies there unconscious, a breathing tube in her mouth and other tubes and monitors encircling her. Bobby, Nick, and Stephanie are sitting in chairs around the bed, Steph holding her mom's hand. Rob is standing at the foot of the bed, and my dad is leaning against a wall along the side of the room.

Before anyone can even say hello to us, Josh lunges for his dad, punches him, then pushes him up against a wall, his arm crushing Rob's throat.

"I will kill you, you son of a bitch," Josh hisses.

Bobby and Nick immediately jump up from their chairs and pull Josh off their dad.

"You think you're the savior here, Josh?" Bobby growls, shoving his hand against Josh's chest. "You disappear for months at a time, have no idea what's going on, and then you swoop in to avenge Mom? Get over yourself, bro. You have no fucking clue."

"He didn't do anything, Josh," Nick says, patting Josh's shoulder to try and calm him down. "It was a car accident. The car's totaled. I saw it."

"A car accident?" Josh repeats, coming out of a daze.

"Yeah, dickhead, a car accident," Bobby says.

"I could never do that to her," Rob says, with tears in his eyes. I've never seen him emotional, and I don't think his kids have either. Everyone freezes in a shocked silence.

Dad rubs my arm and kisses my cheek as he passes me on the way to Rob.

"Let's take a walk," he says, putting an arm around Rob and guiding him out the door.

I go to Josh, touch his face, then take his hands in mine. "Josh, you are here for your mom. Go be with her."

He continues to come out of his fog as he walks slowly over to the bed. He leans down and kisses a spot on Pam's head that isn't covered in bandages or bruises. He sits and takes her hand and tries a smile at Stephanie, sitting across from him.

"Hey, Steph," he says. "Sorry about that."

"It's okay, Josh," she says. "It's how we roll. I'm glad you're here." She looks to me. "I'm glad you're both here."

I walk around the bed and give her a big hug, then go back and put my hand on Josh's shoulder as he holds his mom's hand. "Will someone please tell us what's going on?"

"I thought Josh knew it all," Bobby says, but he's not really mad anymore, just wants to make a point.

"I get it, Bobby." Josh twists around in his chair to look at his brother, as close to an apology as they come in this family. "Can you fill me in please?"

Bobby tells us she was driving at night and hit a deer. The car rolled a few times and ended up smashed against a tree on the side of the road. Nobody's sure how long she was there before someone spotted the car and called 911.

"You know Vermont roads at night," he says.

Stephanie picks up the story, explaining that Pam was unconscious when they found her and they have her in a medically induced coma right now to control the swelling in her brain, which is why she has a breathing tube. The swelling is lessening, and they're hoping to be able to bring her around later today or tomorrow. They won't know about any brain damage until she's conscious. Steph starts crying, and Nick goes over to kneel by her chair, putting a hand on hers. I squeeze Josh's shoulder harder.

Bobby wraps up by letting us know the extent of her injuries— four broken ribs, a broken wrist and collarbone, one lung collapsed from the broken ribs, and a ruptured spleen, which they removed. The rest looks terrible but isn't major.

"We have to wait to see if there's permanent damage from the brain injury," Nick adds.

"Is she going to wake up?" Josh asks, looking at Bobby.

"They keep telling us they're optimistic but can't say for sure."

Bobby and Josh lock eyes for a while, and it seems to be their way of giving each other a hug, crying together, saying how sad and scared they are. I wish they would do those things, but I know they won't.

"Have any of you eaten?" I ask.

"Bobby and I took Dad to the cafeteria a few hours ago. Steph hasn't left that spot since she got here," Nick says.

"Steph, let's go get some food. These guys will watch over your mom, and we'll only be gone a little while. You need your strength for when she wakes up."

It takes a little more convincing, but she agrees to come with me, and I take orders for coffee and snacks. I expect to see Dad and Rob in the cafeteria, but they aren't there. I try to distract Stephanie by asking about her new apartment and her promotion to events director at the museum, and she allows her mind to escape the hospital for half an hour or so.

When we return to Pam's room, Rob is back, but Josh and Dad are gone. Nick gets up and gives Stephanie her chair. He walks over to me and takes the coffee I've brought him. I give him a hug, and we chat briefly, to the degree that feels appropriate in the ICU. I ask after Dad and Josh, but Nick doesn't know where they went.

"I think John wanted to keep the Josh-Dad quality time to a minimum," he says.

"I'm going to go check on them." I squeeze Nick's arm in support. "I'll be back."

I walk through the halls and hear them talking in a little lounge around the corner. I haven't spied in a long time, but I can't stop myself from eavesdropping.

I overhear my dad telling Josh about a conversation he had with Rob some years ago about their lowest points in life. That's how he says it, "at my lowest point," unable even to utter Kade's name, incapable of saying "when Kade died." Rob talked about when he hit Josh, how that was his lowest point, how much he regretted things getting so out of hand, how he'd made himself a promise never to lay a hand on Pam again, and how he never had. I can't help but think about how drunk he and Rob must have been to have had a conversation like that.

"You really think that's true," Josh asks, "not just what you want to believe?"

"I do. The way your dad said it makes me believe it," Dad answers.

"But he didn't want me to know?"

"He has a lot of pride, Josh. He can't admit you were right or that you ended up winning that fight."

They sit quietly for a while, and then I hear the crinkling sound of a plastic chair giving way as my dad gets up, maxed out on emotions. "I'll see you back in there."

I retreat, then take a few steps so it looks like I'm just now walking down the hall. Dad rounds the corner and gives me a hug. I can smell liquor on his breath. Of course that's where he and Rob went. The bar across the street.

"I'm glad you're here, Kai. Josh can use you right now," Dad says, and continues walking down the hall. It's kind of nice to be reminded of how much Dad loves Josh.

I sit down on the cheap little couch next to Josh. "How ya doing, J?"

He looks at me, takes a gasping breath, and starts crying. I take him in my arms and hold him. This is only the second time I've ever seen him cry, and as sad as I am for him, I'm glad he's letting it out. As his tears slow, I feel him relax into me, his head resting on my chest.

"I shouldn't have done that to my dad," he says.

"Yeah."

"Did you hear what your dad said to me?"

"Yeah."

"Spying again, huh?" He shifts on the couch, kisses me quickly as he wipes his face, and pulls me into him, wanting to be close, but also wanting the less vulnerable position now. "Do you think it's true?"

"I don't know, J. I hope it's true."

"Me too. I'm going to believe it for now because it will be easier to be nice to my dad, and I think we all need that."

"Hey, J, I think that's called faith," I say. "Nicely done."

"Thanks, I'm trying."

We sit listening to the muted bustle of the hospital floor.

"Your dad looks like hell," I say. "I do believe he loves her."

"I know, it's just such a fucked-up love."

"Yeah."

Nick comes around the corner to let us know the doctor's arrived to start the process of bringing Pam out of the coma. He looks like a scared little kid. I stand up with Josh, and we all hold hands as we walk back down the hall.

"Josh and I were just talking about faith," I say. "Let's try to have some of that, okay?"

When Pam finally wakes up, she does not have any significant brain damage, nothing wrong with her that won't heal with time. Over the next few days I watch the Tyler family from a new perspective. I see how lovingly Rob and Pam look at each other, which I've never noticed before. It could be a renewed appreciation for having each other, or maybe it was always there and I blocked it because I believed Rob was a jerk and Pam was a doormat. Then I look at my dad, alone, and think about his relationship with my mom. I do remember them being in love, and I also remember them fighting. I don't want to think about Rob and Pam fighting, since that would be a frightening image, but also because I never saw it. Rob was always in charge, never challenged. Pam deferred to him always, unlike my mom, who challenged my dad a lot. I'm watching them now, seeing Rob and Pam in love and Mom and Dad alone, and reevaluating my ideas about which is the better way to go.

I bring it up with Stephanie, who shares memories about Rob and Pam being loving and kind to each other—Rob bringing Pam flowers after work on Fridays, taking her out on dates, doing household projects together. Steph knew a different set of parents than Josh did, coming along so much later. She doesn't remember the abuse, although she knows it happened. Instead, she knows them as a happier couple, one that Josh can't recall.

I also watch Josh with his mom, how sweet he is to her, but also how caring she is to him, even from her hospital bed—brushing his hair gently away from his face, reminding him to go eat, listening attentively to every word he says. I've always known how much Josh loves his mom, but I watch it now as his girlfriend, wondering if he's looking for more of that than either of us thought. I've taken many psych classes, and there's a lot of evidence that people unconsciously look for partners like their parents. I always assumed that since Josh didn't want to be like his dad, he also didn't want me to be like his mom. He admired my mom's strength so much, and I figured he liked that about me too. But watching him here, I start to wonder if maybe he'd prefer I was more like Pam.

I want to talk with Josh about it, but there isn't a good opportunity while we're staying in a full house with his family and going back and forth to the hospital every day. Plus, I am keenly aware of how deliberately all of the Tylers avoid talking about anything difficult. Our first night in Vermont, after Pam was conscious and stable, Josh cried in my arms again in our rental car. He talked about his emotions that day but hasn't talked about them since.

Neither of his brothers have mentioned Josh attacking their dad or anything about being scared for their mom. Steph and I talk a little about her concerns, but not deeply, and I'm reminded that Steph and I don't talk that way, not the way I do with Danielle and Jaimie. All that makes me wonder how much Josh actually wants to talk about things. He tells me he does, but I'm skeptical now, so I watch and wait.

ROUGHING IT

ONCE PAM IS DISCHARGED AND settled back at home, Josh and I hit the road again. Well, not even road, really, more like we hit the trail. We backpack in the Sierra Nevadas for a piece on the John Muir Trail. I've never done hard-core backpacking, and I'm not a fan, even though the scenery is beautiful and I'm sure my photos will be stunning. When I can't help it, I offhandedly complain to Josh, but he's so happily in his element that he doesn't register the degree of my dissatisfaction. To be fair, I try pretty hard to fake enjoyment myself because I don't want to ruin his bliss. As much as this lifestyle doesn't feel like me, it is unquestionably Josh.

We continue doing backcountry stories, lots of camping and rustic cabins. Josh has always been in charge of negotiating with our editor, accepting or declining assignments and pitching ideas for stories we want to pursue. We talk about those choices together most of the time, but I rarely talk to anyone at *Outdoor Adventures*, and Josh typically convinces me to do exactly what he wants, so it's not really a collaboration. I tell myself it doesn't bother me, that he cares more about his career than I do about mine, so it makes sense for him to decide. When I miss my friends or a shower or a night out on the town, I remind myself that none of that matters as much as Josh and me being together. I feel a part of myself slipping away, but then I look at Josh and believe that I'm gaining more than I'm losing.

We do a story about an impressive group of women who call themselves Snow Shoe Goddesses, hiking the Catskill Mountains in the dead of winter. We do a piece about whitewater rafting in the Smoky Mountains and kayaking in Chesapeake Bay. We're in Alaska's Kenai Peninsula, Josh writing about grizzlies and the salmon migration while I take action shots of bears catching and eating fish as they leap out of the water and into their paws.

I hit my wall when we go to Yellowstone National Park in mid-October of 1995. We've set up our tent in the Slough Creek campground on the outskirts of this already isolated park, in search of wolves. Josh is in heaven, and as usual, I try to see it all through his eyes and share in his joy and excitement, but two things make that especially difficult.

First, it's frigid. Josh invested in the best quality cold weather gear, but there is simply no way to stay warm when I'm sitting in a blind in forty degree weather waiting for a wolf to appear. No way to stay warm at night when the temperature drops to twenty-five degrees or lower.

The other thing that makes it hard for me to maintain my game face is that we are camping in the midst of bear country. We string our food up out of reach and take all kinds of precautions to prevent bears from ripping our tent apart to get to our toothpaste or a granola bar we forgot in a bag somewhere. Needless to say, this causes me some anxiety, which grows every time we see a bear.

Our assignment is to write about the reintroduction of grey wolves to the Lamar Valley. Wolf populations had been decimated in the area since the early 1900s, and were all but extinct in Yellowstone by the end of the 1920s. After years of environmental campaigning, wolves had finally been reintroduced to the park this year. We are camping out here in the middle of nowhere because it is our best chance to see a wolf or two.

Josh spends some days sitting with me, waiting for wolves in one of several blinds created for this purpose, but he's mostly out and about, trying to interview people involved in the effort to reestablish the animals in this ecosystem, although he's continually frustrated because people don't show up when they've arranged and he's having trouble tracking them down in this immense park. I spend most days alone, and it is mind-numbingly boring almost all the time.

After ten days, I've spotted one solitary wolf a handful of times, always too far away for a good shot, even with my telephoto lens. Josh's narrative isn't taking shape either, so we're both irritable. I've practically begged him to throw in the towel on this story, leave now before I go insane, but he's not ready to quit. On top of that, our sex life is mostly nonexistent. We've zipped our sleeping bags together to share body warmth, and under normal circumstances we'd be having sex every day. But in addition to being pissed off about being here, spending every day alone, then listening to Josh complain about his hard days, I'm also too cold to take off my clothes. Add to that the fact that the closest showers are at least an hour away and I feel gross. Josh jokes that we could bathe in the creek, but I don't find him funny. The first few frosty nights I took care of his desire in ways that allowed me to keep my clothes on, and he returned the favor. But I have no interest in making him feel good now. He still comes on to me often, but I deny him. Last night, he tried to put my hand down his pants, and I pulled away from him in disgust and barely slept because the temperature dropped into the teens and I kept thinking I heard a bear.

In the morning I'm sour and crabby, and the dusting of snow on the ground does not improve my mood. I demand that Josh take me for a hot shower. He asks if I'll give it up for him once we're both clean, and I give him a look that suggests he'll be lucky if that ever happens again. We drive the seventy minutes to the showers in silence, and I take my time letting the heat and steam melt away a little of my bad temper. Josh looks and smells good when I finally join him back in the car, and part of me wants to kiss and make up, but he immediately puts the car in gear and drives aggressively back to the campsite. I gather my supplies, and he drops me at one of the nearby blinds to watch for wolves all alone in the snow while he drives off in a warm, toasty car to chase down some elusive interviewee.

From time to time, another researcher or park staffer joins me in a blind, and we sit together in silence, waiting and waiting. Today is one of those days. I hope my rage isn't obvious, that it isn't seeping out of my skin and spreading over to the perfectly nice-looking park ranger bundled up next to me, minding his own business, waiting for a wolf to appear. He's scanning the horizon with binoculars, and I'm looking through my zoom lens, and we spot the wolf at the same moment, immediately turning to each other to confirm the sighting.

I start snapping pictures when the wolf is about a hundred yards away, the closest one has come thus far. But this wolf keeps heading straight for us, coming closer and closer as I continue clicking my shutter. She stops for a moment as if she's posing for me, and I take full advantage of her cooperation. I quickly change rolls of film, surprised my fingers work in the cold, and she waits for me. She moves even closer, only about ten or twenty yards away, and I start to get scared. I'm thankful I'm not alone or I would be completely terrified. As it is, I'm thrilled because of how long I've had to wait and because I know these are going to be amazing pictures. I switch to my second camera because the telephoto lens is unnecessary at this distance.

When the wolf finally moves along, I take a deep breath and fall backward against the frame of the blind.

"Wow!" says the ranger, looking at me with a huge grin on his face.

"Wow is right," I say, smiling broadly in return.

We start chattering in a torrent, not caring about being quiet since we couldn't possibly get a better sighting than that one. His name is Ryan, and we talk about wolves and the park and how we got here and who we are. I can't remember the last time I've talked with anyone except Josh, and I realize how lonely I've been, especially because I've been annoyed with Josh for most of the trip, all of which I share with my new best friend. Ryan tells me about his fiancée, who works at the Old Faithful Inn, and their ten-month-old baby boy. We're sitting in Ryan's truck laughing and sharing coffee from his thermos when Josh pulls up next to us.

Josh honks, which sounds bizarre and aggressive in this barren landscape. I say a fond farewell to Ryan and get in the car, looking forward to telling Josh about the wolf. But before I can do that, Josh is grilling me—noticing my flush of warmth and excitement when I got out of Ryan's truck and misinterpreting it, asking how long we were there together, derisively observing my change of mood since this morning and attributing it to the attention from my new friend.

"Don't you dare say one more word, Josh Tyler," I hiss. "You don't know what you're talking about."

We are both quietly seething for the short ride back to the campground. I can't get out of the car fast enough, slamming the door behind me. But of course there's nowhere to go, no way to avoid this fight.

"That was ridiculous," I start, my voice cold and steady. "He was just a nice guy being nice to me."

"Unlike me, is that it?" Josh says.

"You said it, not me," I reply, suddenly sick of always trying to make him feel better.

"I'm sorry, okay? It's been a shit week, a disaster of an assignment."

"Is that supposed to be an apology? Because it sucks." I surprise both of us with this response, and Josh doesn't seem to know what to say.

"Are you even upset about how you've been making me feel, or are you just upset about your story not coming together the way you want?"

He looks away when I ask the question, which gives me my answer.

"I can't believe you," I say. "I can't believe how selfish you are! And what a pushover I am!" I'm pacing between the car and our tent. "Goddamm it, I'm sick of being a lovestruck kid following you around, trying to please you all the time."

"Yeah, I'm sick of that too." Josh sounds mad. How in the hell does he have a right to be mad?

"What are you talking about?" I stop my pacing and stare at him.

"Where did your voice go? Where's your fighting spirit? You've always been a fighter, but you won't fight with me."

"Well, I'm fighting now!"

"Thank God! Finally! Do you know what it's like to listen to your 'Yes, Josh. Okay, Josh,' bullshit all the time?" Now Josh is pacing.

"Oh, yeah, you seem to hate getting exactly what you want all the time. That must be awful for you."

"What I want is a partner. I want you to trust me."

"I do trust you."

"Bullshit! You don't trust me enough to challenge me on

anything! Jesus, Kai! I thought you were going to keep my fucking ego in check."

I don't know what to say because I've never thought about it that way.

"I'm scared," I say.

"I know that," he says, softening, "but I am right here, loving you every day. You don't have to be afraid."

I fold myself into his arms. I know there is more to say, but this feels like all I can do right now.

"I am sorry for being a dick. You deserve better, and I will do better."

"You don't have to be jealous, J. You are the only man I want."

Later, after we make love and are lying together in our tent, I finally tell him about the wolf, and he is almost as excited to hear about it as I was to experience it.

For the next few days, Josh sticks with me in the same blind where I saw the wolf. We take turns keeping watch so one of us can read or nap, and we are both less lonely and bored. I am eternally grateful that finally, on the morning of our fourth day staked out together, my wolf reappears. When I develop the pictures later, I realize this is a different wolf, but at the time, I assume she's my pal coming back to meet Josh. I also have no idea if she's a she, but I'll never know that. She doesn't come quite as close this time, but it's close enough for great photos, and close enough for Josh to be ecstatic. We celebrate by having sex in the car, the heat blasting, both of us stripped naked, me straddling Josh in the back seat.

For another few days, I drive around with him to ferret out the people he's been trying to talk with, but most of them are busy with their work, unreachable or unwilling to be reached, disinterested in interviews that take their time away from the wolves. For the first time, Josh is pessimistic about his story, and I suggest that maybe this time my photos will be the star and his words can take the supporting role. He accepts that, although I can tell he doesn't like it.

REALITY CHECK

A FEW WEEKS LATER, I am ecstatic to be well-groomed again, to be sipping cocktails and lounging in a poolside cabana in Las Vegas with my girls. Danielle splurged on a suite at Caesar's Palace for Jaimie's over-the-top bachelorette party. Jaimie's sister and a few other friends are arriving tonight, but for now, the three of us are relishing being musketeers again.

I've been telling them about my life for the past few months—the travel, the work, Josh—trying to upsell the adventure and excitement and hide the fact that I hate it sometimes. However, they know me too well for that.

"What do you make of this power Josh has over our friend here, Jaims?" Dani asks when I stop to take a sip of my drink.

"Hello," I say. "I'm right here."

"Yes, but you have no insight on the matter," Dani says. "Jaimie, you're the psych major. What do you think?"

"I was a psych major too," I point out, my third piña colada making me less annoyed than I would normally be with this turn in the conversation.

"Nobody's talking to you, Kai," Dani teases. "We're talking about you, which is a totally different thing. Jaimie?"

Jaimie looks at me and shrugs. What can she possibly do to

stop Danielle on a tear? "Kai's life fell apart out of nowhere. She needs something constant, something she can put all her faith in, and she's chosen Josh to be that thing."

That quiets us down for minute.

"Damn, Jaims, that was serious," Dani says.

"You asked," Jaimie says.

"*I* didn't ask," I say, irritated despite the rum. "Can't it be that I love Josh and always have and we are meant to be together?"

"Yes, or it could be that," Jaimie agrees, smiling and putting her arm around me.

"But is it?" Dani asks. We stare each other down for a bit, and then she adds, "This right here is you—pools and parties and makeup and high heels—not sleeping on the ground and peeing in the woods. Is that really what you want? All I'm saying is maybe think about what you're willing to sacrifice for him."

"Everything," I say immediately. "I don't need to think about it. I am willing to sacrifice everything for him."

Dani and I look at each other for a while. I can tell she's thinking about whether to say something else. "Okay then. That's settled. Who's up for a dip in the pool?"

I'm annoyed with her for the rest of the afternoon, but she makes it up to me later that night. We go see the Thunder from Down Under, and she tips heavily to have the most gorgeous Australian man in the show give me a lap dance. She tries to get Jaimie to participate, but she's too strait-laced and declines. Later, we go to a karaoke bar and Dani makes me sing with her—Rick Springfield's "I've Done Everything for You"—to make fun of me, which is her roundabout way of apologizing while simultaneously suggesting she's still right. Classic Danielle move. Later, the three of us sing our theme song, "Ob-La-Di, Ob-La-Da," another classic.

I fly with them from Vegas to San Diego a few days before the wedding to enjoy the beach and fulfill my bridesmaid duties. Dani and I check into the suite Josh and I are sharing with her and her man of the hour, both of whom are due to arrive tomorrow. Except when I call Josh that night, he tells me he's not coming. Another writer broke his leg, and the magazine needs him as a last-minute sub for a cover story about scuba diving on the Great Barrier Reef. I'm as sure they could have found someone else as I am sure that Josh is dying to go. He halfheartedly apologizes for missing the wedding, and I tell him it's fine even though I'm crushed. I'm angry and sad that he doesn't care about being with me at this wedding, these friends of ours that we practically lived with for a year. Doesn't care about leaving me unpartnered in a hotel room with Dani and her guy. Mostly heartsick that he knows this hurts me but does it anyway. But I don't say any of that.

Dani and I are in the hotel bar that night, and she does not let it go so easily.

"Can we please not do this?" I ask when she orders two shots of tequila and two margaritas.

"No," she says. "No, we can't not do this. You need me right now, so start talking."

We take shots, and I start by telling her all the things I want to be true, that Josh loves his job and that he's doing this for both of our careers, to show that we're team players and ready for anything. I say we reached this decision together because we're partners who make compromises for each other. But Dani calls it bullshit because it is. She counters with the truth I don't want to be true, that I do everything Josh wants and that it's his turn to do something for me. She reminds me of all the bold and outrageous things I did while we were at Long Beach.

"You're strong and fearless, Kai, and Josh loves that badass as much as I do."

I tell her I'm not so sure about that. I tell her about our recent fight, and about my reflections on his family, how part of me thinks Josh really wants someone more passive and self-sacrificing, like his mom.

"But that's not you, Kai," she says, and it's like an arrow to my heart. "If that's what he wants, maybe you're not the one for him."

"No!" I almost wail. "I am! I have to be!"

"Kai…" Danielle puts her hand on mine.

"He's the one thing I'm sure of." I don't want to cry, but it's hard, because I'm thinking about other things I used to be sure of.

"He's a part of me, Dani. I already lost a part of me. Josh makes me feel whole again, and I can't lose that. I can't be broken again." And then the tears come as I'm back with Kade, wallowing in the loss and fear that's always simmering right there below the surface.

When I calm down, we do another round of shots.

When the things you're sure of slip away, one by one, some people give up altogether. I know. I've seen that. But some people, like me, hold on even tighter to the certainties that are left, pouring more and more faith into fewer and fewer vessels.

"Josh is everything to me, Dani," I say softly. "I need him."

"You don't," she says gently. "I'm not going to argue with you about it because I understand why you think you do, but you don't."

I tell her that she thinks I'm stronger than I actually am. Everyone has their limits, and I know mine. Which is why Josh going to Australia is so devastating. It has once again confirmed my deepest fear, that he would go right on with his life, with or without me.

Dani disagrees with me again, this time taking Josh's side.

"I've seen the way he looks at you," she says, "the way he

touches your face. He loves you. You matter to him. He wants you in his life." This calms my anxiety a little, because most of me does believe it.

She puts her hand on mine. "You know I'm always on your side, right?" I nod and she continues. "That includes with Josh. I like Josh. He's cool. I just really, really like your spirited self, and I don't want to see her slip away."

HEADING SOUTH

WE'RE HOME FOR CHRISTMAS, SO we get to attend the *Outdoor Adventures* holiday party for the first time. It's held at the Lambs Club on West 44th Street in Manhattan, in the midst of the hustle and bustle of Times Square and Broadway. It's ironic that this party for a magazine about the great outdoors is in the heart of the cement jungle of NYC, in an elegant venue with wood paneling, brass fittings, and leather banquettes. The party and location are all me, even if the magazine isn't.

I meet our editor face to face for only the second time ever, as most of our contact is via phone or email or through Josh. When we join him and the group he's chatting with, Josh knows them all already, and I immediately feel off balance, realizing I should know them too. Josh introduces me, and they are all "Nice to finally meet you" and "The phantom Kai—we thought Josh made you up" and "Heard so much about you." Everyone is very nice and genuinely seems glad to meet me, but I get more annoyed with each response in this vein. When Josh and I find a moment alone, I ask him how he knows everyone, and he reminds me of the times he's made appearances in the office when we've been staying at Mom's and I've been busy with something else. I wonder why I didn't come with him to those meetings, unable to remember if he asked or if we both just assumed he'd go without me, and what that means about the power dynamic between us. But before I can get too far on that train of thought, the managing editor clinks his glass to get everyone's attention for a toast.

He starts with the typical holiday wishes and recaps the magazine's highlights from the year. I'm shocked when he concludes by praising my wolf pictures, featured in the December issue, and everyone claps for me. For me! Including Josh, who looks proud and happy. The managing editor closes his speech by welcoming Josh and me to the *Outdoor Adventures* staff, meaning we are no longer freelance contract workers and are official employees of the magazine, which wins us another round of applause.

Things loosen up as the night goes on and the alcohol intake hits its stride. Josh and I mingle both together and apart, which is nice because I'm getting to know new people, making new friends, and Josh is catching up with Teddy's dad and other people he's met and worked with over the years. I hear them talking about places they've been and want to go, and I can tell that Josh is jealous of the overseas travel, particularly the guys who've been to the Alps, where he's longing to hike. Later, I overhear some guys roasting Josh about his Yellowstone story being a fluff piece and my pictures saving it for him. He catches my eye and looks away, and I can see that he's humiliated and mad, and the rest of my night is ruined because now I'm worried about him.

We almost get through the evening without a big scene, but not quite. Luckily, it's after we're back at Danielle's, where we're spending the night, so she's the only witness to the ugliness. Josh and I both drank a lot at the party, although I stopped drinking once I realized he was upset, so he's more drunk than I am, needing me to guide him on the subway and back to the apartment, arms around each other in what looks like a romantic gesture but is really for physical steadiness and support.

I drop my guard when we finally lie down on the pull-out couch. I'm confident that we've made it through the evening unscathed, even more so when Josh rolls over to start kissing me and peeling off my pajamas. I'd rather he leave the top on and stay under the covers so we can be a little more on the down-low here in Dani's living room, but I let him strip me naked because he's had a hard night and because I do love his hands on my bare skin. He throws the sheets and blanket off the bed to keep me from covering up and goes down on me, clearly wanting to be in control, to make me cry out like I usually do when he engages in this particular endeavor. I moan and groan but try to stay relatively quiet so as not to disturb Danielle. There's a thrill in knowing she could walk out and see us at any second, and I'm sure Josh feels that added excitement too. I put a pillow over my face to moan into it, but he tosses it aside. It starts to feel like a contest, him trying to make me scream and me trying not to. He flips me over and enters me from behind, which almost always makes me wild but tonight feels more about power than love. Josh pounds into me, and I pretty much stop participating. I didn't know you could have passive-aggressive sex, but that's what this is. I can't figure out if he doesn't notice that I'm checked out or if he simply doesn't care. He collapses on top of me after he comes, pressing me into the bed and making me feel trapped under his body. In a moment of adrenaline, I push him off, get up, and wrap the sheet around me.

"What the fuck was that?" I yell in a whisper, still not wanting to wake our host.

"C'mon, Kai, you like it rough sometimes," he slurs.

"I do, when we're on the same page. Not when you're trying to prove something."

"Oh, really?" He stands up, seeming perfectly sober all of a sudden, even though I know he's not. "And what exactly am I trying to prove?"

It's a good play on his part, a strong bet that I won't bring up the party or his humiliation, since my function in life seems to have become making things smooth and rosy for him. I stand there pulling the sheet tighter around me, debating whether that's who I want to be.

"One night," I say softly, and then anger wells up and I get a little louder. "One night being about me, and you couldn't take it." Louder and louder. "You couldn't take me getting praise and attention for ONE STUPID NIGHT!"

"I looked like a fool!" Josh screams.

"How? How exactly did you look like a fool?"

"If you hadn't taken those pictures, they would never have published any of it. Nobody would have seen that stupid bullshit I wrote."

"Jesus, Josh! You took selfish to a whole new level right there! Not only are you mad that everyone loved my photos, you're mad that I took them at all! Not one bit of happiness for me! Not one bit of pride in my work! I'm proud of you every time I read your stories, even when you go off and write them without me. You can't stop thinking about yourself long enough to think about me for one goddamn minute!"

Not surprisingly, we've woken Danielle, who comes out of her room, looks Josh's naked body up and down, then looks at me with a question in her eye. I tell her everything's fine and I'm sorry we woke her.

"Don't be a dick, Josh," she says as she goes back to her room and shuts the door.

"I don't want to stay here," Josh says, pulling on his boxers. "Let's go."

"I can't drive right now," I say, sitting down on the bed with a sigh, noticing that he doesn't say, 'Let's go home,' even though we've been staying with my mom between assignments for over a year. "I need sleep, then we'll go." I pick up my pajamas and head for the bathroom to put myself back together. When I return, the lights are out and Josh is either asleep or pretending to be. I lie as far away from him as I can on the edge of the bed but end up waking in his arms in the middle of the mattress, as if my body was drawn to him without my conscious will. From the pull-out, I see Danielle sipping her coffee at the kitchen counter. Our eyes meet, and I know she's wondering what the hell I'm doing. I'm wondering the same thing.

On the drive back to Mom's, not only does Josh apologize, but he starts a conversation about what kinds of assignments I'd like to explore in the new year. This leads to a whole discussion about what we've liked and not liked about our work so far. We sit in front of the fireplace at Mom's house late into the next few nights and have honest, open conversations about what we want the year to look like. We go into the city together to propose the story we've come up with, a tour of Patagonia, including hiking at Torres del Paine National Park—which Josh has done, but it's one of his favorite hikes ever and he wants to share it with me— and whale watching near Puerto Madryn, Argentina, right on the other side of Cape Horn. Our editor loves the pitch, and we start making plans to leave by the end of February.

We resume reading aloud to each other, first from travel books about Patagonia, then rounding back to fiction in front of the fire and in bed at night. We boldly tackle James Michener sagas, starting with *Hawaii*, since that's where our story officially began. We enjoy a slow, quiet couple of weeks preparing for our trip, and I participate more with the research Josh always does for his articles, learning all about the history and people and flora and fauna of the southernmost tip of South America.

We are gentle with each other, especially Josh with me. We've gotten into the habit of sex in the morning, after Mom's left for work and we have the house to ourselves. For a few weeks after our fight, Josh is sweet and tender in his lovemaking, kissing and caressing me, moving slowly in and out, which is nice, but there comes a point where enough is enough. After we finish one day, as I'm tracing his chest with my finger, both of us still enjoying our postcoital glow, I tell him that as nice as it is, he doesn't always have to be such a perfect gentleman when we have sex. He laughs, which is a relief, repeating the phrase "a perfect gentleman."

"I'm trying to be respectful, ma'am," he says, smiling, then serious. "I was a disrespectful asshole at Danielle's, and I appreciate you having sex with me at all, honestly."

"Babe, me wanting to have sex with you is never going to be a problem. And yes, you were an asshole that night." That makes him smile again, even before I say, "I like it nice and pretty, but I also like to be fucked now and then."

He looks at the ceiling and puts his free arm over his eyes.

"Oh no, not that position," I say. "What's going on?"

"I'm not sure I trust myself to fuck you," he says, not moving his arm.

"Josh, you were all kinds of pissed off that night. You know that was different."

"I don't though," he says, which is a surprise, because it was so obvious to me. He's watching my face now but misreads my expression. "See, you think I'm an asshole again because I don't see it. I am, I know." And his hand goes back over his eyes, which is as much about shame as it is about thinking.

I move his arm away to make him look at me. "Listen to me, J, that night was all about power. You were mad that I was on top at that party, so you wanted to take back control in bed. That's the part that wasn't okay. The being mad and the wanting to control me."

"Okay, I get the mad part. But when we really go at it, that doesn't feel any different to me than it did that night. Part of what gets me going sometimes is the power, the dominating you. That's bad, right?"

Now I lie back and look at the ceiling. He takes my arm and puts it over my eyes. "That's how it's done," he says, then holds my other hand and lies in silence waiting for my response. I think about how what he said should sound disturbing but it doesn't. I realize that I like him to dominate me sometimes. Okay, complete honesty, I like him to have the power a lot of the time, but I try to stick to sex for right now rather than evaluating our entire relationship and having some psychological, existential crisis over my ambivalence about controlling my own life.

I roll over to look at him. "I like that too," I say simply. "I don't know if it's bad or not, but I like when you dominate me in bed." We share a moment where we both seem to debate talking about his domination of our lives in general, but we let it slide.

"So how do we make sure it feels good for you? How do I know?" he asks. "Why haven't we ever talked about this before?"

"Up until that night, I've never felt your aggression as anything but completely hot and sexy," I say, and I mean it. "And let me repeat that I like the sweet and tender thing too."

"Yeah, I got that you liked it." He's back to smiling at me, since I was pretty emphatic when I came a few minutes ago. The slow and steady rhythm of him sliding in and out of me builds tension in its own way, the wanting him to go faster but him holding back and working it until the very last second when the agitation feels almost unbearable, and then it crests and crashes over me.

"You're getting hot thinking about it," he says. "I see your cheeks flushing."

"Maybe," I say. "Whatcha gonna do about it?"

"That depends," he says. "You need to promise me that you'll tell me if you don't like what I'm doing, if it crosses the line into not okay."

"I will."

"Sometimes you don't," he points out, and I know he's not only talking about sex.

"I promise I'll tell you if what we're doing sexually isn't okay." I choose to be very specific so that we both believe me.

"Well, get ready then," he says, rolling me onto my stomach and putting my hands over my head. "Stay like that," he says with the control I'm looking for. He sucks on my ass, and I feel him giving me a hickey. It hurts in exactly the way I like, the way that gives me chills and makes me shudder in pleasure. He pauses to look at the mark and then bites me in exactly that spot, which sends that thrill of sensual pain through me again. That's all the foreplay he offers, and it's all I need. He pushes my knees up under me and pulls me onto all fours, his arm wrapped around my waist. He kneels behind me, with one leg under him and the other planted along the side of my body, giving him more leverage to push into me, hard and fast, sending us both into a convulsing climax within a few thrusts.

And just like that, we're back on track. We have an amazing trip, and Josh writes one of the best stories he's ever done. We see whales and penguins, which are amazing. I welcome the five-day backpacking trek around the Circuit at Torres del Paine National Park, because Josh brought me here specifically to show me one of his favorite places on earth. The wind on the hike is incredibly strong, and whenever we round a corner and a blast almost blows me over, I lean back into Josh and he puts his arms around me as if he's holding me up. We continue reading to each other every night, finishing Michener's *Hawaii* and starting *Alaska*, another of our places. We've decided to continue reading about the places we've been and the places we want to go, and it feels like the first time we've had any kind of plan for our future. I try really hard not to think too much about how pitiful that sounds.

SPEAKING UP

I **PRACTICE USING MY REDISCOVERED** voice when our editor tells us the magazine is planning an issue dedicated to African adventures. Josh of course wants to go for the full-scale safari, weeks in the savannah. I suggest we do a story on the Seychelles, a unique and less-known destination off the east coast of the continent. We go back and forth on this one, but I don't back down, and we end up having a great time and writing an amazing piece on the islands. It doesn't make the cover, but it is a featured piece in that issue. We extend our stay to enjoy the topless beaches and romantic beauty after the work is done.

We get a lot of international assignments now, which we both love. We backpack or stay in a yurt or a hut or some other plumbing-free dwelling in the middle of nowhere, and then we go to a city or town in the area to spend a few days at the end of our assignment, financing our own stay at a hotel or chalet or lodge with beds and towels. The magazine is called *Outdoor Adventures*, after all, so our work is more in line with Josh's preferences, but I fight for spending time in places I want to see along the way. My anxiety subsides a little more each time Josh accommodates me. I see that he does care, I do matter, he wants to be with me and make me happy, and that calms me.

But then something happens that starts the cycle all over again. I want to go home to Mom or visit Danielle, and Josh wants to take some story in the Amazon, so we part ways, and I freak out picturing him living a wonderful life without me. Then he's back, and I can't even put my finger on what starts it sometimes, yet there I'll be, hearing myself saying yes to things I don't want to do, saying it's fine when it isn't. Sometimes I catch myself and adjust course. Sometimes we end up fighting about it and that resets things.

Bobby's wedding brings on the worst fight thus far. We are both pretty drunk, so that doesn't help.

"Man, an open bar is a dangerous thing. I'm not sure they thought that through with this crowd. How much do you think that bill is going to be?" I ask as I flop onto our hotel bed, pretty toasted.

"Well, your dad gave up drinking again, so the bill won't be as bad as it could have been," Josh says as he pulls off his jacket and tie.

"True. Will you take off my shoes? I can't move."

"I'll bet. You didn't stop dancing all night. Did you have fun?"

"I did, other than people asking me every other second when we're getting married."

"Right? What's up with that?"

"Yeah, crazy to think that two people who love each other and have been together for years might actually be planning to get married someday." I'm not mad until I say it, and then I'm furious. I sit up and look at Josh. "Are we ever going to get married?" I'm drunker than I thought.

"Now is not the time to have this conversation." He turns away from me, unbuttoning his shirt.

"When would be a better time, Josh?"

"How about when we're not both wasted?"

"Well, then we'll never have the conversation because you know I'd never ask you when I'm sober. That's what you mean, though, right? Let's not ever talk about it?"

"What's there to talk about? You know how I feel. It's not my thing."

His cavalier attitude further enrages me.

"So it doesn't matter what I want? You'll never marry me and I simply have to accept that?"

"Apparently not." He throws his shirt on the floor. "Listen, I told you right from the beginning that I didn't want to get married."

He walks toward the bathroom, as if the conversation is over. I stand up and block his way to let him know it's far from over.

"Four years ago! You told me that four years ago! Am I expected to know that nothing will ever change? Stupid me! I thought maybe you actually loved me and might want to spend your life with me."

"I do want to spend my life with you." His calm voice is driving me crazy, as if he can't even be bothered with this ridiculous conversation I've started. As if we're talking about nothing.

"You are so full of it, Josh."

"Listen, I am doing my best to keep my cool here, but you need to relax."

"Just relax and go along with your plan for our lives. Like always."

"Goddammit, I hate when you do that." At least I'm getting a reaction from him now. "It's your life. Do what you want. I'm not making you do anything."

"I want to marry you, but I can't do *that*, can I? And your answer is that I can just leave if I don't like it. You don't even care if I stay or leave!"

"Fuck, Kai! You are making up a big drunk story here that has nothing to do with reality."

"Okay, so tell me. Why can't we get married?"

"You tell me why you want to get married. Because we're supposed to? Because it will guarantee happily ever after? You know that's not true! Our parents were miserable! You think if we're married, I'll never leave? You know that's not true either. You lived that one. Our parents did all that. They were married and look what happened."

"Am I supposed to wait around knowing there's no future for us?"

"I didn't say there's no future. I said I don't want to get married."

I feel ugly, hot tears coming on and struggle to hold them back.

"What about kids? No kids?"

"God, can we please not do this right now?"

"So that's a no then."

"No, I don't want kids."

"And that's never going to change?"

"It doesn't feel like something that's going to change."

I feel like he punched me in the gut. Part of me wants to keep fighting because I am so hurt and angry, but part of me feels defeated and wants to find something to hold on to. That meek part of me that's willing to settle for any scrap from him is back in charge.

"Okay, forget marriage, forget kids. Can you please just tell me it's forever?"

"I don't know what forever is. I don't live in forever. I live right now."

Fuck meek! The fighter part of me comes roaring back to life.

"Your *now* is such bullshit, Josh!" I scream.

"Marriage is the bullshit!" Josh is yelling now too. "I don't bullshit you. That's what I'm saying. I'm not going to make you promises that are bullshit, that I have no idea if I can keep. You know me. You know that's not what I do."

"I do know you. I've known you forever. I know that you are a selfish mama's boy who only thinks about himself and what he wants. What about what I want? Can't I have what I want for a change?"

"If what you want is forever, then no. I can't give you forever. I can only give you today."

"See, that's such bullshit! Your no bullshit is such bullshit. You just can't commit because you're scared to turn into your dad."

That takes us from hot to ice cold.

"I can't believe you'd throw that in my face."

"I'm just making sure there's no bullshit. Isn't that what you want?"

"This right here is definitely not what I want. What I wanted was to come up here and go to sleep. You're the one who can't fucking shut up!"

"You want me to shut up?"

"God, yes!"

"You tell me we have no future, and you want me to shut up?"

"That is not what I fucking said! Goddammit, Kai, please stop talking."

"No. It's my life, right? I can do what I want, right? Well, I want to keep talking, so I'm gonna—"

Josh walks across the room and punches a hole in the wall, then a second one.

I turn and walk out and go sleep in Stephanie's room.

There's a post-wedding breakfast for the family the next morning, so I go back to our room to get ready. Josh looks a wreck when I come in, which makes me feel a little bit better. He's sitting on the one chair, staring into space.

"I'm so sorry, K," he says when I walk through the door, but he doesn't move or even look at me.

"Me too," I say. "I am truly sorry that I was so mean. I shouldn't have opened that box when I wasn't prepared to know what was in it. That wasn't fair."

"Please don't think that I don't care whether you stay or go," he says, and now he does look at me. "I hated that you left last night, although I think that was smart. I can't remember the last time I was that angry. I scare myself when I get that mad. Can you understand that?"

"I do, J. I really do. How's your hand?"

"Been better." He holds up his swollen, black-and-blue hand. He can't even open it all the way.

"Oh, babe, do you think it's broken?" I kneel in front of the chair and take his hand in mine, turning it gently this way and that.

"I hope not, but it might be smart to go get an X-ray after breakfast. It hurts like hell."

"I'm sorry. I was being a total bitch."

"That's no excuse. You know that, right?" I nod. "There's no excuse for me being violent. That's entirely on me."

"Okay, I know. So, separately, I'm sorry. You deserve an apology for how I acted too."

"That is true." He smiles at me then. "I don't want to start it all up again, but I need you to hear me say what I said last night. The part you skipped right over in your drunken rampage." He pauses for effect. "I want to spend my life with you. Do you hear that part?"

"Yes," I say with tears in my eyes.

"The thing is that it has to be one day at a time. And probably no kids. You need to think about whether that can work for you.

I want you to be honest with yourself and with me. If that's not enough to make you happy, then as much as I would hate it—really, truly hate it—you have to leave."

"I could never leave you, Josh." I don't even hesitate.

"I don't want you to be unhappy, to go your whole life wanting more than I can give."

"You make me happy," I say. "I mean, not all the time. And yes, there are sacrifices required, and I will miss having those things. But all I've ever wanted was you, and you are enough. You are more than enough. You are everything."

"You're everything to me too, Kai. Please believe that."

"I do," I say, and then I correct myself. "I'll try."

CODA

After the wedding, we're back at my mom's for a while. We cancel our next assignment because Josh broke several bones in his hand and can't write for a few weeks. We need a break anyway, and the downtime helps us heal right along with the hand. There is something liberating about having everything laid out for me. I'm not going to marry Josh, but we are going to be together. It eases my mind knowing that. He didn't say forever, but what he did say was a kind of commitment.

I talk with my mom about not having a family. I can tell she's sad about not having grandkids, but she supports me in letting that dream go, although I'm not sure either of us believes that I'm really letting it go. It's not that I think Josh will change his mind, but it is possible. I'm not giving up all hope.

Jaimie makes a trip to the East Coast for the first time ever to see the autumn leaves and to take advantage of Josh and me being grounded because of his hand. After spending a few days in the Adirondacks admiring the foliage, we meet up with Danielle at Mom's house. After a couple of nights here, we'll head to Danielle's to party in the city.

It's a cold rainy day, and we're all in the kitchen baking cookies, singing along to Frank Sinatra and the Beatles and some tunes from this decade. It feels like we're drunk, but we're not drinking. We're at ease and happy and completely in a zone together.

"Josh, how do you like being one of the girls?" Danielle asks.

"Works for me," he answers, with flour on his shirt and a dusting on his cheek.

"Nate wouldn't be so comfortable," Jaimie says. "It's one of our recurring fights, how he's not at ease with people. I want us to socialize more, but he doesn't like it."

"I always liked Nate," Josh says. "He's a good guy."

"He's a great guy, but he's quiet and shy, takes a long time to warm up," Jaimie says, and I know what she means.

"You're on the quieter side too, Jaims," I say.

"Compared to Danielle maybe," she says.

"Who isn't quieter than that one?" Josh says, and Danielle snaps a dishtowel at him.

"I know I'm quiet, and I don't need tons of friends, but I'd like to have more people in our life in San Diego, people besides my family. It doesn't bother me nine days out of ten, but on that tenth day…that's one of the things we'll probably always fight about."

"You won't always fight about it," I say. "You'll figure it out."

"As a therapist in training, I don't necessarily think that's true. I think most couples have certain things they fight about over and over and over again. They resolve it temporarily or avoid it for stretches of time, but there are pressure points that get them every time."

"That was definitely true for me and John," Mom says.

"Yeah, it was," I say. "I heard you have pretty much the same fight at least a hundred times."

"That's because you were always eavesdropping, young lady."

"Right?" Josh says. "Always sneaking around gathering intel."

"Hey, no ganging up on me," I whine.

"Speaking of ganging up on you," Danielle says, looking at Josh, "what's your recurring fight?"

"Like you don't already know," Josh says, holding her gaze.

"Danielle, I don't want to talk about this," I say halfheartedly, knowing there's no stopping her and kind of interested in what Josh will say.

"I didn't ask you," Danielle says to me, although she's still looking at Josh.

"Josh, you can ignore her," I say, intrigued by their locked eyes.

"Can I really?" he says, caught in their stare-down.

"No, you can't," she answers. "No one ever has."

"That is true, Josh," Jaimie says. "Sorry."

"So what is it, Josh?" Danielle prods.

"That Kai wants to settle down and I don't. That she gets so scared of losing me that she becomes a Josh-pleasing robot and I let her."

"Wow," Danielle says, finally looking away from him and at me. "That is spot-on." She looks back at him. "I'm impressed. Most guys are clueless. You really do know her."

"I do," Josh says, looking at me a little sadly. "It seems like an unsolvable problem."

"It's not unsolvable," I say. "We've solved it. We're not settling down and I'm okay with that. I am going to use my voice and stop worrying about losing you. I'm trusting you and we're fine."

Everyone looks at me, and I can tell no one believes me. Do I believe me?

"I'm serious," I say, hating the pleading note in my voice. "Josh just broke his hand over this, and we figured it out."

"If I wasn't your best friend in the whole wide world, Kai, I would go to Vegas and bet all my money on the fact that you will absolutely, positively have that fight again. But since I am your best friend, along with Jaims here, I will instead join you in your beautiful dreamland and pretend that it's all better now, that you don't care about getting married or having kids, that you love camping and hiking and looking like shit, that you will never again have a panic attack that you might lose Josh. Who's with me?"

"Settle down, Ms. Sarcasm," Jaimie says. "There are lots of recurring, unresolvable fights that aren't the end of the world. Most of them aren't. Some things are deal-breakers and some things are price of admission. I learned that in one of my therapy classes. Lots of annoying things happen over and over in a relationship, and those are the cost of doing business, what you pay to play the game of love. Nobody knows the deal-breakers except the two of you. Other people can't know that or decide it for you."

"That's so true," Mom says. "When John and I would have our same fight over and over, I think it was a price of admission for a long time. I loved so many things about him. He was fun, smart, handsome, and he was such a good father when you guys were little, playing with you all the time, hours on end. And the sex—well, never mind, I won't embarrass my daughter with that. I think I would have put up with the drinking and the avoidance of all things difficult if one of those things hadn't been Kade. That's what made it a deal-breaker for me."

I give her a hug. "I haven't heard you say it like that before, Mom. I haven't heard you say anything nice about Dad in a long time."

"Your dad has a lot of demons, but he also has a lot of goodness in him. I can't usually think of his better qualities because I'm still so mad at him."

"I think we probably will fight about this again," Josh says, obviously ruminating on it. "I just really, really hope it's never as bad as this last one, and I hope it's never a deal-breaker."

I move from Mom to give Josh a hug.

"See, look at all that good honest sharing," Danielle says.

"Aren't you all glad I brought it up? Lift that rug and sweep it all out."

I hug her next. "You are a pain, but I love you. I love you all." I give Jaimie a hug too.

"Okay, you know what time it is," Danielle says, and puts on "Ob-La-Di-Ob-La-Da" and we sing along. Life does go on.

BREATH OF HEAVEN

ONCE JOSH HEALS, WE FLY to Thailand. We are working on two stories while we're here, for two different issues of the magazine. The first is focused on sailing. There's a possibility we could nab another cover with this one, so we're highly motivated to make the piece great. The second story is about the dramatic rock climbing along the shore where we'll be sailing.

We board our sailboat and settle into the plush, if tiny, cabin. We like the captain, Lou, and his first mate and son, Chakan, right away. The magazine chose this American ex-pat to guide us and teach Josh enough about sailing to write the article. Lou started out like Josh, a wanderer and adventurer, then fell in love and settled here, which gives me a shot of hope for Josh. Chakan is twenty-five, born and raised in Phuket, so he gives us the young local perspective on things. Josh spends tons of time absorbing everything he can about sailing and the area, asking all kinds of questions, and helping with everything they'll let him do. I spend my days lying on the deck getting a killer tan, occasionally taking some pictures. I tell them I'm just trying to stay out of the way, and they laugh at me.

The water in the Andaman Sea is an unbelievable aquamarine. The shades of blue change as the sun advances across the sky and as we move closer and farther away from shore. At times I'm hypnotized just staring at the changing colors, and Josh teases that I'm lost in myself, since my name means "sea," which becomes a running joke with everyone on the boat.

Our first day brings us to Phang Nga Bay, which has dramatic cliffs and tall, narrow columns of stone rising out of the clear blue waters, the reflection of orange limestone on the calm surface making the scene even more splendid. Next is James Bond Island, famous for the movie *The Man with the Golden Gun*. Josh and I have fun rolling on the sandy white beach, and I give Chakan my camera to take movie-poster pictures of us.

We spend several days anchored off of Railay Beach, where rock climbing rules. The gorgeous stretch of white sand is sandwiched between impressive cliffs where climbers dangle off rock faces, invert around arches, and explore caves. Josh has a great time interviewing the climbers, and he and Chakan join them in their unnatural maneuvers. I take photos from the safety of the ground, trying not to picture my lover's body smashing against the rocks as he plummets to his death. There is no way to take a bad photo here, as the scenery is breathtaking and the climbers are fearless, putting themselves into unbelievable positions as if posing for a spread of crazy stunts no one should ever try, which they kind of are. Josh has fun, but I'm relieved when we raise anchor and sail on with him still in one piece.

Our next stop is the plethora of small islands surrounding Koh Lanta. I've never seen so many sandy white beaches, accessible only by boat. We go for days without seeing another person, and on one of those days, Lou and Chakan drop us on an island that I don't think even has a name, on a beach that's like something out of a dream, and leave us alone there overnight. They say we have to experience the indescribable feeling that comes from being safely stranded on a deserted island, but we all know we are primarily there so Josh and I can have sex on the beach. As soon as the boat is out of sight, we strip down and stay naked until we see the boat approaching the next morning.

Sex on a deserted beach with the man you love is magnificent, but it's amazing during this entire trip, for a multitude of reasons. First, plain and simple, how could it not be? We are in paradise. We are sexually excited almost all the time. I'm almost constantly in a bikini, and Josh never wears a shirt. We are both tan and glistening with oil and sweat all day, and then we get to shower every night and slip into bed clean and fresh. On top of that, Chakan and I innocently flirt a lot, which gets me hot too. Flirting always has. I'd never do anything about it, and Josh knows that. He likes Chakan, and he knows Chakan doesn't mean anything by it, but it gets him jealous enough to kiss me and touch me a lot to prove to everyone that I am his to kiss and touch. He also doesn't mind when I sometimes let a moan or squeal slip out when he's making love to me at night, evidence of who's doing what to whom. It feels like we're falling in love all over again, not that we ever weren't in love, but we are completely in sync on this trip. We have fun.

After our voyage, we spend a few days in Bangkok. I'd told Josh I wanted to see the city, and he agreed. I asked and he gave, a shift I'm allowing to sink in.

Josh gets the news from our editor that we'll be spending the next few months in Europe, doing a variety of stories for a few different issues. We're both excited, because for all our travels, neither of us has been to Europe. The culmination of our trip will be hiking the Tour du Mont Blanc, which Josh has been dying to do for years.

Josh is naming all the hikes and adventures and little hole-in-the-wall places his hiker friends have recommended across the Continent, while I'm listing all the cities we can't miss. It's nice that we're excited for each other's suggestions almost as much as for our own. I'm not bitter about the backpacking because I'm going to Paris when it's all over. He's not resenting the idea of Rome because he'll be sea kayaking in the Scottish highlands and river rafting on Italy's Noce River.

We chronicle adventures in Norway and Austria and sightsee in London and Venice before backpacking the Tour du Mont Blanc, generally agreed to be the most beautiful hike in Europe, and arguably the most beautiful in the world. I'm unusually eager for this trek because I know it will be beautiful and because I've been getting what I need along the way, so there's no built-up resentment. There's also the fact that we're going to Paris afterward, ending our European tour in the City of Lights.

We start our hike, as most people do, in the French town of Chamonix. The trail circles the Mont Blanc massif, over a hundred miles through France, Italy, and Switzerland. The hike generally takes eleven days, but we're stretching it to seventeen. We're staying at a variety of hostels and B&Bs along the trail, spending multiple nights at certain spots. We want to talk to as many other hikers and locals as we can, immerse ourselves in the community of people who are part of this journey.

The Mont Blanc massif is unbelievably extraordinary. As gorgeous as I expect my pictures to be, I also know they won't do it justice. The panorama, the scenery all around in every direction, will never come through in a photo. That's not to say I don't try. I take a gazillion pictures, since every curve on the trail reveals a new splendor. I also take lots of pictures of other hikers, people staring in wonder and amazement, laughing at the end of the day, contemplating the meaning of life. It is all happening for everyone every day on this trail.

And Josh and I are both in heaven again as we circle the massif. All is right with the world.

THE FALL

I CAN'T BELIEVE THIS IS happening! How can this be happening? I started getting nervous toward the end of our hike because I was late, but I told myself it was all the physical exertion, the altitude, the change of diet—anything but what it is. Now I'm at a clinic in Paris hearing that I'm pregnant. The nurse tells me to stop taking my birth control pills and start taking prenatal vitamins, but I barely hear her. It's like she's talking through a voice distortion machine or like I'm underwater. I already lied to Josh about what I'm doing today. How am I possibly going to tell him?

I'm supposed to meet him for lunch at a café near the apartment we're renting for the week. I stop across the street and watch him sitting at an outdoor table, scribbling something in his notebook. I don't want to join him. For once, I want to be as far away from him as possible, because when I go and sit down with him, I'll have to tell him, and everything will change.

I decide to wait until he looks up. Once he sees me, I'll go to him. Except he doesn't look up. He is lost in his work. I finally walk over to the table. He looks at me and smiles. "Hey, beautiful, I ordered wine." He pours a glass for me as I sit down.

I figure I might as well jump right into it. "I'm not drinking wine because I'm pregnant."

"What?" The smile disappears.

"I'm pregnant, J."

He stares at me with an unreadable look, then turns away. I wait several minutes for him to respond.

"You're not going to say anything?"

"What am I supposed to say?" He looks back at me, his face a blank slate. "How did this happen?"

"Umm…sex, I think." I know sarcasm isn't the best response, but I'm irritated by the dumb question. I try to control my anger by reminding myself that I've had some time to digest the news, while Josh is completely blindsided.

He's looking at me coldly, also clearly trying to control some strong feelings. "I thought you were on the pill," he says, and it feels like an accusation.

"I am on the pill. What's that supposed to mean?"

"Nothing. I'm just trying to figure things out."

"Are you trying to figure out whether I've been lying to you about taking the pill? Is that what you're trying to figure out?"

He doesn't say anything. He won't look at me.

"I can't believe you! How could you think that? How could you think I would do that to you, betray us like that?"

"I don't know what to think right now."

"Well, let me give you some time and space to ponder it all, Josh. It's not like I need you or anything. It's not like this impacts me in any way." I get up from the table and walk away. I can't believe he lets me, but he does. I knew it would go badly, but I wasn't expecting this.

I walk around the City of Love for hours, through the winding streets and alleys of the Left Bank, feeling utterly alone, watching enamored couples strolling hand in hand, sipping wine at cafés, soaking in the romance. Kids are sailing toy boats on the main pond in Luxembourg Garden, which would typically make me smile but today makes me cry.

I find myself heading back toward our flat, but since I'm not yet ready to face Josh, I sit on a quiet pew in Sainte-Chapelle, giving my tumbling thoughts and tired feet a rest, becoming lost in the play of light through the stunning stained-glass windows.

When the light starts to fade, I go back to our place, dreading part two of this conversation. Josh is sitting at our little table with a nearly empty bottle of wine.

"Is that helping you think?" I know this isn't the best way to start the conversation, but I am mad, hurt, scared, and completely let down by him, so I'm not at my best.

"Not really, but since my thoughts are pretty shitty right now, I'd rather not think." He's staring at his wine like a pouting child, not even looking up at me.

"You are unbelievable," I say. "Can you think about me for one second? Consider what I'm going through for just a beat of time?" I feel trapped in this room, filled with angry energy that has nowhere to go.

Josh finally looks at me, and I can't see any love in his eyes.

"What exactly are you going through, Kai? Isn't this exactly what you've wanted since you were six years old?"

"Did you really just say that?" I start pacing the length of the flat, but it's not big enough to contain my fury. "How dare you think this is anything close to what I've ever wanted?"

"But it is, isn't it? Having my baby? You've said it more than once."

"Yes, Josh, I want to have your baby. I want to marry you and have a family together. Is that such a crime? What is so fucking terrible about that?"

"It's not what I want!" he screams. "I don't want a family! I get that this surprised you, but for you it's a good surprise. For me, it sucks."

"You are so selfish, Josh. You think this doesn't suck for me? All I've ever wanted was to make you happy, and I know this makes you miserable."

"You don't care about making me happy. You care about keeping me. You want me happy so I'll stay with you, but that's not the same thing as wanting me to be happy."

"Fuck you, Josh! That is complete bullshit!"

"Oh, good answer, Kai. Strong argument."

"All I have ever done is love you. Always, always, always! And you don't appreciate me at all. I give and you take, and when you give to me it's exactly what you're willing to offer, never a sacrifice. I sacrifice for you all the time!"

"I never ask you to do that!" He's standing now, and we are face to face yelling at each other.

"Yeah, so you've said many times. You would be fine with or without me, either way. I can stay or go. Completely up to me. So romantic. Perfect for Paris."

"So terrible of me to remind you of your free will, to encourage your self-determination."

"Oh my god! FUCK YOU! You are not the better person because you want us both to be free. You are the chickenshit who's too scared to grow up and be a man!"

"I'm outta here!" Josh grabs his backpack and heads for the door.

"Did I hit a nerve there, Josh? Can't even respond to that because there's no way to deny it?"

He turns toward me with rage in his eyes, but he speaks softly and coldly. "I'm leaving because I want to beat the shit out of you right now, beat that baby out of your body. That's what I'm scared of. Always have been, always will be." And with that, he's out the door.

I don't know what to do. I can't even cry. I lie on the bed in a trance, trying to stop the world from spinning out of control. I think about calling my mom, but I can't tell her yet. I want to stay perfectly still, to pretend that once again my world hasn't changed in an instant, but as the realization sinks in that it has, I know I can't just lie here.

I walk down the street to the public phone and call Danielle. When she answers, I give her the facts, and we come up with a plan.

Josh is gone for four days. In that time, I develop my pictures from Mont Blanc and select the best ones for what I think Josh will be writing. I buy a plane ticket to JFK, and Danielle makes me an appointment at a clinic in New York. I write a letter of resignation to the magazine but wait to mail it.

I come back to the flat on my last day in Paris to find Josh there waiting for me. He's sitting at the table, but this time he gets up when I come in.

"You're back," I say, leaning against the door, needing its support.

"I am. I figured if I waited until I knew what to say, I'd never come back, so I'm here, even though I still don't know what to say."

"How about you're sorry?"

"I am sorry."

"You can't know how much you hurt me, Josh, how much you've let me down." I look away. I can't say what I need to say if I'm looking at him. "It's not even about the baby. It's about everything you said. I thought you knew me better than anyone, but you don't know me at all, and that just ruins me."

I'm crying, but not uncontrollably, just tears running down my cheeks, as it should be when your heart is shattering. Josh moves toward me, but I hold up my hand to stop him.

"I do know you, Kai. Don't say I don't know you." His voice

cracks. "I didn't really think you got pregnant on purpose. But I also know you want the baby."

"I do want the baby, and I want you. More than anything." I look at him then, because I have to, because I need him to know I mean it and I have to see his eyes when I say it. "But I'm giving up both." I don't look away because I will miss his face so much and I want to look at it for as long as I can.

"I'm leaving you, Josh. I love you, but I'm never going to get what I need from you, so I'm leaving. I'm going back to New York and having an abortion. I'm quitting the magazine and finding a new job. My heart is broken, but that's happened before, so I guess I'll recover."

"I love you, Kai. I really do." Tears stream down his cheeks, but strangely I've stopped crying.

"Not enough." It's probably the strongest, firmest thing I've ever said to Josh. "If you loved me enough, as much as I love you, you'd tell me to have our baby." I wait for a minute, to give him one more chance to say it, even though I know he won't. "As always, I love you more. I'm sacrificing and you're not, and I'm done with that now. I need you to go."

He stands there looking at me, crying. "You want me to leave?"

"No, Josh, I want to marry you and have our baby, but since you haven't offered that, I need you to leave." The tears are back, and I need him to go before I fall to the floor in a heap and he has to come pick me up. I couldn't bear it, couldn't let him go if he touched me right now.

"I am truly sorry," he says.

"I know you are." I move past him to look out the window as he packs his few remaining things. When I hear the door open, I speak up without turning around.

"Josh, just for the record, your dad wouldn't have left the other day. Your dad would have taken his anger out on me, and that's not what you did. That's what makes you irrevocably different from him."

"I love you and I will miss you more than you know," he says.

LOOSE ENDS AND FRESH STARTS

THE PLAN IS FOR DANIELLE to pick me up from the airport and take me to her apartment. She's made an appointment for the following day to end the pregnancy. But before I board my plane at Charles de Gaulle, I break down and call my mom, telling her everything. I'm not sure she gets the full story through all my sobbing and choking, but she understands the main points and thankfully doesn't push me on any details she missed.

Dani and Mom meet me at JFK together, and I fall into their arms like a marathon runner at the finish line, utterly spent and relying on them to hold me up, which they do. When we get to Dani's apartment, Mom warms up the lasagna she made earlier that morning. We settle in the living room after dinner with glasses of wine, me cuddled up with Dani on the couch, Mom in the fluffy armchair next to us.

"Kai, you know I support you completely, but can we talk about this decision?" Mom asks.

"It doesn't really feel like a decision, Mom. It feels like the only thing I can do."

"It is a decision, though. Probably the biggest one you've ever made."

I start crying, but not in an out-of-control way, in a really, really sad way.

"I'm sorry, sweetie, but you need to own this, to be sure of what you're doing here. As always, I want what's best for you, and you need to be sure that an abortion is what's best."

"What else is there, Mom? He doesn't want our baby. I don't want it without him. It would be a constant reminder that he's not here."

"Are you sure he won't change his mind? It's only been a few days. Maybe you both need to sit with it, process it a little."

"He's never wanted kids. That's not going to change. I thought it would, but here it is, right in front of him, and he doesn't want it. He doesn't even want me enough to want it for me."

"I get where you're coming from, Tammy," Dani says, "but Kai has always known her own mind. She follows her heart, and I think that's what she's got to do here too."

"Yeah, 'cause it's worked out great so far, huh?" I blubber. Mom moves over to the couch and rubs my back.

"It has in moments," Dani says. "You've had an amazing run. You've seen the world, loved the boy you loved your whole life, established a kick-ass career. It didn't last, and it sucks now, obviously, but that doesn't mean it wasn't great. It doesn't mean you were wrong."

"I was always so sure that I would be with Josh, that someday we'd get married and have a family, but I was wrong. And if I was wrong about that big, huge, fundamental thing, what do I know at all?"

"Well, I know you're strong and you can do anything," Dani says.

"I know that too," Mom agrees. "And you know it, Kai. You

might not feel it right now, but deep down you know it. You can have this baby and make it work, or you can have an abortion and move on with your life. Nothing has ever defeated you, and that is saying a lot."

I sit up straighter, anchored by these two pillars of strength on either side of me.

"All of this is breaking my heart," I say. "Looking at his baby would break my heart every single day, and that would defeat me, and I can't do it. I can't love our baby without him, and that's not fair to a baby."

"Okay then, that's your choice, and we're with you." Mom leans over and kisses me on the cheek.

Danielle whispers, "Ob-La-Di, Ob-La-Da."

I almost can't say it, but I do.

"Life goes on," I whisper back.

The next day is the worst of my life. Even worse than Kade because I had no control over that. I'm choosing this, ending the possibility of a little life, a little me-and-Josh. I am also saving my life. It really feels like that to me. Regardless of what Mom and Dani have said, I know I can't live through raising this baby without Josh, or at least I can't live through it well, giving our child the love and attention it would need and deserve. To save myself, I let my baby go.

November 6, 1998
Dear Kade,
Please take care of my baby.
I love you

PART 3

FAITH

FORWARD MOTION

DANIELLE AND I ARE TAKING our usual Sunday run through Central Park, on mile three of our six mile goal. It's a beautiful spring day in New York, not quite warm but without the bitter chill of winter. We've already circled the lake and are now running through trees on less traveled paths, as if we're in the woods somewhere rather than in the middle of one of the busiest cities in the world. I'm comforted by the rich smell of dirt, buried in snow for the past months, now sucking up the sunshine and warmth, preparing for the new growth about to bloom.

As I run beside this amazing woman who has been letting me sleep on a futon in her dining nook for the past six months, I'm filled with gratitude. It's not that I have no money to get my own place. I've saved most of my income over the past few years and am currently waitressing at a champagne bar in Manhattan called Flute, a high-end place with excellent tips. I'm simply staying where it feels safe and comfortable, and Dani is fine with that, enjoying having me as a roommate again.

For a few months, we resumed our college cycle of partying, flirting, and hooking up, but my heart wasn't in it. I hoped that sleeping with other men would help me forget about Josh, but that was a dumb idea that didn't work, and after a few guys—okay, maybe more than a few—I gave up on it. We still go out a lot, but I'm currently on a break from men, instead enjoying getting to know Dani's friends, who have welcomed me into their group.

After our run, we head to our regular café on Columbus Avenue for bagels and coffee. This is why I love New York. A minute ago we were running along quiet wooded paths, and now we're sitting at a table on a busy, noisy street, with the energy and action of the city all around us. In between bites, we comment on the people passing by, noting the fashions, speculating on relationships, admiring cute men and babies and dogs.

Dani and I haven't seen each other much these past couple of weeks, which happens sometimes. Our schedules don't match up, since I work nights at Flute and she works nine to five at Morgan Stanley downtown, now their human resources director of professional growth and development. She's been away at a conference in Chicago for the past week and is telling me about the learning and networking, then about the nonprofessional after-hours escapades, which are more entertaining.

I tell her about my midweek trip to Boston to see Stephanie. It took me a few months to call her after I left Josh, despite her frequent attempts to reach me, so there were relationship repairs to be made there. She understood how upsetting it had all been for me, but she was also hurt and upset that I avoided her for so long. My loving her brother had always been a complicated situation, so there was no reason to think the breakup would be any easier to negotiate. My visit this past week was the final step in getting our friendship back on solid ground. I met her new boyfriend, Don, who she loves, although they haven't said the words yet. She's doing PR for the Boston Tourism Bureau, so she had plenty of ideas for fun things to see and do all week. We laughed, we talked, we reentered each other's lives on new terms.

Though I had a great time with her, I cried on the train ride home. She is still Josh's sister after all, and as much progress as I've made in not thinking about him every single day, being with her brought him back, brought the grief and sorrow back, along with all the thoughts of what might have been. I cried on the train and I cried myself to sleep that night, but I woke up Friday morning feeling refreshed, like the last coating of dust had been wiped away and I had a clean surface to build on, which leads to the next phase of my conversation with Dani in the café.

"I need to get my career back on track," I tell her. "Enough with the waitressing."

"Halleluiah and amen!" she says, which makes me smile. I know how hard it is for her not to share her every thought, and this one has obviously been there for a while, waiting for me to get to it myself.

"I'm not sure what to do," I say. "I loved taking pictures, but that was never part of my plan, that was just to be with him. I'm afraid that going back to photography will keep me tied to him somehow."

After taking a swig of coffee, Dani offers an alternative perspective. "You went traipsing around the world taking pictures of what Josh wanted you to take pictures of, what would best illustrate the story he was telling, and you were awesome at it. Now you can choose a completely different variation of photography, one that fits you."

"It's so overwhelming, though," I say. "I don't even know where to start."

"Maybe start with the pictures," she says, which feels completely right.

That afternoon, we make the one-hour drive to my mom's house to organize years of contact sheets and prints so I can start putting together a portfolio of my work. It helps having Dani and Mom there with me, because going through my photos means reliving my past with Josh and there are tears involved. Mom is comforting and Dani is a taskmaster, letting me wallow for a minute before redirecting me to the job at hand. They both offer input and feedback when I comment on pictures I particularly like or don't, ones that have more meaning or seem more powerful, all of which helps me get a sense of what I want to do moving forward. I've always loved capturing people's experiences—a yearning glance, a knowing gaze, a contented smile. That's what I want to keep doing. Dani and Mom agree.

I spend the week reprinting some of my favorite images, including one of Kade from our camping trip so many years ago. That one isn't right for my new portfolio, but it gives me the idea to make a second album of my most beloved photos, some of which are duplicated in the portfolio, and some of which are too personal. I can't bring myself to include Josh in either album, but there are a plethora of shots from the years we've spent together. He is implied, if not explicitly included, in my whole life.

But not anymore. I shake my head to clear away those thoughts. Not anymore.

Between working late at the bar each night and working on my portfolio every day, I'm exhausted by the weekend. But I'm also excited, which makes me realize how much I've unconsciously been longing to launch my own career, and which assures me I'm on the right path.

I contact my editor from *Outdoor Adventures* and get in touch with some of the photographers I met there. They connect me with other NYC photojournalism professionals, and after months of calls and meetings, networking and interviewing, I'm doing contract work for the style section of *New York* magazine. I hope to be hired onstaff at some point, but I have to prove myself first, which I'm confident I will do. For now, I work as a contractor and continue part-time at Flute to finance my Manhattan lifestyle, which I decide should include my own apartment.

It's been comforting and fun living with Danielle, but I'm ready to be out on my own. I need to feel like an independent adult with my life moving ahead, and getting my own place is a key part of that. I move in early 2000 and enjoy choosing furniture and decorating, finding my own style and making the place feel like my home. Mom brings the things I stored at her house, and I hang several of Kade's paintings, including the one of me on the swing. I leave the one of Josh and me in the back of the closet.

SOMETHING NEW

AND SO, BIT BY BIT, I rediscover myself. A different me, shaped to a new self by this second great heartbreak, but still me. The spark is back. I'm embracing fun for its own sake, not to numb or escape or avoid. I'm a grown-up, independent, assertive woman who speaks her mind and isn't worried about pleasing anyone else. I like myself again, and it shows. Dani and I dress up and go out together on the weekends, often joined by the rest of our crew of friends, and I feel free and relaxed and alive.

I've started dating again, most recently seeing Eric, a successful Manhattan promoter who has a reputation for knowing how to make things happen. Tonight, he's arranged entry for me and Dani to an amazing party at Le Bain, the glittering disco at the top of the Standard Hotel. The guest list is exclusive, even for this always exclusive club, since it's a birthday celebration for a Broadway diva, one of Eric's many celebrity clients. Dani and I are flirting with some Yankees, which is fun, but I'm also exchanging sexy glances with Eric. Although we haven't actually said hello yet, we're acutely aware of each other's attention. He's busy playing host, which is fine with me. He's a sexy, powerful man with a ton of confidence and swagger, so it's foreplay just to watch him work the room. He's tall, with midnight black hair gelled into perfect form and a sculpted body dressed in a tailored Hugo Boss suit.

I leave the dance floor and lean into the crowded bar, trying to get the bartender's attention. Eric appears beside me, and before I know it, I'm served a freshly shaken cosmo, evidence that Eric's been paying attention and already knows my favorite cocktail. I enjoy a sip before he takes my hand and leads me to a reserved couch that looks out over the downtown skyline.

"The view is breathtaking," I say, kicking off our conversation.

"Doesn't compare to you," he replies, his finger lightly tracing my knee. "You're stunning."

"Well, thank you. You don't look so bad yourself." His touch is a stimulating balance of confidence and restraint, a perfect teasing taste of possibility.

"You having fun with those ball boys?" he asks.

"I am. Do you mind?"

"Not at all. I'm working. Have all the fun you like, but you are going home with me." He spreads his hand over my knee and squeezes firmly.

I love flirting with him. He's so good at it. There is so much heat and chemistry between us, and although I take a great deal of pleasure in the mounting tension, I also can't wait to consummate, especially since I haven't had sex in almost a year. He's been a perfect gentleman on our first few dates, with equal measures of patience and assurance of what's in store.

"Going home with you, huh?" My grin is speaking for me, but the flirting is hotter if I put up at least some resistance.

"I like my chances."

He takes his hand from my knee, holds it up for a split second, and shots appear in front of us.

"Is this how you're planning on getting me to go home with you?" I tease.

"Do I need shots for that?" He takes both glasses in his hands, holding them out of reach. "Kai, you are the sexiest woman in the building. Will you please come home with me tonight?"

"Yes, I would be thrilled to go home with you."

He smiles and hands me a shot. We clink glasses and drink.

"I'd like one more of those," I say.

Eric raises his hand for another round, and the server brings waters with our shots.

"Gotta stay hydrated, Kai. All that dancing and flirting with ballplayers."

"Hmm, sounds like you mind a little bit." I want him to mind a little bit.

He grins before answering. "Maybe, but mostly it's a turn-on watching you out there, getting them all excited. Knowing that it's all a show for me."

"It's not all for you. I'm enjoying myself."

"I can tell. That's a turn-on too."

"Damn, you are sexy."

"Back at you," Eric says. A young man comes and whispers in his ear. "Will you wait here for a minute? I have to handle a situation, but I'll be right back. I want to show you something."

I nod and sip my water, which hits the spot after everything else I've been drinking tonight. I'm almost hypnotized by the sparkling downtown skyline, dominated by the Twin Towers lit up in front of me, with the Statue of Liberty way off in the distance.

When Eric returns, he reaches for my hand. "Want to see another spectacular view?"

"Sure." I take his hand and follow him through the crowd. Across the room, we walk down a dark hallway. "Are you showing me the bathrooms, Eric? That's so romantic."

"Have you been in these bathrooms?"

"No."

"Then hold off on the judgment."

There are a dozen or more individual bathrooms, not labeled for men or women, each with only the lowest lighting, as in the hallway. He leads me into one and closes the door.

"Oh my god!" I exclaim as I catch the view. The fourth wall of the bathroom is floor-to-ceiling glass looking out over uptown Manhattan, the Empire State Building glowing brightly. I lean against the glass, looking down at the street far below, then back out at the skyline, easily convincing myself that I'm floating over the city.

Eric moves up behind me, pressing me against the window. He brushes my hair to the side and leans in to kiss my neck.

"Mmm, that's nice," I say. His hands move slowly down my sides, along the curves of my body.

"May I?" he asks, moving one hand up under my short skirt. His other hand is moving toward my chest.

"Oh, yeah," I reply. He slips his hand inside my low-cut top and massages my breast while the fingers on his other hand make me wet and wild.

"So what do you think of the bathroom?" he whispers in my ear.

"I still wouldn't call it romantic, but it's definitely something." I'm breathless but attempting to remain witty and coy.

"I'm not trying to be romantic. You'll know when I'm being romantic. Next time I'll do romance and you'll be swept off your feet, but how about we fuck right now?"

I crane my neck around to kiss him because my body is wedged between his and the window and I can't actually turn around.

He moves back a little to loosen his pants, and I slide off my panties and bend from the waist, bracing my arms on the glass in front of me and resting my chin on my hands.

"Is this okay?" I ask. "This way, I can enjoy you and the view."

"Yeah, this view works for me." He hikes up my skirt and rubs my naked bottom before giving me a light slap, which makes me gasp.

"Is that alright?" he asks.

"It's new," I answer. "And yes, more than alright."

He spanks me again, then lifts my hips, slipping into the wet and ready spot he's prepared. He thrusts in and out, groaning as we climax, not quite together, but close enough.

The next weekend, he fulfills his promise of romance. He brings me to the River Café, a Michelin-starred restaurant tucked under the Brooklyn Bridge, with stunning views of the Manhattan skyline from the opposite side of the East River. He brings me roses when he picks me up, which no one has ever done before. Josh handed me wildflowers once or twice on a hike, and other boyfriends brought me flowers, but no man has ever brought me a dozen long-stemmed roses, fragrant and at the peak stage of opening. He's wearing a perfectly tailored Tom Ford suit and picks me up in a town car with a driver, so the romance factor is high before we even get to the restaurant.

We have a table by the window, and I drink in the view along with the Opus 1 wine he orders.

"I wish I'd brought my camera," I say.

"You're not working tonight," he says. "Tonight is all about me and you. I'll bring you back anytime to take pictures."

It sometimes feels like I'm dating an actor reading a script, Eric is that smooth, but I like it. I like being with someone who wants to impress me and succeeds so definitively. It's nice to be swept off my feet.

After dinner, he takes me back to his place, where he continues the romantic wooing. He has a great apartment in midtown

Manhattan with a fabulous view of the city. He runs me a bubble bath and lights candles in the bathroom and his bedroom, puts on a Sade CD, then climbs into the tub behind me and we settle into each other. When we move to his bed, he makes love to me tenderly, kisses and caresses on my shoulders and stomach and feet building a slow burn rather than a sudden fire.

"You were right," I say after, lying in his arms, wrapped in his Egyptian cotton bedsheets. "You can do the romance thing as well as the fuck-me thing."

"Baby, I am happy to oblige with romance or fucking you anytime."

Dani thinks Eric is a hoot. Eric parties harder than she and I ever have, and she admires his stamina. She also loves the particular parties he gets us into. Whether he's working or not, he has connections all over town, so we go anywhere we want, places Dani has heard about but has never figured out how to get through the door.

Dani currently has a fairly serious boyfriend, so we double-date with them sometimes. Lawrence isn't as into the party scene as the rest of us, but he loves good food and great wine, so the four of us have some amazing meals together. Lawrence is a lawyer who works at Morgan Stanley with Dani, which is how they met, and she likes him more than she usually admits to liking guys, although she's unsure of his squareness factor, thinking he may be too low-key for her. He and Eric both earn a ton of money, and they both enjoy spending it hand over fist, showing off that they have it to spend. Eric likes to shop too, for himself and for me. He buys me clothes, a Louis Vuitton purse, Christian Louboutin shoes, and gorgeous diamond earrings, and I let him spoil me.

The only bumps in the road with Eric are glimpses of his overindulging. He drinks a lot, and what occasionally gives me pause is how much he can drink. We go out to dinner with Dani and Lawrence and have several bottles of wine, and the guys also do shots here and there on the side. And he never really seems drunk, even though the rest of us often are.

He has that addict personality. He wakes up at six a.m. to work out pretty much every day. His drive at work is intense too, managing a successful business that is well known among the city's elite. He does everything with intensity, which completely turns me on. Josh was so chill and noncommittal about everything, and Eric is completely the opposite. He is all-in all the time. When he's working, he's laser-focused; when he's drinking, he's pounding them back; when he's shopping, he's spending a grand. And when we have sex, I am his entire world. I feel adored for once, his passion and attention lavished over me, and I love it.

The good times last until September 2001.

September 3, 2001

K,

It took a lot of cajoling for Stephanie to give me your new address. She told me you wouldn't want to hear from me, and I know you aren't going to want to hear what I have to say, but I wanted you to hear it from me rather than through the family grapevine.

I met someone here in Spain. I've been doing pieces in Europe for a while now, and have made this little town called Tudela my home base. Anyway, you don't care about that. I'm just stalling for time because I don't want to tell you about Marcella. We've been together for a few months, and she's pregnant. She's Catholic and won't consider an abortion or any other option besides having the baby, so we are having a baby. And we're getting married. Tomorrow, actually, so I'll be married by the time you get this. I'm so sorry, Kai. I know this is going to devastate you, and I am sorry, but I have to do this. I'd rather not have a kid, especially like this, but since it's happening, I'm not going to be the loser dad who runs away from his responsibility. I have to do the right thing here, and hopefully we'll end up being happy. Marcella is a sweet, kind person, and I think I can be happy with her. I hope so.

Please don't hate me, K. I never meant to break your heart, although I know I did.

J

THE CRASH

The feeling of dread won't go away. The pit in my stomach churning away when I wake up in the morning and all through the day. At moments my heart pounds against my ribs, the blood pumping through my coronary arteries at a breakneck speed and pressure until it feels like my chest will explode. I stay huddled up at my mom's house, spend days in bed, curled up under the covers, unable to face the world at large. I'm not interested in anything the world has to offer, not because I'm worried about what could be out there, but because I know for sure—grief, devastation, betrayal and loss—and I want no part of it. I'm not sure if I'm depressed or traumatized or simply deeply sad, but I cry all the time and am immobilized by the intensity of my feelings.

Mom tries not to bug me, yet she pokes at me every day or two, inviting me for a walk, encouraging a shower, suggesting lunch out with one of her friends. Sometimes I acquiesce, mostly so she'll worry less, although my fear is ever present, never diminishing, my constant tormentor.

Up until a few weeks ago, I thought I still knew some things for sure. My whole life, I thought I would marry Josh. Even dating Eric, I realize now that a part of me still had some belief that Josh and I would end up together. But Josh married someone else.

I thought I would never witness thousands of people being murdered in one fell swoop, but I was wrong about that too. On September 11, I was in my apartment mourning the permanence of losing Josh, ignoring the world around me, ignoring my phone until the repeated ringing became unbearably irritating. When I realized what was happening, I ran with my camera toward Ground Zero, taking pictures of the shocked faces around me.

I started developing the photos but hit a wall of grief and despair and couldn't go on. I called my mom in wracking sobs, and she came and picked me up and brought me to her house. The magazine called asking for my photos, but I couldn't do it. I couldn't do anything.

A long time ago, I was sure I'd always have my brother too. I thought I'd moved on from that grief, but it comes pouring back over me now. I am lost in loss, the emptiness, pointlessness, and chaos of it all.

Danielle left the city too. She stayed here with Mom for a few days, but her parents wanted her to join them at their house in Martha's Vineyard. The fact that she gave in to that request when she's never felt any emotional support from her parents exemplifies how raw and desperate we all are right now, how none of us are thinking straight.

Mom is so worried about me that she calls Dad and invites him over. I have to give him credit; even seeing how terrible I'm doing, he comes back several times. We don't talk much, because he is my dad after all, but he brings a movie or a milkshake or a deck of cards every time and spends an hour or two with me. It doesn't make me feel better, but it doesn't make things worse.

Eric calls pretty much every day. He didn't leave the city, didn't stop working. Most days, I take his calls, but some days I can't talk. He wants me to come back, to keep him company, to get on with our lives, but I can't see how to do that. For the first time in my life, I have no hope for the future, no hope that I want a future. I can't see anything good in it, anything that interests me. I turned thirty four days after the attack, and I feel like an old woman, worn out and exhausted, drained by life and loss. I feel myself slipping away but can't do anything about it.

In October, Eric comes to spend the weekend at Mom's. This plan was formulated mostly by him and Mom, and I have no energy to resist, so here he is. Mom doesn't particularly like Eric, doesn't like the high-roller lifestyle we share, but she's willing to try anything to pull me out of the muck. Even Dad and Eric.

Eric is a city boy through and through, and although he journeys to the suburbs to see me, he brings the city with him. His fancy clothes and slicked-back hair don't match my sweats and ponytail, so I primp more than I have in weeks, even shave my legs. Hanging out at my mom's isn't Eric's scene, so he convinces me to go out. We drink a lot, and my anxiety recedes. For the first time in over a month, my stomach and my heart are settled, calm. It's all back the next morning, combined with a hangover, which makes it worse, but Eric takes me out again, and the drinking helps again, and I realize this must be how Eric has been coping for the last month. I can't imagine being in New York in those days and weeks following the attack, but perhaps this numbing has been the answer for all those people who stayed. I know my family history. I know I could easily be an addict, and I'm not about to let that happen. But the respite feels good, a break from the constant churning of my body and my mind.

Eric's visit helps revive me. In addition to forcing me to tend to my appearance and get out of the house, the physical intimacy feels good. Sex is always good with Eric, and my inner pain doesn't diminish that. I didn't think I had any desire for anything until he was right here in front of me and that part of me came alive again, and maybe that reawakened my hope that the rest of me can come back to life too.

Eric tries to convince me to return to the city with him, but I'm not ready. He's disappointed but understands. He saw that spark reignite in me too, and he believes it will continue to grow.

The day he leaves, I set up a darkroom at my mom's and start processing my photos. I cry as I look at the faces—the shock, the horror, the heartbreak. I can only go through a few at a time as the pain comes raging back, but it is also somehow comforting. Comforting to be reminded that my pain isn't exclusively my own. It is shared. Our world has been torn apart, not just mine. We are all grieving, not me alone.

I still wake each morning with that pit in my stomach, but it eases a bit as the day goes on. My appetite comes back, and I take my mom out for meals now and then.

I send some pictures to my editor, who loves them. He wants to run a few but also suggests that I think about doing a book. He suggests I contact an agent, a friend of his, to talk more about the idea. In a way it feels like too much, but in another way it's exciting. It's a little piece of a future, although I'm still not sure I want to invest in a future that seems so precarious.

Eric loves the book idea and encourages me to come back to the city to pursue it, but although I feel less anxious, more confident that I will reengage in life, I'm not sure it will be in NYC. I love it, but I'm not sure if I can walk those streets again without reliving the terror. Plus, I can do it all from here, from anywhere. I don't have to go back to New York. Still, that's where my life is—Eric and Danielle, who returned to the city a month ago, our crew and my apartment. Her thirtieth birthday is in early November, with a blowout celebration planned, and I want to be there for her, so I decide to go, to see what it feels like to be back, see if I can return or not.

My anxiety is intense as I ride the train into Grand Central, yet as soon as I'm out on the street, it feels like home. I immediately start crying, standing on 42nd Street sobbing for all I've lost and for all I love, including this city. I take a cab to my apartment, where Eric is waiting.

"Welcome home, baby," he says, pulling me into his arms.

My cheeks are streaked and my eyes are red, so he knows I've been crying, but he doesn't say anything about it. I love this about him. He never asks hard questions, never cares about discussing serious stuff, and that's fine with me at this point. Where had all that talking and sharing and digging deep gotten me before?

Instead of talking, I kiss him. I'm happy and relieved to be back home, and I'm overwhelmed and afraid, but mostly I'm tired of being sad and dead inside. So I let Eric wake me up. Our sex is raw, desperate, filled with longing and need, and I feel alive again.

The party is another thing I hadn't realized I needed. I need my tribe back, and here they are, embracing me, needing me too. We celebrate hard that night, everyone aware of living life in the moment, never knowing when the moment might come to an end.

REBUILDING

Not even a week later, Eric instructs me to prepare for a big night out. He picks me up in a limo, complete with champagne. We are making out in the back, so I don't notice where we're headed until the car stops.

When the chauffer opens the door, I realize we are at the Standard. While the party with the Yankees wasn't officially our first date, it was definitely the night that moved the dial for both of us, and we consider this our place.

It all seems sweet and sexy until we are seated on the same couch where we sat that night and I see the empty space where the towers used to be and all I want to do is leave.

"Please just stay for a minute," Eric says. "There's a reason I brought you here."

"How can everything change so completely in one moment?" I can't take my teary eyes off the gaping hole in the skyline. "You think things will last, but then they crash and crumble away."

"That's kind of why I brought you here. We've both lost things." I know pieces of Eric's life story—his mom died when he was two, and his dad left him with grandparents who were bitter about raising him and died years ago. I've shared about Kade and the basic brushstrokes of Josh.

"The towers are gone," he continues. "Lives are gone. And yet we're still here." He takes my hand and leads me toward the bathrooms.

In spite of the tears, I start to laugh. "Eric, you are smooth, but I'm not sure even you can segue from 9/11 to sex in the bathroom."

He smiles. "Watch me."

He leads me into the same stall we enjoyed before and stands at the window next to me.

"Look." He points to the Empire State Building, lit up in red, white, and blue. "That's still standing, just like you are and I am. Who knows how long it will last, but it's here now, and it's beautiful."

"It is."

"I want to marry you, Kai."

My head snaps toward him to see if he's serious, which he is.

"I think we should get married," he repeats. "Fuck terrorists, and fuck being afraid. Fuck being sad and hopeless. Let's grab on to life and happiness and fuck 'em all."

"Wow, I never thought a marriage proposal could have so many fucks." I'm overwhelmed and stalling for time, but I'm also pretty sure I'm happy.

"You know I do things my way."

"You certainly do." I look at him intensely.

"You don't believe I'm serious," he says. "You think I'm drunk or have PTSD or something, but I've never been more fucking serious."

I smile because I know he threw that fuck in there on purpose. "But we've never even talked about having a future together. It's so out of nowhere."

"So?"

"Maybe the bathroom isn't the best place to talk about this?" I take his hands in mine and try to lead him out.

He stands firmly in front of me. "This is the perfect place to talk about it because it's exactly why you're going to marry me. Everything you've ever been sure of has turned into a fucking shit show. Marry me as the opposite of all that. Ride the wave, baby." He looks a tiny bit nervous, which I've never seen on him before and find endearing.

It is so tempting to stop thinking about all the misery of the past and jump into this fresh new adventure. Irresistibly tempting to have someone want to build a life with me.

"Two questions," I say.

"Shoot."

"Can we have kids? I mean, not right this second. I don't want kids right this second, but I do want kids. Do you want kids?"

"Yes. Yes to kids. Next question."

"That's it? Just yes?"

"Yes. Isn't it a yes or no question? I mean you don't want like ten kids, do you?"

"Maybe two or three?"

"Yes, whenever you want."

My smile is giving away my answer already, and Eric is smiling in return, back to his typical confidence and swagger.

"Second question," he reminds me, then adds, "not that it matters."

"Cocky."

"Like you didn't already know that. What's your pointless question?"

"Do you have a ring?"

"Baby, of course I have a ring. You've met me, right? You think I'd do this without a ring?"

"You would if you just thought of it in the car."

"I bought the ring two weeks ago, the day you told me you were coming in for the party. I wanted you to choose to stay on your own, but I've had the ring in my pocket since the day you got back, just in case you told me you were leaving."

I'm touched by this. He needs and wants me in his life. I matter to him.

"Do you remember the first night we fucked in here?" I ask.

"Obviously."

"I said it wasn't romantic, but it just became very romantic."

"Well, we can't have that," he replies, pushing me up against the window and kissing me hard and deep, grinding against me.

"Eric—"

"Shh," he says.

"Don't you want an answer?"

He pulls away just an inch to look at me.

"Fuck yes, I'll marry you," I say.

When we head back to our couch, Eric gets down on one knee and slips a big, beautiful diamond ring on my finger. He motions for shots and champagne, and we invite our friends to come join the celebration, which lasts into the wee hours.

I call my mom first thing the next morning to tell her the news. She's surprised, and not in a good way. I remind her that I've dated Eric for over a year, presenting my evidence that we should get married, then angry that I should have to convince her. She wonders out loud if alcohol played a part in the proposal, and I'm furious and hurt.

"No, Mom, he loves me and wants to marry me. Is that so hard to believe?"

"Of course not, Kai. Of course he wants to marry you. I can't believe every man in the world doesn't want to marry you. You are exceptional. I'm just surprised you want to marry him. I mean, he's fun and handsome, but…I don't know, honey, I'm just surprised is all."

"You mean that he's not Josh, but there is no more Josh, Mom. There's no more of a lot of things, and it's time to move on. This is my chance for a fresh start and I'm taking it."

Mom tells me all she wants is for me to be happy, and I tell her that I am. She can tell this isn't up for discussion, so she apologizes for her reaction, and I forgive her. We make plans for her to come to the city the following weekend to start shopping for wedding dresses.

Dani questions my sanity in this decision as well, but she understands when I explain why Eric is right for me. I can't love as intensely as I did before because it's simply too scary, too risky, yet I don't want to be alone because that's scary too, so I'm choosing a Goldilocks solution, finding an amount of love that feels just right. Also, Dani's been through 9/11 in a way my mom hasn't, and she understands that extreme measures may be needed to heal.

When I call Stephanie to ask her to be my co-maid-of-honor, she has news as well. Josh's wife miscarried shortly after their wedding. I have no clue how to respond to that. My first reaction is ugly and dark. I'm happy that woman lost that baby, and I hate myself for it. I don't ask anything more, but Stephanie knows the unspoken question and tells me that they're staying married, that Josh is going to try and make it work.

I'm sitting at Eric's dining room table writing a letter to Kade to tell him all about my engagement, the attack, all the ups and downs of the past few months, when Eric comes in.

"What are you doing, beautiful?" he asks.

Only Josh and Jill, my old therapist, know that I write to Kade, but I am marrying Eric. He should know me at least as well as Josh.

"I'm writing a letter to Kade," I tell him.

He laughs. "Your brother Kade?"

"Of course. Is there another Kade?" I'm immediately on the defensive.

"I'm confused. He's dead, right?"

"Don't be a jerk, Eric."

"I'm sorry, I just really don't understand. You write your dead brother? That's fucked up, babe."

I gather my paper and pen and head for the door.

"Hey, hey, where are you going?" Eric follows me. "Babe, I'm sorry, but c'mon, it sounds crazy, you have to admit that."

"I know, but it makes me feel better to write him sometimes."

"Okay, I'm sorry. You caught me off guard. Let me make it up to you. Let me make you feel better." He starts kissing my neck and caressing my back, his hands sneaking toward my ass.

"You hurt my feelings," I say. "That wasn't nice." I'm still upset, but he's excellent at distraction, clearly part of what I love about him.

"You are right. That wasn't nice. Let me be nice to you now. I'll be very, very nice to you, Kai. Will you let me be nice to you?"

"Mmm-hmm," I say in reply.

The next day he brings me a blue box with a silver and gold Tiffany pen and some expensive Italian stationery so I can write to my brother in style. It bothers me a little that I know he still doesn't get it, but I appreciate the lengths to which he goes to apologize and show me I matter even if he doesn't understand.

Eric and I get married on New Year's Day, not even two months later. He has so many contacts, and so many people have canceled plans due to the attacks, that we end up having a surprising number of venues to choose from. Our ceremony and reception are at Tribeca Rooftop, a 1920s printing press building on a cobblestone street in downtown Manhattan. Eric does most of the work on the event side, since he does that all the time. I find a dress and get a photographer friend from the magazine to take pictures.

Danielle and Stephanie are joint maids of honor and the only two attendants. Eric has his two best friends stand up for him. Mom and Dad walk me down the aisle.

Steph is with me in the bathroom after the ceremony, helping me realign myself after I pee, a challenge in a wedding dress. Dani is in another stall.

"I know I shouldn't say this, Kai, but this is weird," Steph says, fixing the bustle on my gown.

I know what she means but don't want to talk about it.

"We planned this day so many times, and there are pieces of it that feel right in line with all that."

"You as my maid of honor, for instance." I hope we can stop there.

"Yes, exactly, but it's weird to see you marry someone else."

Dani is washing her hands, but her eyes are on me in the mirror, watching to see my reaction.

"Steph, I can't do this now. I'm happy with Eric. I can't think about your brother."

"Like you haven't been thinking about him all day," Dani mutters.

I give her an evil look and she stares me down. "Tell me you haven't."

These are my best friends, and even when they piss me off, they know me too well.

"Not all day," I answer. "And I wish I wasn't."

"Okay, but it's best not to ignore ghosts," Dani says. "Let's have a little exorcism instead. Purge Josh Tyler from this wedding."

"Ooh, I love it!" Steph agrees as she turns to leave the bathroom. "Stay here."

"You are a pain, Dani, but I love you," I say, shaking my head.

Steph comes back with a family picture from her wallet and nail scissors she must have had in her purse. She cuts Josh out of the picture and puts his little face in a bowl she also brought back. Then she pulls out a Tribeca Rooftop matchbook and hands it to me.

"Wait, wait, wait," Dani says. She runs out of the bathroom and comes back with three shots. "Light it up, Kai."

Mom walks into the bathroom as I'm about to strike the match.

"What's going on in here?" she asks. "Why is Dani bringing shots into the bathroom?"

"We're exorcising a ghost," Dani answers plainly, as if it's the most normal thing in the world, like it happens at every wedding.

Mom surveys the scene. "Wait for me." She comes back with her own shot. I've never seen my mom do a shot, but I love that she's right here with us. I wish Jaimie was here too, but she's eight months pregnant and couldn't fly.

I light the tiny picture on fire.

"To Kai," says Steph, raising her shot glass as the photo burns.

"To unexpected twists and turns," Mom says.

"Ob-La-Di, Ob-La-Da," Dani says.

"Life goes on." I clink glasses with my tribe.

HAPPILY EVER AFTER?

ERIC AND I HONEYMOON AT the Four Seasons in Bora Bora. We make love morning, noon, and night in our bungalow perched over the water, a few times on the glass section of floor right over the brilliant blue sea. We get massages, eat at the decadent restaurants, and soak up the sun on the breathtaking white sand beach.

I move in with him when we get back, and although the plan is to find a new place to make our own, I quickly settle into his oasis and realize it is unlikely we could find a more perfect apartment. I plan to redecorate to make it feel more like my home, but I never seem to get around to it.

Our first year of marriage is fabulous. We see friends and go out a lot, but we're also busy professionally, each pursuing our own goals in our separate arenas. Eric's business is booming, and I continue to work for *New York* magazine. Most of my time and focus, though, are spent on my book, which comes out on September 11, 2002. I'd signed with my editor's agent friend right before the wedding, and she'd quickly found a publisher. It was important to everyone that the book come out on the anniversary of the attacks, so everything moved at Mach speed. It's not a bestseller, but it is selling well in local bookstores, and what's most important is that I'm proud of it. I formatted the book in two-page spreads, one side showing devastation, the opposite side showing resilience. I paired pictures of sadness and loss, anger and fear, with pictures of love and support, energy and fun. It ended up working beautifully, illustrating the full range of human experience.

Over the next year, I have more time on my hands, and it becomes harder to ignore how much Eric drinks. He goes to Atlantic City periodically with his friends, and I come to realize he gambles a lot too. That isn't new, but I wasn't paying attention to it before. I bring it up with him a few times, but he rationalizes that it isn't causing problems because he never loses more than he can afford, which is true.

The real wake-up comes one weekend when Danielle and I tag along to Atlantic City with his rat pack. In spite of how much he drinks, I've never really seen him completely wasted, which should have clued me in to his level of tolerance, but up until tonight, it hasn't. Tonight, though, he loses thousands of dollars playing poker, then gets crazy drunk. We have the biggest fight we've ever had, which is stupid because he doesn't even remember it the next morning.

He wakes up and heads straight for the minibar, and when I ask him not to, the fight resumes.

"See, this is why I come here without you. I knew you'd make a big deal out of nothing." He turns away from me, mixing his Bloody Mary.

"It's not nothing, Eric." I circle around to face him. "You have a problem."

"My only problem is you giving me shit. This is how I blow off steam. Do you know how stressful my job is? I have to be on, ready for anything, twenty-four-seven. My clients get into all kinds of shit, and I have to bail them out, spin it all to be okay, line up appearances and manage images. Twenty-four-seven!"

"I thought you loved it." My anger softens as I get a glimpse into a part of his experience I don't know much about.

"I do love it. I love the adrenaline rush. And I love this too. I love kicking back with my boys and not managing anything." Eric has also softened. I can see the pleading in his eyes now, replacing the anger. "Don't make me manage you, okay?"

"Do you even remember our fight last night?" I try my best to ask gently, to keep him engaged rather than escalating back into a full-blown fight. "Do you remember the ugly things you said to me? Do you remember throwing up and passing out in the middle of that fight?"

"No, I do not, thank god." He bows his head in shame. "It sounds like a shit show."

"It was. You lost a ton of money last night, Eric. I watched you at that table and you couldn't stop. I watched you at the bar and you couldn't stop that either."

"I didn't want to stop. That's different." He's looking me in the eye again, and I know he believes what he's saying. "I did walk away from the table, if you remember. I did stop. The amount I lost is no more than what I spent on those last few pairs of shoes I bought you. It's no big deal. I know what I can lose, and that's what I lost. Last weekend I doubled my money. That's how it goes."

Eric pulls me in for a hug, and I let him hold me.

"You know my dad's an alcoholic, right?" I say this softly into his chest. "My brother was an addict, and it's part of what killed him. I can't have that in my life."

"Babe, you're overreacting. This is your stuff with your family, and I get that, but it's not about me. I'm fine."

"You're drinking right now and it's ten o'clock in the morning."

"Hair of the dog, babe." He walks over to the sink and dumps the drink, then comes back over to me. "Is that better?"

"Yes." I nuzzle back into him and he holds me close.

"I don't need all this. I just like it. I'll tone it down if it bothers you."

"Can you?"

"Of course I can. I'm sorry for whatever I said last night. Was it bad?"

"Yes," I say, tears coming on again.

"Baby, I'm sorry." I can tell he means it. "What did I say?"

"I said something about drinking being a fucked-up way to get through life, and you said it's not as fucked up as writing letters to dead people."

"Fuck, I'm an asshole." He squeezes me tighter. "I intentionally don't get that drunk around you because I know I can be an asshole. You've never seen me wasted before, right?"

"I've seen you drunk, but not like that."

"See? If I had a problem, wouldn't I be like that all the time, or at least more often? You've known me for years and that's the first time I've been like that."

We settle together on the little couch, with me tucked under his arm.

"You drink a lot, though."

"Sorry, babe, but so do you." I think about that, about how much we drink together.

"I guess you have a point. Can we tone it down? Not drink so much? At least for while?"

"Sure thing. Anything for you," he says. "But not when I'm here. Atlantic City is my free pass, okay?"

"Okay." I feel like he's hearing me and giving me what I need for the most part. He's willing to give something up for me, and that calms my nerves and makes me happy. I'm willing to compromise and let him have his wild weekends once in a while.

"You don't get a free pass for everything, though," I tease, looking up at him with a smile.

He kisses me. "Baby, I have no interest in fucking anyone but you."

"Are you interested in fucking me now?"

"Always and forever." And the intensity is back on me, all of his focus and energy making me feel like I'm the only thing that matters. He's sweet and tender up to a point, and when he senses I've had enough of that, he flips a switch and becomes rough and wild, full of the dominating confidence I love.

We go a while with far less drinking. Instead of sharing a bottle of wine with dinner, we order one glass each. We sip on a cocktail at a party rather than slamming back several. I hadn't realized how much I'd been drinking too, and I'm glad to be aware of it and glad that it's been easy enough for me to rein it in.

Eventually, though, Eric starts drinking more again. His trips to Atlantic City become more frequent, but since I'm not there, it's easy enough to ignore. However, one Friday night, when he tells me he's going away for the second weekend in a row, I freak out. He's only going for Saturday night, for a party, but still, it seems like we're slipping down a terrible slope. We have an ugly fight, and this time he disregards my concerns and leaves the next day anyway.

That Sunday morning, after our run, I bring it up with Danielle, who's shocked that I wasn't aware of this all along.

"I thought we simply weren't mentioning it," she says. "I didn't think you were oblivious to it. Your boy can slam 'em back."

We talk for a while about Eric's drinking habits, analyzing the available data to quantify the problem. Dani helps me see that it's been like this from the beginning, that Eric has pretty much always had a drink in his hand, although we both agree that Atlantic City was the only time he was an obnoxious, out-of-control drunk. We decide it's more apparent now that I'm drinking less, which makes me worried that it was really a bigger problem all along. We also discuss how it's more triggering for me than for most people because of my family history, although Dani thinks that's all the more reason for Eric to make extra accommodations. The fact that he knows my particular background and keeps drinking anyway is evidence to her that it's not in his control, or that he's an asshole who doesn't care about me, which neither of us think is true. We commiserate over his decision to go to Atlantic City despite my clear objections. Dani agrees that was a dick move, but I also admit that I was in naggy wife mode. Before we arrive at the definitive conclusion that my husband is an alcoholic, I change the subject, since I'm not yet ready to land there.

I ask Dani about her rekindled relationship with Lawrence. She broke up with him a while ago because she decided he was too boring, but she's been toning down the partying along with me and is now giving him a second look. He's still in love with her, and they started dating again about a month ago. Dani fills me in on how that's going, which is very well.

When I get home, Eric is there, much earlier than expected. He's never home from Atlantic City before Sunday evening. There are roses and a jewelry box on the counter.

He gives me a hug when I walk through the door. "I'm sorry, babe. I shouldn't have left like that yesterday."

"You shouldn't have," I say.

"I know, but I hate when you get that tone, all bossy and demanding. It flips a switch that makes me want to push back even harder. No excuse, though. I am sorry."

"I hate being like that too. I hear my voice and wonder who the hell I am. I don't want to tell you what to do, but it worries me. Your drinking and gambling worry me."

"I know. There's really nothing to worry about, though. I wish you'd trust me on that."

"I want to. I'll try." I kiss him and let him hold me in this moment of peace. I'm scared to say what's on my mind, but I force myself. "Will you please cut back on the drinking again?"

"I will." He kisses me. "I promise. I'll take a break from Atlantic City too, although you might not want me to now."

"Why wouldn't I want you to?"

"Because I won ten thousand dollars last night," he says, all cool, like it's no big deal.

"Oh my god, Eric!" I pull away and look at the huge satisfied smile on his face. "Ten thousand dollars?" My first thought is to wonder how much you have to gamble to win ten thousand dollars, but I don't say that. We're making up, and he's excited, and I'm not going back into nag mode.

"I got you something to celebrate and apologize." He takes my present from the counter and leads me to the couch, then hands it to me.

"Thank you, and thank you for the beautiful roses too."

"Open it."

Inside the little blue box is a diamond pendant necklace sparkling up at me.

"It's gorgeous, babe." I kiss him. "Thank you." And that's what convinces me to forgive him and pretend that it's all over and everything will be fine now. Well, that and the fact that I want so badly to believe it.

March 27, 2003

Dear Kade,

I know I haven't written in a long time, but I need to tell you something that I can't talk to anyone else about.

My husband is an alcoholic. So now I'm Mom married to Dad. How did that happen? He cuts down on drinking, or even stops sometimes, and I believe things might change, but the change is only momentary. The pattern stays the same. He drinks and we fight, then he stops for a while, then it starts all over again. Sound familiar?

I talked with Danielle about it at the beginning, but not anymore because it makes me feel stupid. I never mention it to Mom because I don't want to bring any of that up for her again. So here I am, in it alone, trying to keep hope alive that someone might choose me for once over doing exactly what they want. Sorry, that's a dig on you and Josh and Dad and Eric.

I love you but you all kind of suck.

FAMILY REUNION

I'VE BEEN STARING IN THE mirror fixing my makeup for ages, stalling because I don't want to go where I have to go. Eric and I are in Boston for Stephanie's wedding, running late for the rehearsal dinner. I've been here for a few days, doing my maid-of-honor duties, helping Steph get ready for her perfect day. Eric arrived a few hours ago, and we made love this afternoon. I need as much reassurance as possible that I am happily married and that seeing Josh will not disrupt my life in any way. He and his wife arrived earlier today, but I haven't seen him yet.

Eric finally gets me out the door. He's on edge as well, which happens when he's not drinking. A good deal of his confidence apparently comes from a bottle. He knows the general outline of my relationship with Josh and knows he's going to be the outsider among the Tyler family. I think he's also uptight about seeing my dad since things are always a little tense between them, although I've never been able to put my finger on exactly why.

When we walk into the restaurant, Eric heads straight to the bar, ostensibly to get us both a needed drink. I see him order a shot and down it quickly before heading back to me with two glasses of wine.

"Please take it easy tonight," I say, which seems destined to be a bad start to the evening.

"Just wine," he replies, pretending he didn't just do a shot, which I pretend I didn't notice.

When I see Josh, the air is knocked out of me. I almost start crying and hate myself for that. I wish Danielle were here with me instead of Eric. I'm supposed to be Steph's support person for the next two days, I'm Eric's babysitter, and I'm afraid I won't get through it all without somebody in my corner, but then Eric takes my hand and gives it a reassuring squeeze. I look at him and he's there for me. Maybe the shot was exactly what he needed to snap back into his confident, competent, sexy self. Maybe it will all be alright.

We greet Stephanie first, and she gives me a tight hug, appreciative of my being here, especially since she knows how hard it is for me to see Josh again. We greet Don, her groom, who is a sweet guy and completely in love with Steph.

I want to head straight to our seats and avoid making the rest of the rounds, but there's no way to avoid it, so we join my dad, who's talking with Rob and Pam. I introduce Eric, and we chat for a while before Josh appears with Marcella. She's slightly taller than he is and slender, with straight dark hair and huge eyes. She would be strikingly beautiful except that she looks bitter or empty or sad inside, although it's highly likely that I'm viewing her as I want her to be.

"Hi, Kai. Long time no see," Josh says.

I am immediately livid at his flippancy. Long time no see? Eric and Josh both recognize the angry fire in my eyes, and Eric steps in, for which I love him. He introduces himself and shakes Josh's hand, then puts his arm around me, and I love him for that too. This is what partners are for, right? To rub ex's faces in the fact that you've moved on? My breath steadies and I relax a bit into Eric.

Josh introduces Marcella, and Dad greets her warmly. I know I should say something, but I can't think of anything nice, so I say nothing at all. Eric continues to run interference, asking about their flight. In her melodic Spanish accent, Marcella tells him about her lack of travel experience, and I'm enraged again because I can't believe Josh is married to a person who's barely been on a plane. I schlepped around the world for him, and he wouldn't marry me.

"Eric, let me introduce you to the rest of the family," I say, and pull him away.

"Smooth, babe," he says.

"Right," I say, then kiss him, because the joking is exactly what I need, and I love him for knowing that. I don't kiss him for Josh's benefit, but when I pull away, I see that Josh is looking, a pure bonus.

Stephanie's talking with her other brothers. We join them, and I introduce Eric to Nick and Bobby, who's holding his youngest of two sons, an adorable baby, in one hand, and a beer in the other.

"Finally replaced my brother, huh, Kai?" Bobby asks.

"Always the asshole, Bobby," says Stephanie.

"Good to know some things never change," I say, trying to act like it's no big deal.

"How about another drink before dinner, babe?" Eric asks, and for the first time in a long time, I agree that's a great idea.

We get through dinner with no problem. Once we're seated, I'm safe from any interaction with Josh. I sit between Stephanie and Eric, good conversation and plenty of wine flowing. Steph has cleverly arranged the seats so that I can't even see Josh, so I'm pretending he isn't here.

After dinner is another story. This isn't a group that just goes home after dinner. I'm talking with Steph and her mom and some of their other friends when I realize most of the men have disappeared. I look around the restaurant and see Josh and Eric sidled up to the bar with my dad and Rob. I squeeze Steph's arm and point to the bar.

"Oh my god," she says. "That can't be good. Mom, go see what's going on over there."

Pam follows our troubled gaze and heads over to break up the grouping, but as usual she's ineffective. As she walks back to us, Josh looks over and meets my eyes before I look away.

"They say they're fine," Pam reports.

"Do you think they're fine, Mom?" Steph asks.

"I think they're drunk."

"I'm going to collect my drunk and head out," I say. "I'll see you bright and early in the morning, Steph. Your wedding day!" I hug her, pretending I'm happy and fine, even though she knows I'm not.

"Eric, you ready to go?" I squeeze between him and Dad, on the side away from Josh.

"Not yet, babe, the night is young. I'm just getting to know Josh here."

He's not as drunk as on the Atlantic City night, but he is drunk.

"Dude, if Kai wants to go, you should probably go," Josh says.

"I know how to give my wife what she wants, Josh, but thanks," Eric says. I can almost see his chest puffing up.

"Really? It doesn't seem like it," Josh says, drunk and puffing up as well.

"Hey, guys, Kai's probably right." Dad steps in for once. "We all want to be fresh tomorrow." He and Rob walk away, hoping the others will follow, or simply avoiding the scene as per usual, but the macho game of chicken isn't over yet.

"You think you know her better than me?" Eric says to Josh, his voice rising. Bobby and Nick look over from down the bar. I'm nervous about where this is headed, but I'm also gratified that

Eric is giving Josh a hard time.

"I've definitely known her longer," Josh says.

"True, but she left you, right? And she's with me now? So as far as I see that makes me the winner and you the loser."

"Yeah, you're a winner all right," Josh says under his breath, just loud enough for Eric to hear, and I know things are about to escalate.

"Babe, let's not finish our night like this." I stroke Eric's arm, leaning into him, exuding my sexy vibe. "Let's go back to our room and finish it on a better note."

This has the dual impact of shoving it in Josh's face that I'm going to have sex with my husband and giving Eric the ego boost he needs, the clear victory without a fight.

"Sure, babe, whatever you want," Eric says, looking pointedly at Josh.

Eric and I have wild, something-to-prove sex that night. The next morning I leave early to help Stephanie get ready. I'll meet up with Eric later at the church, and I'm hoping he'll stay away from Josh, but I don't say anything because I don't want to start a fight or plant any ideas in his head.

The wedding is perfect, and Stephanie is a beautiful, blissfully happy bride. I avoid eye contact with Josh all through the ceremony and dinner. I make my toast and Steph cries, so all success there. I'm drinking more than usual, knowing I need help getting through the night. Eric agreed to take it easy, but I see him slip away for another drink whenever he thinks I'm not looking.

On one of Eric's trips to the bar, Josh asks me to dance. What can I say? I've always been terrible at saying no to him. So now we're dancing and I'm torn up inside because I love it and I hate him at the same moment. At first, we're quiet, because really, what is there to say?

"How have you been, Kai?" he finally asks, although I already wish he hadn't.

"Fine, Josh, you?"

"Okay, I guess, but I miss you. I wish we could be friends."

I stop dancing, look at him for a long minute, then turn and leave the dance floor, leave the room, leave the building. I walk without direction, circling the parking lot, just to be outside and away from him and everyone else, afraid the volcano of anger inside me will erupt and ruin the wedding. He follows me.

"Kai, stop," he says. "Please talk to me."

"Fuck you, Josh!" I continue walking to no place in particular as he walks beside me. "You want to be friends? That is the stupidest thing I've ever heard you say! I thought you hated bullshit, Mr. Authenticity, Mr. Honesty, Mr. Tell it like it is."

"I'm sorry, okay?"

"Sorry for what? What does that even mean?"

"I'm sorry about our baby." That stops me in my tracks, almost doubles me over with physical pain, a blow to my core.

"I'm sorry we didn't work," he continues. "I'm sorry I got married. All of it."

"Why, Josh? Why did you marry her when you wouldn't marry me?" I'm crying hot, angry tears. He tries to hold me, but I push him away and take a step back. "Don't touch me. Answer me."

"She was pregnant."

"I was pregnant! Why did you want that baby and not our baby?"

"I didn't want any baby, but she was going to have him no matter what, and I didn't want to be the dick who walks away from his kid. Then I couldn't be the dick who left when she had a miscarriage. It's not a great marriage."

"Don't tell me that." I start my agitated pacing again, Josh matching me stride for stride. "I don't want to know that."

"You can't tell me you're happy with Slick. There's no way he makes you happy."

"Shut the fuck up, Josh!" I stop walking so I can yell directly in his face. "You were the one who was supposed to make me happy, but you didn't. You broke my heart!"

"You ended it," he yells back. "I never wanted you to leave."

"But you let me go! You were the love of my life, Josh, and you just let me go. You didn't love me enough, and that just about killed me because everything in me believed that eventually you would." I turn to walk back inside, but Josh grabs my arm. I see Eric barreling toward us, but Josh doesn't see him.

"Please, Kai. Please stay with me."

"Get your fucking hands off my fucking wife!" Eric pulls me away from Josh with such force that I trip, scraping my knee and palm. As I'm falling, he's pushing Josh, who slugs him in the face, and then they're both swinging away, landing hard punches, with me screaming at them to stop as I pick myself up off the pavement. Bobby and Nick run up and pull them apart, but not before both of these men I've loved are hurt and bleeding.

Nick walks Eric away and I follow, but I turn around to say, "Go home, Josh. Get your wife and go home." I mean it more than I've ever meant anything.

I want to take Eric to the ER, but he won't let me, so we go back to the hotel and I get ice from the machine to put on his nose and eye and jaw and hand. We haven't said anything to each other about what happened. I change into pajamas, turn out the lights, and climb into bed next to him.

"Is he the love of your life, Kai?" Eric asks in the dark, flat and emotionless.

"He was," I say. Somehow, in the dark, it's easier to be honest.

"So what about me?" he asks, sounding more sad and vulnerable than I've ever heard him.

"You're my husband, and I love you." I want to take his hand, but it's holding ice to his face.

"But I'm not the love of your life."

"That was a stupid thing for me to say. I don't even know what that means."

"Sure you do," he says, rolling away from me, letting the ice fall to the floor.

We lie there in silence for a while. I try to fall asleep before the conversation goes any further, but I don't succeed.

"Do you still want to be my wife?" he asks, facing the wall.

"I want you to stop drinking," I say, as it seems to be the moment to lay it all out there.

"I want you to love me more than you loved him," he says, ending the conversation.

When I wake up in the morning, Eric is gone. He's left a note saying that we'll figure things out when I get home.

There is a bon voyage breakfast this morning before the bride and groom leave on their honeymoon, and I understand why Eric wouldn't want to show up for that, especially with a wrecked face.

I find Stephanie right away and apologize for the drama and for leaving without saying goodbye. She dismisses me in her honeymoon high, happy enough with her experience of a near-perfect day. She's glad the fight happened in the parking lot and not on the dance floor, because she knows things could have been worse.

Nick and Bobby join us, and Nick reassures me as well. "With this family, there was bound to be a fight. Could just have easily been me and this fool."

"Your guy looked like a wuss with his hundred-dollar haircut and Armani suit, Kai, but he can throw a punch," Bobby says. "My brother's face looked like shit. Very impressive."

"Thanks?" I say.

"I never laid that good a punch on Josh," Bobby adds.

"That's not the point here, Bobby," Stephanie says, rolling her eyes.

"Where is Eric anyway?" Bobby says, looking toward the bar. "I wanted to compare his face to Josh's."

"He left early this morning," I say. "Something came up for work."

"Yeah, I'll bet," Bobby says. "Something came up for Josh too."

"He isn't here either," Stephanie says, to make sure I know that.

"Who cares about Josh? Kai's married to Rocky now," Nick jokes.

"Oh, yeah! That was Rocky and Apollo there," Bobby laughs.

"Nice, guys." Stephanie wraps up the conversation. "Let's sit down. They're starting to take breakfast orders."

Dad asks if he can sit with me, which is sweet. We talk about work and the Yankees while we eat, and when the plates are being cleared, he surprises me by starting a difficult conversation.

"Are you okay, Kai?" he asks. "Really?"

"No, Dad. Not really." I feel like crying but don't want to because first of all, we're at a breakfast with about thirty people, and second, I don't want to scare my dad off. I need him right now, which is really weird for me, since it's been a lifetime since I've felt like that.

"Is Eric okay?" he asks.

"I don't know. He left before I woke up."

"Why'd he leave?"

"He heard me tell Josh he was the love of my life."

"Oh." Dad obviously doesn't know what to say to that, probably because there's nothing to say.

"I wanted to talk to you, Kai, before the boys had the fight, but now I'm not sure if I should. You have a whole other mess to deal with now."

"What, Dad?" My marriage may be falling apart, but right now, the only relationship I care about is this one with my dad, hearing what he wants to say to me. I never thought that would matter to me again, but in this moment it matters more than anything.

"When we were at the rehearsal dinner, at the bar after, I was watching Eric doing shots with Don and his friends. I've noticed his drinking every time we're together. He drinks a lot, and he's never as drunk as he should be. I know drinking, Kai, and I recognize that."

"Dad," is all I can say. I'm floored. He's only mentioned his drinking problem once or twice, always painfully, when he's been working the steps. And here he is, bringing it up to help me and Eric.

"Eric isn't me, and I don't know him well enough to judge anything. I'm just saying it's a tough habit to put down, and if it's a problem now, it may always be a problem."

I stare at him, deeply moved.

"And maybe you don't need to deal with that problem again," Dad concludes, exhaling. "That's what I wanted to say."

"Oh, Dad." I hug him tightly. "Thank you." I want to say more, but I don't know how. I've never talked with my dad like that. I'm trying to think of how to start, what to share, but he's done.

"I've got to get going now, Kai," he says, getting up. "Good luck with everything."

I get up and gave him another hug, although he's stiffer now, back to his usual self.

"I love you, Dad."

"I love you, too, Kai."

When I get home late that night, Eric is out. He comes home drunk at about two in the morning and passes out in our bed. He's up and gone at six a.m. for his morning workout, and I realize we could go on and on like this. He could be a functioning alcoholic for the rest of his life—succeeding at his job, staying in shape, loving me in a certain way. I could just not say anything and live like this forever.

But I know I'm not going to do that.

When he gets back from the gym, I tell him we need to talk. He asks if we can do this another time, since he has an important lunch meeting and needs to get to the office and prepare for it. I would normally accommodate him, but today I don't. He knows what's coming and would rather avoid it forever, which is what we'd do if it was up to him.

I start by apologizing for not loving him enough. I know how that feels, how awful it is, and I am truly sorry. I am realizing, too, that neither of us loves ourselves enough, and this is the moment I decide to change that for me. I don't say that to him because it sounds mean. It sounds like I'm picking me over him, which is exactly what I'm doing, but I don't need to elucidate that for him.

It is a sad conversation, but there are strangely no tears. Eric pours a drink, then showers and leaves for work. I call Danielle, and she takes the day off to come over and help me pack. I have movers take most of my stuff to storage and the rest of it to Danielle's. Roomies again, but only briefly this time. Lawrence recently moved in with her, and as welcoming as he is, I don't want to get in their way. I'm proud of Danielle for taking this step, for letting someone try to love her, and I'm not about to make that any more challenging.

I don't feel as devastated as I expected. I'm sad and I have a lot of regrets, but I don't feel hopeless or defeated. I actually feel empowered. I am going to move forward in my life without a man. I am going to find a great apartment, focus on my career, enjoy my friends, and figure out who I am all on my own.

I only get derailed for a brief moment when Stephanie comes home from her honeymoon and calls to tell me about it. After listening to her recount her romantic holiday, I tell her that Eric and I split up, and she is quiet for a long time. Then she tentatively tells me that Josh has also left Marcella.

"I wouldn't have mentioned it if you were still with Eric," she says. "But now it feels like you need to know, like maybe it means something."

I'm silent for only a split second. "It doesn't mean anything, Steph. Josh and I are over, whether we're married or single. We are done."

I think about our conversation for a long time after, and for the first time, I feel like it really doesn't matter to me what Josh is doing. I have no interest in him. It feels disrespectful to Eric to think any more about Josh. If I'm going to grieve a relationship right now, I'm going to grieve my marriage. I've given Josh enough of my energy, and I feel really, truly done.

My mom suggests therapy, and I go. I learn so much about myself and feel stronger and more confident than I have in years. I don't need alcohol, and I give it up for the most part. I don't need men or sex, and I take a break from those too. I am happy and content all by myself. My dad and I don't have any more deep talks, but we see each other more, do things together for fun. He comes to the city for Yankee games and to join me for a Broadway show now and then.

In addition to my work at *New York* magazine, I start thinking about what else I can do with my pictures. My 9/11 book sold modestly, and I think about doing something else like that, but it doesn't excite me or feel quite right. So instead of deciding, I chose simply to spend time taking pictures of things that call to me and decide what to do with them later. I spend the next year doing exactly that. I take assigned pictures for the magazine, and the rest of the time I take pictures of whatever I feel like.

I redirect my faith and certainty toward myself, toward believing in me. I'll figure out what to do. I will make myself happy. I will find my path all on my own, and I'm actually looking forward to the journey.

May 12, 2006

Dear Kade,

I can't remember when I've been so nervous. Tonight is the opening of my first gallery show! Hopefully not my last! I wish you were here, Kade, although I wonder if it would be happening if you were. You were always the artist, as if only one of us could be. I was the friendly, happy, smart one. But really we were both all of those things, or at least we could have been. Given more time, I think we would have realized that we were more alike than we were different. I had the idea for this show a long time ago, but it was hard because I kept thinking it should have been you. You should have had the gallery show. Then I realized we could both have had gallery shows. We could have done this together, side by side. Not taking anything from each other, but enhancing each other, sharing our strengths and talents. I know we did that for a while, and I miss it. I miss you. All this time later, and I still miss you. Obviously I always will. Yet I am also living my life, filling the holes as best I can, learning how to make my own self happy.

Love you always

WEIRD AND
WONDERFUL

ALL I CAN THINK AS I look around the room is that this is a weird and wonderful night, one that I have planned and worked toward for over a year.

I am standing in the Leighton Edmund Gallery, white walls covered with my photographs. The marble floor is polished to a glistening white as well, and I see the crowd in it, reflected beneath themselves, all of us appearing to float in this white cloud dotted with my work. It's all a bit surreal, difficult to believe that I am actually here, in this small but well-respected, up-and-coming Chelsea gallery filled with my pictures and so many of the people I love.

Additionally weird and wonderful is that the room is packed not only with friends and family who have come to support me, but also with strangers who are admiring my work and buying photos for the exorbitant prices the gallery director suggested but I never though anyone would pay.

The cast of characters is delightfully hard to believe. Eric's here, he and I somehow managing to maintain a decent relationship after we split. I wouldn't say we're friends exactly—there should be another word for it—but we talk and see each other from time to time. He's become my pro bono publicist, helping me find this gallery and promoting my exhibit, and it's thanks to him that the room is as full as it is. He's not staying long, since his new girlfriend is eager to move on to a party that isn't all about his ex-wife.

In another part of the room, my mom and dad are chatting together easily. They each have dates this evening, Mom accompanied by a sweet guy she's recently started seeing, Dad with a woman he's been with for almost a year. It's still strange and a bit unsettling for me to see them enjoying each other's company, but it also makes me happy. It's certainly better than avoiding each other, all the angry tension, nice that they can now engage in a pleasant conversation, although god knows what the four of them are talking about. I see Mom laugh, and I shake my head in wonderment.

Danielle slides up beside me and hands me a glass of wine, reminding me to look as if I'm drinking but not to actually drink, since I have to be on my toes to talk with critics, journalists, and potential buyers. Dani is my right hand this evening, not that she isn't always, but tonight it's official. Eric coached both of us on the important players, so she's offering me both emotional support and logistical assistance, reminding me whom to talk to, keeping me moving and schmoozing, helping me stay focused on cultivating interest in my work rather than hanging out with our friends, which I would rather do. I'll return the favor at her wedding to Lawrence in a few months; I'm already planning a wild bachelorette party and helping her pick flowers and food.

"Your parents look like BFFs over there," she says.

"It's so weird. I can't remember them being so nice and connected. Did they even talk at my wedding?"

"Not that I remember." Dani is looking around the room.

"Who's that woman over there taking notes?"

Neither of us recognizes her, so Dani heads over to find out who she is and what she's writing.

I stand in front of my favorite photo of Kade. This one isn't for sale, but I wanted him here. Soon I'm overwhelmed with emotions, feeling like an imposter, thinking once again that Kade should have been the one to have a gallery show.

"You are an artist." I hear Josh's voice inexplicably beside me, telling me exactly what I need to hear.

I turn in confusion. It's been two years since Stephanie's wedding. I'm over him, but there's still history here, drops of emotion that don't completely evaporate. My eyes well up. I used to hate how easily I cried, but now I accept the tears as a part of who I am and how I express myself. I no longer fight the inevitable.

"I'm sorry, Kai. I didn't want to mess up your night. Steph told me about your show, and I wanted to see it. I'm so proud of you and happy for you. I thought it would be okay if I came, but maybe that was selfish."

He turns to leave, but I pull him to me and hug him. "I'm glad you're here. You are a part of a lot of these pictures, a part of the journey that led me here. It's just all so overwhelming—the show, my parents, you. I wasn't the artist, Josh." I'm crying into his chest, just a little, and it feels good.

"But you are, clearly." He kisses the top of my head. "You and Kade were always more alike than anyone recognized."

"I wish he could have seen that, seen his strength and potential."

"I know. Me too."

"Josh?" Mom says, with Dad right beside her, my parents moving in to head off any emotional precariousness on my part. They greet Josh and barely have time to start into a conversation before Dani reappears, also in protection mode, saying a quick hello to Josh, then pulling me away.

"Where did he come from?" she asks.

"I have no idea."

Josh chats with Mom and Dad and their dates, and they make their way around the exhibit while Dani keeps me busy with journalists and critics who seem mostly positive about my work. Eric heads out, and I can't tell if he's seen Josh or not. I thank him for all his help and support and realize that I am finally genuinely more grateful for what I have in my life than I am grieving for what I've lost.

As I'm circulating through the crowd, I overhear Dani talking privately with Josh on the other side of a partition displaying a recent photo I took of a mother and daughter playing near the Alice in Wonderland statue in Central Park, the sun shimmering on the little girl's white-blond hair, making her look like an angel with a halo. The smile on her face and the innocent love in her eyes add to the cherubic effect.

I've stumbled upon their conversation in the middle, so I'm not sure how it started, but Dani has obviously asked Josh why he's here, and he's telling her what he told me about wanting to see the show.

"Listen, Josh, I like you, always have," she says. "You're a cool guy and I've seen how happy you make her. Thing is, I also saw how you almost broke her. You can't do that again."

I walk away then because I don't want tonight to be about that, don't care enough about Josh's response. A reporter for *amNewYork*, a small daily paper, starts talking to me, asking me about my series of late-night Time Square photos, which keeps me from any second thoughts about going back to eavesdrop on the rest of Dani and Josh's conversation.

Mom and Dad say goodbye as the room is emptying, both of them praising my work and the success of the night. I've lost track of Josh, which makes me a little sad but also satisfied that I'm able to lose track of him.

"Oh my God! That was the best!" Dani hugs me tight. "Could it have been any better?" Lawrence is finally beside her, having patiently relinquished her attention to me all night.

"I can't imagine wanting to change one single thing," I agree.

"Even Josh?"

"Even Josh."

"Where'd he go?"

"No idea," I say, proud of my indifference.

We check in with the gallery director, and I'm thrilled to learn that I sold quite a few prints tonight. After reviewing details about the remainder of the weeklong exhibit, the three of us head out.

Josh is leaning against the wall of the next building down, looking over and smiling when we exit. It's a pleasantly warm, beautiful New York City night, the street still humming with activity. It could just as easily be eight o'clock instead of midnight. You never know the difference in Manhattan, and I love that.

"Hey, Josh," Dani says. "We wondered where you went." She introduces him to Lawrence, and they shake hands.

"Too many people, but I wasn't ready to leave." He produces a bottle of champagne. "Any interest? Continue celebrating your brilliance?"

I hold his gaze for a full minute, then look to Dani. "What do you think?"

"Oh no, I owe this man his reward for waiting all night." She gives Lawrence a sexy smile, then looks back to me. "You are on your own here." We hug and she gives Josh a look before walking away with a breezy, "Don't do anything I wouldn't do," which leaves a wide range of choices.

"So what do you say?" Josh asks, waving the champagne bottle back and forth. "For old time's sake?"

I move in close to him and put one hand on his chest, the other on his cheek. He lays his free hand on my hip. I kiss him lightly and it feels just right.

"For old time's sake," I say, and lead him to my apartment.

We make love that night, and it is tender and sweet and lovely. Every good thing it ever was.

The next morning, we go to the café down the block for brunch. It's a neighborhood favorite and packed with chattering New Yorkers, but instead of feeling loud and crowded, it's warm and homey. We catch up on each other's lives, and it feels natural and easy to be with him. We laugh hysterically as he describes last summer at the Cape, watching Bobby chase his three young sons around.

"Can you imagine the irony of Bobby yelling at his kids for wrestling in the water? Telling them to stop fighting? I was busting up. And me laughing made them do it more, which was awesome!"

He tells me more about Bobby and his family, about Nick's job and his fiancée. We talk about Stephanie's adorable baby, Charlotte, how sweet and funny and perfect she is. I tell Josh about my work at the magazine and my friends in New York. He tells me that he's been interviewing for jobs teaching journalism and writing at a few small colleges, and I choke on my coffee.

"Okay, okay, I know," he says, laughing my reaction and at himself. "I'm ready for roots. I never, ever wanted roots, but now I do."

"Well, I never thought I'd hear that." I know I'm surprised, but I'm not sure what other feelings are lurking there as well. Perhaps wistfulness that it's come too late for us.

"Yeah, I never expected to say it. Want to hear something else I never expected to say?"

I nod as I take a bite of my omelet.

"You may want to finish chewing first so you don't choke again." He smiles and waits for me to swallow. "I've been in therapy. Can you believe that? Me, in therapy?"

"Yeah, what could you possibly have to work through?"

"I know. I should have done it a long time ago, but I thought it was a weak move. Real men handle things themselves, ya know?"

"Yeah, the men in our lives were great at handling things."

"Right? Anyway, it's been helpful. I'm less afraid of who I could be and more comfortable with who I am."

"That's great, Josh. Me too. Been in therapy, less afraid, more comfortable with myself."

"Well, look at us, mentally healthy."

"On our way at least." It's nice to talk with him like this, like friends who've known each other forever, no more bitterness or dashed hopes or unrealistic expectations.

We finish breakfast and are lingering over our coffee, feeling guilty for taking up the table for almost two hours when there are people waiting out the door and on the street.

"I suppose we have to leave at some point," Josh says.

"I suppose so."

We head out onto the crowded sidewalk in front of the café. There are families strolling along toward the park or back home for naptime. It's easy to tell which ones are which. Most of the crowd is milling about waiting for a table.

Josh pulls me to him and holds me tight. "Everything should have been different for us. I wish I'd listened to you, followed your lead once in a while, loved you more and better."

"Shoulda, woulda, coulda, Josh. We had a good run while it lasted. Your life just wasn't my life. And the life I wanted wasn't yours. I wish it could have been different too, but we are who we are. Neither one of us can be something we're not."

"Goddamn, you were always this voice of wisdom, even at ten years old." He continues to hug me. "I have always loved you, you know, even when it wasn't how you wanted."

"I know. Me too, always loved you but not always how you wanted. For a while there, though, we loved each other exactly right."

"Yes we did."

We kiss and finally separate.

"See you around, Kai."

"See ya, Josh."

There are no tears as we part that day. Is it because we don't say the word goodbye? Is it because I don't think it's goodbye forever? I don't think so. I think the joy of our time together is greater than any sadness I can let in right at that moment.

June 5, 2006

K,

I loved seeing you the other night. I loved touching you and holding you again. I can't stop thinking about you, and I have a proposal. Will you see me again and hear my idea? I love writing to you, but in the interest of time, you can text me your answer. Let's move forward, okay?

J

A NEW BEGINNING

JOSH PICKS ME UP MIDMORNING on Saturday. He's packed a lunch and is taking me for a picnic somewhere outside the city, but that's all he'll say. It's strange that I'm not anxious at all, not overthinking it or wondering what will happen or what it all means. I'm content with my life, in a place to enjoy Josh but not need anything from him. He knows me, and I know him, and that feels cozy and comforting.

We drive across the George Washington Bridge and up the Palisades Parkway. It's a warm day, and we have the windows cracked to let in the scented springtime air. We're surrounded by green—grass, trees, bushes. In all my travels, this is still the prettiest highway, cute and quaint in a way you wouldn't expect so close to the huge metropolis on the other side of the river. We chat a little and listen to music, no pressure to talk but talking when we have something to say. After about forty-five minutes, we get off at an exit I know intimately.

"Josh, where are we going?"

"We're going home, K," he says, which makes me smile, a smile that's deep inside me, not just on my face.

I have questions that I decide not to ask. Instead, I enjoy the familiar sights of my hometown and the feel of every turn on the mountain road that I know by heart, that I could drive blindfold-ed, the road that leads to the one place I've lived that was truly my home.

"What are we doing here?" I turn my smile to him.

"Shh. You were doing great at just trusting me."

I sit quietly as Josh drives up the rutted, steep, curving drive-way, past the blooming daffodils and mountain laurel blanket-ing the side of the hill. I roll my window down all the way and breathe in the scent of my roots—dirt and flowers and pine trees, rotting leaves buried under snow all winter. We park in the emp-ty driveway of my childhood home, which looks different than in my memories—smaller and with a new back porch some other owner built. Josh puts on his backpack with the picnic supplies, takes my hand, and leads me into our woods. I know where we're going now, but I have no idea why and no idea if we're trespass-ing. I follow along anyway because it feels so good to be here.

He leads me to the mossy spot where we had many import-ant conversations, lays out a blanket, and motions for me to sit down. The house may look different, but the woods are exactly the same.

"I'm going to get right to it," Josh says, pulling me abruptly out of my reverie. He kneels in front of me and offers me a ring. "Kai Martin, will you marry me?"

"Josh…" I have no idea what to say. My head is spinning, and the scene becomes surreal, like I'm watching it without actually being part of it. I listen as he tells me the house is for sale and he's put down a deposit, that he wants to live here with me for the rest of our lives. It's hard to know how I feel, probably because of this out-of-body sensation. I take some deep breaths and settle back into myself. I expect to feel overwhelmed or ecstatic or angry, but I don't feel any of those big emotions. I feel quiet, which allows me to think.

Do I need Josh? No. I am certain of that, and that certainty grounds me.

Do I love him? Yes, of course I love Josh Tyler. I always have. Another thing I know for sure. The problem was always that I loved him more than he loved me. Is that still true? This is where my certainty ends.

"I know there's no reason for you to believe in me right now, but I want to prove that you mean the world to me," Josh says. "That's why I want to buy this house for you. It's why I went to see your dad and asked his permission to marry you."

I let out a quick little burst of a laugh. "What did he say?"

"You know your dad. It was something profound like okay."

I picture the conversation and realize how much it matters to me that Josh had it. We both know he doesn't need Dad's permission, but it means a lot that he took that step.

"I wrote to Kade too, and talked to your mom, just to cover all my bases."

My eyes well up, mostly happy tears, but also that familiar, nostalgic sadness.

The surreal feeling sweeps over me once more when he tells me he wants us to have kids. He apologizes again about our baby and says he'd like to try making a baby together on purpose this time. When I question the dramatic turnaround, he explains that he's spent the past year in therapy analyzing why he let me go and the answer he came up with was that he was stupid, which makes me laugh again and pulls me back into my body. He admits he was afraid and all that too, but mostly he realized that he was immature and selfish and stupid.

"I appreciate it now, K," he says, "all the love you gave me and the sacrifices you made. I regret more than anything that I didn't appreciate it then. I regret that I let you walk away. I regret that we didn't have that baby. But I can't change the past. I can only change the future, and I want that future to be with you. Marry me, and I will spend the rest of my life appreciating you and loving you as much as I wish I always had. I'm all in. Forever."

Tears are flowing as he says all this. Blowing my nose helps convince me it's real, reminds me I am an active participant in this pivotal moment. It also helps me stall for time so I can consider what I want to say. I think about asking him if he really wants to get married but firmly stop myself because this isn't about what Josh wants. It's about what I want. So what is that?

I push down on the moss, feeling it give way beneath the pressure of my hand. I let go and watch it rise back up.

"You're offering everything I always wanted," I say. "This house, you, us married with kids. It's like a dream come true." I pause, trying to understand my deeper hesitation.

"But?" Josh says.

"But I'm not sure it fits anymore. I'm not sure it's what I want now." He droops a little, and I touch his shoulder. "Let me think, okay?"

He brushes a tear off his cheek and looks at me. "Think away." He zips open the backpack, pulls out a water bottle, and takes a long sip.

I lie back on the moss and put my arm over my eyes. "Is this how it's done?" I ask, trying to provide some levity.

"Looks about right," Josh says.

What do I want? I ponder it all for a long time, feeling the sun on my body, hearing the rustling of leaves in the breeze.

I've wanted to marry Josh since I was a little girl, but I'm not a little girl anymore. I thought marrying Eric would fill the empty spot inside me and give me the security of forever, but it didn't do either of those things. I consider the anchor that weighed me down for so long, that the men in my life always chose something over me. My dad and Eric chose booze. Kade chose death. Josh chose freedom. For a long time, that defined me, the knowledge that I was not the thing that got picked, but I realize now that in the end, I've always chosen me. When the critical moment comes, I choose me. And I'm proud of that. I didn't need anyone to pick me because I was good enough all on my own.

Of course, I wasn't on my own. I've had my mom. And Dani and Steph and Jaimie. But I've got me too, and I know that now. So I don't want to marry Josh because I don't need that anymore. In fact, it's important for me not to stay trapped in the scenario I laid out for myself when I was six years old. I don't want to do something that feels like I'm supposed to do it.

Still, here I am, in these woods I've known and loved my whole life, with this boy I've known and loved my whole life. And it feels entirely right. It doesn't feel forced. I don't feel any pressure around it. It just feels like it all fits. I sit up and look at him.

"I don't want to get married," I say, and he looks crestfallen. "But I do love you." I kiss him softly. "I love this house, these woods, this place, but I don't want a version of my old life. I appreciate the grand gesture, really I do. But I don't want to go backward. I want to move forward."

"Can we do that together?" he asks, worry furrowing his brow. I notice lines on his face, not the boy I loved, but a more weathered man who I still love.

"I'd like to try," I say. "But we have to take it slow, build trust that we can do it differently this time."

"Okay," he says, taking my hand. "Slow it is. You lead the way, K. I am following you this time around."

"No more leaders and followers, J." I squeeze his arm and lean my head against him, feeling grounded and happy and sure. "How about we try being equal partners this time?"

He takes my face in his hands and kisses me deeply.

"That sounds perfect," he says.

June 10, 2006

Dear Kade,

You will never guess where I am. I'm sitting in our woods, on the Big Rock, and I can almost feel you here. Josh just offered me marriage and our house, but I declined both. It feels completely right to be back in these woods, and it also feels right to leave them. It feels right to be with Josh but not to get married, although a baby might be nice. We'll see. I'm not sure what will happen next, not exactly sure of what I'm doing. I understand the risks of loving people deeply, the pain of heartbreak, but I'm not scared any more. I have faith in myself that I'll figure it out and be okay, whatever comes.

I sent Josh to wait in the car while I came here to write you this letter. Josh is a part of me. You are a part of me. Mom and Dad are part of me. But I am also whole all by myself. That's why I'm sitting here alone, feeling you and Josh and all our history, but not feeling lonely. I'm feeling myself.

That's all I know, and it is enough.

I love you, Kade, always and forever

ACKNOWLEDGMENTS

There was a lot of magic and serendipity involved in the creation of this book, particularly the magic of Kai telling her story through me, of having her and Josh living in my head for a few years. I barely believe I wrote this novel, and couldn't have done it without each and every link in a chain of amazingly supportive people.

First and foremost, thank you to my mom, for being my biggest cheerleader, for reading about twenty versions of the story, and for introducing me to Joy Johannessen, who is not only a fabulous editor who tucked and tightened this story, but who also encouraged me in my journey overall, including suggesting I apply to the Community of Writers Workshop, where I went from someone who wrote a draft of a novel to feeling like I might actually be a writer. I cannot express my gratitude for Joy! (she'd delete the exclamation point, but I'm leaving it)

Additional appreciation for my experience at the Community of Writers, where I met two sets of wonderful women. First, my Baes...Claire Boyles, Re Marzullo, and Sabrina Sarro. Before I attended one moment of the actual workshop, I knew I'd found my people, and you have been my people ever since, providing encouragement and support that has kept me going throughout this process. Thank you! I also met Caroline Kim and Swathi DeSilva through the Community, and we have been a writing group for years. They have helped make this story richer and the characters more real. Thanks to them for keeping me writing consistently and giving honest feedback.

A huge thank you to Anna Dorfman, who created such a beautiful cover. I loved many iterations of possible covers and am sad that I could only pick one, but this is THE ONE and I love it most of all!

Thank you to the team at Books Fluent and Books Forward for helping with the logistics of making my story into an actual book and hopefully convincing people to read it.

A general thank you to the (lower case) community of writers I have met over these past years, so many of whom have been exceedingly gracious and generous with advice and support. Thank you to those of you who took the time to read my book and write endorsements that made me cry…Lee and Susan and Amy and Claire and Caroline and Bob.

And now for my personal, sentimental appreciations. Thank you, Grandma, for being my lifelong pen pal, for teaching me to love reading, and for being my model of a strong, determined, independent woman who reached a point in her life where she did whatever the hell she wanted. Speaking of…a second thank you to my mom for demonstrating a lot of those same qualities, for always believing in me, and for molding me into the woman I am today. Thank you to my dad for showing me that creativity and fun are important parts of life, and that a person can always evolve into new versions of themself. Thank you to Sean and Keri, my first and always partners in life, who grew up with me in Kai's house and played with me in Kai's woods.

Thanks to my kids for inspiring me, each in their unique ways. Thank you, Christopher, for embracing your creativity and living your dream of being a musician. If you can do it, so can I. To

Casey, who reminds me of Josh in Josh's best moments, thank you for reading and giving feedback and for always bringing positive energy to the room. Thank you, Jake, for demonstrating what courage looks like, for being scared and doing hard things anyway. When I'm filled with doubt and fear, thinking of you motivates me to keep going.

Last but never least, thank you to Ken. You are the solid ground from which I can launch into all kinds of crazy endeavors, always knowing that I have a safe place to land. You encourage me. You believe in me. You love me. And that has helped me soar. Thank you.

Most of all, thanks to those of you who are reading. It has all led to you.

BOOK CLUB DISCUSSION QUESTIONS

1. As a child, Kai is certain of a great many things. Later, she doubts everything she thought she knew. Eventually she discovers faith in herself and the world. What do you think moved her from one to another? Where do you feel you land, more in the realm of certainty, doubt, or faith, and how did you get there? What about Josh? And Kade?

2. Kai's relationship with Josh has many iterations. Were there times you did and did not want them to end up together? What was it about Josh that drew Kai to him early on? Do you think those reasons stayed the same or changed throughout the story? Do you think things will work out for them?

3. Kai and Josh's experiences in their families of origin impact their romantic relationship. How do you think certain choices they made as adults were linked to their experiences when they were young? How about for you?

4. There are three unique depictions of marriage in the book, Kai's parents, Josh's parents and Kai's with Erik. What did you think were the strengths and weaknesses of each of them? What did you think about Jaimie's observation about recurring arguments and dealbreakers versus price-of-admission (pages 269-271)? Have you experienced these things in your relationship?

5. Kai's mom, Tammy, is a force to be reckoned with during much of the book. How did you feel when she was strong

and when she wasn't? Did those same feelings come up when Kai was strong and not, or did you respond differently to their different struggles?

6. Tammy talks with Kai a few times about reasons being different than excuses, the first of which happens when Kai yells at Stephanie during dinner (page 25). Do you agree that reasons are different than excuses? How so or why not?

7. Tammy provides advice, guidance and support to Kai at several points in the story. What did you think of their relationship overall? How did you feel about how Tammy supported each of her children, and would you have liked for her to do anything differently?

8. How did you feel about both Kai's dad and Josh's dad? Did you have any empathy for them? Were there any ways in which they were good fathers? What did you think when Kai's dad shared advice about Erik's drinking toward the end of the book?

9. What did you think of Kai's friendship with Danielle? With Steph? What were the strengths and problems in those friendships? How did they help Kai grow and thrive, or not? Talk about friends you've had who influenced your life in big and small ways. Who do you go to when you need support? Who is it you most rely upon?

10. Being a twin and then losing Kade is a defining part of Kai's story. What did you think of their relationship? How did you feel about Kade's struggles?

11. Did you learn anything about addiction and/or other mental health challenges by reading this book? Did it change your perspective on any of those things? Do you have any personal experiences with mental health struggles?